THE
ELEVEN MILLION
MILE HIGH
DANCER

ALSO BY CAROL HILL

Jeremiah 8:20

Subsistence U.S.A.

Let's Fall in Love

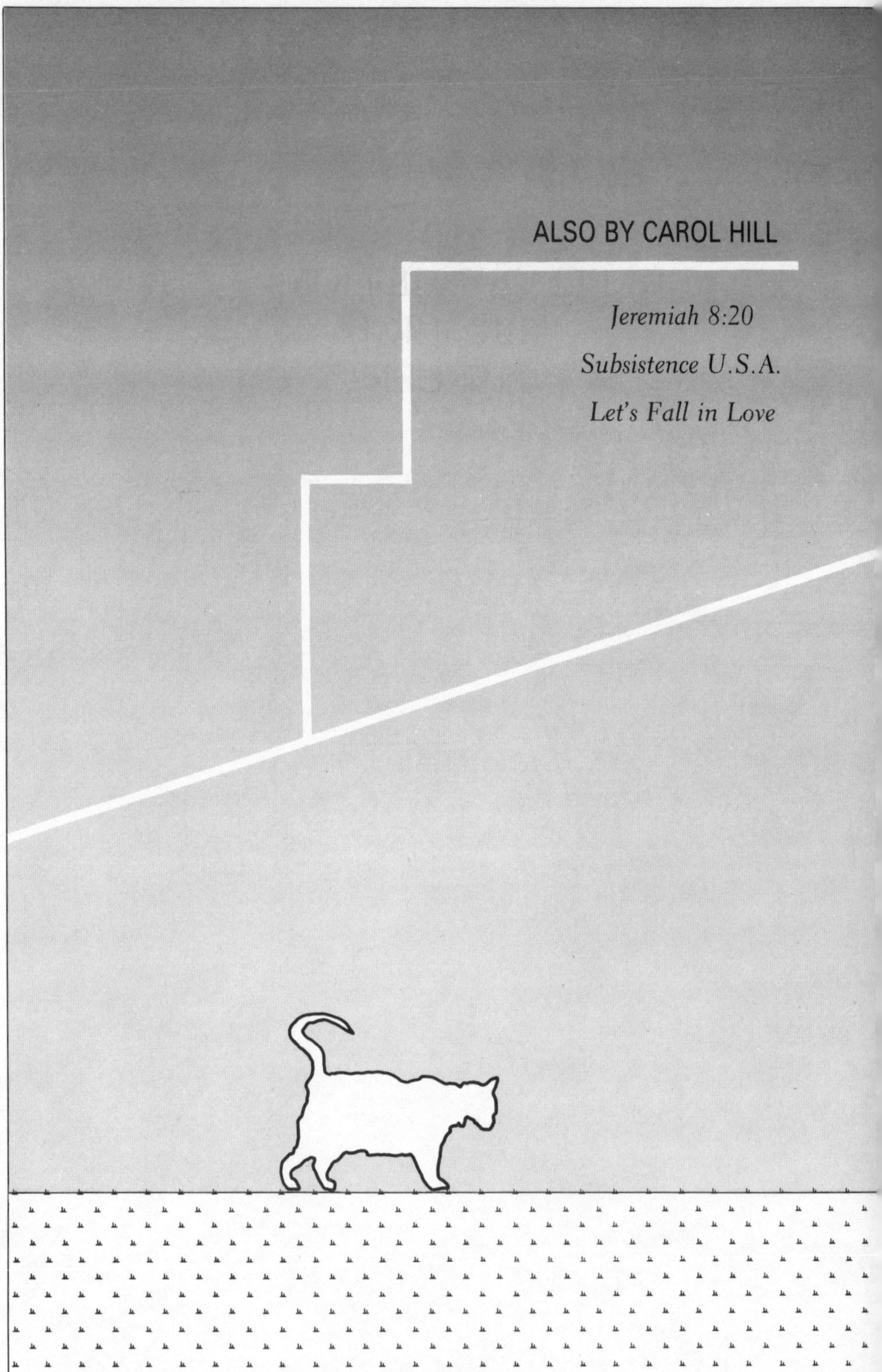

The ELEVEN MILLION MILE High Dancer

by
CAROL HILL

A William Abrahams Book
HOLT, RINEHART AND WINSTON   NEW YORK

Library of Congress Cataloging in Publication Data
Hill, Carol.
The eleven million mile high dancer.
"A William Abrahams book."
I. Title.
PS3558.13845E4   1984   813'.54   84-566
ISBN 0-03-070699-8

First Edition

Designer: Kate Nichols
Printed in the United States of America
1 3 5 7 9 10 8 6 4 2

Grateful acknowledgment is made for permission
to quote from the following work:
Lines from "Snow White and the Seven Dwarfs" from
Transformations by Anne Sexton. Copyright © 1971
by Anne Sexton. Reprinted by permission of
Houghton Mifflin Company.

ISBN 0-03-070699-8

For Jerry
who loved, encouraged, supported,
challenged, and inspired

and

for my Mother
whose sense of wonder and love of language
probably started the whole business

Acknowledgments

I would like to thank my friend and agent, Liz Darhansoff, for her continuous enthusiastic support, and her colleague Nancy Meiselas for such thoughtful commentary. I am very much indebted to my editor, William Abrahams, for his hard work, imagination, and indefatigable enthusiasm, and to Mr. Robert L. Saxe who read the physics with a physicist's eye and a generous sense of poetic license. The original idea for the title comes from an illustration in Heinz Pagels' book, *The Cosmic Code*, where it is used by Dr. Pagels as an illustration of Einstein's special theory of relativity. Any errors that occur in this final version of course belong exclusively to me.

NOTE TO READERS

All the quoted scientific material in this novel is true. Further explanation can be found in the Afterword.

Ground Speed

*If a man could pass through Paradise in a dream,
and have a flower presented to him as a pledge that
his soul had really been there, and if he found that
flower in his hand when he awoke—then Ay!—and
what then?*

—Samuel Taylor Coleridge, *Anima Poetae*

Dancer

She saw her now. The Dancer. She glided through the starry heavens, a *glistening sinuous amber, bright, then dark, a darkening scarlet reaching until it set her spinning, spinning now into a violet so deep, so rushed, so beaming it took her breath away. The Dancer there—a thousand stars shone through her eyes, galaxies spun down, around her thighs, and between, within, the vortex, moving, sinuous. Still. And then the rush, the movement like a rainfall, rainfall in your mind, striking heat, striking the light, heat lightning pinning you down, striking you blind with its beauty. That was the power of the Dancer. Or so they said. So they waited. Waiting to see her again. Waiting. Such was her power. Or they awakened suddenly in the night, feeling she had kissed them, her wet mouth glittering, steel diamonds on their lips. Sometimes they cried. They awoke crying in the night with a pain that made them want to die. For some. For others it was worse. Some went nuts. Swore to it. The men. Couldn't handle it. So they said. Spewed out their brains, the logic left, sticking like resin to the backs of their tongues. Their mouths made sense, working slowly, but their minds, their minds were shot. All reason. They became clerks. Some of them. Simple accountants. People didn't talk about it. That power. Her power.*

She herself, the woman who was going now, thought it was in the movement. It was so dazzling, she drew you in and then . . . Then there was no telling. At least none of them did. But this time it would be different. Because of the men. Always, before, it had been the men who went. This time it was a woman. And a woman had a different way of knowing.

1

Strange reports. Patterns in light sources that contradicted everything. And gravity waves. Swore they'd found them. Speculations confirmed. People didn't quite know what to make of the reports: they were hard to believe. Some people didn't. It was whispered the findings had been stolen from the Russians. Others said the Russians invented them in order to be stolen. No one was certain of anything. Except this: The two Soviet cosmonauts who reported them had absolutely, completely, and totally disappeared.

Amanda Jaworski, America's leading lady astronaut, in her bright blue boots, her red-and-white-striped shorts, and her blue-and-white-starred top, strolled confidently along the halls of the space center. She smiled at the looks she got.

She's gorgeous, General Farkheimer thought with a sigh. He wished she wasn't *so* appealing.

"What thighs," said Louise Studebunker, the general's secretary. "I'd give anything just to have one of them." She sighed.

"What good would one do?" the general said with a huff, turning in the door.

"I'd settle for one," said Louise over her typewriter. Louise was four feet eleven and had briefly calculated that if you took both of her legs and put them one on top of the other they might just come up to Amanda's one. And nowhere close to its architecture.

Amanda passed them. "Good morning," she said with that dazzling smile, swinging her roller skates over her shoulder, her blue boots making a sharp *click, click* down the hall. Louise watched her retreating form, in those brief, tight, striped satin shorts, swinging in the way that Amanda had, a kind of rhythmic lilt in the swing of the hips that kept Louise and the general watching her in a kind of trance as Amanda kept clicking down the long hall and people came to the doors of their offices to say good morning and to watch Amanda walk, her long blond hair flipping on her back as she nodded to the left, good morning, nodded to the right, good morning, people standing in the doorways just to say good morning, five, ten, fifteen trilling good mornings, until the entire long hall of them stood there in the doorways staring, their heads tilting right good morning, their heads tilting left, and then again, back and forth in a happy metronome as Amanda's hips swung in tune to the *click click click* from the floor. This instant orchestration was only one of the effects Amanda immediately produced.

The other one was war. Some people hated Amanda. They said she was "unheard of." Sergeant Delko, her trainer, was one of these people.

"Ouch," she would say when he zipped her into her flight suit, catching her breast in the zipper.

"Your tits are too big for these suits; they shouldn't let you go up," he'd say, lowering the zipper and stuffing the material in.

"Stop squashing me!" she would yell, furious, for she was in a three-hundred-pound space suit and couldn't move to get at him.

"Don't worry," he'd say; "if they're like your head, they're pure rubber. You'll bounce back," he concluded, zipping her up with a savage cry.

Delko was barreling down the hall toward her now. He was glowering, and screaming as usual. He must have spotted the shorts, she thought.

"Who the hell do you think you are in that getup?" Delko screamed. "Wonder Woman?"

But Amanda only smiled. Of course, she thought, she did look something like her, except she, Amanda, had blond hair and no magic bracelets. And she wasn't Wonder Woman. She was America's leading lady astronaut, and she would be the first person on Mars. Delko was fuming because Amanda had designed this outfit herself, after rejecting out of hand a pair of ballooning, ugly, blue-and-white-striped overalls with a set of red stars on the pocket.

"You've got to wear red, white, and blue," Delko had screamed, throwing the overalls at her.

"Those things are ridiculous," she said, throwing them back. "I look like a clown." But that was only half of it. The desert that surrounded the space center was exceedingly hot, and Amanda insisted on shorts. Besides, they were easier to skate in. Amanda definitely liked skating. They let her do it because the space center, spread out over three square miles, was more like a runway than a hallway, and the skating was great for her leg muscles. Delko of course objected.

"You'll ruin your knees," he grumbled as he walked her outside, hating the attention she was getting. To get even, she skated up the curb and leaped over a fire hydrant, turning to smile at him.

"Bet you can't do that, Sergeant," she said, leaping again 360 degrees and skating backward on one leg.

"Big deal," he grumbled. Sometimes he hated Amanda so much he almost lost his breath. He had dreams that she would burn up in the launch. But she wouldn't, he knew. Too much luck. Partly it was this quality she had. He wouldn't know what to call it exactly. Some people called it femininity. No one knew precisely what femininity was of course. They just knew Amanda had it. It seemed to Delko it was indecent somehow, this quality she had, and certainly in an astronaut. And a physicist at that. An astronaut, a physicist, and an extremely good pilot. It was this combination of achievements with this other feminine thing that disturbed him. Delko of course didn't know what femininity was either. He only knew he didn't like it. He sensed in it some statement of purpose that got him riled.

But that wasn't the worst of it; no. There was something worse than that. It was her mind. Her mind, Delko thought, shaking his head. All the dreadful things he could imagine that could be visited on him in this world had been assembled in this one place: Amanda's mind.

It was Amanda who had been responsible for teaching the other astronauts how to meditate.

"Technology isn't enough," she had cried. "We must learn body control through our minds. The mind is the pathway to outer space and inner peace."

It was this last remark and things of that ilk that drove Delko absolutely crazy. Insane. It was Amanda after all who had been responsible for the arrival of what he called "the bathrobe people." It was bad enough that they arrived, but then they stayed. She was always ruining things: now she had these little Commie chink bastards in yellow bathrobes in here, walking all over a good old American boy's army base. Walking barefoot and giving meditation classes. She was turning the whole goddamn air force into faggots. She was faggotizing the whole space program. That's what she was doin'. Hell, far as Delko could find out, not a single astronaut had gotten into Jaworski's pants. If you couldn't get into her pants, he didn't know how the hell they thought they could get into the stratosphere.

But Delko knew nothing of love. And Amanda *was* discreet. Hotchkiss, the handsome and dashing aerodynamic engineer, was definitely in pursuit, and she had explained to him as best she could explain that she was not technically, theoretically, or otherwise available, due to her enchantment—for that seemed at times the *only* word—with the devastating likes of Bronco McCloud. McCloud was a jet pilot who gave devilry new fame. He was, it was said, a handsome devil, a daredevil, devil-may-care kind of devil who had the reputation of being one of those Terrible, Wonderful men who caused women, often at precisely the same time, great joy, as well as despair.

He was called "Black" Bronco, because of his thick and curling hair. And of course, something more.

2

Amanda was not thinking about McCloud this morning for a change, nor Hotchkiss either. She was troubled by the reports. It was not unusual for a subparticle physicist, which was Amanda's training, to be receiving classified reports. In fact Amanda thought one could hardly take a good look at the nucleus of an atom (where the subatomic particles were) without getting someone *very* excited. But it was unusual for there to be so much secrecy about the reports from outer space. After all, she thought, she was the one that was going out there. Didn't they want her to know?

But she had been looking around her carefully, and there had been too many little messengers of late, too many red envelopes in and out of Farkheimer's office not to make her uneasy. And it wasn't just the space program. Hotchkiss had told her they were sealing everything up: the army, the navy, and the air force as well. He didn't know what it was. All Amanda knew was that she did overhear Farkheimer on the phone: "I don't know where. Somewhere out on the desert. It's got the brass excited as all hell." Then he hung up.

She needed to think about it. Tim Purse, the new radio astronomer, had promised to show her the radio-telescope readings. She had a lot to think about now. She'd go skating. She did her best thinking on the move.

"I have perfect balance," she would say, and she would tear off into what she admitted was a bit of a show-off thing, but nonetheless something she loved to do—a spin. It was in the middle of one of these spins that the thoughts came to her about singularities.

Singularities, to a physicist, and to other people as well, were the most intriguing thing of all. A singularity, simply put, was this: The point at which all the laws broke down. All the laws. The laws of physics, of thermodynamics. Where a thing was supposed to be hot and get hotter, in a singularity it got cold. Where gravity was so dense a thing would fall in on itself—commonly called a black hole—and forbid even light to escape—such a thing, it now turned out, might conceivably allow light to escape. Different laws prevailed.

She remembered the latest Nobel speech: "We are pushing back the edge of the observable universe." And the farther they pushed it back, of course, the farther back it went; different laws prevailed. How much different would it be then, when she actually got out there? Would the computer pictures put together by sound, by radar, turn out to be radically different from things she would see with her own eyes? That she didn't know. But she would do her best to be prepared down here. She wanted to know as much as she could, exactly how things were being put together.

There were other scientists at the space center who had been brought there specifically to brief her on the Mars shot. She liked the one she had met this morning, Purse. A frail, bespectacled parody of the devoted scientist, he had whispered to her that they had just installed the most powerful new radio telescope in the history of the world, and that he, Tim Purse, had been called in to "read it." It was true, she knew that there were findings out there that nobody could explain. Tim Purse insisted these things were valid.

She thought perhaps Hooper would find out something for them. Hooper was being sent to the moon in a few days, and Amanda was going to the Cape for his launch. She herself could hardly wait for her own trip to Mars. She thought somehow the answer to these puzzling reports could only be found farther out there—even beyond Mars. The point where the physicists wondered about black holes and time symmetries and even singularities. She didn't want to think about singularities now. Not in light of *those* reports.

3

The most profound changes in our conception of the physical universe came about in the twentieth century. The discovery of quantum effects, by Planck, Einstein, Bohr, DeBroglie and others, led to quantum mechanics, a radically new conception of matter and a description of the physical universe in which the classical passive observer is forced into active participation in the phenomena he is trying to describe . . . it is no longer possible to speak of a reality that is independent of our knowledge.

—Erich Harth, *Windows on the Mind*

"Know what, Rufe?"

"How's that, Eb?"

"You ever seen anything like that before?" Eberly asked. Eberly weighed three hundred pounds. He was the fattest sheriff in the West.

"Nope, never did," Rufus said. Rufus weighed one-eighty. They were sitting on the small oak porch, watching the moon set over Texas. The moon had lit up the desert with a strange silvery light. It was not a normal light. It was a light that was light and that was night all at once. And what they saw enacted there, what brief demonstrations occurred on that sand basin, struck them full of wonder.

And something more. The silence hung between them and made them shift in their chairs. It was not just the silence. It was the sense of something coming.

"Think we ought to tell anybody about it?"

"No, I don't," Rufus said, drawing on his pipe.

"Think they'll say we've gone loco?"

"I do, Eb."

"You think maybe we gone loco, Rufe?"

"It's within the realm of possibility," Rufus said.

Eberly started in his chair, alarmed by this formulation. Every once in a while Rufus would talk like that. "It's what?" Eberly said, scowling.

"It's within the realm," Rufus said.

"Realm . . . what in hell's a realm, anyway?"

"It's a . . . well, it's a place, that's all."

"What kind of place?"

"Oh, just a place."

"Well, if it's just a place, how come you don't just say it's a possibility, how come you go puttin' this here realm on it?"

"Don't know, Eb."

"You gotta watch yourself, Rufus. You reading them books again?" He attempted to move up out of the chair, but his weight was too far back. With a wheeze, he just managed to shift it forward, so the back of the rockers went almost straight up. He didn't fall, though. He just balanced there, somewhere between getting up and falling down. "I told you about it before, and I ain't gonna tell you about it again," Eberly said, panting now with the effort of hauling his three hundred pounds straight up. "It's no good for you; you're gonna get them. You don't wanna get them, do you?"

"What's that, Eb?" Rufus was dreaming.

"Strange ideas. That's what. Once you get them they start spreading like contamination. I've seen it happen. Once it hits a territory it goes faster than a plague. Whole country's suffering from this contamination, and now they're blowing it West. Right outta all that eastern air pollution, that stuff is spreading something fierce."

"How do you figure that, Eb?" Rufus said.

"I watch the news," Eberly said.

4

Rufus looked at the sun and spit. It was going to be a hot day, even for Texas. Something was wrong. It smelled like rain. How was it it smelled like rain without a cloud in the sky? Sun burning faster than a bull's balls, too.

Rufus was standing about three miles south of a huge salt lake one hundred miles west of Waco. He was leaning against a split-rail fence on the edge of town consisting of a general store, a gas pump, a café, and a post office. That was Reno, Texas.

Still there was something, something wrong with the sky. Rufus could see it. Something going on all right. He turned and went toward the gas station looking for a drink. He swung into the café and was relieved to see Eberly seated at the bar, and the old Indian they called Dr. Tom. Old Tom never said much, but he cured snakebite, frostbite, premature ejaculation, and warts faster than any man Rufus ever knew.

"Evenin'," Rufus said, sitting down. There again.

"What's the matter with you, Rufus?" the sheriff said. "Sun gettin' you? It's only ten o'clock in the mornin'."

"Must be the sun," Rufus said, feeling confused. Knowing it wasn't. Weather was crazier than a hoot owl in a storm. He turned to Dr. Tom. "You smell rain, Tom?"

The Indian's face barely moved.

"Well, go outside and see for yourself," Rufus said, surprised at the uneasiness in his voice. "I tell you, forty-two years in Texas I've never seen anythin' like it."

Tom went out and Rufus followed him. Eberly, easing off the bar stool, waddled out to join them. The three stood on the edge of the small worn oak porch and looked out at the desert.

"Jesus," Eberly said. "Ain't never seen that before."

The sky had turned green. Just once Rufus had seen it like that, up in the mountains near the desert outside of Santa Fe. But it had been raining then. He looked at Tom. Tom's face didn't move. The old Indian seemed to be sniffing the air. Then he bent down, leaned down to the earth, and laying flat out, pressed his face into the sand and listened.

"What in hell's he doing?" Eberly asked. But Rufus raised a hand.

"Shhh," he said. Goddamn Indians could hear the grass grow.

It happened before any of them saw it. Rufus had been staring out across the salt lake, silver and shimmering in the terrible heat. Eberly had been looking at the thermometer and wiping the sweat off the back of his neck. It was making his skin crawl for some reason. The thermometer read 112 degrees and it was only 10:15 in the morning.

A sidewinder had crawled out from under the porch and now was approaching the Indian's head. The days had been so dry he was covered with the dust as he slithered across the two feet of dry earth, soundless except to the Indian. Rufus turned as he heard the rattle, turned suddenly, the sidewinder at his boot, too late as the snake shot forward to the Indian's neck; suddenly, strangely, as if in slow motion, its head kept going clear across the Indian's neck, sailing forward, landing three feet ahead while the rest of the spiraling snake snapped and quivered to the ground.

Old Tom had cut his head off in the middle of a strike.

"Jesus goddamn Christ!" Rufus said.

Eberly, his mouth open, just stared. He had watched, but could not believe.

"How *old* are you?" Rufus said, astonished now as the Indian smiled and returned his knife to his belt.

"Ya ain't got no teeth, so I can't tell," Rufus said. Jesus Christ, he must be a hundred years old if he's a day, and he moved faster than the goddamn snake.

"Don't usually see sidewinders out so early," Rufus said.

"It's hot," Eberly said, seeming to melt now, the fat pink rolls on the back of his neck glistening like a pig over a roast. He looked out across the desert. Miles away he could just make out one of NASA's huge silver tractor-trailers moving across the highway with its silvered rocket cargo.

"They're s'posed to send one of the big ones up today," he said. "It's goin' to Venus, I hear. Hell, it can't be any hotter there. What do you think, Rufe?"

"I think it might be hotter," Rufus said.

The Indian spoke. He said something to Eberly that sounded to Rufus like "Iwa Chichuawa."

"What'd he say?" Rufus said.

Eberly had still not closed his mouth. He seemed stunned.

"He said," Eberly said, pausing, "he said the world is comin' to an end." He looked at Rufus. The old Indian had walked off now down the road.

"He ever said that before?" Rufus asked.

"Not that I ever heard."

"Well, I don't like it," Rufus said. "I don't like it one goddamned bit."

Eberly personally blamed it on all that monkeying around they were doing in space. Ever since that NASA come to Texas there'd been nothing but trouble. Should have kept the whole damn thing in Florida, Cape Canaveral. Let them have it. Sent them up there, didn't see why you had to have all this here scientific stuff, mission controls and all. Why it was ruining, positively ruining, the great state of Texas.

Even in Washington, D.C., people were starting to say that something strange was going on. In fact, there were so many strange things that you almost couldn't keep up with them. Things had gotten so bad of late that even the president of the United States lay there, unable to sleep. And this was a president everybody said could sleep through anything. The Middle East blowing up—he went on vacation. South America blowing up—he took a nap. Russia invading Poland—he went for a swim. The man had cool. They called him Daddy Ice. Well now, Daddy Ice was tossing and turning. Yessir. Even a man capable of ignoring the most fundamental things in life, even such a fantastic man as that was beginning to think something was up. And he started wondering. Fact was, he couldn't get a decent explanation. Up until now he had always gotten an explanation. The government was particularly ingenious at explaining things. Now the president of the United States lay awake at night staring at the ceiling wondering if maybe he was in the midst of a coup so powerful it was taking place without his knowing it, a coup so powerful that it had infested every nuance of government and thought. Sometimes at night the president thought he was being lied to, that he wasn't being told the facts, that the lies had gotten so complex, so intricately woven that *sometimes* the liars themselves didn't know they were lies. Sometimes at night the president thought that. Sometimes he thought it was just political—that the CIA wasn't telling him everything. He tossed again. The fact was there were always reasons. Hell, he knew that. Everybody knew it. Reason that the nuclear reactors blew up, *blew up*, for god's sake, and wiped out one-third the population of Utah, well, there was a reason for that, wasn't said to be a lie. Nobody *lied* about the danger of building that particular kind of plant. No, that was said to be a miscalculation, that's all. A surprise. A desperate surprise.

It was true that Utah was a shit-ass state, as far as the president was concerned. Nonetheless, it troubled him, losing one-third (well actually only 18 percent died, right off; the other 10 percent lived three months and then died of radiation sickness; and hell, 2 percent were still living, although they weren't going to live much *longer*, unless it wasn't as bad as the *press* made it out to be). Still, it troubled him. It didn't look good. Looked like he was losing his grip. That kind of national disaster. Got everybody all excited. Still, the thing that bothered him most when he thought about it was *What had happened to the Indians?*

Had the Russians, as the CIA reported, kidnapped the ten thousand members of the Oswego tribe one night in helicopters from the Palomar plateau?

Had they, as the Department of the Interior said, "died out naturally due to the inability to adapt to modern life," all ten thousand of them died out naturally *overnight*? The president wondered about that.

Had they, as Strategic Special Security, Center for Unexplained

Phenomena, said, had they been taken away by UFOs? And why would the UFOs take the Indians? Hell, nobody wanted the goddamn Indians. Nonetheless, it was a question of national pride. Just 'cause you didn't want your own Indians was no reason you wanted anybody else stealin' 'em.

Sometimes at night, when the president thought about these things, he thought maybe he wasn't being told the truth.

The strange things had all been revealed in the file now called "Secret File 3000 CUP." CUP meant Center for Unexplained Phenomena. Three thousand had been arrived at because they thought it would take about that long—to the year 3000—to get the unexplained explained. Some historian with a computer had figured out that nothing remained unexplained for longer, on an average, than one thousand years, except those things you called NEP. NEP were Never to be Explained Phenomena, which, somebody had taken the trouble to work out, would be in the odds of three million to one of ever being explained. But these were good times, historically speaking. Optimism ruled. The NEP file was small. No one was thinking that it was possible that NEP would someday overtake CUP. No one wanted to think too much about NEP.

As far as explanations go, the president personally leaned toward outer space and UFOs. If it'd been up to him, he would have scrapped the whole goddamn space program. Didn't belong up there. No point messing around in it. But it was too late. You *had* to fool with it now. Otherwise the Russkies would be takin' potshots at you from the moon.

How had it all begun? All the trouble. The president thought it had really begun with that damn report out of Cononga County.

It was just after midnight during a routine check by the Cononga County Police Department along Route 41. There were oil fields all out along the route, and from time to time reports of vandalism at the wells. There were private guards on duty, but the county had agreed to send a car out every hour after midnight. It paid off. Sometimes they caught trucks of Mexicans sneaking by when the weather was bad. So it was a routine check, except that Harry Walters, who was just a rookie, a kind of smart-assed type for a cop, some of them thought, had brought his high-powered binoculars, ones he used weekends when hiking. These were equipped with special red lenses for seeing at night. He had just picked them up, out of boredom really, since they had passed the Quanto Company gates and had not seen anything and were just heading back to town. He'd picked them up and just looked around, and that's when he saw them.

"Holy shit," he said, letting out a long whistle.

"What is it?" Sergeant Thomas asked.

"I dunno . . . it's people climbing straight up into the sky," the rookie said, and handed the glasses to the sergeant.

The phone rang, shattering the silence. It was 1:50 A.M. and Jenkins, the deputy sheriff for Cononga County, answered. It was Sergeant Thomas.

"What's up, Tom?" Jenkins asked.

"Nothing unusual—got a report some Indians tried to break into the Mount Hopkins Observatory. Caught three of 'em; two of 'em got away."

"How'd they get up there?" he asked, curious. Roads were closed due to spring storms, flash floods, and rockfall. There was eight feet of snow still unplowed from a blizzard a week ago, and because of avalanches all access roads to the observatory were impassable.

There was a pause. "They scaled it."

"It's eighty-five hundred feet straight up that cliff. What do you mean they scaled it?"

He shrugged. "They did it."

"What'd they want?"

He shrugged again. "Nobody knows. Found them climbing the telescope."

"What happened to the ones that got away?"

"Dunno. Looked like they were climbing up, up into the sky."

"You been drinkin', Tom?"

"Nope," Tom said.

"You think I ought to wake the sheriff?"

"I think you might," Tom said, " 'cause we don't know where they went. They went up but didn't come down."

Eberly didn't like being hauled out of bed at 2:00 in the morning, especially to hear about Indians that went up but didn't come down. Nonetheless, there'd been just too many things of late. Too many. Ever since he had sat out there that night starin' at the moon with Rufus.

Time to take steps. Huffing his way into his pants and shoes, hauling his suspenders over his shirt with great effort, Eberly personally blamed it on all that monkeyin' around they were doin' with space.

5

Amanda was a terrific pilot, Delko begrudgingly admitted, and she went after the risky stuff. He was surprised, sometimes, at the things she talked people into letting her do. And a lot of things went wrong. But she always got out. Never saw her get hurt yet.

"You got a lucky star hanging over you," he would say, shaking his head.

"Maybe so," she'd reply, smiling, and leap over another pump. "But maybe," she'd say to Delko, "it's 'cause I got my period. It always gives me an advantage."

It drove him absolutely crazy that she made such a big deal about getting her period. Lord, you'd think she'd be embarrassed about it. Not her. Big fucking deal. Didn't know what the hell was wrong with her hormones anyway. Anybody else with that training, any self-respecting American girl with that kind of physical training should've stopped menstruating. Instead, *this* broad, when they tested her, tested *better* on all the stress tests, *mental* and physical, when she had her period.

Delko even told his wife about it, who said, "I don't believe it."

"It's true," Delko cried in despair. "Everything that's supposed to work against her, she makes it work for her."

"She's weird," his wife said.

"That's what I keep telling them," Delko said. "But they still insist on sending her up."

"Why? Why send up somebody *weird?*" his wife said.

" 'Cause she's better," Delko said gloomily. "I hate to admit it, but she's so much better."

"What's better?"

"Her reflexes. Her timing. Her eyes. She's got special eyes, some kinda tennis stars got eyes like that too. Fifteen/fifteen in each eye, and extra wide peripheral vision."

"I thought there was something funny about them," his wife said.

6

"I love it. I love it. I love it," she cried, upside down, her toes toward the sky, surrounded by swirls of cerulean blue. Amanda Jaworski, America's leading space lady, rocketed straight up to the sky—swung around and around and around. She leaned to the left, she pitched to the right, past Mach 1, passing Mach 2, at 1,500 MPH. The experimental flight plane pitched to the right, dipped down, straight down, into a spin, spinning, spinning, and then into a dive at dizzying speed—the "black-out" cone, as the pilots called it. All the time, though, her mind was fixed on what she must do, her mind straight, as her eyes riveted on the controls, concentration like steel, fighting the blackout. She knew exactly, precisely, what to do.

On the ground, the ground-control boys were in pools of sweat. Eddie Nevelly had the sweat coming down like sheets, his eyes blinking faster than windshield wipers as he cursed *Jesus fucking Christ she's never going to make it, she can't get out, she can't get out,* screaming into the silent mike, "Abort! Abort! Amanda, my God." All communications were out as the silence fell around Eddie's screaming, as still as stone. The control room watched the monitor, the spinning descent of the plane, turning and barreling toward the ground, nose down, plummeting like a screwdriver. She was a goner. One sharp intake of breath, by all ten men at once, as miraculously she ejected, she was *out*, out and flying free upside down, feet wound around the chute, a strong updraft holding it open, and she was fluttering down, while below her the orange explosion, the gaseous mass, split the ground at 1,250 miles an hour.

"My God," whispered Eddie, as the zoom on the monitor showed a close-up of Amanda. She was smiling. And then she waved.

"I don't goddamn believe it," someone said, for all of them. Nobody had ever ejected at five seconds to zero. Nobody had ever done anything at five seconds to zero and made it.

"I never seen such luck in all my goddamn life," Eddie said slowly. They all turned toward each other, the group relaxing, inhaling again. It had been a nightmare. America's leading astronaut lady had had a bad accident in an experimental test plane. Something had gone wrong up there in that F-16, and one minute thirty seconds after takeoff she was in a dive. The boys in the control room knew about dive. That dive was the kind of thing you didn't come out of. Not at that altitude. Nobody had ever ejected out of it. Not that kind of dive.

"You know Amanda," Eddie said. "She'll tell you luck had nothin' to do with it. She'll tell you it's 'cause she's a girl." He started to smile. "You know, she says women have this special kind of timing."

They all smiled then, with relief, with the terror wiped momentarily from them. Some of them thought, briefly, about this girl Amanda. If pluck were the key to the universe, this girl held it in the palm of her hand. But as all of them knew, it would take more than pluck. It would, in fact, take luck. Not one of them knew if there was enough luck in all the stars to make it to Mars and back.

NASA had *never* taken on a risky project; that is, one that hadn't been adequately tested. But the pressure was on. The girl was going up because of the Russians. The Russians would beat the United States to Mars if she didn't go. But it was risky as hell. Five top scientists had quit in protest. "We're not ready for a manned flight," they said.

Delko watched Amanda walk in the gate to cheers. He didn't cheer. He looked at her. Fearless. Stupid and fearless. That smile. Smiling, after a narrow escape like that, like she was thinking about something terrific.

Amanda *was* thinking about something terrific. She was thinking about love. About the complexities of it. About timing. About trains. About passion and probability. About Hotchkiss, and the way they met. Meetings, she believed, had implicit properties that determined the structure of everything that followed them. Like colliding neutrons and protons, the initial contact determined things to come.

They had met on a train. She was wearing a hat. It was night. Another train passed while their train was standing in the station, or was it that they passed another train while *it* was standing in the station? It was impossible to tell. It is characteristic of motion on high-speed trains that it is not possible to tell whether you are moving forward or backward or not moving at all. One deduces one's position and one's direction simply by the appearance of things outside the windows. This is a very important fact to remember: The relative motion of things, especially when strangers meet, and kiss.

It was thought, a while back, that romanticism, along with other traditional points of view, could never stand the impact of modern particle physics. That for years the "shadow" had been falling. "Between life and death (beat) falls the shadow." "Between reality and illusion (beat) falls the shadow." Then it turned out the shadow wasn't a shadow at all, that the only thing between reality and illusion was this charge of photons, particles of light, bombarding electrons like crazy. Broken down it went like this: the minute you threw light on a subject, you affected it. Therefore the only way you couldn't affect it was to keep it in the dark. Of course, in the dark you couldn't see it. This was of no importance to the man in the street, who went about turning lights on and off the way he had done for years. It was in the laboratory that the world of subparticles—things smaller than atoms—was shown to be an absolute snake pit of uncertainty. If scientists couldn't predict, if they couldn't measure, how in hell could anyone ever be sure of anything? For those who were comfortable knowing that anybody who ever was sure was a damned fool, this wasn't a problem. But for those who planned and measured effects, this was something they planned to spend some time figuring out.

The woman on the train was one of those people. She was a blond-haired blue-eyed deep-chested particle physicist. She was wearing a very décolleté dress, and the handsome naval officer with very blue eyes had just lit her cigarette. She thought, considering the hat, the veil, the train, her gloves, and the fact that they both had blue eyes, that she definitely should have a cigarette. It suited the scene. Of course she did not ordinarily smoke, so this little effect was brought off with considerably less élan than she might have wished. She was aware that *he* was aware of her plunging décolletage. Perhaps it was this awareness that caused her to say the following thing: "The earth, and the sun with it, are spinning around the Milky Way at over nine thousand miles a minute."

Hotchkiss could barely take this in, impaled as he was on the dark shadow just inside her left breast. He couldn't imagine what it was that he should be so fascinated. Hell, Hotchkiss had seen plenty of tits in his day, but there was something about that shadow, dark, curved, smoky; he could almost smell it, it seemed warm to him, the slight mound of breast rising from it, gleaming like a pearl; he could almost, yes *taste* it. . . . Hotchkiss sat up. How long had he been staring at that broad's chest? He lifted his eyes. She was staring at him. Smiling.

Hotchkiss blushed. He couldn't remember if he'd ever done that before. He didn't think so. No doubt about it, this broad was really getting to him. She was what you'd call a dish, a doll, a knockout— those things men used to call women back in the fifties. Not that this was the fifties, but Hotchkiss thought it anyway. He had been talking to her before dinner, as they gathered in the cocktail lounge, and the more she talked the more fascinated Hotchkiss had become, although to tell the truth, in the beginning it was not the way she talked so much as the way she walked. The whole chassis seemed to be aligned in the most intriguing way. But then, he couldn't be sure. Perhaps it was the action of the train. But he did talk to her, and as he did, he found himself trying to assess the exact color of her eyes. He thought they were blue, almost turquoise. They were *strange* eyes, they did not reflect the light in any ordinary way. Beautiful eyes, they were; but *her*? My god, Hotchkiss thought to himself after a few minutes of conversation, this broad is out of her mind. She was far out, so far out Hotchkiss had trouble keeping up. Halfway through, he thought Maybe she's just crazy. She was a physicist, no less, a pilot, and enrolled in the NASA astronaut program.

He didn't think they'd ever send a woman into space. Not after the Russians' fiasco. Oh, they'd sent one up all right, brought her down, married her off to a cosmonaut, tested her reproductive tract, shut her up, and closed up the women's space program. They did it for history and genetic impact. Now it was done, and to hell with it. Hotchkiss thought it was of interest only in that this creature before him was *most* unusual.

As they left the dinner table, he wondered where they could go. Perhaps to the bar car. He realized then that he had been so bewitched he didn't even know her name. He asked her, touching her arm. She turned to him and said slowly, sweetly, like she was rolling something wonderful and warm over in her mouth, "Amanda."

Oh God! he wanted to cry, I want to kiss your tongue. But of course he didn't. He would have to get to know her.

Amanda, meanwhile, had for reasons she couldn't precisely locate, settled her attention on this man Hotchkiss's hands. They were large, tanned hands, and they seemed to her quite beautiful. She felt, as she spoke to him, that she was watching only the hands wrapped around the glass. They fascinated her, they seemed huge, they seemed gentle, they seemed quite *interesting*, and as he turned to ask her something and she spoke, she knew she wanted to say, I want to kiss your fingers, but of course she didn't.

Somehow delicately, deftly, they wandered together through the cars out onto the tiny observation platform. They could feel the night whisking by.

"It's a lovely night, isn't it?" he heard her say.

He touched her hair.

"This is the first time I've had a dress on in over a year . . . I've been in training," she said, swinging around. The white silk skirt lifted up gently, like a cloud.

"It's hard to believe the moon is two hundred and twenty-eight thousand miles away, isn't it?" she said.

"You think a lot about speed and direction, don't you?" he said, without taking his hand from her hair.

"Speed and direction," she repeated, "it's everything . . . it tells you everything you need to know . . . if you can find out."

"Everything?" he said, bending closer to her. Was it perfume or was it her? She smelled of spring rain.

"Yes, everything. People are born at different velocities. You have to get in touch with your own speed." She was whispering now, "If the earth is spinning around the Milky Way at five hundred and forty thousand miles an hour and you don't feel that, how fast do you think you're spinning?"

"Fast," he said, bending down toward her neck, "very fast," and he sank, then, into the dark curve he had been seeking before.

"Oh," she said, quite surprised, "is that usually the first part of a woman that you kiss?" She seemed more curious than outraged, so Hotchkiss took a chance on the truth.

"No, actually," he said, "it isn't. I just couldn't help myself." His hands were still on her hair. "I usually start here," he said, bending to kiss her mouth.

To Amanda it seemed that he kissed her forever, that the kiss, like the speed of light coming from M87, had started fifty million light years ago and was still reaching her. It felt to her like it was the longest kiss of her entire life, and so she was surprised, amazed, in fact, that when they stopped for air, or whatever the reason is that people stop, she was quite astonished to hear herself say, "I see . . . where you begin, and where," she paused, "do you usually end?"

"That," said Hotchkiss, smiling, "is a very leading question."

And Amanda thought this was indeed true. She thought she should escape. But she wasn't interested in escaping. And just then they hit a curve, and call it fate, call it centrifugal force, she was thrown into his arms.

It would be important, were it possible to determine such things, to know precisely whether in fact it was fate or centrifugal force, as this incident of being *thrown* on a curve into the arms of a man who has just kissed you in such a manner is an extremely telling moment. It was coming, from Amanda's point of view, at a perfectly dreadful time in her P.L. (personal life), which was already careening like a car out of control. In fact, she breathlessly decided something definitely was wrong. She had been and was, up until this very moment, absolutely madly in love with another man, and she could not, absolutely could not, entertain the complexity of an even passing infatuation. Even one as passing as one on a train. She made up her mind. She would let matter take its course until they reached their destination. Then she would say goodbye, it's been nice falling into your arms around curves, or whatever the appropriate thing might be to say. Amanda had not really wanted to fall into Hotchkiss's arms, had not wanted to find his hands quite as fascinating as she did, but she suspected somewhere she was suffering from the side effects of her passionate involvement with a whirling tornado known as Bronco McCloud.

It was said of Bronco that women stuck to him like molasses. This annoyed Amanda somewhat because it seemed that people always talked about him in relationship to food.

"Ohh, his hair," one of his admirers had screamed, referring to his thick black curling locks, "your hands run through it like it's pudding."

This had caused Amanda to take another look at Bronco's hair, which she thought did not resemble pudding at all. And then there were his eyes. Amanda had seen many different colored eyes before, but she had never seen eyes like this: gold eyes. That is to say they were called "topaz," but Amanda could see there were gold flecks in them, and it was, she thought, those gold flecks that explained the devastating light that shone there. He was trouble, all around.

7

One of the more bizarre consequences of quantum uncertainty is that matter can appear more or less out of nowhere.
—Paul Davies

The lone blue pickup truck tore across the darkening desert. Spumes of dust whirled out from behind the wheels of the truck, spiraling higher and higher, like a small tornado. Behind the truck, the sky was black as the night. It was high noon and the sky was closing like a curtain. Eberly turned the lights on.

"It looks real bad," Rufus said.

"Dammit, Rufus, I see what it looks like," Eberly said, pressing his foot to the floor. "We're gonna make it, though." The truck tore through the canyon heading for a small natural bridge of rocks at the far end of it, less than five miles away, which would protect them from the black sky gathering quickly behind them.

(*"They're going to see,"* said the first one.)

(*"No, they won't,"* said the second.)

They rounded the far end of the canyon racing toward the rocks, now only three miles away, when the truck came to a screeching, dead stop, throwing Rufus against the windshield and spinning the truck on its side.

Head bleeding, Rufus stared. Eberly stared. And then it was gone. There was nothing.

"Jesus, Mary, Joseph, and Goliath," Eberly said. "Rufus, did you see it?"

"Yes, I did," Rufus said. His voice was very quiet. They got out of the truck and pushed it back on its wheels. The storm was about to hit just as they got the truck righted and got the windows rolled up. In seconds, everything was black, the dust howling outside the windows, Rufus said later, like the devil himself. It was the sound that was as bad as anything, Rufus always said. In spite of all the times they had been in the desert, it struck fear in them to be caught in something like this. In minutes the sand had almost completely covered the truck. Then, just as suddenly, it was over. They got back out of the truck, and with their hands they began to clean the mounds of sand from all around it. They swept it from the hood and cleared the wheels.

"Why'd you jam the brakes on like that?" Rufus said.

"I didn't put no brakes on," Eberly said. "We hit somethin'. Felt like a wall."

Rufus looked at him. "I didn't see a wall."

"I didn't see a wall either," Eb said. "I *felt* it, though."

"I could have sworn I saw you hit the brakes, Eb."

"Maybe," he said, "after I hit it."

"Hit what?"

"Whatever kinda wall it was out there we couldn't see."

Consciousness, it turns out, is a slow phenomenon . . . some experiments by Benjamin Libet strongly suggest that about half a second elapses before we can become conscious of an event our senses have picked up. This is a long time, considering it takes only a few hundredths of a second for a stimulus to go from peripheral sensors—for example, touch receptors in the skin—to the cortex and about a tenth of a second to react with some predetermined motor act to an anticipated event.
—Erich Harth, *Windows on the Mind*

It was while they were clearing the wheels that Eberly saw it. He bent down and picked it up. It was a small cylindrical object, about two inches in diameter. It was smooth and unremarkable except for the fact that they had never seen anything remotely like it. It was glowing a purplish color until Eberly picked it up. Then it stopped glowing abruptly and looked like a small smooth stone.

"You think that thing we saw dropped this?" Eberly said.

Rufus didn't say anything. He was looking off somewhere.

"Rufus?"

"It's just a stone, Eb."

"It's a stone now, Rufus, but you saw it was something else before I picked it up."

"I don't think we ought to say anything about what we saw, Eb," Rufus said. "And you know why."

"I ain't sayin' anything," Eberly said. Then he put the object in his pocket and they got back into the truck.

What they had seen was blue. It was about eleven feet high. It was enmeshed in steel, and it looked like a gladiator. It had a helmet with a pointed top and a jaw of steel. It was shooting something from its arms in all directions. "It was all weapons, Eb," Rufus said. "Its arms, its head, legs—everything. I could see it."

"We only saw it for a second," Eberly said. "Maybe less. You think it's the army, the Russians—or you think it's something from outer space?"

"Don't know," Rufus said.

"Maybe we ought to tell somebody."

"Maybe not."

And they didn't.

"I think it was a rocket," Eberly said later.

"It had legs, Eb."

"Only looked that way, Rufe."

"Eyes. It had eyes. I've never seen a rocket with eyes," Rufus said.

"A man can't be sure of anything he sees on the desert. You've been out here long enough to know that."

"Been out here long enough, that's for sure," Rufus said.

8

Night launch. The rocket was there, white and gleaming, steam billowing around it like an iron horse, red fires lighting the bright white cone pointing straight to the stars above. A night launch was always dangerous, Amanda thought, hurrying across the base. The crowds that had gathered on the Cape were getting larger. It was a warm night. At T minus two hours thirty seconds they started to cough. Then the wind swept it in from the beach. The stuff was getting so bad it began to thicken the air so they could hardly breathe. Slowly it brought them down. First the old ones fainted, then a few children. No one got too excited. It was summer after all. The heat. They tried to ignore it, but their breathing was getting harder. At T minus thirty minutes, only the young and strong were standing, waiting, hoping for takeoff. T minus twenty-eight minutes and still counting when the wind came up suddenly, swirling the steam and fires around the launch with a terrible howl in the air that seemed to come from the sea; the sea, a wild animal now, was releasing this red clotted mess into the air; and they couldn't breathe, all of them gasping, stumbling, crying, running for the buses, the tears streaming down their faces, coughing and hacking, falling to the ground. Amanda felt it, heard it, saw it, and knew what it was. No doubt. Red storm. She knew she had to get to her car.

She started to run, but the running made her breathe harder, and the stuff was collecting inside her, closing off her air. Finally she had no choice: she hit the ground and started digging frantically, covering herself in her jacket, holding it over her head and digging out a small hole for her face, and burying her head in it. The dust was all around her now, thick and swimming. It made a terrifying sound, an unnerving whistling howl. She was hacking and coughing and telling herself to keep her face down and stay calm. Not to panic. It would be over soon. You felt like you were dying, but you weren't. No one had actually died from it. Yet.

Red tide was a tiny microorganism that normally occurred in a polluted sea; it had risen now, into the air, turning the night sky red.

When it was over, Amanda was gasping and desperate. She could feel the stuff in her eyes, her ears, her mouth, coating her lungs, the inside of her mouth, red and thick and terrible like a blizzard of blood-soaked cotton.

Get to my car, was all she could think, and when she felt a break in the wind, she raised herself up, past the bodies hacking and rolling around her, ran to find her car coated with the stuff, the seats, the cushions floating in it like a car that had sunk into a red sea. She reached it, hurled herself inside, and drove like a madwoman at desperately high speed, coughing and fighting for consciousness.

There were hundreds of cars and buses lined up outside the NASA hospital as she roared past, driving right up the front steps, nearly crashing into the glass doors, opening the door of her car and falling out, collapsing as two gas-masked attendants with a stretcher reached her side.

"It's Jaworski," one of them screamed. Several million dollars of highly trained astronaut was lying there in cardiac arrest. They rushed her inside.

Amanda Jaworski, America's leading lady astronaut, was in cardiac arrest for two full minutes before they pounded her back to life.

When she recovered, the first face she saw was Hotchkiss. "Hi," she said.

"Amanda." He was sick with worry, she could see that. "What in hell happened?"

"I—I almost don't know," she said. Her blue eyes, he thought, her magnificent turquoise blue eyes were gray now, gray with confusion and fear. "I forgot something at the lab . . . so I went back. I was in there longer than I expected to be, and when I came out, that storm, that strange stuff, was starting."

"You should've stayed in the lab."

"I was halfway across the launch site," she said. "When it got bad. I thought I could make it. God, it was awful. I was never caught in one before."

"I'm glad you're okay," he said. His hands were shaking. Her head turned as her blond hair fell across the pillow catching the light. Hotchkiss's heart fell to his knees.

"I'm fine," she said. She was quiet. *Very* quiet. "Except I really had these . . . these incredible hallucinations."

"I never heard of that effect before," he said.

"No," she turned to him, looking very concerned, "as a matter of fact, neither have I."

"Are you sure?" he asked her. There was no answer. "Amanda?"

"I can't remember," she said, astonished. "All of a sudden, just like that," she snapped her fingers, "I can't remember any of it." And then she did. Something. Something about Hooper.

"Hooper," she whispered, "did he get off okay?"

"He's off," Hotchkiss said, touching her arm. Amanda had been given a sedative and had been asleep for hours. Hotchkiss was not about to tell her that already they were worried about Hooper. The radio contacts were all off schedule, and when they got them, half the time it sounded like nonsense. They were looking to blame the Russians. They thought maybe the Russians had put some kind of scrambler into the system. Or something worse.

9

When Amanda had arrived back in Texas she did not want the handsome Donald Hotchkiss to think she was ungrateful, for after all he had come to her bedside when she had been stricken, but she did very much want to see the Terrible Bronco. He had not come to the hospital, but he sent her a plant. The plant, she had noted in the hospital, was awfully *small* and not the kind of plant that would particularly cheer you up if you weren't feeling well. Still, Amanda was amazed he had thought to send it at all. Oh, she knew he'd be thinking about her if he had heard. But it was not like McCloud to send things. If you asked any woman who knew him at all they'd roll their eyes, shrug, shudder, and say, "Oh, he's terrible, can't count on him at all." That's what they would *say*. Privately and personally they were, all of them, down to Louise Studebunker, the general's secretary, crazy nuts in love with McCloud. When it came to women, McCloud was a terror.

He was a terror and yet they kept hounding his door. Amanda had heard of McCloud's charms for years and had concluded she would never even like him. They had been introduced once or twice to no dramatic effect, until one sunny day on the airfield they ran quite literally into each other. Perhaps it was the sun, which blinded her. Perhaps it was the airfield. Amanda decided it was probably the airfield that did it. All that coming and going. All that upping and downing. The sun was in her eyes, when his voice, a voice like soft gravel, rolled against her ear and said, "Hi."

"Hi," she said, feeling a spin. He *was* good looking, she thought. How had she not noticed before? And of all the most clichéd things, he had a hairy chest. It was *quite* a hairy chest, and it peered out between the buttons of his flight suit in a *most* attractive way. There were gray hairs in it, she noticed, which served only to heighten her interest. She didn't know really quite what had hit her, but it appeared that it was a powerful electromagnetic phenomenon that made it impossible for her to leave his force field. In a countdown of ten, she felt herself thinking, I want to be yours forever. Instead she settled for coffee. The impact of McCloud was such that her coffee cup shook in her hands. It was like all the storybooks said. She was a wreck. Bronco was not doing too well either. He was used to a different flight plan, spotting a target, diving for it, obliterating it, and taking off again. He never missed. However, in this case, McCloud was feeling quite differently. Things were out of control. The atmospheric pressure was unique. He didn't want to take off, again. Or ever. And he was at a loss for words. This truly surprised him. He said to himself, "This is me, Bronco, man with a thousand lines, stories, poems, routines. A man who gets by with his smile." And here was this man, the killer-diller of womandom, holding hands (yes, by the second cup they were) with this adorable, admittedly adorable, but nonetheless definitely weirded-out astronaut broad. First and foremost, McCloud did not go for girl astronauts. He did not like jocks. He went for girls in dresses, and he had a saying, "You never chase it until you can see its legs." And here he was holding hands with a girl in a flight suit. Good grief! She might even be flat chested. Within hours (it took them five to have thirty-three cups of coffee) McCloud realized he was into a dangerous thing. For openers he had never had a bill in a coffee shop for thirty dollars just for the coffee. Secondly, he didn't give a shit if she were flat chested or not. Whoever she was the whatness of her held him and he was ready to do business—if it meant he had to bore right through that flight suit.

Instead, he realized he had to get to know her. No. He wanted to get to know her and then he wanted to hold her in his arms as the sun went down. Until then, at a loss for words and all, he attempted conversation.

"So," he said, feeling stupid. She was feeling stupid, too. She didn't think she'd ever said so many stupid things in an hour to anybody in her whole life. Really stupid things like "It's nice out today, isn't it?" What made it all even stupider is they both started to say the same thing at exactly the same time. And then they laughed.

Bronco was saying to her now, "So how do you feel being the first woman to conquer outer post-moon space?"

"Oh," she said, blushing (this was the worst: she had never blushed before), "I'm not out to conquer it"; and then she added, before she knew what she was saying, "I just want to fall through it," and then she blushed again, as if she had just told him of the terrible yearnings welling up inside her.

He said something fabulous like "Oh," or something very savoir faire like that, she thought, while she let her thoughts wander toward this conquering thing. Should she have said she wanted to conquer space? No, she decided. She was a fierce women's-rights advocate, but this conquering business was all wrong. Her trajectory required a different attitude in orbit.

She was personally and firmly of the opinion that historical circumstances had nothing, absolutely nothing, to do with the fact that it was *men* who were always going forth and conquering things. Usually, in the form of exploration. Magellan was conquering the straits, Cortez was conquering Mexico, Caesar had conquered everything. Whereas nobody really thought of Queen Victoria as conquering anything. And after all, she had commanded the largest empire in history. Amanda thought it was the word *conquer* that was the cause of it all. That Love Conquers All should have been footnoted; especially in women, it came with the bloodstream, Amanda believed, the need to be conquered, and it was this early intrauterine attachment to romantic love that too often determined the life-style of the female of the species.

By the end of two weeks, there was no getting away from it. Amanda was madly in love with Bronco. And she found it particularly irritating that a woman of her intellectual achievement should be so addicted. If she could have regarded herself as a dumb blond, which she felt assuredly she might have prior to women's lib, she could have accepted it and even enjoyed it. But now, with herself well on the way to achieving award after award in particle physics, it made her feel madly, uncontrollably doomed to know that one look from Bronco McCloud and she was finished, an absolutely crumbling lump of surrendering massive molecules. She had spent several hours talking with psychiatric types about the problem. Some said it was a mother problem. Some said it was a father problem. The ones that didn't say that said she had a dependence problem, which was because of either (a) the mother or (b) the father. Such conversations were always illuminating but nevertheless did nothing to dim the light that began to shine in her at the first hint of interest in Bronco McCloud's eyes. She had seen many many more dramatic eyes, but there was something, she thought, perhaps some mysterious power that manifested itself in the precise color of Bronco's eyes, which entered her nervous system in such a way as to render her electromagnetically helpless. She had once, in a fit of daring, in fact, used this description of herself in a psychiatric test, and apparently because it was a NASA test it had thrown them all into quite a frenzy, and there had been special meetings to decide what to do with her because she already was in advanced astronaut training.

The worst things had gotten started when she had written an essay in answer to the directive "Describe yourself," and she had gone outside under a tree and told them she was a "mass of boiling contradictions," and that she had decided some time ago that she was full of such contradictions and would continue to be so and that that was who she was. She said that furthermore, contradiction was endemic to the temperament of a person, who was accorded equal power in her emotional and (this is what got them finally, she later decided) intellectual development, to say that she accorded equal power to Frank Sinatra and Werner Heisenberg. She thought perhaps it was because they were men that they couldn't get the Frank Sinatra part, but she knew she had caused Big problems when she said "He makes me melt." It was the word *melt* that did it. They didn't like this concept of an astronaut person "melting" in relationship to anything whatsoever. Perhaps, she thought later, it brought about too much anxiety about the ability of the heat-shield tiles to hold. She didn't know. Personally she thought melting was quite wonderful and that more people ought to take it up.

A problem had developed now in her relationship with McCloud. It was what Amanda called the "sun problem."

The "sun problem" was this: Amanda wanted to watch the sun come *up* in McCloud's arms, and McCloud wanted to watch the sun go *down*. Normally this would not be a problem that could not be worked out, except for the fact that it led to a piece of evidence that could not be worked out—the reason for McCloud's sundownsmanship, and absence of sunupsmanship, was this: McCloud was married. This fact seriously interfered with the otherwise boundless reaches of her passion, Amanda felt, especially as it came as such a shock. The psychiatrist she talked to about it said, How could it be a shock when she admitted that McCloud wore a wedding ring. Amanda said he was wearing flight gloves when they met, but upon careful questioning conceded it was difficult to conceive that he had been wearing flight gloves the entire first week.

That was when she found out. Bronco was devastated to the degree that he had not lied: he assumed she knew. He could not and would not ever lie to her. He regarded being married as something that had happened to him and was an indelible part of his bloodstream—like having measles—and was part of his history. He failed to understand why she was getting so excited about it.

Amanda, on the other hand, was quite excited. She had asked one of the other women about McCloud, without revealing her own feelings, and had gleaned even more disturbing information. It appeared that not only was McCloud married, he was *extremely* married. Rumors were that he was so married he had five wives—three in Texas and two in New Mexico—and over thirty children. McCloud roared when confronted with this and rolled off her couch onto the floor, clutching a can of beer. "Five!" he screamed. "One is enough!"

"But I would love to have thirty children," he said, winking at her. And he smiled. And she smiled. He *would* love to have thirty, she was sure of it. There was something tribal about him, but she was glad to know it had not expressed itself in the wife business. As it was, the one was enough.

"It's going to cause problems in the long run," the psychiatrist had suggested, and Amanda, crying, had said she knew this was so. The fact was, after so brief a time, Amanda would have to say they were still in the short run. She didn't know when the long run would begin, but she was sure they weren't even near it yet, and already it was making its influence felt. The short-run problem was this: she wanted more of

McCloud than she could ever get. It was this, she thought, that had led to her losing her balance on that curve and falling into Donald Hotchkiss's arms. Otherwise she felt fairly certain that her Eustachian prowess was such that she never would have fallen.

10

The Milky Way Galaxy of which mankind is a part is made up of a hundred million suns; roughly one for every nerve cell in the human body.
—Charles J. Lumsden and Edward Wilson, *Science*, March 1983

Splashdown 0800. Ninety eyes scanned the sky. The weather was bad and getting worse. Ten-foot seas were sloshing over the bottom deck, and anxious faces lined the rail of the ship.

They were waiting now for Hooper. Today Hooper was due back from the moon. Half of NASA was worried, too. There were rumors everywhere that Hooper'd had his brains fried.

The ordinary procedure was for the doctors to wait on the ship, but this time Levinson insisted on going out in the launch. The seas were very bad.

Levinson looked around before he stepped down the ladder. He wasn't the only one who was worried.

"Here he comes!" It was a gasp and a yell all at once as the dark silver streak bulleted out of the clouds and plummeted toward the sea, accelerating to fifteen hundred miles an hour as it hit the surface of the water, one-quarter mile off course, heat shields flying, scattering like dust in the wind. Storms had hit the capsule, tearing it to shreds, pocking it, like gunshots. They were worried now, in the launches, as they closed in, that if there were a leak in the capsule, Hooper would go down with it.

They got to him just as the capsule, filling with water, rolled over for the last time, Hooper's face in his space suit rolling in the water, breathing through his air supply as his capsule filled, his eyes rolling up at them as the frogmen yanked open the hatch and Hooper swam forth. It was the look on his face, they said later, they'd never forget.

"Hooper? . . . You okay?" Dr. Levinson said, helping him into the boat. They had each of them asked the same question. Indeed, this person gave every appearance of being Hooper, the first man to enter the dark regions beyond the moon and return. But the expression was so vacuous, the entire appearance of the astronaut so wraithlike in his white suit, his face so twisted behind the bubble mask, like a drowned man floating face up in the sea, there was something, well, so absolutely bizarrely weird, that the rescue crew, all four of them, were temporarily transfixed. They helped him out. He had a certain quality, that's all, was what they would say afterward.

Amanda slept, dreaming of zero Gs, the light effortless swim of space, while they hooked electrodes up to Hooper's head and frantically turned the dials.

Hooper was lying on the table, that strange expression on his face. Dr. Levinson looked nervously at the EEG machine. The rat they'd sent up with him was hooked up, too. Marshak, Levinson's assistant, was so nervous he ripped the paper out of the machine just before it was ready. There was no escaping it. The lighted tube went *blip-blip-blip*. Cathode ray or paper, the story was the same.

The brain waves of Hooper leapt across the paper from the machine, a crazy staccato of signals, ranging from what might have been sheer madness to bliss to nothing. Blank reams of nothingness. Whatever it was that he had seen out there, only Hooper had seen it. The rat was perfectly sane.

11

A one percent net imbalance between positive and negative electricity in the human body would blow your head right out of the solar system.
—Nigel Calder, *Key to the Universe*

It was 0900 on the morning of March 18 that the President of the United States opened a letter from a special FBI courier marked "For Eyes Only." He opened it and read the first page, stopping to take a deep breath in between the lines. "There is no available explanation for the kind of electrical wave pattern measured in this astronaut's brain. It is reasonable to assume some extraterrestrial effect has occurred that has influenced the ability of our machines to register this properly, because it is impossible for anyone to display these brain charges and not explode. The further contradiction is that although the charge is enormous there is no indication of brain activity. The memory aspect of the brain has been totally eliminated. Whatever the cause of this action, it has not occurred in any other living thing sent into space."

That was the first report. That was bad enough. He figured some astronaut went crackers, that was all. Wasn't the first time, wouldn't be the last time. The next one really got him upset: the document told him that evidence had been found to support the theory of a previously discussed Soviet plan that involved, once again, a kidnapping. But not of the Indians. It seemed the Soviets were into snatching. It was called "The Snatch Plan." What exactly they were going to snatch no one seemed to know. But it had to do with space. It would, whatever it was, the report said, "strike a devastating blow." The suspicion was that the Soviets might attempt to kidnap America's great woman astronaut, Amanda Jaworski, before her flight to Mars.

It gave him a strange feeling, because he rather liked that little astronaut girl (well she wasn't exactly little), and his face flushed as he recalled the tall willowy liquid-motion blond who had set his heart a-flutter.

He had met her a short time ago in the middle of a big snafu: she was supposed to be taking up the shuttle the next day and she had flat out refused to do it. Said something was wrong with the propulsion system and she definitely wasn't going to use it. She said in her opinion the rockets were "fatigued." Until they changed one of the rockets, she wasn't going up. Period. Needless to say, the NASA brass was most embarrassed. They figured when the president got out there he could talk her into it, but instead, when he arrived, he was told she was in a meditation class. She'd sent a note to his attaché asking him to join her in the class and telling him to be sure to take his shoes off.

His aide at first told him not to go. "She's got a monk in there with her, from Tibet," the aide said.

"What in hell for?" said the prez.

Delko, who was mortified by this entire disregard for protocol, found himself attempting to explain Amanda. "She, uh, thinks he understands the 'nature of things.' She thinks what's wrong with the space program isn't the rocket. It is the 'nature of things.' I told you all along that broad is weird."

The president, angry then, had barged into the room, where he found Amanda sitting on the floor, eyes closed, with a small, rather energetic-looking man in a saffron robe. They did not even blink when he entered, nor seem surprised.

"Good evening," the yellow-robed man said, nodding, "and welcome."

"Hi there, Mr. President," Amanda said, smiling her ever-dazzling smile. The president, wowed by the conviviality of his reception, was momentarily stopped in his tracks. The only thought coursing through his brain was that that little astronaut girl sure was one hell of a cutie.

"Sit here," she said softly, patting a little mat beside her, and the president, normally a very unshook man, felt himself getting all wiggly inside.

"Well uh," he said, turning to one of his aides. "Should I?"

"Should you what?" said the aide, who, according to speed registries, was on one of Amanda's exceedingly slow tracks.

"Sit there," the president whispered, pointing.

"Oh," the aide said. "Why not?" It was a day of bold moves for the aide.

"Look here," the president said, sitting next to Amanda, "we have a rocket out there, little lady, and sure as hell we've had our share of snafus, for sure, but it's ready now, and you've got to get out of this here temple with this fella and go out there and drive it."

To his astonishment Amanda leaned over and whispered in his ear, and when she did it was the most embarrassing thing that had ever happened to him in public life. So much for the autonomic nervous system. He just thanked his lucky stars he was wearing big, baggy pants. Of all the damn things!

It wasn't just what she said; it was the way she said it. It had all these little moans and *ummms* in it, at least the way he heard it. What she said was, "Just a minute; something fabulous is going to happen," and she gave his hand a squeeze.

"The problem is," Amanda said to the president, "he's going forward and you're going backward."

"You can't insult the president that way," Delko said, whispering loudly.

"That isn't an insult, it's just a description of direction. He's going backward instead of forward.

"Of course," she said, "forward is really so much better for you, all around, but you'll get to it. If backward is all you can do, well," she shrugged, "we'll make the most of it, won't we?"

"Are you crazy?" Delko yelled. "You better apologize right now, telling the president he's backward."

"I didn't say he was backward; that wouldn't make any sense at all," Amanda said. "I just said it was his direction." And she smiled that absolutely drop-dead bedazzling smile again.

In Washington, the Special Commission on Atmospheric Effects had been called into an emergency session: Red Tide. Red tide was a phenomenon based on a very small microscopic species of plant life. Under the proper conditions of tide force, water temperature, and air temperature, the plant could grow at a ferocious rate, turning the sea red for hundreds of miles. At first, the tide appeared to be not much more than an annoyance, although it posed a threat to fishermen. It took the oxygen out of the water, and the dead fish would wash up, polluting the shore. The tide stung. You couldn't swim in it, and in the worst of times, under special circumstances, with the right wind factors, the microorganism would rise into the air, causing severe inflammations of the respiratory tract. For miles around people would gasp and cough, clutching their throats at the unseen invasion, choking on their breath as the invisible dust storm tore through their throats, leaving them gasping for air.

It had been just two weeks ago that the red tide had hit so violently that a special group of VIPs had to be taken by special air-conditioned ambulances and treated at the local hospital. They weren't treated for hours because the hospital was *jammed*. They all thought they'd been gassed. Eventually they were all dismissed and given antihistamines for red tide, but it had been embarrassing. A red storm had never been so severe.

The secretary of the army called the Nuclear Project Commission and told them to keep from dumping their local wastes for the next three weeks. The secretary knew it was the high water temperature issuing from the plant that was responsible.

"We got to put it somewhere," was the reply.

"Well, bury it in Oswego County. Don't put it in the ocean until after Pluto's up."

The plant reluctantly agreed. They had worked hard to get nuclear power approved for the state and they didn't want to upset the secretary. Secretly they would continue to seep small amounts into the ocean. The secretary just didn't realize the stuff was *dangerous*. Radioactive waste. There wasn't *room* to bury it in Oswego County. But that was somebody else's worry. Somebody would take care of it. In the meantime they would *have* to continue to leak some of it into the ocean. The Gulf Stream would take it to England. Let the Brits worry about it. That had been three weeks ago. Yesterday, the second red storm had erupted. Dr. Baker, the commission's head, was saying, "Our current information provides no data to suggest the causes of these storms, which occur only in the Cape Canaveral area, most intensely around the launch site. There is more here than red tide. This raises the most obvious question as to who or what might be influencing the weather."

Solipsovich reviewed File 411: Plant Nineteen, Cape Canaveral, Florida. He made a notation and then he called Rhinelander. Rhinelander told him that despite orders to the contrary, he knew they were continuing to dump nuclear waste into the ocean. The red-tide program was good yet for weeks. Good. It would perfect the confusions of his plan.

Solipsovich then turned to File 11. Yes, it would take 150 people to launch the Pluto. But once the countdown was at twenty-seven, at twenty-seven seconds down, once that countdown was started, it took fewer people than that. Solipsovich sat back, lit a black-market Cuban cigar, and permitted himself a secret Soviet smile. Yes, it took much less than that. Solipsovich knew it was possible to launch the spacecraft at countdown twenty-seven with less than that. Yes, Solipsovich knew the one thing that not even an idiot American general could know, and after countdown twenty-seven, it was possible: only one person in the computer room. And Solipsovich knew who that would be.

It was not until several hours later that Solipsovich would learn that fate had played for once into history's hand.

12

Thus relativity theory has taught us the same lesson as quantum mechanics. It has shown us that our common notions of reality are limited to our ordinary experience of the physical world and have to be abandoned whenever we extend this experience.
—Fritjof Capra, *The Turning Point*

It was a week after her T–38 flight. Amanda was crossing the airfield when Tim Purse came running up to her. The man's face was white and he was trembling. He kept looking over his shoulder.

"Look, I . . . I must talk to you," he said. "You seem like a very nice person and I . . . I—Oh my goodness," he said, when she turned around to stare at him.

"What is it?" she said. She knew these radio astronomers were nervous types, but this one was *shaking.* "I've got to take this plane up. What did you want to say?"

"We have to meet," he said to her, whispering, "secretly. I might have to send you a letter."

"Well, what is it?" she persisted.

His eyes were as wide as saucers. "What I heard," he said, " . . . out there."

"Well . . . what was it?" she asked, getting exasperated. "What did you hear?"

"Well, it, it's not what we *thought.*" He looked over his shoulder. "You *can't* go up there unprepared—you *must* talk to me, but it's a *secret.* My God it's—" Delko was stomping across the field, and Tim

Purse spotted him. "I'll talk to you soon. Don't tell anyone," he said, spinning on his heels and leaving.

"Wait," Amanda said. She felt somewhat peculiar and at the same time curious. Why the man seemed absolutely beside himself. These radio astronomers were odd, all right, but she decided to say nothing.

"What's that creep doin' out here?" Delko said gruffly. "He's s'posed to be out with the dishes."

"Dishes?"

"The radio dishes . . . out in the valley. He ain't s'posed to be up here."

"I don't know," Amanda said.

"Well, what'd he say to you anyway?" Delko said suspiciously. "I hear they been pickin' up stuff nobody can decipher."

"Nothing," she said. "He wanted to know where he could get a hamburger." And she turned away.

It was bothering Amanda, what Purse had said. Amanda loved being America's first lady astronaut destined for Mars. She loved the training, she loved space, she loved exploration. Exploration, she felt, was almost a spiritual as well as a practical necessity. But what she didn't like was the military influence. There were secrets. She knew it. Knew for certain now. The last three manned space flights had carried a total of nine astronauts. Nine. And nobody had been able to talk to any of them. And now her pal Hooper had come back and they wouldn't let Amanda see him. She'd talked to the capsule communicator for the last three flights, Mary Washburn, who had said, "Well, you know when they were incommunicado with us, all the tapes were still running. They taped everything. But they self-destructed, they said, on landing."

When she asked Delko, Delko said there were no tapes. General Farkheimer said they self-destructed because the heat shield wouldn't hold. She didn't believe any of it. There were tapes, she was certain. Why would they deny it? And why wouldn't they let her talk to Hooper?

"Know what, Rufe?" Eberly said.

"How's that, Eb?"

"You know what the trouble is, Rufe?"

"No, can't say as I do."

"Trouble is head rot," Eberly said. There was a pause. Eberly had posited this thesis before. Not an altogether complex idea; nonetheless, it always took Rufus a few minutes to consider it.

"Head rot, Eb?" he repeated. Partly he repeated this slowly out of consideration for Eberly's passion. Diagnosis was not a normal part of Eberly's perception of the world, so that when it was offered it consumed and assumed more passion than it might from a more analytic individual. This, Rufus felt, required some acknowledgment.

"How bad you figure it is?" Rufus said.

"Head rot?" Eberly said. "Hell, takin' over the entire government, White House; it's spreadin' from out there in the East. All that pollution in the cities, it's rottin' their brains out, and they don't know it."

"That's what you figure?"

"You got a better explanation?"

"No," Rufus said, because as a matter of fact, he didn't. Maybe head rot was the cause. Seemed as good a likelihood as any.

"An' it's spreadin'," Eberly said.

"Spreadin'?" Rufus said. "How fast you figure it's spreadin'?"

"Mighty fast. And here's how," Eberly said. He drew out a pencil from the bar and began to draw on a napkin. "See," Eberly said, drawing a stick figure. "This here's the smart man, got it?"

Rufus nodded. He got it.

Eberly drew another figure. "And this here's the stupid man, got it?"

Rufus nodded again.

"Now, when the smart man talks to the dumb man, who wins the argument?"

Rufus shrugged.

"The dumb man, and that's how head rot spreads," Eberly said.

Rufus pondered his line of reasoning. Eberly's mind could not be said to interest him, but its contradictions occasionally engaged his attention. "How you figure that?"

"Well, a stupid man can't understan' a smart man, 'cause he's too stupid, right?"

Rufus nodded, figuring this might be so.

"So the smart man tries to get the stupid man to understan' what he's sayin', right?"

Rufus nodded again.

"Wal, if you're talkin' to somebody stupid, you got to get down to their level to explain it, and pretty soon if you talk to enough stupid people, you hang around that there level so long it catches up with you, and it's harder to go back up to your own. After while, you just stay down there 'cause you get tired goin' back and forth, back and forth. And that's how the smart man gets dumber . . . by talkin' and thinkin' stupid all the time. That's head rot, and that's how it spreads."

Eberly drew a line between the two figures, one with the arrowhead pointing to the smart man, and one with the arrowhead pointing to the dumb man, thus completing his composition. Eberly clearly felt that these excursions into thought were works of art, for he carefully signed the napkin in the corner, *Sheriff Eberly*. Such efforts in diagnosing the national ill were sufficiently remarkable that the bartender, Silas Pond, would tack them up behind the bar. There were already three napkins devoted to explanations of head rot.

Now, since there was at this time nothing else to say about Head Rot, Eberly asked the whereabouts of the Kid.

The Kid was Alice Thwaite's youngest, Henry, and he'd gone off to college, of all things, and come back that summer looking for work. The Kid couldn't stand the sheriff and the sheriff couldn't stand the Kid either, but they were attracted to each other by this mutual disregard to such an extent that the sheriff was always asking for the Kid and the Kid always wanted to know where the sheriff was at. Eberly had gotten the Kid a job for the summer in Silas's café, the Arroyo. Personally, Rufus found the Kid a trial. Kid was always saying, "Hi, Rufs." Rufus couldn't stand anybody calling him Rufs. "Hi, Rufs," the Kid would say, "let's hunker down here and have a set-to." Rufus didn't know where the Kid got off talking like that. "Hunker down," the Kid would say, "let's hunker down," as if a man spent all his life in a squat, as if a man could only think in a squat. Well maybe, Rufus thought, it had a grain in it, meaning a grain of truth, meaning a grain of salt.

Still, the Kid provided them with cause for new discussion. It was the Kid had told them about the bump. He told them he had studied a science course and found out there was a bump, two hundred feet high, smack dab in the middle of the Indian Ocean. Eberly didn't believe it.

"Don't see how you're gonna have a bump out there, 'cause then the boats have to go uphill! How the hell you gonna have a boat go uphill?"

"There's a bump," the Kid said, "but it's not like that, Sheriff. [The Kid always called Eberly 'Sheriff.'] It's a long, slow bump. You can't see it, you can't feel it, but you can measure it."

"Two hundred foot high I say you got to be able to see it," Eberly said. "How's it come about again, you said?"

"Gravity," the Kid said slowly, pretending he understood it. "The moon has this pull, see. It pulls on the earth and right at that spot, the way the earth spins and everything, it pulls that one part up real far so it pops out."

Rufus suddenly had a vision of the Indian Ocean as bubble gum, and he let out a laugh.

"You're not very scientific," the Kid said. The Kid, as far as Rufus could guess, probably wasn't very scientific, either. Unless he'd come a long way. Always possible. Some people came a long way. In a short time. Woulda had to be a *long* way in a *short* time. Only last month the Kid was making soup sandwiches.

Rufus screwed up his eyes and looked at the Kid intently. Was it possible this Kid understood the nature of gravity, then? He didn't know, but he thought a person who understood gravity should look different from this. Rufus looked deep into the Kid's face. He concluded he didn't. Musta heard it somewhere.

"My roommate," the Kid said, hearing the unsaid doubt, "is a physicist. A genius. He told me all about it."

"An' you believe it?" Eberly said. Eberly believed nothing but his own prejudice. Eberly would deny all evidence, conviction, fact, and history. Eberly was always right about everything, but just recently, very recently, had suffered a minor disturbance. It was minor, but for Eberly this particular minor disturbance was like the pull of the moon on the Indian Ocean. That day out hunting with the Kid and seeing that owl—it bothered Eberly. And nothing, but nothing, bothered Eberly. Anything he didn't like, he usually shot at it and got it out of the way. But that damned owl was bothering him. Eberly, in his groping way, had come up against the cosmos. Fat Sheriff Eberly, stupid, prejudiced, and mean of spirit, had to grapple with fact. What it was was that this mother owl, settling on her eggs, obeying the strongest instinct to mother and protect her nest, was in fact crushing them. The thin shell of the eggs worn down by pesticide and insecticide now cracked at the slightest motion. The wind, perhaps, could crack these shells. The feathers of a protective mother rustling over the eggs would crack and destroy them. The gentlest touch, the profoundest instinct, had now run straight into history. There was no protection for the egg, no assurance for the young.

Eberly's life, of course, had been defined by fear. Such fear inspired him to shoot at everything unfamiliar. The unknown was his enemy. But he couldn't shoot the mother owl because now he had seen it.

And last year he'd seen it, too. A terrifying thing, if you thought about it. Jesse Brown, a farmer, died from drinking his own cow's milk. Drinking milk from his favorite Holstein, rippling the pure white milk out of his pet cow's udder, fresh and warm, and washing it down with fresh baked cornbread, corn fresh out of his fields, grown and kept by his wife in pristine ceramic urns. Farmer Brown, the cleanest, the most careful, the best of them all, the most reverential, had drunk a glass of milk. And died.

Buried him three months later from radiation sickness. And then his wife. And his two children. Government said it was a shame. Didn't know how, didn't know why. Just a shame. Something must have drifted over the fields, something from the plant drifted down through the streams too. Brown should have seen it coming, the government said, when he saw the trout lying dead in the stream. An accident here, an accident there. These things cannot be helped. Something must have drifted.

An attitude, perhaps. An attitude that everything could eventually be fixed. But not radiation, that could not be fixed. But they didn't know that. They thought it could. So they let it drift. A little here, a little there. It was a shame. It shouldn't have happened. But what more was there to say? It certainly wouldn't happen again. Best not to let the public know about it. Wouldn't be good. Might get them excited. Folks might get ideas. Want to shut down the plants. Lord knows they needed the plants. Why did they need the plants? Why, they were there 'cause the Commies had them . . . that's why. And why not? Nothing would go wrong that couldn't be fixed. A man dying 'cause he drank his own cow's milk scared the bejesus out of Eberly. And the owl. Scared the fuckin' shit out of him. What was goin' on, anyway? What in the name of hellfire was going on? Who could he blame it on? The Commies? The Commies were good, but didn't seem right. Couldn't blame it on the Republicans 'cause he'd voted for 'em. Couldn't blame the niggers or the wetbacks 'cause they didn't have nothin' to do with it. Was a shame, actually, that you couldn't blame nuclear power on the niggers. Seemed almost right that you oughter be able to. But niggers was stupid. And nuclears was smart. Physicists and all them there brains there.

'Course now Eberly wondered. How smart was that? What *was* smart if the smartest people were spendin' all this time blowin' every living thing off the face of the earth? Head rot, maybe. Was that eastern head rot had got 'em. Had to be that. Head rot. Yes. That was it. From eatin' rich food back East. Rich food and foreign wine. Did it every time. Yes. Eberly leaned back in his chair and sighed a sigh of relief. Head rot was at the root of it, of everything.

As far as the Kid could see, this Eberly was about the biggest slob he'd ever met. The Kid smiled. He'd scared the shit out of him Saturday up in the mountains.

Eberly was leaning over staring at the eggs, and the eggs were crushing under the weight of that poor frantic momma bird, not understanding, and Eberly was watching this, and the Kid said, "See, Eberly, insecticides. It leaches the calcium out of the birds' eggs."

"What do you mean?" Eberly said, his eyes wild.

"I mean," the Kid said, "you eating the same wheat, the same corn that owl's eatin', and it's gonna pull the calcium right outta you, too. . . ." He paused dramatically. "You see them eggs, crackin' and splinterin' like that?" Eberly nodded. "Well, same thing's happening to your bones, Sheriff. Maybe not this year, maybe not next, but some year you gonna sit. You know, you got them main sitting bones—pelvis they call it; you gonna sit, and it's gonna crack and splinter just like those eggs. . . ." He paused a moment as Eberly paled. "And then you know what? With no pelvis, nothing to hold you up, you gonna fall down and then your organs gonna pop, 'cause they ain't gonna have no ribs to hold 'em in and protect 'em; you gonna die with your guts splattered like a bug against a windshield."

Bug against a windshield. Eberly wished the Kid wouldn't give examples like that. Couldn't forget it.

"I eat meat," Eberly said finally. "Don't eat no corn, no grain, don't eat no owl food."

"That's good, if it's true," the Kid said skeptically. "On the other hand, there's no way around it, Sheriff, unless you stop eatin' entirely."

"How's that?" Eberly said, feeling he had it beat.

"What'd you think they feedin' them steers? They feedin' 'em plenty of grain. It's no good, Sheriff, you can't escape it. My roommate, the physicist, says so." The Kid took deep satisfaction at the fear in Eberly's eyes.

The Kid did not know what, if anything, to make of Rufus. Rufus sometimes seemed like he *knew* something. Something special. Other times, most of the time, he just seemed to the Kid like a bigoted ole bastard.

Rufus sat down on the steps of the Arroyo Café and took a long draw on his pipe. Something was going on out there in the desert, and it was definitely more than weather. He saw the Kid watching him from across the street, trying to decide whether or not to come over and talk. Rufus knew what he was thinking; he was thinking Rufus was a bigoted ole bastard. Rufus knew everybody thought he was a bigoted ole bastard. Personally he didn't give a good goddamn what they thought. Fact of the matter was, Rufus wasn't bigoted. Rufus thought he hated everybody equally. Everyone was regarded by the Rufusian cold eye with equal disdain and contempt. Rufus said mornin' and Rufus said howdy, but he didn't smile till he knew a man five years. Rufus loved his hatred; he locked into it like a man finding an oasis in a desert. His whole life had been confused until he found that cold spot, gleaming with suspicion and distrust, and held it. It held him together, Rufus knew. It kept him peaceful through friendship and love and harbored him in disappointment. Not that he ever felt much in that department. No, he had not ever really suffered disappointment, he told himself. Not so's he couldn't stand it. Rufus attributed this to primal wisdom, that he knew his terrain. He was born in the desert near the mountains and grew up thinking life was pretty much a case of the wild horses. They were the first things he loved. Sometimes you could catch them; sometimes you couldn't. He liked the wild look in their eyes, but the herds had thinned out now almost to nothing.

Rufus had, some years ago, due to the only disappointment he had ever acknowledged, turned toward the stars. They relieved him with their beauty and the final assurance that the object of his search, his secret aim, was light years away.

When he was eight, Rufus had sat in the mountains all night, with his father and a loaded gun. The gun was for the bobcats, and Rufus wished they would never come. He hated killing things. His heart leaped at the first sound of the hooves coming across the desert. He and his father would wait in the cold mountains, with the moon turning the rocks to silver. They would wait all night for the horses. And then one night, the only magical night Rufus had ever had, they captured one.

His father threw a golden lasso over a wild tossing head, a small black mare, and they took her home. Rufus loved the horse. He watered it, fed it, and groomed it and talked to it. He told the horse his dreams and his nightmares. When he woke sweating in the night, he ran through the cold air to the stable and lay in the straw. The mare would nuzzle his hair and whinny that she knew.

They had a record player in the trailer where they lived, and his mother had one record she played a lot. It was called "And They Called the Wind Maria." Rufus named the horse Maria. He didn't know whether it was after his mother or the wind, but when he took the horse out at night and they stretched out into the wind across the cold desert, with the stars clear in the sky, he knew he was one with the wind and the stars. Once on a history test after he had correctly identified the four elements—earth, air, water, and fire—he said the earth was like his father, the wind was like Maria, the fire was his mother, and his body was the air. When they were together, Rufus wrote, you had everything you'd ever need.

The teacher wrote "Fanciful," and deducted a point. He did well in school, but such tendencies kept him from distinguished accomplishments. At the end of the eighth grade he lost heart, somehow. His father died, the wind got colder, and his mother moved to Waco. They took Maria, and Rufus occasionally went to school, but he liked farm work better. His mother died soon after, and then the mare as well. After that, he didn't go to school. With the wind and the fire gone, he tilled the earth. He tilled the earth—it soothed him—until the droughts came, and then he bought a gas station and pumped gas. Seemed as good a thing to do as anything. But he found it hard to breathe.

Farming had gone commercial. Everything was going commercial. Things were going, period. Only thing to do was pump gas.

He knew what the old Indian meant: world coming to an end. His world had come to an end when he was eighteen. With all of them dead, he decided to open a gas station. He took up smoking, drinking, whoring, and playing cards. Nobody disliked him, but nobody liked him much either. Except the women. The women who stayed the nights with Rufus knew. They knew he had loved something once, a long time ago. Many nights now, Rufus turned to the stars. When he heard the horses were up in the hills, he would go out and wait for them. A lump would come up in his throat when he heard them run by, but he never had a horse again. Sometimes the black mare would come to him when he slept and tell him not to worry. She was the only one who knew that he ever did.

Rufus had sat one night in a bar with Eberly and the Kid from the university, and the Kid had told him that some French writer had said that the reason life didn't mean anything was because we knew we would die, life didn't make any sense. The Kid was all excited about it. Privately, Rufus didn't think you had to be French or a writer to figure that one out. Privately also Rufus thought the writer didn't quite hit it. It wasn't so much things dying, it was that you loved them. A lot of horses had died in Rufus's world, and none of it bothered him in the way he couldn't make sense of it until the mare died. The nonsense of it, the terribleness of it all came from the twist in the heart. The French writer, the Kid said, said the nonsense of it came from knowing a man was going to die himself. But Rufus personally didn't think that was so much it. He didn't know, of course; he'd never come close to it himself. But he didn't think he worried too much about it. Maybe he was too young. Maybe you worried about it when you got close to it. But for the other business, he personally couldn't take the nonsense part of it, the twisting pain inside that made you sweat all night long, wake up with the desert in your mouth, and a sandstorm in your mind—confused, lost, and drowning, drowning in the same wind that had once given you glory. The terror of the sandstorms was more than a man ought to be expected to take. A man like Rufus was not used to terror. Things elemental had gotten the upper hand.

Selling the farm and taking to pumping gas was all unnatural to him. He hated the smell of gas. The pumps gleamed with a porcelain finesse that reminded him of refrigerators, stainless-steel preservers. Gas and oil—the Texas dream clicked off at so many dollars per gallon. They'd scream shortage, yet Rufus saw the trainloads backed up for miles. Shortage or excess, the price went up. It was all right with Rufus. He didn't mind messing with it. Sometimes he missed the soft smell of the horses, but he felt safer here, where the price was fixed.

In Washington, they reviewed the evidence. The evidence suggested that the Russkies were just as upset as the United States about the reports from out there, but that might be a plot, too. Maybe they weren't upset. Maybe they were just pretending.

What they didn't know was that in Moscow the Soviet Commissar on intercontinental ballistic missiles had just interviewed two more cosmonauts and he was preparing to slit their throats.

Amanda was watching the morning news. At the end of the newscast she padded over to the refrigerator to get some milk. It was 7:30 A.M. Time to wake up Schrodinger. Schrodinger was Amanda's cat, and he was not in any ordinary sense of the word an ordinary cat. Schrodinger was named after the famous physicist Erwin Schrödinger. Now people who know about particle physicists, which admittedly are not very many people, would understand why this particular cat had this name. Schrödinger was a scientist who proved, for people who are interested in such things, that occasionally a thing can both be and not be at precisely the same time. People who absolutely loved and absolutely hated a person at the same time might understand such things. But in any event, the original Schrödinger was a scientist and had proved scientifically that a cat could be both alive and dead at exactly the same time.

Amanda's cat Schrodinger seemed living evidence of this thesis. If not dead, he was very close to it most of the time. He did not sleep in the sense that most cats *sleep*. He fell into catatonic states, commonly known in human circles as narcolepsy, at the drop of a pin. Nothing short of a pack of baying hounds could rouse Schrodinger from his stupor. He was awake, Amanda had once calculated, exactly one hour out of each twenty-four. It was divided in the following way: Amanda woke him for breakfast at 7:30, and because she felt it incumbent upon her, as his owner, to provide some assistance for his problem, she forced him to walk around the apartment for a period of twenty minutes. She pulled a string, a yellow one, in fits and starts and cried, "Come on, Schrodinger, come on," attempting to engage his interest, which collapsed periodically, and he would quite literally collapse with it, his four legs splaying out from under him in four directions, much more like a puppy than like a cat, and lie there unconscious. If the count got to ten, Amanda knew all hope of rousing him had disappeared, so she would frantically knock him on the head, throw cold water on him, and do whatever might be necessary in order to rouse him to at least get him to walk for fifteen minutes. It was necessary to keep him ambulatory during this time in order for him to get to the cat box and make his morning toilette.

This done, he would leap from the cat box, and often not three feet from it, fall fast asleep.

Schrodinger's total passivity during the semi-coma was so colossal that during parties people would throw Schrodinger around as if he were a pillow, without any possibility of waking him. There were times, in the middle of such parties, when Amanda, seeing her cat thrown across the entire thirty feet of her living room to be caught idly by a leg or the tail, and then tossed back, felt that even in a coma, Schrodinger's dignity was being assailed, and she would call a halt to it. Occasionally she discovered that some people actually thought that Schrodinger was a stuffed toy and were quite horrified when they discovered he was a real, living, albeit sleeping, cat.

"Why, I've never seen anything like it," they would remark, declaring his oddity with a faint air of superiority.

At such times Amanda would say, "It's something mysterious. I think it's narcolepsy. People have it too, you know," and then she would tell them all about it. "Narcolepsy," she would say, "is a mysterious disorder that causes a person to fall completely asleep at any given moment, even while walking or talking or driving a car." In fact, Amanda knew of a story that was quite a terrible one, when you thought about it, although of course it did make people smile. It was the story of a physicist whom people said suffered not from narcolepsy but from being so very boring that he not only put others to sleep but himself as well. One night during a dinner party, in which people were so very bored they were paying no attention to him whatsoever and paying a great deal of attention to themselves, the famous physicist fell asleep in the middle of a sentence and his head fell smack into his soup bowl. Because no one was paying the slightest attention to this, it was not until the butler attempted to remove the soup, and with it, the famous physicist's head, that they discovered to their horror that he had drowned. Some said it never would have happened if the soup had been hotter. Or even colder. But a lukewarm soup had finished him off, and this, they all felt, was the real tragedy of the situation. Amanda herself imagined it must have been quite an awful *lot* of soup in his bowl, and therefore it must not have been at all good, in order for him to drown in it, but people said this was not at all right because everyone knew that to drown it takes only an inch. It was for this reason that Amanda served Schrodinger his water in a long flat lasagne dish, with only a half inch of water in it, lest the same fate befall him.

The other forty minutes of Schrodinger's waking life was spent between 6:00 and 6:40 when he had his dinner and took a brief stroll all on his own onto Amanda's veranda, where he would make a few feeble efforts at swatting a moth, pouncing on a stray ant or two, and then precisely at 6:40 he would slink inside and collapse into his coma. Amanda thought the moth swatting was some sort of heroic attempt on his part to cheer her up, as it was clear that he himself had no real hope of catching one.

There were some people who said to her, "Why don't you get a more interesting cat?" and at such times Amanda would feel quite defensive because actually she found Schrodinger quite interesting. In fact, she was totally captivated by this cat. Nonetheless, she could see what people meant; but for other reasons it was out of the question. After all, she loved Schrodinger. It was just one of those things; it couldn't be helped. And Schrodinger loved her. It was something she knew. Besides, he didn't sleep all the time. He was up one hour a day. And, she knew, he always woke up whenever Bronco McCloud came to the house. As McCloud crossed the threshold, Schrodinger was up, alert and hissing. It was sheer jealousy and it was impressive to Amanda that Schrodinger was capable of such passion that it would actually wake him up.

When Hotchkiss came, Schrodinger didn't move. Occasionally, Hotchkiss would yell into Schrodinger's ear, "HI SCHRODINGER," but there was never a flinch. "He must be deaf," Hotchkiss would say. "Either he's deaf or he's dead," Hotchkiss would conclude.

Amanda felt deep inside her that if life had been more sensible she would be in love with Hotchkiss and not McCloud. Although she did find Hotchkiss to be an altogether attractive person, she did not find him devastating. Bronco McCloud was devastating, in the most literal sense of the term. It was quite exciting to be devastated by McCloud, and he knew it. His business was devastation, not love. And this was why women adored him. Although Amanda thought he was not the kind of man you would want to be with if you were tired or you had gained weight or anything like that. McCloud was for your prime. He was out to steal it. To take and leave nothing but the moment. This was the deal. Amanda knew it. And still . . . she decided it was worth it. The moment was worth the price. Until, of course, she fell in love with him. Then everything was torture. And it was made sublimely tortuous by the fact that McCloud, who made it his business never to fall in love with anybody ever, was also falling in love with Amanda. Two people out of control in the business of devastation could not fail to be exciting, which they both enjoyed. Its longer-range prospects would cause pain, they both knew, but there was nothing to be done. Like skydiving, they would both hang on until the last possible minute before pulling the cord.

13

Schrodinger had not always been this way, and finally, at Hotchkiss's insistence, Amanda had taken him to a vet. After a look at Schrodinger, he said, "Good grief, why are you bringing me a *dead* cat? I'm a vet, not a taxidermist." The vet stared at the stiff paws shooting straight out from Schrodinger's little body. He poked him with disdain as he said this.

"Oh," Amanda said quickly, "he isn't dead. He just plays dead."

"Really?" the vet said in disbelief. "I've seen dogs do it, but I've never seen cats do it."

"Well, he isn't playing, exactly," Amanda hastened to add. The vet looked at her. Clearly the man was convinced Schrodinger was dead. "He can't help it," she said. "He has something like narcolepsy. It's very mysterious. I thought maybe you could help him."

The vet looked at her again. Then he poked Schrodinger. "What do you mean, mysterious? This cat is dead."

"No . . . no, he isn't," Amanda said. "Try your stethoscope."

Which the vet did. With head bent over, ear to Schrodinger's chest, his face was pure amazement.

"That's incredible," he said finally. "How long has he been this way?"

"His whole life. I mean, since he was little. Every day he wakes up for breakfast and dinner. Otherwise, he's like this," she said. Then, as if to make it better, she said, "Sometimes he even purrs. He has a terrific purr."

"Really?" the vet said. But Amanda could see he wasn't interested.

The fact was, she had run into this kind of thing before. People didn't like to be around problems they couldn't solve. So they usually recommended her to a specialist. Which this vet did.

"Actually," the vet was saying, "I think this is a case for Harry." He handed her a card.

"Harry?"

"He specializes in cat brain surgery. Maybe he has a tumor."

"Oh, I don't think so," Amanda said. "What makes you think that?"

"He has an awfully fat head."

"Oh yes, well, that's just the way he looks." Amanda did not like the insulting tone leveled at poor Schrodinger, and immediately she reached onto the table and grabbed Schrodinger into her arms.

"Thank you," she said to him as he opened the door, and Amanda carried Schrodinger through the waiting room of shocked faces explaining, embarrassed as she did, "Oh, he isn't dead . . . he just looks dead. It's something mysterious." At last she slipped quietly, mercifully, out the door. When she got to the street, she put Schrodinger into his carrier, since otherwise there were just too many questions to consider, and took him to the specialist.

The specialist, after poking about in total disbelief at Schrodinger's unmoving body, said, "Well, this pussycat is tense. Very *tense*."

"Tense?" Amanda said, thinking this must be the least of it.

"Yes, by golly," the vet said. "This is one hell of a tense cat." He poked him again. "It's muscular tension, all right."

"But I thought," Amanda said, "that cats were supposed to be relaxed."

"Relaxed?" the vet yelled. Amanda wondered why he seemed to be shouting. "Of course they're supposed to be relaxed. This pussycat must have a lot on his mind! We're going to do some tests here and find out what's on it, by golly."

The vet disappeared with Schrodinger into another room, and when he came out some minutes later, he was trailing charts and graphs. "This is amazing," he said.

He had been doing research on "cat dreams," or the amount of electrical activity in the brain of a sleeping cat, and said that there was no doubt that Schrodinger was "dreaming up a storm."

"It's an absolute volcano in there," he said with some admiration. "No wonder he's exhausted all the time."

"From the mental activity?" Amanda asked, surprised.

"I have to think so," the vet said. "This cat might be a genius."

"Well," Amanda said, beaming, not quite knowing what else to say. She was glad the vet had said it first. She had known it all along. It was something she would keep between them. She could not, after all, offer as an explanation for Schrodinger's passivity that he was exhausted from his mental pursuits. Nonetheless, if one were looking for explanations, this seemed to be a good one.

Actually, all of the vets had remarked, "He has an awfully fat head," to which Amanda had reluctantly assented. It was true that Schrodinger's head was quite wide in relationship to the rest of his proportions, but Schrodinger was altogether a very large cat indeed, and Amanda felt somehow, possibly out of her adoration for him, that he worked together, aesthetically speaking, in quite a pleasing way.

The vet who did the brain-dream research said to her, "I've never seen a cat's brain like this. I think he has two frontal lobes. And his right hemisphere is enormous."

"Oh," Amanda said, "are two frontal lobes uncommon?"

"It's unique," the vet said. "I've never seen a cat with two. And a right hemisphere like that is extraordinary. Does he do very smart things?"

"Well," Amanda said slowly, finally opting for the truth, "not in any noticeable way, really. Of course," she quickly explained, "it would be difficult to know, really, because he's asleep all the time."

"Oh yes," the vet said. Then, during a proprietary moment, the vet put his hand on her arm, and looking intensely into her eyes, said, "You know, I think he has a very rich inner life."

This startled Amanda. She thought actually that a rich inner life would benefit almost everyone. Almost everyone except Schrodinger, that is. She thought that if anything, what Schrodinger needed was more of an outer life, which is why she had brought him to the vet in the first place.

"But he never does anything," she said. The vet, moving so close to her that she had to take a step back, but she couldn't because the wall was behind her, said, "But someday he *will*." He had pronounced this, breathing in her face with an almost messianic fervor, and Amanda decided that he was a person who had spent altogether too much time studying the brains of cats.

She excused herself and prepared to pick up Schrodinger, who was already asleep, when the vet said, "Would you care to donate him to research?"

The hardest part for Amanda regarding Schrodinger was the sympathetic looks she got from her doorman and the elevator men. At first. After a while they began to think she might be right, or else she was definitely out of her head. "The girl with the dead cat" was how they talked about her when she wasn't there. "Is it dead?" she had heard one say to another when they hadn't seen her come in.

"Sure, it's dead," the other man had said. "You ever *see* it?"

"Nah, I ain't seen it. Louie seen it. Louie said he saw it walkin' around there once."

"Not a chance."

"She says it's alive though. It's got some mysterious thing wrong with it."

"That's what she *says*; it must break her heart," the doorman said. "You know women are like that. They can't face things sometimes."

"It don't stink though," the first man said.

"No," the other one said, joining the puzzle. "I noticed that."

"And Louie says he also heard it purring, even though it looked dead."

"Yeah?"

"Yeah." The first man had stopped sweeping now.

"Louie said that?"

"Yeah. He swore on it."

"Well, now," the doorman said, and turned back to the elevator.

Sometimes out of their embarrassment they would turn to Schrodinger, who, it seemed to Amanda, always went into his stiffest fits in front of them, and say, "How you feelin' today, fella?"

Amanda wished that she had not told Hotchkiss about Schrodinger's condition being the result of excessive electrical activity in the brain. Now when Hotchkiss walked into the house to find Schrodinger, wherever he had collapsed—which in this case was in the Swiss cheese, which Amanda had left on the terrace and which had by now, one o'clock in the afternoon, melted all over the sleeping Schrodinger—Hotchkiss would lean over and yell into Schrodinger's ear, "How ya doin', boy? You better ease up on those calculations, Schro." Smiling he would pat him on the head, although this morning because of the cheese, he had to assist Amanda in combing the cheese out of the cat, or the cat out of the cheese, as it were.

There were times, Amanda ashamedly admitted to herself, when she wished that Schrodinger were different. Up until his mysterious illness Schrodinger had been more or less an ordinary cat—that is, from other people's points of view. From Amanda's point of view, of course, he was always quite extraordinary, but he hadn't been weird. Schrodinger had only been weird since he was three months old. She noticed it one bright cold January day when she came in the door and found him there lying stiff as a board. Needless to say, it struck terror in her heart, but she soon discovered he was purring. Several local vets had not solved the mystery, and she had by now rather gotten used to it. The fact of it was that Schrodinger even in his stupor was of enormous comfort to Amanda.

Amanda was normally an extremely bright and happy person. But she had what she called her "moments." And these moments were actually quite terrible. It was, she thought, like falling into a well, a well of despair from which she could not exit. She did not know the cause of such things. They seemed to come on her like lightning, like blows from a future or a past, beyond all reckoning or control. Such times she would take to her bed. Too weak to do anything else, she would lie there waiting for it to pass. At such times Schrodinger would wake from his stupor and come and lie in her arms, licking her face and purring, and when she would open her eyes she would see him there, his face searching her face, his green eyes full of concern.

"I'm okay, Schro," she would say, petting him, and then feeling better he would come and sit on her chest or her back, the part nearest her head, and begin to purr in the incredible way that he sometimes could, until it made Amanda's ribcage positively rattle, which produced an uncontrollable giggle.

"Schro!" she would cry, shrieking and throwing him off, "you're too much!" and he would raise his tail then and trot off, concluding his work had been done. He looked enormously pleased with himself. You could tell cheering her up was his forte. Such things could not fail to make her smile. And although it might seem an extremely ridiculous thing to say, or even to *think*, Amanda did feel that Schrodinger was the only one who ever had, or *would* understand her. So as Schrodinger had come to comfort her in her despair, she felt a very special obligation to see him through his mysterious illness. In fact, if anything, she felt it was some sort of dreadful discrimination to love anything just because it was conscious, so to speak. People would say, "Why don't you get rid of that cat?" And Amanda would think, How silly. You love a thing whether it's alive or it's dead, after all. Dying doesn't end the loving of it, and so the same was true of awake or asleep. It was probably more *fun* to love something that was awake, but you had to see things you loved through their less interesting phases as well.

"I wouldn't say it's less interesting," Hotchkiss would declare. "It's just ridiculous. That cat is always out. Zonked. You have a cat who is up, being a cat for an hour a day. The rest of the time he lies there vibrating."

"Purring," she said.

"Vibrating. It's just like having an air-conditioner that blows hot air. It's just noisy. And you have to feed it."

Despite such protestations, Amanda knew that Hotchkiss was fond of Schrodinger, as it was impossible not to be. For the brief time, and even Amanda conceded it was *quite* brief indeed that he was awake, he made the most of his charms.

Although Amanda appeared to the NASA people (and to almost everyone else) to be the essence of perfect balance, inside herself she knew there were times when she was a minefield at the core. These roaring passions that would erupt astonished her. "I have no medium speeds," she would sigh at breakfast, curling her toes around the rung of her chair and thoughtfully stirring her coffee. When she loved McCloud it was so fiercely she thought she might, on occasion, expire from it. At other times, she definitely contemplated murder. This was because McCloud was clearly a wicked man.

Now a wicked man was almost an anachronism, Amanda thought. Men, these days, were not *wicked*; they were hostile, self-destructive, or uncooperative. McCloud was none of these things. Or they were supportive, understanding, and sexually unconflicted. Bronco was none of *these* things either. He was wicked, by which Amanda meant he was terrible and wonderful all at once. There were those, of course, who only concentrated on the terrible part. "An unpleasant aftertaste," was how another of the women pilots had put it. This pilot, whose name was Miranda, bragged about an "affair" with McCloud, which only put Amanda into a rage. The rage was evenly divided between the fact that such a transaction had occurred and the consummate nerve of referring to a one-night transgression as an "affair." McCloud greeted the news from Amanda with downcast eyes.

"What can I say?" he said, looking genuinely sad. "It was before I knew you, and besides," his eyes glanced sideways, "she forced me into it."

Amanda didn't know whether to laugh or cry, for although he was laughing, she suspected in some way it was true. He ducked as Amanda threw the nearest object, which was in this case the toaster, across the room. Amanda reflected on these incidents, for they brought out aspects of her personality that had heretofore eluded her. She had never considered herself a violent person, a toaster thrower for instance, or an anything-else thrower. She was not a thrower. But when Bronco implied, and he always implied, what an extremely varied and active sexual life he had, she quite clearly felt the impulse to kill.

On the whole she was much more capable of hating Hotchkiss than McCloud, although she had never thought of murdering him. She thought of escape. If there were anyone unhateable it should be Hotchkiss, but she sensed his intentions toward her, and in some way it undid her. She resented it.

The love she had for Hotchkiss was guarded, the love for McCloud unbound. One of the reasons was this: McCloud's eyes were as magical as McCloud's arms; in them and among them, they had rewritten history. In Bronco's arms she had never been unloved, she had never been forsaken, she had never been forlorn.

With Hotchkiss, all was not perfection. Perfection had a way of eluding a determined purpose, which Hotchkiss had. There was a kind of tension in Hotchkiss, emanating from his fascination with Amanda's "Amanda-ness," as he called it, and a feeling that welled up in him that he must someway protect her from the furthest reaches of it. Amanda sensed this, too, but instead of giving her courage, it produced quite the opposite effect. There were times with Hotchkiss when Amanda felt threatened with something that prior to meeting Hotchkiss she would not have dreamed she could have felt: a loss of self. In this way she sometimes felt that the kind of love Hotchkiss had for her actually bordered on punishment.

Certainly any girl concerned for her future would have nothing to do with the likes of Bronco McCloud. McCloud promised nothing; and therein hung it all. This failure of a future, this essence of unreliableness—here was passion's secret noose. Amanda tossed and turned at night. She thought that for women, the likes of McCloud would hang them all. She knew she would give up everything for the joys of McCloud's love. True this was no idle passion; this was no will-of-the-wisp thing without meaning. The meaning of this was this: with McCloud and McCloud only could she give herself fully. Why this should be she really didn't know. But somewhere in his sweet momentariness, like the pause of a butterfly on a flower, Amanda found herself. The staunch reliability of Hotchkiss, Hotchkiss's very depth, that he would rescue her if need be from the jaws of death itself—this life-giving action was totally ignored by the female heart. The female heart, she thought, if one approached it that way, was giving hell to time. No future, no past, only the now, snatched at the heat of passion, was the gentle sex's way of saying fuck you to hands of time. Time, time, time, the enemy, time ending the race, the dare, the choice; women more than men, although all of them for sure, but women were timed: a time to bleed, a time to stop, a time to bear children, a time to stop; aspects of femininity were built so rigorously into a clock as to force an urgent stand against such a terrible oppressor. *Now* and *only now*—what a way of getting even. She didn't understand it. She knew only this: it was a dangerous game and required an elastic nature Amanda knew she did not have. Hotchkiss's cool eyes contemplated her now; Hotchkiss was out to possess her, and would not stop until he did. Walking next to him now she could feel faintly this ambition, sense he would suck the very breath from her bones. With McCloud things were different. Passionate yes. But free. No threats of destruction here. Amanda would melt, yes, they would meld, yes, and then she would return quite sated to her very self. But with Hotchkiss the exit was unruly. Precarious. Uncertain. She felt the power of his hands pulling, pulling, until once again she knew the abyss. Where death was pleasure and pleasure was death she did not know for sure. She was not even interested, really, in finding out. Hotchkiss was for her a dangerous man. Underneath that cool, rational gaze, his courage, and his love, underneath those smooth benign surfaces, a primal terror lurked. Hotchkiss was a capturer and he was out to capture. Her.

14

Amanda did not put the two events together in her mind, at this time. She did not, in fact, do that until much, much later. But this morning she was making herself a peanut butter sandwich. Amanda was fond of peanut butter; her hope was that she would eventually persuade the flight food people that peanut butter was an excellent thing for outer space and she would be allowed to bring it. In case she failed, however, she had upped her consumption of peanut butter over the last months.

The cover of the jar was off. That was strange. She never left it open, because Schrodinger liked it. She could see now that he had been in there. It was a new jar, and his paw marks were right on top.

"Really," she said to herself, "this is disgusting," and she scooped out the top, which Schrodinger had messed with, and made her sandwich. She knew it was *odd* that the top was off the peanut butter, but she did not think any more about it at the time. It was after eating that sandwich, approximately two and a half hours later, as she was strolling across the airfield with Delko, that she heard *it*.

She heard this kind of electronic sound, a beeping sound, and then the word. Clear and indisputable. The word was *nerp*.

"*Nerp*," she heard.

"What?" she asked, although in truth she didn't know why she said What? because she was quite convinced that no one, at least no one there, had said it.

"*Nerp*," she heard again. Definitely electronic and high-pitched.

"What's that?" she asked again. "Didn't you just hear that?"

"What?" Delko said.

"That sound . . . it sounded like *nerp*."

"*Nerp*? No, I didn't hear no *nerp*," Delko said. "You're mentally unstable. I told you that long ago. They ought to haul you off this flight."

Amanda said nothing more and proceeded toward the lockers. Well, she'd heard it all right.

She hadn't thought very much about the NERP question until several days later, when at a meeting with Farkheimer and two members of the Joint Chiefs of Staff who were visiting the space center, she heard it again. Loud and clear—"NERP NERP NERP." She heard it three times, and she said, carefully stifling her impulses to say What what what? "Uhh . . . did you hear a noise or anything?"

"No," they said to her. "We didn't hear anything."

"Ummm," she said.

And then she heard it again.

"Well," she said, "there was something. I have excellent hearing."

"Practically bionic, that girl," Farkheimer said, grinning proudly.

Amanda felt an increasing need of explanation for this NERP phenomenon, which was happening whenever she was around Delko and occasionally one or two other NASA personnel. It was that electronic voice, as if Delko and whoever else it was were suddenly a video game that talked and the word it spoke was *nerp*. That would be all the *nerp* she would hear, then a pause of as much as five minutes, then another *nerp*.

One night she said to Hotchkiss, "Donald, did you ever hear of a NERP?"

"A what?"

"NERP. N-E-R-P."

"NERP?" he said. "No, I never heard of NERP. What is it, some kind of early-warning system?"

"I don't know," Amanda said. "I seem to keep thinking about it."

Several weeks later, as the word kept beeping in her ear when she was being introduced to people, Amanda thought she ought to consider telling a psychiatrist about it. But she put this off, too, after going to one of the medical staff and insisting on an electroencephalogram, which, they said, revealed only that all her brain functions were perfectly normal.

Amanda thought that actually she would not have pursued the NERP question at all except for that meeting at the airfield. The NASA people, during one of the shuttle flights, had gotten the president on hand, and Amanda was presented to him once again as the first lady astronaut for the Mars shot, due to go up in six months. The president and his wife shook hands warmly with Amanda and it was just as she was shaking his hand that she heard it, *NERP*, loud and clear, and she found herself saying, "What?" and the president simply smiled and said, "Proud of you, dear."

Amanda had a sign on her office door that read NOTHING IS SOMETHING. This sign seemed to irritate Delko. This particular morning he arrived early and saw an open book on her desk. She rushed in just as he was about to start reading.

"*The Mind and the Brain!*" she said astonished. "How marvelous you're interested, I thought you only read lurid mysteries."

"I read detective stories, not that," Delko said. "This is a stupid book. Just what I'd expect, *The Mind and the Brain* . . . is that stupid or is that stupid? It's like saying the brain and the brain or the mind and the mind. I figured you're reading it because you know you're unbalanced."

"No, it isn't, and the book isn't stupid," Amanda said. "And I'm not unbalanced. The brain and the mind are *not* the same thing, as eminent neurophysiologists now know. It is in fact one of the great, and I emphasize the word *great*, fabulous mysteries of all time, but they do not really know precisely what the mind is. But it's not the brain, they do know that," she said, glaring at him, for she had just spent an hour in Farkheimer's office, defending herself against Delko's report that she was "showing signs of mental instability." She was livid that she even had to give up the time for such a defense. Delko, it was no secret, was much more anxious for Mary Washburn to take over this mission than he was for Amanda. He had resigned himself to the fact that they were sending a woman, but he would try to do what he could to prevent Amanda from being the one. His big problem, and this is what Amanda knew so well, was that no one else in the astronaut program could learn as quickly as she. She didn't know what to call it—a kind of photographic memory, or simply consuming drive—but all that anyone had to tell her, even in the most complex procedures, was one time. And she got it. This remarkable ability put her ahead of everyone else. The race was with the Russians, and Amanda was going to help the U.S. win. So it would take some powerful proof from Delko to keep her off the shot. But he was working on it, so of course she could never let him know about the NERP sounds. Amanda kept banging her desk drawers, trying to keep her temper as she thought of her ridiculous conversation with Farkheimer. Ridiculous. She pointed to the sign on her door. "I had to explain that, too, you know," she said to Delko, "because you reported the sign too."

"Now is that a stupid sign or is that a stupid sign? *Nothing is something.* You're s'posed to be some kind of scientist."

"I am a scientist," Amanda yelled at him. "I am a physicist. Subatomic particle specialist. And if there's anything I know I know that there is no such thing as nothing. The void is not a void. The void is full. There is no such thing as a vacuum, Sergeant," she was still yelling, "except in your head, perhaps! Yes!" she said, "you defy even modern physical theory. You have a vacuum, where none has ever existed before! Shall I tell you, Sergeant," she said, rounding the desk, "why nothing is something? I'll tell you why, because when you get right down to the nitty gritty of an atom, smack into the tiniest piece of matter we know anything about, there isn't any matter. Do you get that? There is no stuff, it's not material—you and I, Sergeant, are composed of atoms and we are certainly material, are we not?"

Delko gazed at her with total irritation. He didn't understand a goddamned word she was saying.

"Right we are. We are here, we are seeable, touchable, and we are made up of atoms, that in their ultimate composition we cannot see or touch. We have only patterns and energy. That is what there is at the heart of an atom. Patterns and energy. No *stuff*. Nothing, in your terminology, is not only something. It's everything."

"That's why I reported you," Delko said steadfastly. "You're overworked. They should postpone your mission. Otherwise you'd make more sense."

And they stormed out then, the two of them, to go to a training session, two small dots in the macrocosm, doomed forever to have absolutely no knowledge of the other.

Amanda decided to make a secret appointment in her effort to understand the NERPS. The psychiatrist said that auditory hallucinations were not an uncommon phenomenon under periods of extreme stress, which was one that talking with the president of the United States conceivably might be. Amanda explained there was no stress. She thought, in fact, that the president of the United States deserved respect out of the tradition of the office, but she personally thought he was a total dope, and so did everybody else who knew anything about anything. She could tell by his eyes that even the psychiatrist seemed to agree with that.

She liked the psychiatrist, the secret one that none of the NASA people knew about, because the psychiatrist did not think she was crazy. She suspected the psychiatrist thought *Delko* was crazy, but he would never say so. She told the psychiatrist she might come back and talk to him, because with Delko always telling her she was crazy, sometimes she was beginning to think so herself, and it was very helpful for someone, other than Hotchkiss, to tell her she wasn't. The psychiatrist said it was all right, she could come whenever she wanted to, or not come at all if she didn't want to, and he would help her know she wasn't crazy. Then he would turn and stare out the window as if he were looking for something, something unknown and foreign to them all.

That night, as Hotchkiss and Amanda sat watching television, Hotchkiss thought she seemed upset.

"What's wrong?" he asked finally.

"Delko is trying to keep me off the shot. He's promoting Mary Washburn. He wants everyone to think I'm nuts."

"He's never liked you. But then," Hotchkiss added, "I thought he didn't want *any* women going up."

"He didn't!" Amanda said, getting out of her chair and pacing the floor. "He *hates* the idea of a woman going up. He says they're irrational, emotional, et cetera."

"Well he's just a sexist bastard," Hotchkiss said quickly, which was not, he soon learned, the right thing to have said.

"Oh! You're missing the point! Of course women are emotional, of course they're irrational, at least some of the time. At least they have the *capacity* for that—and thank God they do! Where did Descartes get us—with all his 'Cogito Ergo Sum' crap?"

Hotchkiss looked up at her, astonished. "I don't know," he said. "Where?"

"Here. Now. Sitting on top of nuclear power that could ruin you, me, and the future of the planet. He got it all wrong, all wrong, which wasn't so bad; but if he had been a woman, he would have gotten it right."

"Now who's being a sexist bastard?" He thought that occasionally Amanda was quite capable of fully believing that women were vastly superior to men, and at such times she pointed out to him that the masculine tendency toward rational, linear, logical thinking processes might look good but was wrong. "Wrong, wrong, wrong," was her favorite phrase in such discussions. "Logic misses the point. The point is experience." When Hotchkiss would protest that this wasn't very scientific, she would launch into a series of arguments that he found quite impossible to follow. Nonetheless he got up now and followed her into the kitchen.

She was making peanut butter sandwiches, her favorite thing.

"Okay," he said, "I'm ready to hear from a lady scientist why Descartes was wrong."

"I've told you again and again, thinking alone won't do it. People with terrible impulses often think very effectively."

"No, I mean the part if Descartes had been a woman. I mean what's all this women's superiority crap," he said, banging open the refrigerator door. Fact of it was, sometimes he thought she had a point, but it wasn't a point he really wanted to think about.

"I didn't say they were superior, I said they experience rather than analyze, it's a different way of apprehending realities. You need both ways, I've always said that."

She swung back into the living room, carrying a glass of milk and the peanut butter sandwich. Schrodinger, stimulated by either the conversation or the peanut butter, of which he was inordinately fond, roused himself and Amanda picked him up and put him in her lap. Hotchkiss followed her out of the kitchen, still thinking about Descartes. Privately and personally, he didn't give a damn about Descartes; nonetheless she had touched a nerve.

He sat there watching her eat the sandwich. He wondered how it was that he thought that she ate this sandwich quite beautifully. It was unusual to think of a person eating a peanut butter sandwich as doing something beautiful, but he thought the way she ate it, especially when she took a dab of peanut butter and licked it off her fingers, was actually quite a marvel.

"So tell me," he said, when he could tear himself away from simply watching her, "what would have been different if Descartes had been a woman."

"Well he wouldn't have *said* that, or *thought* that, not to mention he would have had a much better time."

"I don't get it, "Hotchkiss said.

"Well he would have thought the opposite," she said, finishing the milk and peanut butter with a gulp. "It would have been *I am, therefore I think*, not the other way around. And he would never have thought the body was a *machine* if he'd been a woman. I mean with all due respect," she said to Hotchkiss, "anyone who has ever had a period knows you're not a machine. I mean it's very primal and spiritual all at once. It centers you in the most incredible way. I do my best thinking, my very best feeling, everything, when I menstruate."

"That's a lot of blood hocus-pocus," Hotchkiss said. "I thought women hated it, it messed them up."

"No, it doesn't," Amanda said. "I mean I feel sorry for him."

"Why? Descartes?" Hotchkiss asked, amazed.

"Yes. I mean he must have suffered a terrible mind-body split, and he's publicized it as if it were a good thing." She sat back then, waiting for Hotchkiss to argue. He wasn't going to argue though, he was going to mull it over. She might have a point. He hoped she didn't have a point. But she might. The problem was, if she had a point, he thought the solution was going to be very complicated indeed.

15

Delko had heard rumors they were going to send that chimp up—342—on Amanda's Mars trip. Said he was some kinda genius. He was the one the Russians had tried to kidnap. They were using chimps now to take the landers down. This 342 had made a successful rock-collecting mission to the moon, and had his pictures in all the papers. Good, Delko thought, send the two genuises up there, the chimp and Amanda, and never let 'em back. Now, however, there might be a delay. Three-forty-two had broken loose and stolen some ambassador's car, and Hobbs and the state police were out looking for him and sending out a highway alert.

Beedle Hobbs, Jr. ("just call me Beedle"), was having a fit. Nobody could believe that damn chimp, old 342, the terror of the army, the navy, and the air force, was on the loose. NASA, whose top security had failed them, couldn't believe it, and certainly Beedle, who was the only one who truly knew what a dirty-minded, ornery, and no-account maverick that chimp was, could not believe it. "Three-forty-two is his name, and space is his game"—that's how Beedle used to introduce him, and he was the envy of every national, international, and even extraterrestrial space program. No question about it, this chimp was the End. All the astronauts, cosmonauts, and other nauts in the world could keel over dead and that chimp could take it up, turn it around, dock it, send out the satellites, and take it back.

And now he had escaped. Or so they thought at first. Some blamed it on Hobbs. Others blamed it on the FBI. This chimp, of course, was not into any ordinary escape. No. He had stolen a diplomat's car and was last reported on Interstate 91 doing ninety-five through Jacksonville.

Now, after his near-miss kidnap by the Russians, he was headed for a little entertainment. Beedle could understand his thinking. Still and all, the police were having trouble and NASA was having a fit. Not to mention the Russians, whose double agents, posing as policemen, were cursing under their breath that the KGB had been outwitted by a monkey.

Well, it wasn't the first, and it wouldn't be the last caper by 342. Some part of Beedle, annoyed as he was, appreciated 342's basic sense of the theatrical. Of course there were loads of TV cameras all over the place already. Three-forty-two would love it. Damn chimp loved publicity. He always pulled *something* just before a launch, so as to set himself in the public's mind. At first, they tried to keep it *secret* how much work the chimps were doing on the launch, but this 342 was a regular publicity agent. After the previous caper, he held a regular press conference on it all. It was no *accident*, the caper. Beedle knew that. No sir. That chimp deliberately stole the air force plane, because he was one hell of a *pilot*. Had a regular air show up there—old 342 up in one of those jets spinning and turning, doing tumbles and wing-over-wing acrobatics that knocked their socks off. And then of course there was one *finale*. Three-forty-two sorta specialized in finales. Somewhere he got hold of some confetti, and he was spraying it as he came down. Next to bananas, 342 *loved* confetti. Bailed out halfway and landed in the top of a cottonwood, but with his background and all he had no trouble getting out of his harness and swinging through the trees. They had some time catching him after that. That was for sure. He had a good time playing peekaboo with them all—flashing his little face through the trees and then screaming and running for it. Eighteen hours is what it took them. They called it the old cottonwood roundup.

"Well," the sergeant turned to Beedle, "I've tried everything else. I think we're gonna have to gas him."

Beedle had been thinking.

"Hell, don't gas 'im," Beedle said. "You'll wind up gassin' the whole county. You'll get everybody *but* him."

"Well, what're we gonna do?"

"Well," Beedle sighed, "I been thinkin' about that. I think the only way to catch him is to hold a press conference."

There was a pause.

"A press conference?"

" 'Fraid so," Beedle said. "He's a sucker for publicity."

Eberly swung into the Arroyo Café and pressed his fat form down into a chair at the counter. Almost everybody was there, everybody meaning Rufus, Old Tom, the Kid—meaning Mrs. Thwaite's boy Henry—and Silas. Eberly knew they'd be talking about the Indians. Hell, goddamn government man had called him up at four in the morning to tell him about it. What was he s'posed to do? He rode out there anyway, with Shawcross and a couple of others, and hell it was weird: nothing there but a bunch of empty tents, abandoned pots blowing in the breeze. *Nothing*. Not a trace.

"Jesus," Eberly said. "Sure left in a hurry." It looked to Eberly like some big vacuum cleaners had come along and sucked 'em all right up. "Food was cookin', fires were lit. Never saw no Indians leave a place like that."

Horses were tied up; the teepees stood as usual in that strange cool wind; there was the occasional shattering sound of a clay jar rolling across the hard stone surface of the plateau.

"It's cold up here, Chief," Willington said, looking around. He was very nervous.

It *was* cold. Lordy, it was colder than *anything* Eberly ever knew. They had to get back in the car and turn the heater on. It wasn't just the Indians. Something terrible was going on up there, and Eberly hadn't been sure he wanted to know about it. Now, in the Arroyo Café he overheard them; he wished they'd stop talking about it. The four of them sat at the counter, knowing he had just come in and still keeping on talking like he wasn't there. They knew he didn't want to hear about it.

Harry and Clem were cleaning up the service-station floor when the Mercedes pulled in. It was red hot, steam coming out of the engine, and you could smell the rubber as he jammed on the brakes. Harry looked up first.

"Jesus, looka that Arab. He gonna bust that thing he don't slow down."

They were looking at a white 1958 Mercedes Benz convertible—a magnificent machine in excellent shape—and they were also looking at the driver, a short and rather odd-looking man, who appeared swathed in a very large burnoose. Oddly enough, the top of the car was down but the windows were rolled up. The driver was looking around nervously and beeping the horn *incessantly*.

"Impatient son of a bitch," Clem said, wiping off his pants and slowly ambling out to the pumps. The driver was now *leaning* on the horn.

"Take it easy, take it easy," he said, rounding the back of the car, and as he did so he heard the engine start. Just as he reached the driver's window, the car shot off, accelerating quickly, and careened onto the road, sending an oncoming truck jackknifing into a ditch one hundred yards from the station. The driver, fortunately, was thrown clear, and sat dazed in a meadow right beside the air pump.

"Lookee that," Clem said, pushing his hat back in a daze. "Damn crazy Arab, he's gonna get hisself killed."

"You ain' kiddin' me none," Harry said, "and the damnedest funniest-lookin' Arab you ever did see."

They stood there, transfixed, the two of them, by this momentary visit, startled by something more than the surprising impatient action of the car. What it was exactly they were not to discover until the following day when the *Mason Herald* showed a front cover photograph of a figure in an Arab headdress with the following headline:

PRIZE CHIMP ESCAPES

IN ARAB HEADDRESS—

CRASHES CAR

There, staring out at them from the center of the newspaper, was the face of a smiling chimp, swathed in a very large burnoose, arm up, seemingly *posing* for the photographer.

The story continued:

Space program's prize monkey today escaped with an Arab diplomat's car and his headdress and caused a wild goose chase down Route 91, causing three major accidents, and wound up on Tom Reynolds's farm, the car squashed like an accordion. Fortunately, the chimp, who goes by the name 342, was found hanging from the branches of a nearby tree and miraculously escaped without injury. His keeper, Beedle Hobbs, explained that the animal was fond of fast cars and planes, and was in fact an excellent driver unless under duress. Mr. Hobbs said, "He's under a lot of pressure lately, with the space shot and all. They been putting pressure on him for Mercury now, and he got to cut loose once in a while. Sure am sorry about the ambassador's buggy."

"You seen that monkey drivin' that car?" Silas said, pointing to the TV. Eberly had seen it. Some smart monkey. Had to give him credit. Now that he had Eberly's attention, Silas turned to Rufus and said, "You know, they cleaned out them Indians, clear out of the reservation."

"What're you talkin' about?" Rufus said.

"They moved 'em."

"What do you mean, they moved? Indians ain't about to move off the reservation."

"Well, they did."

"Who said?"

"Tom. Tom told me he moved 'em out."

"When?"

"Last night."

"Where to?"

"They took 'em to the airport."

"The Indians? They took the Indians to the airport?" Rufus said.

Silas looked at him, trying to decide whether he was surprised or jealous. "Yessir, tha's what I'm trying to tell you. Took their goats and their sheep, too."

"What for?"

"Get on a plane."

"Well, where they going?"

"Russia."

"Russia?"

"Yep. Heard tell they got 'em some kind o' deal, some part of Russia taking the whole damn tribe. Tom says they originally Mongolians. He sending them back to Mongolia."

"You're kiddin'."

"Nope. 'At's what Tom says. Russians came right in here and kidnapped the whole damn bunch of 'em."

"It's stupid."

"No, it ain't."

"What'd Russians wanna be doin' kidnappin' Indians?"

"They gonna get a ransom, that's what."

"Ain't nobody gonna pay that. Ain't nobody wants the goddamned Indians anyway."

"Mebbe not. But you can't have no Russians kidnappin' your Indians like that any time they feel like it. Ah mean, if they were kidnappin' Mexican Indians, or something, that'd be one thing. But they're kidnapping American redskins. You can't have it."

"No, I guess not," Rufus said. Privately he thought something was up. Wasn't nobody kidnapping American redskins for no ransom. Must be something else. They all turned and looked at Eberly, but Eberly wouldn't look back. He just drank his coffee, blew his nose, and drank his coffee some more. Sure was an embarrassing thing—to be sheriff of Cononga County with ten thousand Indians on a reservation and wake up in the mornin' to find 'em *gone*, with no *trace* at all, and nobody seein' nothin'. Why, it was like somebody reached in and picked your pocket.

16

It was breakfast time. And it was happening again. Hotchkiss swore to himself that he would stop asking Amanda, "Where'd you go?" because he felt that this gave a kind of authority, a kind of credence to what was *strictly an imaginary experience*, he was certain. Hotchkiss wasn't crazy, or anything like that, but still, he couldn't help it. He wanted to know.

And she would tell him quietly, not triumphantly or anything, just "Well, this is what just happened. This is where I went." And at those moments, just at the moment of her telling, Hotchkiss, with all his heart and soul, absolutely believed her to the living end. That was a phrase Amanda was fond of: "the living end." Some people, Hotchkiss noted, said, "the dying end."

Sometimes, although she only appeared to be traveling for a few minutes, Hotchkiss observed that when she came back, it would take a very long time to recount everything that had happened. Whereas as far as he knew she was gone fifteen, sometimes thirty seconds, but never more than two minutes, it sometimes took her hours to describe to him all the things that had happened. Hours and hours. One time it took the entire weekend. "I must have been a witch—I mean, maybe I still am a witch, because how else could I do this?" Amanda would say.

"Amanda," Hotchkiss would answer wearily, struggling for an explanation, "you are not a witch. Don't you know, for heaven's sake, whether you are a witch or not? Don't you have any *confidence*?" He didn't like thinking he was in love with a witch. That would make him a lunatic, which he most assuredly wasn't. Hotchkiss was not only not a lunatic, he had absolutely no intention of becoming one, and so he set to the task to bring Amanda's flagrant imagination, for that is all in Hotchkiss's view it could possibly be, under control. He thought it was dangerous, actually, that Amanda the last few weeks seemed to be quietly accepting all this "out of the body" routine, witchcraft, traveling in outer space, voices, the whole kit and caboodle of what Hotchkiss would come to call "the standard nut-job vocabulary." The problem was, and it was really a problem, was that other than these "funny things" that happened to Amanda, she didn't seem like a nut-job at all. She was, in fact, a *scientist*, which made her ready acceptance of these strange phenomena even more puzzling to Hotchkiss. She was a practical, straightforward person, practical enough to be sure that nobody, but absolutely nobody at the National Aeronautics and Space Administration ever found out about her "travels."

Hotchkiss wondered when it had started. After all, Amanda had not always been like this. But recently she would wake up in the middle of the night, sit bolt upright in bed, and say, "Someone's trying to reach me."

This would startle Hotchkiss, who would also sit straight up and say, "What do you mean?"

Amanda would say, "I don't know what I mean."

"How can you not know what you mean, Amanda? You just sat straight up and said 'someone's trying to reach' you."

"I know what I said," she would reply irritatedly. "I just don't know what I mean."

"How can you say something and not know what it means?" He was tired and exasperated. After all, it was three o'clock in the morning. "You're dreaming," he would say. "Go back to sleep."

"It's the strangest thing," Amanda would say, getting up and going to the window, looking up at the stars. "I feel like someone's trying to reach me."

"Well who, Amanda? And why are you looking at the sky? Are you trying to tell me you can hear anything on a fourteen-hundred-megahertz band? You know that's the only radio band they think any kind of extraterrestrial life could contact us on. Are you having a fantasy, Amanda, that you are a radio dish?" His tone was quite sarcastic. He didn't like it, he just didn't like it at all. Sometimes she went too far.

"No, I am not a radio dish," Amanda said. "I told you, I don't know what it is; it just doesn't feel like a dream." Then she punched the pillow. "I suppose it is though," she would say, punching the pillow very hard. "I suppose it has to be." Then she would lie there, awake and unable to go back to sleep.

Hotchkiss was remembering the time they had gone to Egypt to see the pyramids. Amanda had stomped around the pyramids yelling, "Oh what a waste. This is terrible, terrible, simply dreadful." She would look at the tomb drawing of the thousands of slaves laboriously pulling the stones along the sand, a recently uncovered drawing that indicated this might have been the way they were built, and she would wail, "Oh no! They did it all wrong! What a waste! Why didn't they use the crane? Dreadful, simply dreadful!"

"Dreadful? You think it's dreadful? It's one of the great achievements of Western civilization."

"But you don't see . . . there was such an easier way. I mean, using all those slaves to do that work. . . . It's inhuman. They should have used a crane." That kind of remark in a highly trained scientific person would normally be unsettling, but Hotchkiss was used to it. It wasn't as it seemed.

"You know, of course, Amanda, they didn't have cranes then."

"Well, that's precisely what I mean. I mean their brains weren't any smaller. They should have had cranes. I mean it's criminal, really."

"Amanda," Hotchkiss said, "the crane didn't exist in ancient Egypt. There wasn't a crane until someone invented it."

"That's just what I'm saying," she said. "You don't pay attention. It's always been there, in people's minds, waiting for them to discover it. The crane was sitting there all along. They just refused to see it. It's a question of how you look at things."

"I suppose," he said, shrugging.

Sometimes he didn't follow her thinking, but he was left to overcome his embarrassment with the guides who would murmur, "Doesn't she know they didn't invent the crane yet?" He would at first attempt to hastily explain, "No, see . . . she thought they should have invented it. I mean, she thinks they could have invented it . . . that the crane was there all along, waiting to be invented." And then he would excuse himself and run after her.

The Egyptian trip with Amanda, like most trips with her, went along those lines. She looked at things differently. Like just now they were discussing the fact of almost infinitesimal time, the time it took for a subparticle to travel across the nucleus of an atom. The time was one billionth of a trillionth of a second, or, one might say, a very short time indeed. That is to say, from our point of view. From Amanda's point of view, which could at any given moment change, it was this: "Just think. It might be living out its entire life—love, marriage, children, and the movies—and to us it's not even the blink of an eye."

Before Hotchkiss could explain it was not likely that a subatomic particle would be going to the movies, much less engaging in sexual activities, Amanda would beat him to it, saying, "Well, I don't mean actually going to the movies, you know, but whatever a subatomic particle's equivalent might be."

The impact of these thoughts were such that Hotchkiss, over a cup of coffee or taking a stroll or whatever, would find himself occasionally wondering what the equivalent of a movie in the life of a subatomic particle might in fact be. He thought this emphasis on perspective was partly due to Amanda's training as an astronaut. She spent so much time contemplating stars and planets that were millions of light years away that she would occasionally be given to thoughts such as this. "Imagine, if there were such a thing or an event that made the universe, and it were conscious, we would be like"—she snapped her fingers—"less than a second in its experience; you know what I mean?" she would say, getting up and roaming about the kitchen, for Amanda liked to cook when she was thinking.

One of the terrible things about being an astronaut was what she called the dreadful food they had on board. Of course there were those in the program who found Amanda more than difficult, as she had rejected all of the food and said, "If you can't give me a decent Bolognese sauce, hold the pasta concept and give me sandwiches." They thought this unfair and overly demanding, and the food consultant was quite miffed. A lot of people were miffed. Amanda was too beautiful, too charming, too joyous, to make anyone, except Delko, totally angry, but she got them miffed. Willful. They said she was willful, when Amanda thought it was just that she had strong opinions. That was all. Also, she pointed out to Hotchkiss sotto voce that the nutritionist's palate was in his socks, as far as she was concerned. "Even his oatmeal cookies," she hissed; "they reek of ginger." She would say softly, "Don't get me wrong. A little ginger in the right place is a wonderful thing. But ginger in an oatmeal cookie is just awful. Oh dear, oh dear! Awful!" she would say, shaking her head as much in disappointment as in consternation. And this was characteristic, too. She was as interested in determining the best recipe for an oatmeal cookie as she was in contemplating the speed of subatomic particles.

Amanda was thinking this morning about Schrodinger's attitude toward death. She thought he seemed almost quite frightened of it. Occasionally they found dead things in the fenced-in yard where he was permitted to roam—moths, mice, an occasional bird. That is to say, Hotchkiss found them, or Amanda. The only time Schrodinger found one, he came screaming into the house in a state of fright; when they went outside they found a dead bird, a chick that had fallen from its nest and struck death on the stone.

"He's overcivilized," Hotchkiss would say. "He's an animal, after all, even if he's a peculiar one. He ought to be trying to kill birds, mice, and all that. Even the way he swats those moths, like they're balloons. He hasn't a prayer in hell of ever getting one." Hotchkiss's voice was full of disdain.

"He's just highly evolved," Amanda said staunchly. "His instincts have been sublimated."

"Admirable," Hotchkiss said, scooping up the poor dead bird in a bag. "You realize, however, he is so evolved that if it weren't for you, he would be finished. In the wild he couldn't survive. Okay, the dead bird is gone, you can tell him it's safe to come out now."

Schrodinger in typical fashion had put his head and as much of his trembling body as would fit into a large paper bag on the floor in the living room.

Amanda turned to contemplate his shivering rump.

"Schro," she said softly. "Schro, it's okay. The bird is gone. No more dead bird."

Slowly, very slowly, with her encouragement, Schrodinger backed out of the bag. He did this smoothly, however, and it reminded Amanda of nothing less than a 747 pulling away from a ramp. Finally he was out and turning around.

Hotchkiss had entered the house now and paused to stare at him. "Look at those eyes," he said. "They're like saucers. He's scared to death."

"Of death," Amanda said.

"What?"

"He's afraid of death," Amanda said. "Aren't we all?"

"Amanda," Hotchkiss said, "death is a concept. Animals don't have any idea of death. They don't know they can die."

"He knows," she said. "Besides, some of them know. What about the elephants?"

"Oh no," Hotchkiss said, leaving the room. He didn't want to hear about the elephants. Amanda always brought up the elephants when it came to death. Although he had to admit it was a remarkable thing. It suggested that elephants had ideas, or at least a system of meanings that was not unlike human beings. The male elephant, the head of the herd, upon seeing a female who is dying, has an instinct to mount her. It is his last animal effort to bring to life his dying lover. Amanda did not stop thinking about this. The first time they saw this incident in a film, she had burst into tears. Elephants, Hotchkiss had to admit, were more than interesting. It was clear from the film that their behavior in relationship to the dead elephant could only be described as mourning. However, he thought, going from observations of elephants to Schrodinger's concept of death was a leap he was not prepared to make.

17

"What in hell is going on?" Ellis was saying—or yelling, rather—into the general's face. "Did you lissen a' what that damned fool was saying? Well, did you? Nobel Prize winner and all that?"

Normally the general would not have taken that kind of language from anyone. But then Ellis was not anyone. Ellis was the dyed-brown-haired, six-foot-two eighty-seven-year-old president of the United States, and he was at the moment, as far as the general was concerned, definitely showing signs of Losing His Grip. Definitely, the grip was going.

Ellis was still yelling, only now at the following: the chairman of the Joint Chiefs of Staff, Robert Doover; the chairman of the Joint Commission on Interballistic Strategy, James Hodges; the foreign secretary, Dellwood Phipps; the secretary of state, Arnold Lewind; his press secretary; the secretary of defense; the general of the NATO division in northern Europe; and the secretary for internal security. He was yelling, in fact, pounding on the table with his fists, and in the general's view, about to go over the edge.

Not that he wasn't, in the general's view, entitled to such a desperate position. Events of the last twenty-four hours would have been enough to drive a saint to sodomy, as they used to say back in Kansas, which was where the general was from.

The world, which was more or less used to being in a more or less mess, had definitely undergone some changes in those critical twenty-four hours. The worst of it was that no one could make any sense of it. No sense of it whatsoever. The president and his men had just come from a meeting of the best minds in the country, the best scientific minds—eight of the Thinkers, Nobel Prize winners all. It was quite harrowing, actually. The general thought one of them was about a fraction away from the "little green men" theory of the cause of the universe. The general was not the kind of person who usually worried about such questions as the nature and origin of the universe. The general worried about farting in bed and offending his mistress, and hence worried about his diet, the circumference, length, and mighty impact of his prick, which he suspected but could not admit might be waning in his sixty-seventh year; and the general worried about Russkies. Always had and always would. In World War II it had been the Japs and Krauts, and ever since then the Russkies. He thought privately Ellis was too soft on the Russkies, but then that seemed like a question for another era. Compared to what they were confronted with now: No Sense. It made No Sense and there was No Answer. That scientist with the beard, the one who spoke too slow and careful, had impressed the general until he had to listen to his theory. Nobel Prize winner and all. Damn well believed that the earth had been visited by another planet; some superior civilization had come to earth with these here bacteria, planted them here and just watched them grow up out of the slime. Well, it was a real knock in the hinges as far as national pride was concerned. Bad enough to think you'd come crawling out of the primordial ooze with some damn ape for a grandmother, but this? To have been planted, as it were, by a superior civilization, like the whole earth was some kind of garden, some kind of little terrarium for these superiors—it was downright insulting.

And then he remembered the clarity, the conviction with which the scientist spoke.

Finally, the general said, "What about the evidence?"

This apparently was the wrong thing to say, as Ellis now began to bellow like a bull whose balls got caught in the chopper. The general's eyes widened. Never heard a man bellowing and hollering like this one now. Seemed that what Ellis was saying was he didn't believe the evidence. Hell, the general didn't believe it, either. None of them believed it, that was the whole trouble. Nobody could *believe* it. Yet, it seemed to be true. There was no getting away from it. It was like somebody coming on to tell you the earth was flat. You wouldn't believe it, but when they got through with their lines and maps and calculations and all, well, you'd know it was true. You just wouldn't believe it, was all.

Of course, there was more at stake here than intellectual convictions. There was strategy. Because if the scientist and the others with him were right, the signals were coming from some such civilization. But if not, it might be a Russky plot.

"I mean," Ellis was bellowing, "can you tell me, General, what the fuck is going on?"

Even the general winced at this. He was a man used to the worst of talk, but still, the president of the United States using the F word. It upset him, it shocked him, it seemed unworthy of the office.

"Sir," he began to say, and then thought better of it. Hell, he'd known Ellis when he was ten years old, behind the garage, pulling his thang like it was taffy to make it longer. Knew him and grew up with him, and now he had to call him Mr. President. But he thought privately that Ellis should have learned a thing or two and certainly not say fuck.

However, he did concede that access to the Oval Office meant that in times of great pressure one did require epithets more powerful than "O!" or "Gosh darn it" or even "Feathers!" as the president's father, old O.J., was wont to give out with. The general sighed. Somewhere there was a relationship between power and language, and he knew that "Feathers!" was outside the parameters of it—at least as long as Ellis had the Saudis under control.

But really Ellis had nobody under *control*. Talk was all over Washington: crime, corruption, payoffs, the future of the national security. It wasn't good. One had to learn to balance these things. He knew Ellis didn't have *it*. Never had had it. What the hell, most of the presidents didn't have it, but they managed anyway. But now . . . nowadays with all of this coming to the fore, it would have been useful, indeed extremely useful, to have had *it*.

The general had never heard anything like this, never in his entire life. And to have all those scientists *agreeing* about it. Of course, they couldn't release it, not to the public. *Absolutely not.* Already probably somebody had tipped off some damn reporter. Goddamn reporters all over the place, like fleas and lice getting in where they shouldn't be and making people scratch and bleed. He'd have outlawed it privately. Constitution or no damn Constitution, he'd just have outlawed the whole goddamn press corps. Freedom of speech, freedom of the press were just a lot of liberal rot—certainly when things got serious. And things were definitely getting serious. Quite serious. Serious enough to make all those things outlets of the national security. Folks had to be told what you wanted them to know, not a whit more and not a whit less, especially in a democracy.

The general moved one leg from one side of the chair to the other. He permitted his back to collapse slightly against the fine printed fabric of the wing chair. His teacup slid perilously against the saucer in his lap. He had not realized that for perhaps fifteen minutes he had been sitting rigidly, unmoving, as Ellis bellowed at the room. His tea was cold. It was quiet in the room now. Of course the story would not get out. Not something like this. And even if it did, they'd all say it was just crackers. That's all—crackers and nuts. Bunch of crazy scientists. He shifted uneasily in his chair. Well, if it would be so easily dismissed, why then did they all regard it as so dangerous? Dangerous and incomprehensible and disturbing. All those things that Ellis personally, he knew from experience, did not like.

Ellis was not alone.

In a remote outpost of the Soviet Union, in the small cabin in Vladivostok, which was the outpost of Internal Security, amidst the falling snow the commissar of the International Communist Party prepared to shoot two Soviet cosmonauts. He had changed his mind about slitting their throats and decided instead that they be shot at point blank range, in the face. Blowing their brains out was the solution, since the brains were the problem. No coward's death for them.

He had already discussed with Internal Security how they would "integrate the information" into Soviet society. When and how to start the "erasures" from the official history. First the photos: all pictures of Zamayt and Solipsovich would be airbrushed. All records changed. When these two cosmonauts might be missed . . . but they might never be missed, he knew. Certain questions in certain realms would be asked. He did not seriously believe things would go much beyond that. Besides, it would take awhile. Like the other incident. They had done very well with that.

But still there were slips. The public had found out. Admittedly, ten years after it happened, but they had discovered the disaster. Now he would have to execute Zayatin Zamayt and Solipsovich quickly. He would come up with something. They had gone crazy. He had told them that what they said and what they said they saw was impossible. At first he thought they were suffering from Western interrogation, but then he was forced to conclude their minds had snapped. Snapped.

Dust spirits, Zamayt had said every time he had a memory of his dead sister, which kept getting stronger as he approached the moon. She swirled past the clouds, twisting like a tornado, the form getting clearer and clearer until, *voila!* Like a miracle his sister spoke from the lunar surface.

And then this business about NERP. *Nerp nerp nerp,* the cosmonauts kept saying. What was this NERP? What language was this? When they interrogated the cosmonauts they said nothing. They just looked into their eyes and cried *nerp nerp nerp.*

Execution on the spot, known in the execution trade as "cerebral cortex." The only possible answer. Nonetheless, it was disturbing—not the execution, but the conviction with which they spoke. Two crazy cosmonauts. Despite all the planning. And those words—*nerp nerp nerp!* What could it possibly all mean?

18

It was a big day in Reno. The Kid was bringing the roommate, the Genius, into Reno to meet his mother and get a piece of her apple pie, and to meet the sheriff and whoever else happened to be at the Arroyo Café that day. Since Rufus and Tom and Silas had heard so much about the Kid's roommate, naturally they were there. Rufus wanted to take a good look at a genius, and when the Kid walked in with him, there wasn't one of them was surprised.

The Genius, as geniuses were reputed to be, looked just like one. He was skinny, he wore glasses, and he had the proper expression, as they came later to call it. He had a dazed quality. He blinked and squiggled around in his chair a lot and didn't seem to say anything until you asked him a question. As nobody in that group, especially Rufus, was given to initiating conversations or questions, not too much was said. The Kid introduced the Genius all around, and then they all just sat there feeling uncomfortable, waiting for him to emit appropriately geniuslike remarks. As it was, he didn't say anything other than he wanted another Coke. He also said he didn't want anything to eat because he had already eaten Mrs. Thwaite's apple pie. The accumulated uneventfulness of this occasion was wearing on all of them. After only a few minutes Rufus was surprised to see Eberly lean forward and say, "Hey, kid, lemme ask you somethin'."

"Yes?" the Genius said, relieved perhaps that someone was saying something.

"You ever hear of moon mirages?"

"What?" the Genius asked, starting to smile. Rufus thought Eberly might get insulted. He knew why he was asking him, though.

"You know how folks see mirages on the desert in the sun—well, if the moon was bright enough, wouldn't it be the same?"

"Hmmm," the Kid said.

"Well," the Genius said, and he seemed to be thinking about it. "Well, the moon is reflected light, it's not direct light."

"What?" Eberly said.

"It's still sunlight," the Genius said, "but it's reflected off the surface of the moon so it looks like the moon is giving off light."

"You wouldn't be kiddin' me now, son, wudja?" Eberly threatened.

"No, I don't kid anybody," he said, "and nobody kids me." This last had such an old cowpoke bravura about it they were all temporarily taken aback.

"Well now," Eberly said. Then he looked at Rufus. Rufus wasn't going to say anything. He was thinking. Everyone knew about sun mirages, especially in the salt flats: the salt sparkled like a million stars and people got to thinking they were looking at the sky sometimes. They saw gods there and chariots and men with melting wings. Rufus had heard about such things. Could moonbeams, then, cross you up as good as the sun? This genius was saying the moonbeams were all reflections, like mirrors. Perhaps it had been the moonbeams, then, playing mirror games with them that night looking out into the canyon. And the sounds they had heard there all echoes, echoing so loud they filled up the moonlight with their sound. Echoes. They heard the echoes. Mirages, they saw those. But from what? Not from the heat. An echo had to come from a sound. And all that was with them was the silence. And those strange things they figured had to be all in their minds.

The silence had fallen again. Finally the Kid said he thought they'd go out and look at the Genius's project. That lit the fire.

"What project?" Sheriff Eberly said.

"Oh, it's just something," the Genius said, shrugging, refusing to elaborate. This, of course, immediately corresponded to a deep need in Eberly to be nosy.

"What kind of something?"

"It's a rocket," the Kid said. "He's buildin' this rocket out here he says can go faster than the speed of light."

"Not faster," the Genius said. "I *can* make it go faster than the speed of light, I think, but I'm not planning on it. I'm planning on it going up to ninety percent of the speed of light."

"You don't say," Eberly said, coming alive and sliding off his perch on the stool. "How fast you figure that be?"

"I know how fast," the Genius said. "It's one hundred and sixty-seven thousand miles a second."

"A what?" Eberly said.

"One hundred and sixty-seven thousand miles a second," the Genius said.

"That's impossible," Eberly said. "Ain't nothin' goin' that fast."

"What you buildin' the rocket for?" Rufus said.

"I'm readying it for donation to the space program or for emergency escape in case of nuclear war. It's equipped with a space lab and everything. It can support a small community in space for two hundred years, using solar energy alone."

"What makes you think it'll work?" Eberly said.

"I know it'll work," the Genius said, "but I can't get anyone to believe me, because they can't understand the formulas."

"Why's that?" Eberly pressed on.

"They're not smart enough," the Genius said, sighing. "I'll have to wait until I can find someone who is, or just do it."

"You oughta explain it to me, so's I could explain it to 'em," the sheriff offered confidently.

"You're not smart enough either," the Genius said, innocently tempting fate. "It's nothing personal," he added, seeing the dark look on Eberly's face. "It's just that you're too old. Anybody over twenty, their brain cells decrease every day. It's a scientific fact. You look at least fifty," the Genius went on, "so you're down millions already." He looked at Eberly steadily. "I'm only fourteen," the Genius said, "so I haven't lost any."

"I'm only seventeen, so I'm good for another three years," the Kid said, turning to Eberly. "If he explains it to me, Sheriff," he said, "I'll explain it to you." He paused. "I don't mind if it takes a long time." The Kid looked at Eberly coolly, secure in the advantage of time.

Rufus looked at Eberly. He could see that everything this Genius here said Eberly seemed to take seriously. He leaned back now, the sheriff, and then ignoring the Kid said to the Genius, "Well, mebbe most folks dies off. Mine ain't died off, I can tell. I come from good stock. Three generations in Texas."

"It doesn't matter what your ethnic heritage is," the Genius said. "It's a fact that all human brains lose hundreds of cells a year after age twenty, and even more after age thirty." He said this calmly, with no malice.

"Well, lemme tell you somethin', son," Eberly said. "It don't matter none how many we got dyin' off. I could've had ten million a day died off and you know why?"

The Genius, puzzled, wrinkled his brow. "Why?"

" 'Cause this here brain's a Texas brain, that's why. And everything in Texas is bigger: our cattle'r bigger and our women is prettier, and natchurly it just goes along our brains is bigger. So a few cells here and there ain't gonna cut into it none."

"It's not the size alone," the Genius said slowly, as if he were explaining something to a child. "It's the number of folds. The more folds, the higher the intelligence, because it's a big brain stuffed into a skull like a small shell and therefore it has to fold in on itself, like a fire hose," the Genius said. Everyone was staring at him.

"Yeah," Eberly said, adjusting his cowboy hat. "Well, that's what I was tryin' a tell ya: a few cells more or less don't matter 'cause there's a regular accordeen up here," he said, pointing to his head.

"Well, Sheriff, that accordeen up there figure out what happened to them Injuns yet?" Silas asked in an uncharacteristically provocative way.

"We gonna find 'em, don't you worry none," Eberly said, feeling only slightly defeated.

"Hey, son," Silas was saying, "what's a person to do, losing all those brain cells? Anything you can do about it?"

"Oh yes," the Genius said. "You could ingest huge quantities of choline. Choline goes straight to the brain. It enhances your synapses."

"Your whats?" Eberly asked.

"Synapses. The jump at the nerve endings. Choline is necessary for the synapse. You get a lot of it in eggs."

"That right?" Eberly said suspiciously. Rufus could see he was taking it in. "Where else you get it?"

"I don't know," the Genius said, confessing ignorance and granting them all temporary relief. Eberly continued to ponder.

"Tell me somethin', son," Eberly said, getting mean. "You got a license to build that thing?"

"What do you mean, a license? I don't need a license. It's on my old man's ranch."

" 'Course you need a license," the sheriff said. "You need a rocket license."

"I never heard of this," the Kid said suspiciously.

"Well, you need it. Everythin' you build in Cononga County, you needs a license for it."

"It's not in Cononga County," the Genius said. "It's in Reno County."

Eberly looked strange. "Reno County? Well then, you definitely needs a license. My friend Sheriff Johnson says you need a license."

"For a rocket ship, right?" the Genius said, smiling.

"That's right," Eberly said.

"Well, this isn't powered by rockets. This uses laser light." He sat back looking satisfied. "You can't need a license for building a laser-light missile, because there's never been one before," he said smugly.

"Looks like he got somethin' there, Eb," Silas said.

"Well now, I think we got to go take a look at it," Rufus said suddenly, joining the fray.

"Look at it?" Eberly said. "What you want to look at it for?"

"I want to look at it," Rufus said.

"It's not ready to be looked at," the Genius replied quickly. But he was overruled, and so it was that all of them piled into the back of Eberly's pickup truck and went to look at the Genius's laser ship, which could go ninety percent of the speed of light.

Eberly took one look at that gigantic silver spectacle smack in the middle of the R.T. Ranch and he said right off, "I knew you needed a license for it."

"What kind?" asked the Genius, who Rufus really thought was some kind of wise-assed kid.

"Driving license. Any vehicle that goes over thirty-five miles an hour or is over ten feet long, excluding only wagons, carts, and bicycles, you need a license for it."

"It might not have a pilot."

"How's that? How you gonna operate it?"

"I'm working on it," the Genius said, getting out of the truck. "Up until now you needed a pilot. I might still need a pilot, but I'm trying to do without it."

"Hey . . . there!" Eberly shouted as he saw a little man in a bowler hat and a trenchcoat round the bend of one of the silos and head out across the fields and over the hill.

"Who in tarnation is that?" Eberly said.

"Oh, that," the Genius said. "He's a very nice man. He's given me the money for building the rocket. He's very shy, though. He only talks to me. He doesn't even want me to tell anybody he's giving me the money."

"That right?" Eberly said, smelling secrecy and hence excitement.

"Yeah . . . you know he's worried about the NASA people and all that."

"The NASA people?" Rufus said. "What's he worried about exactly?"

"Well," the Genius said, "they knew I wanted to build it, but they couldn't get the money to give me. One of them there thought it was a real work of genius," the Genius said, his boot toeing the ground.

Rufus, watching this, wondered at the sudden modesty. It was clear to him the Genius thought he was a genius, too. Looking at the length of rocket before him, Rufus was about to reach the same conclusion. It didn't look like some cockamamie thing a kid would put up in a backyard. Well, it was cockamamie looking-ish: it stuck out in all kinds of places and had disks and circles and sails; it was peculiar looking. Nobody ever would call it a rocket exactly, but the way it was put together was totally professional.

"You didn't do that with no hammer and nail," Rufus said. "Who built it?"

"Oh, Mr. K., my friend, the guy who went over the hill, he sends me workers. They built it. I gave them the plans and they built it. But it won't be ready for at least five years," he said with a sigh. "It's stupid. They're too busy with weapons technology to make the parts. They told me if I went into weapons research I could get everything built in a year."

The Genius turned to them. "But I don't want to do weapons research. I want to make things that go places."

"Who's this asking you?" Rufus said thoughtfully. "The NASA people?"

"No," the Genius said, walking away, shrugging, and pointing to the barn, "somebody . . . he said I could make anything I want." He turned to them. "He said he's with the Government. He recruits people." He pointed to the hangar. "They're weird people. They never say much." He shrugged again. "Well, what do I care."

"Your daddy know about that?" Eberly said.

"My daddy's dead three years now," the Genius said. "Ever since I started building the rocket. They do all the work over in the main shed." He pointed to a long low hangarlike-looking building at the far end of the pasture.

"That right?" Eberly said, squinting. "Wal now, I'd like to take a look at that."

The small party of five, the Kid, who had been strangely silent, Rufus, Eberly, and Silas, led by the Genius, stomped out across the pasture. It was the damnedest thing, Eberly was thinking, that a kid, genius or not, could put together such a complicated-looking piece of equipment.

When they got to the shed, the Genius and the Kid pulled on the latch door, ringing a bell. Soon a tall, gaunt man arrived. When he saw the group, he yanked the Genius inside and shut the door.

"Whut in hell?" Eberly said, feeling outraged, precisely at what he couldn't be sure, but then the door opened and the Genius was shoved out.

"He says," the Genius said, looking a bit shaken, "you can't go in." He shrugged. "I never brought anybody by before, so I guess they didn't figure I would. I didn't know it wasn't okay."

"Why in' it okay?" Eberly said, pacing up and down now. He was the sheriff after all. Not used to not being admitted, especially to some old barn. "Hell, that ain't the White House, you know," he said. "It's just an old barn. Why cain't we go in there?"

The Genius looked perturbed. "He told me not to let anybody in there ever. Otherwise they'll cut off my money. So please don't."

The Genius's manner was so childlike they were all surprised.

"All right then," Eberly said.

They walked back toward the pickup truck uneasily, caught between the Genius's discomfort and that of Eberly, who was not used to being shut out of anywhere. It was getting dark.

Silas said, just before they reached the truck, "That thing you built. Think it could ever go up there?" He pointed to a bright star right over their heads.

"That's Alpha Centauri," the Genius said. "It's four point seven light years away. I'm building something now that—"

"Now just a minute," Eberly said, "how far is that in regular time?"

"Well, light travels at one hundred eighty-six thousand miles a second," the Genius said slowly, "so think that in a minute it travels sixty times that, and in an hour sixty times that, and in a day twenty-four times that, and three hundred sixty-five times that in a year, so that brings us to . . ."

"Never you mind," Eberly said. "It's mighty far, I can see that."

"Oh, that's not far," the Genius said quickly.

"Ain't far?" Eberly said. They had all stopped walking now. "Whut's far then?" He insisted on an answer, sensing something more at work here than numbers.

"I don't know," the Genius said thoughtfully. "There are galaxies very far out . . . the closest galaxy is there—Andromeda." He pointed to a silky band in the sky. "That's the closest galaxy, and it's two point two million light years away."

"Wal, I guess they ain't never goin' to get there anyways," Eberly said. "Sounds like one of those places you cain't get there from here," and he chuckled.

"I could get there," the Genius said, "if I could invent a tachyon-drive engine."

Eberly looked at him. "Why don't you go and invent it then? Make you famous overnight." He was eager to encourage the boy. There was a kind of raw excitement in this that reminded him of the old Rodeo days.

"Because they haven't been able to discover the tachyon yet," the Genius said with a sigh. "I may have been born too soon."

They continued to stare up at the sky. It was a clear night, and there were many stars out.

"What you gonna do up there if you could build it anyways?" Eberly said. "Ain't nothin' to do up there, is there?"

The Genius looked at him. "I want to see what's going on."

"Cain't you jes' look through the telescope?"

"It's not the same," the Genius said, beginning to feel exasperated. "All you get with a telescope is the light, you don't get *it*."

"What do you mean, you get the light, you don't get it?" Rufus said.

"Well, the light that left Andromeda, for example, left there when we were all walking around as apes."

"Not me, I wasn't walking around as no ape," Eberly said.

"Well, whatever you want to call it, at that point in our evolution, the light left Andromeda. It's just getting here *now*. We're looking at Andromeda's history. That's why they say looking out into space is like looking back into the past. The light, the information so to speak, we get in the future, even in ten years, is still Andromeda's ancient history."

At this Rufus felt uneasy. He liked looking out into space. He didn't much go for looking back in time. He didn't think he was so different from everyone else, in that he looked up, hoping for things to come. The past he thought was safely behind him. He never expected it to be falling down on him from the stars.

They stood there for some time, saying nothing. They were in fact stupefied, by the numbers, the distances, and all they implied, and by the Genius's confidence that he could actually penetrate the mysteries of the skies above. Eberly was still looking up.

"How many stars you figure you got out there anyways?" he said finally.

"Well, in this galaxy alone there's about two hundred billion, which is no surprise. I mean this galaxy is about one hundred thousand light years across, but who knows? There's evidence that there's billions of galaxies in the universe."

"Millions and billions," Silas mumbled, "how you ever going to get hold of that?"

Eberly took his hat off and scratched his head. "Goddamnit, till you started talkin' this way I used to think Texas was just about as big as anythin' could git. And now I'm losing faith."

"Don't lose faith in Texas, Eb," Rufus said, and they piled back into the truck, looking at the sky, and thinking about the stars, the Genius, and his billion numbers. It was the kind of thing, each of them thought, that you would never understand, but you couldn't stop thinking about anyway.

"How far's Orion?" Silas said, pointing to the sky and hanging out of one side of the truck. It was a constellation he could identify. "Two thousand light years," said the Genius. Eberly was steering and hanging out of the other side. The truck kept veering off the road everytime Silas cited a new constellation and the Genius called out the numbers. Eberly kept looking and driving and Rufus stared straight ahead, letting it all sink in.

19

Amanda knew she couldn't tell anyone about what was happening to her, except maybe Hotchkiss. At first, she thought maybe it was something she ate. Then she thought she might be having hallucinations, knowing all the time it wasn't that at all. But having no explanation whatsoever made her uneasy. Very uneasy. The only thing she had conceded to Hotchkiss so far was how terrific it would be actually to discover something that no one really knew about before. She had alluded to this quite obliquely one morning during breakfast, as that was when she and Hotchkiss often had a long time to talk.

She alluded to it in the following way. "I mean wouldn't it be terrific," Amanda said, "to be the first person to think of something no one ever thought of before?" Hotchkiss waited, wading through the enthusiastic flood with which this observation was expressed and wondering what she was really up to. "I mean, imagine this guy who discovered the hammer. Here were all these people sitting around for centuries pounding rocks with rocks. For years, hundreds of years, pounding rocks with rocks. And then Eureka! this guy puts a handle on it. And it's a hammer! Well," she said, her eyes alight, "isn't it fabulous? I mean it must have been simply mind-blowing to be that guy."

Hotchkiss considered this. He didn't know actually how mind-blowing it in fact was. He pictured some grunting Neanderthaler who probably for years and years thought the handle got in the way. But he envied her point of view. It *might* have been utterly mind-blowing; it might have been the equivalent of a Hollywood premiere in the thirties. But somehow he couldn't see it. The hammer was important, he knew. But somehow he'd rather watch Carole Lombard in a white mink stole emerge from a fancy car.

Still, he suspected something more. It was one of those days, Hotchkiss thought, when she was *almost* telling him something. He personally didn't think she was actually that passionately into hammers.

20

Amanda and Hotchkiss were having one of their many heated discussions about Schrodinger.

"Who ever heard of such a thing? All he does is sleep, watch television, and wait for the sound of the can opener. You even had to cook those herrings for him."

"So what," Amanda said. "He doesn't like raw food. You don't like it either. You hate sushi."

"Sushi?" Hotchkiss said, aghast. She was so good at missing the point. "Of course I hate sushi. I am a human being. He, may I remind you, is a wild animal, or a domesticated wild animal. A million years ago he was a big fierce jungle tiger. Now look at him. He's a flop. He only eats out of cans. He's a case against evolution."

"He's highly evolved!" Amanda said with some irritation.

"And I say he's a flop. The harbinger of disaster. A cat that only eats out of cans—he doesn't know how to survive. If Darwin is right, that cat is the end of the line."

"He's onto something new," she said, angry now. "A higher consciousness. Schrodinger's kind, when it multiplies, will prevail. You'll see. I'm confident," she said, moving then around the counters of the kitchen in that way she had, so it seemed to Hotchkiss she was always somehow teasing him, her behind appearing first—rounded, bending around one turn—then her chest dropping full in front of him as she poured coffee, turning and teasing about the kitchen in this most remarkable way she had. She told him again about how Schrodinger was "the herald of a new era."

"My ass," Hotchkiss snarled, as she picked Schrodinger up and cuddled him. "He has about as much chance of prevailing as a tiger with a can opener."

And then these discussions, like so many before, would end unresolved—Hotchkiss feeling uncomfortable, terribly uncomfortable, as though he were caught with the two of them in a system of belief that defied all logic, reason, and reality. That would be bad enough, but what bothered him was *them*—Amanda and Schrodinger—for they were in this together somehow, and she was right; for there were times, indisputably, when despite Hotchkiss and reality and logic and reason and everything else, one had to confess that Schrodinger was more than the sum of his parts—a cat. Whatever it was that was going on, what got to Hotchkiss so was that in the midst of this mystical soup the two of them shared, this ongoing faith in magic, mystery, and secret powers, they were having an absolutely marvelous time. Their interest and confidence in this system of exchanges with the world was constantly renewed by the absolutely terrific kick the two of them seemed to elicit from this seemingly zany enterprise.

The scientists had now tested the last of the experiments from Hooper's capsule. Within hours, they were on the hot line to Washington.

In Washington, the president's national security advisor got the reports and thought he was about to get a case of shingles.

Within twenty-four hours, the NEP (Never to be Explained Phenomena) file had nearly *doubled*.

> *The crucial feature of quantum theory is that the observer is not only necessary to observe the properties of an atomic phenomenon, but is necessary even to bring about these properties. My conscious decision about how to observe, say an electron, will determine the electron's properties to some extent . . . in atomic physics the sharp Cartesian division between mind and matter, between the observer and the observed, can no longer be maintained.*
>
> Fritjof Capra, *The Turning Point*

Amanda was at a dinner party to which many prominent physicists had been invited. Amanda was happiest in the company of the other sub-particle physicists who were considered crazy like herself. "Brilliant," everyone said, "but nuts." One of them, Dr. Bernard, was extremely "far out," even from Amanda's point of view. She listened to him now.

"It is perfectly logical to assume that during those times when the 'mind is absent,' while waiting for a bus, while being bored in the middle of a dinner party conversation, you know how far you can travel. It is my belief that you can in fact reassemble, that in fact you have left your place at the party, experienced what you think you see, and returned, but you yourself are traveling faster than the speed of light—and so it is quite impossible to be detected by the others at the table. It is one of the ironies of modern physics that at that moment it is quite impossible for you to be seen, even by yourself."

Amanda Jaworski's mouth dropped open as she stared at him. She had heard he had wild ideas; she never thought they would converge with her own. She was in the middle of her salad and she knew it was unruly, to say the least, to have it hanging out of the side of her mouth like that, but she was stupefied. There was this Nobel Prize winner telling about invisible travel to other places. She knew. She understood. She wanted to ask him more. But she was being distracted.

"Don't you find that, Miss Jaworski?"

Was he looking at her directly with a special knowledge? Did he *know*?

"Well, I, I've never heard the theory propounded before, I mean by a scientist," Amanda said, feeling nervous. "As you know, most physicists reject telepathy, and," she hesitated, "teleportation. But it certainly is possible, I guess," she said, sliding away.

"Oh, this is so fascinating," a lady sitting next to her said. "Do go on."

Amanda looked at the Nobel Prize winner uneasily. If he were crazy, which he wasn't, she thought, the only really crazy thing was to be talking publicly about this. It was the kind of thing you kept to yourself. He was going on.

"When people are lost in thought," he said, "of course they are lost. Truly lost. The shell remains here, the body remains here, but the molecular structure, the experience, has actually traveled; it is traveling at fantastic speed, faster than light, much faster. The experience goes out and comes back. During such times, the sensory apparatus here is dimmed. That's why when people are lost in thought they can't hear you, they don't see you. They are literally *elsewhere*."

"Oh, time travel. How very interesting," the lady said, speaking with her mouth full of pâté. "Is it true that in the far reaches of outer space an astronaut could return to find his children *older* than he is?"

"Not only possible," the winner said, "inevitable. Time slows down at very high speeds. Tests prove it again and again. Of course, people have difficulty accepting this, but at a future point in society, they will have to accept it. The time for the astronaut would, at those speeds only, be much slower than here on earth. We would age, he wouldn't."

"I see," she said very agreeably. "Well, could you explain it *exactly*?"

"Of course."

Amanda winced. Good grief, he really was going to try to explain the second law of relativity to this lady munching her pâté. The winner started his mini-lecture, and Amanda escaped before the lady could ask her what it must feel like to think about going to Mars.

Amanda didn't know if it was a coincidence or not, but the day she stumbled onto the super-classified tapes was the same day she came home and found the first of the "foot drawings."

There in *amazing* detail were perfect replicas of her feet, in her *worst* slippers.

"Now, who in the *world* . . . ?" She moved to the couch and studied the drawing. Who in the whole wide world would draw pictures of her *feet*? And leave them for her, like an offering?

Although Amanda was desperately trying *not* to see McCloud, she found this too impossible to do. She would tell herself it was neurotic, adolescent, counterproductive, pointless—call it what you will—but then he would call her and she would be off again.

She knew somewhere in McCloud there were lots of worlds. The things that he hated in himself, even these Amanda loved. She thought that someone as wonderful as McCloud really was (which she felt she knew better than anyone, even McCloud) should never be hated by anyone, especially by himself. But McCloud was harsh; he felt he wasn't strong enough, man enough, tough enough, bold enough. He felt he only dreamed enough. He dreamed of Excalibur, she knew, of the magic sword that would change his life, restoring him to his lost powers, enabling him to finally invoke his secret wonder. She also knew he would not search for it; he could only long for it. She knew what McCloud dreamed. What Hotchkiss dreamed she could only guess at. What McCloud dreamed of she could not give him, no one could give him. He would have to find it himself. Or not. McCloud dreamed of glory, strength, and faith. He would be king. Nights he returned to Arthur's court in an attempt to find his place. There were days, she could tell, when he actually heard the sound of the armor in his ear, when he found Guinevere's eyes had singled him out and he made ready. But the horse was never saddled, the call never came.

This morning Amanda had a school visit. She was immensely popular with kids on the lecture circuit. The only problem was sometimes the parents complained. She had to limit the number of speaking engagements she could accept. Amanda would explain the second law of thermodynamics in its utmost simplicity: an increase in disorder in the universe. Using a large bell jar she would fill half of it with salt. Then she would put a thin layer of pepper on it.

"Now you see, you have all the salt in the bottom and all the pepper on the top. What the second law of thermodynamics says is that everything in the universe, assuming . . . what?"

They would all raise their hands.

"Assuming the universe has a ceiling and a floor"—in other words, a closed system.

"You start shaking, and it gets . . . what?"

They would yell, "MESSIER."

"Can it ever get back to the point where all the pepper is on the top?" she would ask.

They would chant back, chorusing, convinced, "ABSOLUTELY NOT."

So much for entropy. It was not difficult for the cleverest of them to extrapolate the message that the world is getting messier. They made their own uses of this, she noted, and many times after an appearance the parents would angrily call the school and say that so-and-so refused to clean up his room because of the "second law of thermodynamics." It would, they argued, simply get messy again.

Amanda privately thought they should be thrilled at such a conceptual grasp of entropy, but somehow they weren't.

At breakfast, Amanda sat there, her pale, gold skin gleaming, the sun raking her arms with its light falling in thin, even blades through the shutters like a knife. Amanda, crossing one leg with the other, the high-heeled sandal pointed exactly precisely on one knee, the short leather skirt above her thighs, too far above, he told her, looked like a motorcycle moll in the leather, but she said, "Shut up, it's fashionable," which was what Amanda said a lot these days. With legs like that you had certain rights, Hotchkiss admitted. Certainly one of the rights was to be fashionable and to wear skirts that ended in the middle of your thigh.

Personally there were times when he thought Amanda was out of her goddamn mind. Like now. Hotchkiss was experiencing what he liked to call "time fallout," which was his way of saying that people were changing too fast for him, things were changing, their minds or mental processes or whatever you wanted to call it. Hotchkiss couldn't keep up. Especially with these space freaks. There was a certain kind of physicist, Hotchkiss thought, whom necessity dictated that he regard suspiciously. Like Amanda, at times. At other times, he thought she was this real normal girl. She liked strawberry sodas, high-heeled shoes, men, lipstick, convertibles, long hair, bright toenail polish, particle physics, quarks, entropy, speculations regarding the speed of light, Darwinism, and archaeology. Now these last few things were not necessarily the province of what one came to think of as an ordinary girl; Hotchkiss was cognizant of that. But still there was enough of the norm in her to give him a complete tumble, a total astonishment, when in the middle of breakfast, which was when it often occurred, Amanda would stare and he would stare at her stare and say, "It's happening?" and she would nod, just briefly. It wasn't so much a nod as a wave good-bye, and she was gone. She couldn't see, she wouldn't hear, for several minutes, and she would swear to him that she had just had an out-of-the-body experience, that she had become someone else, and he would stare at her, buttering his toast with some modesty, for in the face of these travels, buttering toast took on an even greater simplicity than one at first supposed, and he would observe that she came back quieter, more reflective, than before.

It didn't seem to *really* bother her, he noticed.

"Look, it's just something that happens to me, so," she shrugged over her strawberry ice cream soda, which was what she sometimes ate for breakfast, "I have to accept it."

"Maybe it's chemical," Hotchkiss offered helpfully. "You know, maybe from spending so much time in the space simulator, maybe it does things to your thyroid, you hallucinate. I'm sure there's an explanation."

"Yeah," she said. "You know, this ice cream has real strawberries in it," she said, closing her eyes. "This stuff is fabulous."

"You don't seem, Amanda," Hotchkiss said, "really concerned about this." He was annoyed, as he himself was extremely concerned.

"Well, of course I'm concerned," Amanda said simply, sucking the last white froth off the whipped cream on her spoon, "but you know when I get the feeling I just feel like I go away—like I'm traveling. It's like *hearing* something. I feel, well, almost *called.*"

"Good grief, you sound like a doctor with a beeper," Hotchkiss said, a bit huffy.

"Well," she sighed, "what can I tell you? For reasons I don't understand, I got stuck with this. It just seems to have come over me in the last two weeks."

He found himself distracted from the urgency of the journey by the sheer shining softness of her shoulder and the softness of her lower lip. When he recovered from his temporary involvement in that he said, "When are they calling next?"

"You know they never give me a time," she sighed, putting her hand on his hand.

"Yeah, I know," Hotchkiss said glumly. They would wait for the voices and they would come or not come. As simple and complex as that. But until then, until the heaven-sent strangeness came to her, he wanted her earthbound self, the very earthy core of her exact center; he wanted that, and as he found her hand moving up his arm, along his neck, and then her lips, soft against the crevice in his neck, he knew she wanted that too. Except here too in love their views were different.

"I fly," Amanda said to him. "I'm all air and nothing." And Hotchkiss rather was all materialization, bound to blood and bone, as elemental as rock. The thereness of it all was a shock to him, filling him from the very bottom of his soles. Whereas for her she floated free far and away, escaping from his grasp at the very moment of consummation, drifting toward ghostliness and ether—gone, gone, gone. That was how different they were. And Hotchkiss one night wrote a poem and said it was like smoke making love to fire. Sometimes he could think of things like that.

If this was just Amanda, Hotchkiss might have somehow convinced himself that she was just crazy. One crazy person. But it was more. Much more. He had heard the NEP file had doubled. And then there were other things, too many things. Indians disappearing in the middle of deserts, people reporting rocket ships up in Greenland. (The psychiatrists said it was the weather, the atmosphere. Everybody, Hotchkiss observed, when they didn't know what else to call it, called it the weather. Of course there was something to that, too. The weather was very peculiar. July days in December. Things like that.)

And then other people said it was the Russians, some sort of Commie plot. Hotchkiss personally wished at times it would all go away. And yet he was drawn to it. Drawn to something he felt when he was around Amanda, some mysterious complex, some strange magnetism, that would lead his thoughts this way. The fact of it was that Hotchkiss was the kind of person who just went plumb crazy when there wasn't a reasonable explanation to things. Hotchkiss was known as the best troubleshooter in the whole NASA organization. For everything. "He just has a way of looking at it," Commander James had said. "He cuts through everything and he unlocks the problem." Hotchkiss, too, was a scientist, an engineer, but of a different order of mind. If the subparticle physicists wanted to get hung up with the fact that you could not observe something without affecting it, that was okay with him. He accepted it. So what. It applied to subparticle physics. But what was going on was that people were mucking around, trying to make it some kind of metaphor for life, when in fact Hotchkiss knew that life was cold and clear and as definite as steel and concrete. You couldn't control it—Hotchkiss didn't think that—but you could certainly see it, feel it, taste it, and touch it, and if something went wrong, really wrong, you could always figure out a way to fix it.

Now Amanda, he knew, temperamentally did not believe this is the way things are. Amanda thought that if things went wrong, you had to change your attitude or your understanding or something, and then you would see the problem. The in-theres and the out-theres of Amanda drove Hotchkiss crazy. It was all one big slosh, as far as he could tell. Its only recommendation was its consistency. Still, Amanda herself was one hell of a pilot. And he was proud. His girl was going to be the first woman to land on Mars.

"I'd rather go to the moon," she said, somewhat dejected, one night.

"Why?" he said, surprised. "Nobody's been to Mars. You'll be first."

"I kind of dig the moon," she said. "It gives me good vibrations."

"It gives you vibrations?" Hotchkiss asked, holding his breath. It was going to be one of those evenings.

"Yeah, I feel it moving, like I feel its gravity and its smoothness, and the very lunarness of it. I know about the moon because I'm a woman, and I know about water and the tides, whereas Mars, Mars is tougher for girls."

"Very scientific," Hotchkiss said. "Extremely scientific."

"And it's far," she said. "It's nine months to get there."

"Well," Hotchkiss said sympathetically, "I can understand your reluctance about that." The moon was a hell of a lot closer. Still. The first of anything was an important milestone in Hotchkiss's mind.

"But," she sighed, "maybe I won't go."

"What do you mean you might not go? You're going. You're scheduled for takeoff in ten days."

"I know," she said, "but one of the voices called me and said there might be an interference."

"What kind of interference?"

"They didn't say. . . . They said there was a possibility there would be an interference and I might not take off."

"Oh." Hotchkiss had learned to accept the correctness of the voices, whatever their origin, so he sank dejectedly into his coffee.

Amanda had run into McCloud, and she told Hotchkiss of this. She was beginning to wish she had not. She had never seen him in such a cold, pitiless rage. Hotchkiss said to her, "I thought that was over."

"He came back," she said. "I only spoke to him."

"I don't share," he said, looking at her in that clear, kindled way he had. "So choose." Hotchkiss's fury was lethal; the room was shaking with the finality of his words, and Amanda was too. She hated Hotchkiss then, for his ultimatum and his rage. But she was caught in it too, and buffeted by its force.

So she chose. She told McCloud she would not see him again. That was two days ago. Ever since telling him she had become obsessed.

She could not forget a single detail. The way his belt wove through his belt buckle. The way his wristwatch lay on the night table; the way he strapped it on. The precise fall of his light blue shirt as he tucked it into his pants. The worried casual confident I-don't-worry-about-a-thing, worrying-about-everything look in his eyes. The way he drove his car. This loving was ruthless and relentless. It poured adoration into everything. She could not believe that there was such a thing as buckling your pants in a wonderful way, as opposed to just buckling pants. She could not in fact imagine McCloud without the masculine paraphernalia she remembered from her childhood. Keys, rings, belt buckles, cigarettes, lighters, jackets, ties carried on the backseat. Hotchkiss had none of this. Hotchkiss wore jeans and a T-shirt until it was too cold, and then he wore turtleneck sweaters. McCloud had once worn jeans and cowboy boots, and the shock to Amanda was total. If he was devastating in his paraphernalia, what she called his "grown-up" clothes, he was equally so in the jeans. The first time she met him this way she was so shy at how wonderful he looked she could hardly speak.

And what of him with her? What were the circles of his enchantment? Bronco hardly knew. He knew he couldn't wait to be with her. He wanted her pressed up close to him, against him, and yet somewhere he was beginning to know something that, if anybody ever told him, had ever suggested to him, could have made him roll off the bar stool holding his sides. Something had gone deeper here than he ever guessed. He would awake in the night, shaken, and start to write poetry. If he could dismiss himself as a silly lovesick fool, which he felt part of him was, it would have been one thing. But this was serious. She said she wouldn't see him again. But he knew she would. There was this power between them: with her in his arms he felt that everything had always been perfect, everything always would be perfect. They were perfect. With Amanda with him, love *was* revolution. Perfectly they strolled the surface of the earth. What Bronco knew, deep in the bottom of his beer, now crackling out a pack of new cigarettes, was that he, Bronco McCloud, one of the biggest womanizers of them all, was now interested in a woman—one woman. Loved one woman. And McCloud was in shock, because he couldn't handle it. There were times now, Bronco thought, and this was what astonished him, that he was afraid. Afraid of sex. He had been using it all his life, and now that it had *him*, he was learning its power.

Amanda thought it made her a coward, or worse a traitor, to feel this love for McCloud cached so inside her like this, but there it was. It did not make her love Hotchkiss less; it did not make her love Hotchkiss more; it did not prevent her from loving Hotchkiss either, in quite a different way. Hotchkiss flew through her like a bolt of lightning, fast and furious, and then was gone, grounded somewhere by some element other than Amanda. He broke through her, unleashing her, fusing with her, but he never stayed. McCloud seemed to be there from ever forever, staying and playing like an old, very special song. It was the song that lay there finally, this ancient melody sweet on her bones, a song of love and sadness. Tears fell down inside, salted melodies of time. So these days Amanda was torn between two men. And *not* torn, but holding them both somehow, like the hemispheric brain itself: divided and sharing, feeling on one side, sight on the other, and then somehow in its electric miracle, fusing and interchanging. But in the brain, when she thought of this, she thought it must be clear. In her heart it was not. Her heart was a muck, and the muck ached. •

21

Amanda thought Hotchkiss should make more of an effort at increasing his patience with Schrodinger. There were times when Hotchkiss could overcome his exasperation with Schrodinger only through song. One evening after a particularly chilling battle when Schrodinger refused to eat any of the three kinds of canned catfood Hotchkiss had put down, Hotchkiss had yelled, "He's spoiled rotten! He won't eat tuna, turkey, or chicken. Now what am I supposed to do?"

"Try roast beef," Amanda called from the other room. "He isn't spoiled. He's having a bad day. On bad days you have special needs."

"He doesn't like me, that's what it is. He doesn't like me—and to tell you the truth, I'm not crazy about him, either. He's sick. Perverted. You've humanized him or something. He looks at me like I'm a rival."

"He doesn't look at you that way," Amanda would say, coming in from the shower with the towel draped around her and brushing her hair, "and he doesn't hate you, and you don't hate him either. In fact you love him; you just don't want to admit it." She would bend then, so prettily, so sweetly, peering into the refrigerator, the round bottoms of her behind peeking so beneath the towel, and Hotchkiss would be quite overcome, overcome with so many things at once he would find it difficult to say. Usually he acted by putting his hand on those very round parts.

She would sweep him away. "Really!" she would say, straightening up, but he could see the fire in her eyes.

And then he would seize Schrodinger and, twirling him about the room, burst into song in his incredible baritone: "You made me love you, I didn' wanna do it, I didn' wanna do it. You made me sighhhhhh for you," and at this Hotchkiss would get quite theatrical, holding the astonished Schrodinger with one hand and beating his chest with the other. "Yes I do, 'deed I do, you know I do. . . . So gimme gimme gimme what I sigh for, you've"—and at this he would press his nose against Schrodinger's—"got the brand of kisses that I die for," shrieking at the top of his lungs until Schrodinger leaped from his arms and Amanda fell giggling uncontrollably into a chair.

"See that?" Hotchkiss would say. "He's upset. He thinks I'm making a pass."

"Don't be silly," Amanda said. "He couldn't possibly understand the words."

"He understands the words to 'Old Black Magic,' " he said, referring to the song Amanda sang to Schrodinger on occasion and which always brought forth the most astonishing purrs of all.

"What makes you think that?" she said. "He just likes the tune."

"Nope," Hotchkiss said, pouring a drink, "it's the words. He knows the words. He knows he's magical."

"Really?" Amanda said, somehow thrilled and pleased as she accepted the drink from Hotchkiss. "Do you really think he's magical?"— meaning, of course, "as magical as I do?"

"Definitely," Hotchkiss said, raising his glass in a toast and looking very serious as he leaned over to kiss her, the kind of no-doubt-about-it kiss that is only the first of a long line of kisses. He said, kissing her again and again, "no doubt at all."

The agency was down on Amanda. This wasn't the first time. They had been down on her ever since she bought the Mars-mobile. They thought

_____ 104

it was "unfitting" for a serious scientist and a lady astronaut to be riding about in "that thing," which they insisted on calling it, causing such a commotion. It was the commotion, Amanda suspected, that really killed them. Why the space division needed a PR arm, which is what the agency was, Amanda didn't know. Oh, she knew they were always starved for money—people would rather spend money developing hydrogen bombs than exploring outer space—but still and all. She also noticed a new energy on the part of the agency since Hooper returned from the moon shot. It was one of those things. It was supposed to be top-secret classification that "something" had happened to the astronaut on that run, but of course in the way that servants in old English families used to know everything that happened in the house, in the same way the mechanics who "handled" the bobbing capsules in the sea and unloaded the astronauts onto the deck knew there were many people involved, and no matter what anybody said they could all see the expressions on their faces, they could all see how they were *acting*; everybody knew something mighty weird had gone on up there.

Amanda herself attempted to speak to Hooper, but they wouldn't let her near him. They saved him for the parade. Put him in the back of a bubble-topped limo from which he waved, like an automaton. After that he was whisked off somewhere for "further study." Amanda didn't like the sound of it. Not a bit. And now there were other rumors. Rumors about the chimps. That they didn't dare send any more people up there until they "verified" what was going on. They were going to send the chimps up. Or, better, *the* chimp—342. He was the only one who could handle a mission of that complexity. If even *he* could, could a chimp remain operable for the nine months it would take to reach Mars? Amanda wondered. She had also heard they were sending 342 up with her, although they hadn't said they were. Why would they keep it a secret? Because they didn't know themselves. She wouldn't mind actually; she wouldn't mind the company, even if she couldn't talk to 342. She smiled. She could play chess with him though, when things got rough.

The fact was, Amanda had her own doubts about the Mars project. Nine months! An eternity in a space capsule or any other confined space. And then the eeriness. Once past the moon, it would take a full $11\frac{1}{2}$ hours for her voice to travel back to the earth. She smiled. Imagine saying Help, and $11\frac{1}{2}$ hours later they would get the message. It was full of things like that. But it wasn't as if she seriously debated it. She was going. She was thrilled with going. It was that something lately had begun to bother her. Some strangeness had crept into remarks about the Mars shot, something not quite right. But it was a race. All other things were subordinate to the race. She had to let the other thoughts go. The Russians were racing to get to Mars, too. They were almost ready, word had it. It would be a race until the very last minute.

22

Donald Hotchkiss, professor of aerospace dynamics, was teaching a special advanced class for engineering students. Five students from M.I.T., Berkeley, and Stanford were allowed into Hotchkiss's course after having passed rigorous tests. Three had come for three years. Each year they hadn't been able to find two others, so rigorous were their standards. This year Donald had been forewarned. They had found a fourth. But he wasn't a college student. He was a kid.

The spectacled blond-haired half-pint stared at Hotchkiss from the first row. He had the kind of face you wanted to smack, that's all there was to it. A real snot-nosed face. Hotchkiss had heard of kids like this before, but he'd never met one. This kid was only fourteen. He had found an error in one of Bohr's original radium-fusion calculations when he was nine. Things went on from there. He had now undertaken a review of Einstein's theory of relativity and was up, really up, Hotchkiss had been warned, on everything in subparticle physics.

"So why's he want aerodynamics?" Hotchkiss had asked.

"He's not just a theoretical physicist," the general had explained. "He's a crazy kid. Wants to build things."

"What kind of things?" Donald had asked.

"Planes, I guess. Flying things," the general said.

So that was how this genius kid got to be sitting smack in front of Donald's nose. He looked at the eyes. The eyes, lying like two mites behind three inches of glasses, told it all. Those eyes, Donald thought, had been squaring hypotenuses since they were two.

Okay, he sighed. He'd put up with it. It would probably be worth it. This kid could probably teach him a lot.

Amanda insisted that Schrodinger had therapeutic qualities, although Hotchkiss observed that such qualities resided more in Amanda than in the cat. He had to admit that Schrodinger could cure Amanda when he found her in "one of her states," as she put it, a kind of quick malaise that would fall upon her, a sudden slumping that would cause him to say, "Are you tired?" And she would say no, she wasn't tired, she just suddenly felt "occupied." He would insist, "You mean preoccupied."

And she would say, "No. But I am feeling *occupied*, which means some feeling has taken up residence in me, and thus occupied I have to wait for it to leave." She had these sorts of notions about things and she would be quiet and, he could see, sad. Miserable, he would put it. He would want to change it for her when he saw this, but he was powerless to do it. But Schrodinger wasn't. At such times—not at the beginning of the time, but somewhere along the time—Amanda would pick Schrodinger up still sleeping and lay him in her lap, stroking him, and she would chant very quickly, seemingly overcome by her feelings for him, "Oh I love youiloveyouiloveyouiloveyouiloveyou." Schrodinger would thus awaken from his stupor, purring like a 747, his tail making circles round and round like a helicopter's prop. Schrodinger seemed in flight at this, his face, even Hotchkiss had to admit, was smiling, for lack of a better word, and, with his tail-whirling body purring, Schrodinger would awaken in a sea of pleasure. This seemed to please Amanda no end. "Look," she would say, "it's like a miracle. Love wakes him up."

Hotchkiss would hold his head and say, "It isn't love. He just likes being petted." Nonetheless he had to admit that it seemed to change Amanda's mood. He thought, rationally speaking, that there was much too much attribution of magical powers to Schrodinger altogether. Nonetheless, he was at a loss for explanations of a certain sort. It was true the first night he had sat by Schrodinger and done some calculations Hotchkiss had not gotten the answer. But Amanda had said, "You're not sending him the right *vibes*. Think, I love you, Schrodinger. Try to send him love."

Hotchkiss had laughed. Then one night when she was out, he decided to try it. Carefully he lifted Schrodinger up in his basket onto the table and brought out the figures and the plans. He tried to think, I love you, Schrodinger, but this was harder than he imagined, because it was quickly followed by, This is idiotic. Nonetheless, Hotchkiss desperately wanted the solution.

"Try to think it," Amanda had said. "Sometimes even when I don't mean it, it works."

"You always mean it. You adore him," Hotchkiss had grumbled.

"No," she'd said. "Sometimes I don't. But even when I'm faking it works."

All right. Hotchkiss was faking. When he had about given up, after an hour of feeling like an ass, doing his silent invocations of, I love you Schrodinger, he heard a slight rumble. It was Schrodinger. He was starting to purr. This encouragement, it seemed, made Hotchkiss think all the faster, I love you Schrodinger. His excitement was mounting. It was, at a primal level, quite thrilling to think you had awakened anything from such a state resembling death, and perhaps it was this thrill that drove him on. Hotchkiss didn't know, but true enough, Schrodinger purred away. An hour later Hotchkiss had completed the calculation. He had the answer.

By the time Amanda came home, Hotchkiss had put Schrodinger back on the floor and was busily making coffee.

"Well," she said, coming in excited, full of shopping bags and boxes, "I got the most gorgeous cobalt-blue jacket. It is fabulous. Wait until you see!" and she began to undo the boxes.

"I finished the calculation," he said simply and proudly. "It works."

She turned ecstatic. "You did it?!"

"I did it," he said, proud.

"Oh Donald"—she threw her arms around him—"that's so wonderful." It was, he thought, actually quite wonderful. Then stepping back, she said, "Did Schrodinger help?"

He shook his head, feeling quite guilty about the deception. But he was too embarrassed to admit that perhaps Schrodinger *had* helped. In fact he was so mortified at the idea that Schrodinger *had* that he couldn't deal with it at all. He called it to himself "a friendly coincidence."

"I did it myself," he said, feeling like a liar.

"Well that's fantastic," she said. "Wait until you tell the others!" Her eyes were shining. It was at that moment and why at that moment Hotchkiss didn't know, he could see her love for him, he could see her joy in his achievement, but then, just at the moment he could see it so clearly, an old ghost stole across this view. He saw McCloud: there. If she loved him so, how could she have ever loved another? He watched McCloud steal across this landscape covering its bright blue and green with shades of gray, paling it, his jealousy wiped across his joy, diminishing it.

"What's wrong?" she said. "I'm so happy for you and you look angry at me."

"Oh, I'm not," Hotchkiss said, lying again. Then he felt sad. This lying had to stop. It was contagious.

Amanda poured the coffee and stopped opening packages. She was quiet for a time. Something had happened. Too many messages were in the room. She couldn't figure it out. Why, if Hotchkiss had suddenly broken through, was he unhappy with her? She thought suddenly of McCloud. She had never made *him* unhappy, she was sure of it.

Hotchkiss now was manfully attempting to be cheery. He was making tea. But a gloom had settled, and he knew somehow it was his doing.

23

Amanda was at a dinner party, daydreaming.

"What?" she said. It took her a minute to realize that the man across from her, a journalist, was asking her a question.

"I said, isn't it true that there is some concern that the vastness of space, its absence of delineation, is of special concern to women astronauts?"

"Huh?" She knew this utterance was far from brilliant, but she was having trouble, a lot of trouble, taking in what he was saying.

"Aren't you worried you're going to freak out?"

"I, uh, I don't think so," she said.

Would she? she wondered. She didn't know. She wasn't worried. Freak out. For God's sake, she had never freaked out—well, except maybe that once. In the solar simulator. Yes. Better to have forgotten that. They all freaked out in there. Hell, it got so hot, and it was so dark, and it was so hard to breathe you were smothering, for God's sake, it was so red, like red-black in there, and of course she freaked out. She thought there might have been an accident. Still, today she was *convinced* there had been an accident. Richie, who was running the simulator, told her it was fishy. But it took thirty-five minutes in an oxygen tank for her to come through. She couldn't breathe. It wasn't smoke, but she couldn't breathe. The temperature got too hot. Something happened in there and they didn't want to take the blame. That's what it was. Blame it on women. On some "incapacity."

"Well," the journalist was saying, "I was reading this fascinating piece about frontier women and the tendency toward severe depression."

"Yes?" Amanda said, feeling wary.

"Well because it was limitless, you see, absolutely without boundaries, just endless prairie, a nothingness, they went crazy. They said it was 'cabin fever,' but actually there's a theory that it was agoraphobia. They say it's threatening to women because they have a concept of themselves as a space."

"A space?" Amanda said.

The table had turned their attention toward this exchange now. They sensed on the edge of it some sexual revelation. Since this was always the most interesting thing to people, they had their heads, their ears, and their cocks cocked, as it were.

"Well, because a woman's concept of herself is as a space. You know, as a nothing, a void, surrounded by a body. Inner space, you know, so outer space is threatening, like she could disappear."

Amanda looked at the man. Then she said, "Mr. Levitt, I believe?"

He nodded.

"Do you realize that the million brightest galaxies—do you understand that number, the *million* brightest galaxies—not stars, are all within a billion light years' distance from the earth, and each galaxy contains billions of stars. Does that freak *you* out?"

"No. It's difficult to conceive, I admit, but it doesn't freak me out."

"That's because," Amanda said calmly, "you haven't conceived of it. When the conception takes place, you will freak out. In fact, your intellectual understanding would require a freak-out, don't you see?"

He stood there looking at her.

"So far it's only mumbo jumbo to you, but when you get it, you will freak out. Regardless of your 'inner space.' "

Her tone quieted them all. It was true in a way: at the far end of the table the ladies thought of it, suddenly clutching their throats. They didn't choose to think about it. Millions and billions and inconceivable, yes, inconceivable, distances. But she was going on, that woman at the end—the lady astronaut.

"It is also inconceivable," Amanda went on, "that there couldn't be a duplicate planet—a *duplicate*. We can't be the only one in all of that. Statistically it's impossible, if you think of it that way. If only one star in ten thousand has planets, that would add up to ten million planetary systems in a galaxy the size of ours."

"No, you mean to say you believe this science-fiction fantasy that there is a 'parallel world,' one exactly like our own?"

"I'm saying it's possible," Amanda said. "Why not? It's as possible as it is impossible. There certainly could be a mirror world."

"It's absurd," the journalist said, sitting on the edge of his seat and running a finger around the inside of his collar.

"You mean you just don't want to believe it," Amanda said calmly.

"What?" he said, annoyed.

"I said," she spoke slowly and evenly, "that that is what people say when they don't want to believe things. They never say, 'I don't want to believe it.' They say instead, 'That's impossible.' "

"Clever sophistry," the man said. "I'm disappointed to find anyone in the science program of this government who is as fanciful as you are. It distresses me, frankly, that the program tolerates such an unscientific attitude."

"Ummm," Amanda said. And then she said nothing more. Of course it bothered them. This possibility of freak-outs. They should know how much it bothered the astronauts. Nobody talked about it much, but they all thought about Hooper. Hell, they all knew Hooper, and it just didn't seem possible that Hoop could lose his marbles. Privately Amanda thought he hadn't, but Hooper had seen something out there they didn't want him telling to anyone.

Amanda could barely overhear the conversation of the physicist at the other end of the table. She loved physicists. She found them imaginative . . . talking about worlds faster than the speed of light, invisible worlds that existed and moved so fast they couldn't be measured, but they had measured changes in the electrical fields so they knew they existed. All these wild, wild speculations, all of this "without proof"— which she felt akin to. It made sense to her. It "felt" right. She didn't know why. However, Amanda occasionally thought that maybe people who said such things, and the man at the end was that sort, had a point: that women, somehow secretly regarding themselves as "empty space," were more prone to gravitational pulls—such as that of McCloud— than a man might be to a woman. It was the influence of McCloud, like gravity around a black hole, that could cause the female of the species to go into such a spin that eventually she fell in, on herself. It was only by her wildest efforts of will that a woman might keep orbiting sufficiently far enough to avoid the dangerous McCloud force. This is what Amanda thought, although not all the time. She only thought these things when she felt fanciful, not when she was actually "thinking," as in conclusions.

Amanda had spent the morning teaching a group of high-school students the fundamental principles of relativity. She had been giving this lecture for years, and although she understood it on paper, she did not understand it really. That is to say, she understood what it meant and, furthermore, she even believed it, but at the same time she found it quite inconceivable, incomprehensible. Nonetheless, it had to be taught, because somewhere along the line, even though they all knew the truth of it, someone might come along who could actually assist them in grasping it.

"There is no space," Amanda began her lecture, "that is not spacetime. This was Einstein's great contribution," she went on, seeing their smiling faces. She knew why. It gave them all kinds of science-fiction fantasies. And why not? She personally could neither accept it nor deny it. "Think of it," she said, pointing to her desk and picking up a large rubber sheet, "as a large rubber sheet." She then placed the sheet on four hooks, so it hung suspended from four corners. "Think of everything in the space as an action, which curves space." She then threw a small metal ball—it looked like a billiard ball—onto the sheet. "And you will see how it bends. That is the nearest I can give you of a visualization.

Light bends, and time bends space, and gravity bends space, so that space is actually a curved element."

"Why couldn't it be straight? How do you know it's a circle?" someone asked. Someone always asked that.

"Because everything goes in circles," Amanda said. "The earth spins in a circle, on its axis in a circle; the heavens revolve, so to speak, in a circle; the Milky Way revolves again in a circle, and of this," she said finally, "there can be no question. The entire business is entirely circular."

She smiled herself at the pun. Circular! Indeed, as if anyone could ever adequately explain their way out of certain theoretical constructs. She knew she would get a flurry of questions about "parallel" universes, time travel, and the rest. She answered them quite simply, "We don't understand certain phenomena yet." What did she personally believe? they wanted to know.

"Well," she would say, feeling it would be too embarrassing to admit that not only didn't she have the faintest idea but she was quite content not having the faintest idea because somewhere she had the supposition, more than that, a conviction, that they—meaning he, she, him, her, and the entire scientific caboodle—were going to be stood on their heads in the outer reaches of space. The distances were so vast, the laws that governed them so unknowable.

This was something one quite naturally thought about. It was the radio astronomers who took up a lot of her time these days. These days, she had more time, because she had to give up McCloud. Things could not go on, and she had decided not to see him at all or talk to him. She decided that any proximity to McCloud could only lead to one thing, that anywhere in the vicinity of him she was, for all practical purposes, in forces beyond her control.

Hotchkiss, of course, knew all about it. Well, not *all* about it. Hotchkiss knew about McCloud, whom he regarded as an ass, and McCloud knew about Hotchkiss, about whom he felt likewise. McCloud had been in such situations before, but he had never been in love. About the only thing that dissuaded him from pursuing Amanda more intently was the raw, real fact of his own cowardice.

He knew that although he was madly in love with Amanda and that he was insanely jealous of Hotchkiss, that in the end they would leave each other. There was, as they say in the soaps, no future in it, in that Amanda and McCloud were both traveling at very high speeds toward each other, and the end, in McCloud's view, was annihilation. Now certain forms of this annihilation he found quite exciting. Disturbing, perhaps, because McCloud, in love, had encountered forces in himself that left him quite bedazzled. Still and all, the greater force, when confronted with love, was for McCloud to head for the hills, as they used to say in the navy. At first he attempted to think this was part of his savoir faire, his girl-in-every-port philosophy, but this he now knew was not true. The fact was closer to fear. He was afraid of loving Amanda, and as much as he burned with the excitement of doing so, he thought somewhere he would burn out. He thought, and he told her this, that they would both be two small cinders staring out at each other over the desolate plain. Amanda, when she could, reluctantly agreed. She did not want to be married to McCloud. She did not want to go to parties with him or live in a house with him or do any of those normal things that people eventually did. She wanted to consume and be consumed by McCloud, and then when he left her, exhausted and stranded, she seemed only to want to endure the exquisite pain of longing for him until she saw him again.

"It's the velocity," she would say. "I can't hold up under it. No woman in the world has a heat shield that could endure."

This flattered McCloud no end, of course; he saw himself as some sort of Saturn rocket. Hotchkiss also saw himself as a Saturn rocket but of an altogether different variety. Hotchkiss had a crew. McCloud was all charge and power with one aim and one aim only: to burn out all his engines. This has its appeal, and the part of Amanda that shared this interest was the part they shared together in a consummation that approached the divine. The terrible thing was when he left her he felt sick. He then felt he did want to marry her and live in a house with her and do all those things normal people seem to do, and Amanda felt the same. But there was never time to find out, because the speed was too great and the impact too magnificent. They could not endure, under the impact of their passion and their fear. And they could not endure the steady determination of Hotchkiss, who was resolute. He was resolute, he was confident, he was out to capture Amanda, and there was a part of her too, with a longing look over her shoulder at the incomparable McCloud, that wished to be captured and do the normal things that people do. This did not mean she found Hotchkiss dull. This was not it at all. It was rather she found being with him only real, whereas everything with McCloud was real in that it was not false, but it was too much real to endure. McCloud, she had decided, was for her astral plane. For the earthly one she would see about Hotchkiss.

When she and McCloud parted she could feel the lead in his heart. She kissed his eyes and said, "I'll never love anyone like I love you," and he knew she wouldn't, knew she couldn't. They agreed to meet in a year, when it would be safe to remember what they once had. And so it ended. But some nights the loss of McCloud swept through her and the tears fell down *inside* her eyes, burning all the way to her toes.

She did not know if she could or would *love* Hotchkiss. Her heart belonged to McCloud, but that was like pledging yourself to the moon. And this man Hotchkiss with his large hands and his determination was gaining on her. There was no doubt about it. And his force field gave her *excellent* positive charges. There was no doubt about that either.

24

"I know you realize, Colonel," Lieutenant Calhoun said nervously, "it is top secret that that champanzee is going *up*."

"Of course I realize. What is *wrong* with you, Lieutenant? Do you think I'm an asshole?"

Privately Calhoun did. All he said was, "I just wonder if Beedle Hobbs, with his personality, is really the one to handle a top-secret mission."

"Not to worry, Lieutenant. Hobbs won't even know."

Beedle Hobbs was a good ole boy. He respected the army. He tried to cooperate. But he thought that almost anything in the world would have been better than pulling "monkey duty," as they called it at the base.

Still, that had been at first. Monkey duty was monkey duty, but things had changed. Beedle's reputation and his feelings about himself had undergone a slow evolution, because Beedle had come to be associated with a Star. One chimp, and one chimp alone, known as 342, was making NASA history. A chimp who clearly knew how to handle his own career. And Beedle's as well. Needless to say, Beedle had come around to this slowly. In fact, he had come to recognize the importance of this ornery chimp only very recently. He knew Babcock had turned 342 over because he was unmanageable. Hell, at first Beedle thought he was unmanageable, too.

He reflected on this now, did Beedle, as he contemplated his face in the mirror. He did this every morning, as if by the ritual of plugging in his razor to recharge its batteries he could recharge his own. He leaned into the mirror, his brown-haired, brown-eyed, nondescript face trying to menace his own image, intimidate the mirror. Beedle would stand in front of the mirror every day and say his name this way: "Beed (pause) UHL." The "UHL" part came out of the depths of his stomach, roaring like a German guttural. So it became "Beed (pause) UHL," and he said it and said it and said it. It was tough. It was mean. It was hard. Everything a fella should be. Beed-UHL smiled. It made him happy. He tried to mask his disappointment when folks just called him "Beedle."

Hobbs was lost in reverie this morning. He'd come a long way with 342. He remembered the first night he became aware of 342's special quality. The damn chimp was supposed to get four bananas the night before the Mercury shot, but Hobbs only had three. It was raining out and cold, and it meant Beedle had to go all the way over to the warehouse to break out a new box of bananas. He was tired. It was pouring out. One banana more or less was no big deal, he figured. Let Reynolds do it in the morning. Damn chimp wouldn't miss one goddamn banana. Or so Beedle thought.

Things got worse from there on. Number 342 had a fit over the fact there were only three bananas. Screaming, yelling, hollering, banging the bars of his cage, jumping up and down like thunder and lightning, popping the cage with every jump till Beedle thought he was going to break it open. Then it was war.

"I'm tellin' you, you son of a bitch," Beedle said, slamming a stick into the cage, "I'm not gonna go out there to get you your one goddamn lousy banana. You ain't hungry anyway, so just shaddup!

"SHADDUP!" Beedle screamed at the chimp.

"$#@%&&&*!" the chimp screamed back at Beedle; and this was the way it was going when Shawcross walked in there and found the two of them screaming at each other in the basement, the chimp in a foam around his mouth, screaming and jumping around his cage, and Beedle in a foam, too.

"Jesus, Beedle," Shawcross said, "what in hell are you doin' to him?"

"What am I doin' to him?" Beedle screamed, his face red. "Whaddaya mean, what am I doin' to him? What's he doin' to me? I been locked up with him twenty-four hours for a week!"

"Calm down, Beedle," Shawcross said. He had seen this happen before. Personality clash they called it, between Beedle and Number 342. He knew 342 was a rough one. Also the smartest one. But he was scheduled to go into special training. Hell, he was really upset now. Couldn't have him in this kind of state nohow.

"What's the matter, Beedle? What's he want?"

Beedle, chagrined, shrugged his shoulders. "He wants a banana."

"What for? It's eleven o'clock at night."

Beedle sat down on an orange crate, defeated. He was licked and he knew it. "I was s'posed to give him four at eight o'clock when he finished his nightly check-out. I only had three, Charlie, and it was pourin' out. . . . He don't even want it. He just wants to make me go and get it."

Charlie looked at him unmoved. Beedle knew it. Charlie was acting like the damn chimp was the Holy Grail. Beedle knew he'd have to go out and get it now.

"You got to get it, Beedle. I am surprised at you. You know you can't go frustratin' him like that, especially since he's got to go in for special testing tomorrow."

Beedle was a weary man. It is not a nice thing to be bested by a chimp. He went to the door, got the raincoat off the hook, and plodded out into the storm. He walked the 1.2 miles over to supply and brought out a bunch of bananas. They were ripe. Maybe he'd have one himself. He locked the door of the warehouse, the searchbeam sweeping over his rainy figure, and plodded back to the chimp house. He didn't even know why they called it the chimp house. It was *his* house. Three-forty-two was the only one in it now. Shawcross was sitting there reading the paper when he walked in. Shawcross was disturbed. The chimp was quiet now, though, picking his fingernails or some other disgusting habit he had. He had quite a few, Beedle knew.

Beedle took the bananas out of the bag and knew he'd have to give the chimp his before he ate one himself, so he did. As he handed it through the cage, the chimp swiped it from him with a vengeance.

"See?" Shawcross said. "He must be hungry."

"He ain't hungry," Beedle said, resentment beginning to boil over. He sat down next to Shawcross and began to peel the banana. He should have known better. The chimp started screaming. Shawcross looked at him.

"He wants yours. You better give it to him," Shawcross said.

"What're you talking about? They're both the same . . . he's just spoiled rotten."

"Give it to him, Beedle," Shawcross said.

Beedle, now furious, shoved the banana toward the cage, and the chimp shoved the one he had had, with a big bite out of it, toward Beedle.

"I ain't takin' any banana you been eatin'," Beedle said to 342. "Eat it your goddamn self."

The banana fell to the floor of the cage and the chimp picked it up and hurled it suddenly smack into Beedle's face. Beedle turned and reached for the stick, but Shawcross grabbed his arms and held him.

"Easy, Beedle, easy. . . . Look, you got to stop takin' this so personal or I'm gonna have to report you."

"It is personal, goddamnit," Beedle said, seething. "I can't wait to get rid of this bastard."

Calmer, he finally sat in the chair in front of the cage next to Shawcross. Periodically he would steal a glance at the chimp. As the final insult, which Beedle could have predicted, the chimp was eating the banana daintily, just the edges of his teeth nipping into it. He wouldn't eat it, Beedle knew. He was just going to wave it like a sword all night long, pronouncing his victory over Beedle and his kind.

25

Soft Error soft error soft error—the words were being whispered down the corridors. The computers on the latest Mars lander, "The Flying Dutchman," were down. The information had just come in to the Jet Propulsion Lab's imaging team, and Amanda had been ordered to report "immedjitly," which was the way Farkheimer had screamed it over the phone. He wouldn't even tell her what they'd found.

The words *soft error* sent a chill through her that was also, in an odd way, a kind of thrill as well. Soft error meant simply this: nothing was wrong or broken in the computer. The parts were simply so small that something as unpredictable as a wave of light could interfere with its execution. A *hard* error meant the computer was broken, it could be fixed. But light, coming from X rays, gamma rays, or cosmic rays, could affect the results of these computers significantly. She knew they might hesitate to send her up until they had the final report of the latest imaging network from Mars. As far as they knew, Mars was covered with dust and ice. Amanda was due to land on Solaris Luna, which meant "Lake of the Sun." In the month she was due to arrive, January, it would be warm. The mean surface temperature in the area of the lake would be 60 degrees, as Mars would be nearest the sun. Amanda herself wondered what that would do to the ice.

But now, this was something new. What they found was that the surface of Mars was like a piece of Swiss cheese. There were holes in the ice.

Was it so? Or was it soft error?

Amanda was feeling uneasy. There were too many strange things going on. And Hooper on top of it. Hooper dying suddenly like that. "Cardiac arrest," the brass said. Everyone else wondered. That was the problem. No one really believed it. The funeral, a week ago, was the weirdest funeral she had ever attended. She thought there were too many things disturbing her.

When Amanda felt disturbed about what she called real things, she would sit down and attempt to figure them out. When she felt disturbed at other times, when those wells of sadness would descend, when the strange fatigue enclosed her, she would simply collapse onto the bed or the sofa or wherever she was and let the tears fall. She did not know why she was crying and she did not want to know. It was an old, faint song—one she didn't want to hear. At such times Schrodinger would inevitably awaken and come to her. Sometimes he would just lick the tears from her eyes and start to purr; but other times he got so frantic she would have to cheer up immediately before he went completely out of control. She thought Schrodinger was altogether too sympathetic to her. She didn't dare let him see how upset she really was for fear he might go to pieces before her eyes.

The psychiatrist had very gently suggested to her that perhaps she cried when she felt she was *too* different, that she would never be understood. Most of the time, of course, she didn't feel different at all; she felt strong and full of courage. But there were other times when she felt so utterly stranded by what she saw, and pain would surface. When she couldn't make herself clear to other people, she would feel invisible, as if she not only couldn't be seen but also couldn't be heard. And feeling like this, she would want to drive out and see her parents. She loved her parents; that was clear. But they had certainly never understood Amanda. They looked upon her as a kind of antique treasure; a beautiful but foreign object that suggested cultures and forms of expression they only vaguely understood. They didn't want to understand either. She made them nervous. They simply wanted to be proud of her and say she was theirs. So she didn't know why when she felt that she wasn't making herself clear she would want to see her parents. But she did. She would take the Mars-mobile and go for a long, fast drive.

It was a terrible affectation, and Amanda knew it, but the Mars-mobile, her car, was more than she could resist. Only an astronaut could drive it. Sleek, silver and black, designed like a futuristic Bat-mobile, the car was almost a rocket: it accelerated from zero to two hundred mph in ten seconds. It was the one place she had put all of her money. The fact was, whatever money she had went into the car. One of the engineers on the space program had first approached her years ago about building this famous experimental "car." She worked with him on the design, and when the "thing," as they called it around the base, first rolled up, people came out to see it. They couldn't get over it. The seats were pushed way back, and the "joy stick" was a shiny alloy of cast aluminum and bronze. Amanda had to admit, when she drove up to shopping malls or movie theaters, the car, coupled with her exit (wouldn't you know there was an ejection seat, a "shallow exit" it was called, that just sort of opened the door and delivered her upright onto the sidewalk), caused people to gawk and gape and ask a million questions. Amanda had to admit she loved the attention.

As she drove along the slicked roads she turned on the radio, which was beamed into a satellite. It was a huge gleaming neon radio with stations from Japan and Germany; for reasons she didn't understand, she liked to listen to the Japanese announcers discuss American music. She tuned into her favorite Japanese station.

Her parents lived in Sand Springs—a tiny town in a small oasis, surrounded by desert—and she had not seen them in quite a while. Later when she reflected on this she would find it difficult to say why exactly she had such an overwhelming need to see her parents at that moment in the rain at eleven-thirty at night. But she did. At least she felt an overwhelming need to drive her car out into the desert around Sand Springs. So she immersed herself in Japanese sound coming to her through her earphones. It was getting ridiculous, yes, but she had gotten earphones for everything, even listening to the radio in her car. Technically they were illegal, because you might fail to hear a beep behind you, but hers had an electronic "carry over," which meant any external sound above 10 megahertz (which is what a normal shout or squeal or horn would be) would be heard. It was raining so hard and she was so lost in the music that she failed to notice the truck following her. After quite a long while she decided to pull into a diner. She had been driving for hours and felt the need for coffee. When she ran in the door, shaking the water off, she felt them turn and look at her, two men at the end of the counter. She thought she recognized them. Part of the mechanical team, she thought. Then, no, she wasn't sure. She sat down and ordered coffee.

Amanda didn't know why but she felt compelled suddenly to turn around and look at the two men. They were huge, she noticed. They had turtleneck sweaters pulled up around their faces, and scarves, and hats that pulled down. It was cold on this desert at night but certainly not that cold.

As she turned to look at them, the head of one turned around and his eyes stared at her just for a second before they turned back. It made her blood run cold. She had never seen eyes like that before. Not on anything human. When she went to pay her check, she suddenly thought of the waitress all alone with the two men.

"Will you be okay?" Amanda said. "Do you want me to call anyone?" She tilted her head in the direction of the two men.

"Why of course I'm okay," the waitress said. "Why wouldn't I be okay?"

"Those *men*. They're so strange." Amanda saw the two men staring at her. *Nerp*, she heard next. Then again. *Nerp*.

"What men, honey? There's nobody here but me and you," the waitress said.

Amanda dropped a dollar on the counter and tore out of the diner and leaped into her Mars-mobile, hardly noticing that the rain had stopped. She gunned the car across the desert at 140 miles an hour, flooring for 150. Behind her in the rearview mirror she could see the lights of a truck gaining on her.

Amanda, driving furiously now, reached over to the glove compartment for her gun. Something was going on. The truck was no ordinary truck. She was doing 165 and the truck was gaining. She swerved off at the next junction and the truck sped on behind her. Nothing should be out on the desert that late, but down the road in the glare of her lights she saw a car parked across the road, and outside it, a man in distress, signaling. There was no time, the speed was too great to head into the sand, so she screeched to a stop and took out her gun. It was a trick, she was sure of it. As she opened the door to leap to the front of the car, she saw that the man in front of her lights was Hooper.

"Hooper!"—it was barely a gasp—"Is it you?" It certainly *was* him, but he was dead, wasn't he? And she had gone to his funeral, hadn't she?

"NERP!" he yelled to her. "NERP! NERP! NERP!" and he pointed to the oncoming truck, which just at that moment, as Hooper yelled and pointed, vanished—just like nothing—into the air. Disappeared, just like that.

"What in the name of . . . ?" Amanda said, under her breath. Her mouth was dry with fear. She turned to talk to Hooper, but he had disappeared, too. Car and all. Shaking, she got back into her car and drove toward her parents' house, all the time checking in her rearview mirror.

Maybe this is it, she thought. I've gone over the edge of something . . . or something. Maybe somebody drugged my coffee. She thought
all this, but she didn't really believe it. Not for a minute.

She gunned the engine, the clouds broke, and a downpour came.
Lightning shook up the desert and the sand howled, and as she looked
at the sky over the desert it was past midnight, and the sky looked as if
it had turned green.

Amanda continued on to her parents' house, surprising them, said
nothing, took a shower, and called Hotchkiss.

"Hi," she said cheerfully.

"Hi," he said. "It's one A.M. I have a simulator session at six A.M.
I think you're gorgeous, but is there anything special? Or do you just
like to talk at this hour?"

"Oh . . . I was just thinking about you." It occurred to Amanda
suddenly that the phone might be—or not only might be, but probably
would be—tapped.

"Hotch . . . I really want to see you tomorrow morning. . . . It's
important."

Hotchkiss was thoroughly puzzled. He said simply, "Okay. Where
and when?"

"I'll meet you at nine A.M."

There was a pause. Hotchkiss was waiting for more, some suggestion
of emotion, need, an explanation. Instead, nothing.

"Bye," she said, and he heard a click. It was the damnedest thing:
at that moment she sounded so far away, so very, very far away. On
impulse he dialed her house. No answer. Where was she anyway?

When she hung up the phone she leaned back against the pillows.
Her hand on her head, she could feel her temples throbbing. Something
was going on. What? was the question. Either the men in the diner
fixed her coffee, which was unlikely, or she was hallucinating, which
was also unlikely, although things like that did happen to perfectly normal
people in certain atmospheric conditions, such as a storm. Or else Hooper
was alive and real.

But she had gone to Hooper's funeral. It was a closed casket. Tragic.
And she had overheard. Overheard them saying they didn't believe it
was Hooper in the casket.

Amanda turned back the sheets, smoothed down the pillowcases,
and turned on the TV in her room. There was no way she could fall

asleep easily tonight. Hah! she thought as the announcer moved in on something; now I really am hallucinating. Then she started to giggle. The announcer was talking about the high incidence of ghosts in airplane crashes. There were interviews with the crew of a certain flight, who were all too eager to explain the various visits from ghosts of former flights, ex-copilots and pilots.

"The flight experience alone," the announcer was saying, "can in some cases produce heightened effects; these can be sensory as well as imaginative. We all know the jokes"—the announcer seemed almost to blush—"about extramarital affairs on airplanes." Amanda leaned toward the TV set, smiling despite herself. "Well it appears that there is strong evidence to suggest that a sexual experience in the sky would be more heightened than one on the earth."

"Hah!" Amanda laughed out loud. This was too good. Anyone who could manage really satisfying sex in an airplane john deserved everything she could get, was her reasoning. "Heightened awareness, you aren't kidding—people think they are going to *die*, ninny, why did you think—"

"Amanda . . . Amanda."

Oh God, she heard her mother below calling her. Embarrassed at her thoughts, only her thoughts, Amanda gathered her robe about her and went downstairs.

Her mother's face looked almost ashen.

"What is it?" Amanda said coming down the stairs. "What?"

"There's someone," her mother said, holding the edges of her bathrobe near her throat, "there's someone at the door who says he must talk to you."

"Who?" Amanda felt the blood drain from her face. She knew.

"There." Her mother pointed toward the kitchen screen, locked now against the intruder who stood on the other side, soaked and menacing, as the rain drove the water through the screen.

"Hoop," Amanda felt herself gasp, then moving forward, "Hoop, you must come in," and as she opened the door a woman suddenly appeared behind him in the drowning rain, a woman who grabbed Hooper under the arms. Hooper's eyes rolled toward the top of his head, as the woman explained to Amanda even as she lifted him up, lifted up the entire man in her enormous arms, "They got him before I came. . . . They know," she said, holding the crumpled Hooper in her arms, her eyes glazed with fatigue, holding him in the pouring rain.

"They found out and they . . . they got him." Tears welled in her eyes and joined the rain on her cheeks as she turned her back to Amanda and made her way toward the truck.

Under her breath Amanda thought she heard herself say, "What in the name of God . . . ?" Her seeing Hooper had been real, Amanda thought now for sure.

When the fear left her she came to her senses. "What am I doing?" She dashed through the screen door, nightgown, slippers, and all, through the teeming rain, and down the driveway. The pickup, without lights, was just pulling into the street, and Amanda, running like a gazelle, caught it now and banged on the window demanding that the driver speak.

"Stop this, stop this. Let me see Hooper." After what seemed like hours in the driving rain, the window lowered.

The woman with the white face and red lips said, "Forget this. Tell no one. Forget it all, Amanda. Hooper is dead. Or they will kill you too. Remember when you go up; whatever you see, keep it to yourself. They will not believe you, Amanda, and they will have no choice but to destroy you." Her eyes were cold. Pitiless. "He tried to tell them; they wouldn't listen. I—I must go now."

"Who are you?" Amanda said, more frightened, more bewildered than she knew.

"My name is Marilee. . . ." Her head turned to the soaked, still body next to her. "We nearly made it. Don't tell," she put her finger over her lips. "Remember, Amanda, don't tell," and she gunned the truck suddenly, leaving Amanda reeling, then falling into the soaking mud along the side of the road.

Her mother was running from the house now, with an umbrella and her father.

Her father bent over her to pick her up out of the mud. Her mother in her nightgown stood there. Between the blasts of lightning, her face, blurred by the concern and the rain, looked like a neon sign, a horrified neon sign blinking on and off through a hotel blind. The lightning was coming like that, in long even streaks, and then sudden flashes, flashes that lit up the entire sky, lit it up in the most horrible ghostly way.

Amanda saw then, in a flash of light, a huge ship, like a dirigible, pull up its gangplank and rise from the desert floor. All around her was the smell of burning.

"What happened?" her father said, helping her walk.

"I—I . . ." Something was stopping her, something had suddenly landed like a fist in her belly, some thought. "I don't know," she said, and then she turned to her mother, knowing in advance the answer. "Did you see him?" she said.

"Who, darling?" her mother said.

"The—the man . . . the man at the door," Amanda said. She could not stop the trembling in her arms. *I am not crazy*, she said to herself. Don't let this get you, you *are not a crazy person*.

"Did you see the man at the door?" Amanda turned savage, now to her mother, her voice raised. "Well, did you see him?"

"Darling, I—I saw you were up . . . you were in the kitchen, so I came down to see what it was . . . I came down and you were at the door."

"You didn't see anyone?"

"I—I heard a noise, darling. I did; I heard a noise and I thought maybe there was a dog at the door. I told you there was something."

"A dog?" Amanda said. "You thought it was a dog?" And as Amanda stared at her mother she thought, It's true. *She has forgotten what she has seen.*

Her father's arm was around her. "You'll catch your death out here," he said. "Working so hard you get those nightmares. . . . You can't sleep."

"A nightmare," her mother said, scampering behind him. "Yes, terrible to have nightmares."

In the evening paper she would read: UNIDENTIFIED COUPLE FOUND DEAD IN PICKUP TRUCK IN CANYON. Storm had forced them off the road, both parties unknown, no ID, supposed "drifters" to be buried in potter's field. "Oh, Hooper," she gasped.

In the morning Amanda dressed, greeted her parents cheerfully and assured them she had not caught cold, ate her two fried eggs lustily, reassuring her mother that the "nightmare" was over, and gunned the Mars-mobile to the base. She was nervous, no question she was nervous when Hotchkiss walked into the cafeteria.

"Let's go for a walk," she said to him. And he nodded. Okay, what was up with her anyway? Nonetheless something in him melted at just a glimpse of her. He could tell she was on the edge of being wrecked, despite her attempt at calm.

As they walked out into the desert, the sun coming strong already behind the mountains, Amanda was grateful there was no wind. It seemed easier, somehow, to think without the wind.

"Okay," she said, "now I'm going to tell you some things, and I'm going to ask you some things, but before I do that I need to ask you to look me in the eyes and tell me something."

"I like to look in your eyes," he said.

"No, this is serious."

"I'm serious."

"Do you think I am capable of going crazy?"

He looked at her a long moment. Finally he said, "I dunno."

"You don't know?" she said, amazed. "What do you mean you don't know? What kind of answer is that?"

He shrugged. "I don't know if you are or I am or anybody is. I don't have any experience in that line. I don't know what it takes, is all I'm saying."

"Well, I am not asking for scientific proof, just an impression."

"As an impression, no. You don't look like the type; on the other hand you don't miss much."

"What's that got to do with it?"

"I don't know, but I do know this," Hotchkiss said, turning to her and putting his hands on her shoulders. It amazed her—Hotchkiss, such a simple type, with such a seeming understanding of more complicated things. "I grew up near an Indian reservation, and I used to talk to those witch doctors. Never understood much of what they were saying, but those Indians, you know, they would go crazy now and then. I mean it wasn't so uncommon. They were always fooling around with weeds and drugs, and I figured that was it, but this old Indian said to me one day—I'll never forget it—he pointed to the sky and he said to me, 'What do you see?' and I said, 'Clouds.' And he asked me three times did I see anything besides clouds, and I said no, and he looked at me and he said, 'You will never be crazy, so don't worry about it.' Then he sighed and he said, 'On the other hand, you will miss much.' " Hotchkiss laughed. Amanda was bewildered and annoyed.

"What has this got to do with anything?"

"Oh, Amanda, look. You would have looked at the same clouds and seen cowboys and Indians and dinosaurs and magic wands and who the hell knows what else. You've got this real peyote head, we would call it; you've got a conjuror's mind in an engineer's head. I don't know but that's only one part; the other part of you sees it fast. They trained you faster'n any other astronaut in the program in fifteen years. Smart, I think they call it. They only have to tell you once, and you *get* it. They say you're real damned smart. But you freak 'em, too. They think you're too fucking original sometimes. You mess up their systems. You make it better, yeah, but they don't always want to go your way. Hell, Amanda, you know you got 'em buffaloed. And they don't like it. And they don't like you. Now you ask me could you go crazy, and hell I don't know." He turned to her, those cornflower-blue eyes and hair like gold, his face assessing the potential of her mysteries.

Hotchkiss's honesty occasionally moved her, and this was one of those times. She walked on a few paces, the prairie flowers crunching under her red leather scrolled boots.

"I saw Hooper last night," she said.

"Hooper's s'posed to be dead," Hotchkiss said.

"I'm glad you said supposed to be. Why'd you say that?" she asked, turning to him.

He looked at her. She was counting on him so.

"Well, I can tell you this . . . at Hooper's funeral nobody believed it was him."

When she had told him the rest, Hotchkiss walked at her side silently for a while. A prairie dog out of nowhere skittered across their path. Then a jeep loaded with equipment passed them.

Then he squeezed her hand. To their mutual astonishment this caused Amanda to burst into tears. She could not believe it, but she *did* believe it; someone as logical as Hotchkiss had actually understood. She could feel, in the circle of his arms, that he didn't think she was crazy at all. As they were about to turn back, the sky darkened suddenly, the way it can do on the desert, and the wind whipped up into a torrent.

"Hell," Hotchkiss said, grabbing her hand and starting to run, and then they saw it—a black twister coming down through the canyon between the mountains.

"Oh God, we'll never make it," she screamed, and it seemed to her before she knew what happened that Hotchkiss had pulled her down on the ground and was lying on top of her.

He screamed, "Keep your head down," and the wind was over them, around them, and through them. She felt the wind pull her up into a cone, felt Hotchkiss separating from her, felt herself spinning spinning spinning into a blackness and then nothing.

She didn't know later whether it was before the nothing or after the nothing that she heard the voice loud and clear say to her, "Amanda, do not go into the simulator." She heard this. Loud and clear.

When it was over, she felt someone near her, pulling her arm. It was Hotchkiss. "Amanda, God, are you okay?" He was slapping her face. He was covered with dust, and bruises were all over his forehead and his eyes.

"Okay, okay," she said, holding off his hand. She struggled up and looked about. The twister had deposited her about twenty-five yards from where they started, beyond the buildings on the other side.

"Are you all right?" she said to him.

"Yeah . . . by some miracle." Her left side ached. She thought her arm was broken. "Jesus Christ, I never saw anything like that . . . not out here. . . ." It missed the base by ten feet, but it leveled the TV quarters of the press room. Amanda, still feeling dazed, looked about. The equipment was mangled, twisted like junk in a junkyard.

"My God," she said, "I hope nobody was in there."

They took off at a run.

Amanda had "forgotten," she *thought*. That is to say, she no longer consciously remembered the voice that told her not to go into the simulator.

She wasn't scheduled for simulator training until Thursday. All she knew was that, for some reason, she was uneasy about the simulator session on Thursday.

Also, she didn't want to start getting paranoid, but that night when she got home, she found the third foot drawing. There were her feet, unmistakably in the stages of nail-polish ten, the tenth day when the polish was all off her pinky toe, and one-third off her big toe, and there was the drawing, carefully and, she thought, almost lovingly recording the daily changes in her toes.

As they were about to leave for dinner at a restaurant, Amanda, in a fit of guilt, said to Hotchkiss, "Why don't we take Schrodinger?"

He looked at her. "What for?"

"Well," she said, uncertainly, "I don't think it's fair. He never gets out at all."

"He wouldn't know the difference if he did," Hotchkiss said, vaguely insulted by the suggestion. Still, in a reluctant way he understood. "Well, it's just around the corner. We'll have to put him in something. You can't let people see him."

"Oh, I know . . . I have just the thing," Amanda said, and she took out a wicker basket, which Hotchkiss ruefully observed they used for picnics, lined it with towels, and placed Schrodinger into it. She then put a towel over it, leaving it loose so he could breathe.

"Maybe he doesn't even need to breathe," Hotchkiss said.

"What do you mean?" Amanda asked, miffed.

"Well, like those Indian gurus, you know, you can bury them alive for several days and they don't need air or something."

"Oh . . . I should ask Bar-Makdihani—I'm sure he would be fascinated with Schrodinger."

As they entered the restaurant, they saw Farkheimer, his wife, and a friend. Donald said, "They think she's a Russian agent."

"Farkheimer's *wife?*"

"They think the Russian satellites are taking pictures of her nude. The whole base knows—it's top-secret classified. He's crazy about her. Very protective. She takes nude sunbaths."

They had dined well. Hotchkiss was feeling expansive. Amanda looked quite fetching in a blue silk dress around which she had flung, he thought quite miraculously, a long string of glitter beads. It gave her a faint gypsyish air, and he liked it. Everything had gone quite well. Schrodinger, as one might expect, caused no fuss, until they had ordered dessert. It had been a sublime moment for Hotchkiss. He was savoring the last of the wine, the very last was lying on his tongue, like a good-night kiss. The waiter had hustled off, when the woman at the next table, unable to contain herself, leaned over and said, "I've just been so curious all night. . . . Is that a baby in there? He's so quiet."

Amanda, for reasons unclear, blushed, which provoked the woman further.

"Oh I bet it is a *new* baby," she cooed. "Can I just take a peek, a tiny peek?"

"No," Amanda said suddenly flustered, "you can't. . . . I mean, I mean we can't disturb it," she said, trying to be nicer.

"Well, you're just a nervous mommy," she said, leaning over. "I'm just going to—"

"No!" Amanda said again, as the woman lifted the coverlet and quite predictably screamed.

The scream was of the "AGHHHH" variety, the woman backing up several steps screaming actual words now to the effect, "It's dead—oh my God, it's dead!"

There was quite a commotion in the restaurant now, to which Hotchkiss, Amanda noted unfavorably, was not responding at all well. He was sitting there, his head in his hands like a guilty kidnapper. The woman, in her hysteria, had become quite inventive, and like many inventive, hysterical people, quite convincing as well. There was enormous fuss and chatter. Someone was yelling angrily, "Call the police!" and the headwaiter paced nervously, eyeing them, asking everyone to calm down, as he, clearly thinking they were murderers, was afraid to approach the table.

"Look," Amanda said, "it isn't a baby, . . . it's a cat." And she held Schrodinger up for the entire restaurant to see.

"A dead cat!" a man hissed at her. "That is absolutely disgusting. You are a *sick* person!" he said, approaching her. "Why did you kill that cat?" His eyes glowed.

The woman who had discovered Schrodinger was sitting with a handkerchief holding her head. The rest of the table was standing in guilty accusation of Amanda. Hotchkiss was just sitting there, his head in his hands. Occasionally Amanda would hiss to him, "Do something, for God's sake . . ." But he did nothing. Hotchkiss was in a storm, waiting for it to pass.

Amanda was now making an impromptu speech to the restaurant, and it went this way: "This cat looks dead but he isn't dead . . . he—he's part of a research experiment—sort of—I mean he isn't dead—it's something mysterious . . . if there's a doctor here with a stethoscope you can see—he isn't dead at all."

"He's dead all right," a man yelled. By now the restaurant had become a theater. Every eye was on Amanda and Schrodinger.

"Is there a doctor here?" she said sweetly. She was sure there was, but no one volunteered.

"Well," she said, bringing Schrodinger over to the yelling man, "you can listen to his heart—he's purring."

The man, in astonishment, finally leaned over. His verdict was awaited by the tense audience, and his face finally cleared as he said, "It *is* purring."

Amanda, smiling, petted Schrodinger. "You see, it's just this mysterious thing he has. He goes into comas."

"Isn't that something . . . ?" another woman said, approaching the table. "I have an orange one. What color are his eyes?"

"Green," Amanda said, thinking by now it might be okay to sit down. She was glaring at Hotchkiss, who no longer had his head in his hands. Schrodinger was put back into the basket, and people came over to look at him. Hotchkiss was drinking his coffee.

"Let's get out of here," he said.

"It's not my fault," Amanda said.

"I know, but I feel like I'm in a sideshow or something," Hotchkiss said, unable to bear another murmur or another startled outcry.

They paid the check, and Amanda, feeling some sort of obligation, waved a feeble good-bye as they gathered Schrodinger up and left the restaurant. Perhaps it was the cold air, or heaven knows what, but as they did, Schrodinger suddenly recovered. A meow was heard, and when Amanda looked down there he was, fit as a fiddle.

"Oh!" she said. "Schrodinger's awake. At this hour! It's a miracle."

"Why couldn't he wake up in the restaurant?" Hotchkiss mumbled. "Then everyone would have thought it was cute."

Amanda said nothing, simply scratching Schrodinger's head as they walked along, Hotchkiss manfully carrying the basket as Schrodinger licked his hand.

26

As he shaved that morning in the mirror, the reflected glory of his days moving him to reverie—for Hotchkiss was quite capable of finding himself *superb*—Hotchkiss thought about how much he loved Amanda. This seemed to him a remarkably simple thing. He did not know what love was, nor did he wonder. He knew simply that he loved her. This was enough for him. He wanted to be with her, and her alone, all the time. He wanted to experience what for lack of other words he had taken to calling the "very Amanda-ness of her."

He had been so uncomfortable the night before at a formal dinner, sitting next to a beautiful, charming, lovely, engaging creature named Leslie. He had been amused, charmed, and distracted by the lovely Leslie, but through it all he had missed Amanda. He did not know exactly what it was about her. He knew he found himself wondering at her all the time. That Amanda pouring orange juice would say, as the juice dribbled down the lip of the spout, "Can you *imagine*, somebody actually figured out a law for that?"

"What?" Hotchkiss would say in the morning-blearied attitude that was part of his world.

"That liquid will fall along a curved surface in an absolutely predictable way. A guy named Henri Coanda, who pioneered studies of jet-propulsion dynamics, discovered it; the principle is called the Coanda Effect, when a liquid or gas flowing over a curved surface tends to cling to its curvature. Now isn't that amazing?" What was amazing to Hotchkiss was that Amanda was so amazed, struck dumb, he suspected, that *anyone* had ever figured *anything* out at all. Mystified, bewitched, enchanted, and attracted by the world of "laws." That nature had its explanations just "knocks my socks off," as she would say, whereas for Hotchkiss a thing was a thing. Oh, he had his curiosities and he had his pleasures, but he took root in another series of assumptions about the world. The world *was*, as far as Hotchkiss was concerned, and he and his engineering pursuits would find a way to make it work even better. Performance and efficiency, the well-oiled hinge—this was part of his scheme. But Amanda? Amanda was all Gadzooks!—the world of a particle physicist gone berserk: Holy smokes! Egads! Look at this! Eureka!

For Hotchkiss, despite his knowledge of physics, the world was still here, and there. He had not made the quantum leap. But Amanda had been *born* in a river of electrons. Where the river ended and the marsh began it was difficult to tell; where the tadpole ended and the frog began it was difficult to tell; where the Bible's "begats" ended and history began was difficult to tell. Amanda was awash in history, science, and explanations; time had clicked on in her mind in a totally different orbit from Hotchkiss. Her eyes held prisms he had only dreamed of. He knew this.

Amanda's amazement was to him, amazing. He cherished her discovering, even as he said to himself, as he looked, a tree was a tree. Neither more nor less. To Amanda, with her neutrinos, her particles, her bombardments, her matter and antimatter, a tree was "actually a field of concentration," like a random and arbitrary assortment of "visible molecules"; where the tree ended and the things around the tree began, Amanda could not be sure.

On the wall of her bedroom was a black-and-white picture. It was the kind of hazy, muddled black-and-white picture that when you first looked at it you thought it was a tree, because what you tended to focus on was this white tree in the midst of this black ground. But if you concentrated on looking only at the black, at the background, soon the tree disappeared; you didn't see the tree at all, but only the forest. Where Amanda had gotten the picture he didn't know, but she "loved the trick," as she put it. Hotchkiss, for reasons that were unclear, was irritated by it. It seemed to him in the interests of convenience, respect for the basic order of things, that the picture should be either one thing or the other, certainly not both, and more than that, that whatever one saw should not, in his opinion, be a "trick."

"Don't you see?" Amanda would say. "Evolutionarily speaking, the eye is really simply the front part of the brain, which sticks out through your skull. It's the frontal brain; it can play as many tricks as the rest of the brain. Let's look at the phenomenon of eye witnesses." She smiled and bounced next to him on the couch. The pun seemed to please her.

"First of all, let's discuss murder and accidents."

"Do we have to?" Hotchkiss pleaded.

"Well, we have to," Amanda said, "because it's there, in the midst of disaster and death, that people's eyes play all kinds of tricks. Things that were never seen are seen. Things seen are forgotten. Now read this." And she would curl up next to Hotchkiss when the lights were low and read to him from *Modern Criminal Investigation*.

"Now, don't you see?" she said. "Four people witness a murder, and they all 'see' something different. Nobody 'sees' the same thing."

"So what?" Hotchkiss asked. "Who cares? What difference does it make? Something really happened, and just because you have 'inaccurate observers'—"

"No!" she cried, leaping from the couch. "Observing is inaccurate, that's the whole point!"

"Oh," he sighed, and leaned over to kiss her, "you've been spending too much time in particle physics." He shut her up with a kiss, the only thing he could think to do. They drove him crazy, the particle physicists, with their mumbo jumbo that a photon of light (ah yes, photons, they were nuts for photons) contained energy, and the energy it contained moved the electrons in the thing it shone upon, so that, in the world of quantum physics you could not see—i.e., put in the presence of light—anything that did not change by the fact that you were observing it. They seemed to make a great deal of this, Hotchkiss mused, and saw all sorts of meanings in it that eluded him. Hotchkiss was a practical man. But Amanda? Amanda came from a different order of things. Amanda knew this herself, first the neutrino, then the *quark* and then the gluons. Every time they thought they had it, a new subparticle was discovered that blew it all to bits—the theory and the *laws*, as well.

"The lecture this morning," Amanda said, addressing the class of students, "is about a very beautiful Dancer. She is very tall indeed . . . she is eleven million miles high." There was a hush after she said that, then a giggle. "Now the Dancer is going to show you how to understand Einstein," she said. "Would you like that?" There was a big chorus of yeses, although Amanda wondered if they were really interested in understanding Einstein or saying yes. She proceeded to draw the Dancer on the board, and as she did so, she felt that strange peculiar sensation she had had on occasion before. Actually when she thought about it she did not know why she insisted this Dancer was beautiful, it was only really an illustration about time and space. But Amanda knew she was.

"Okay," she said, "you're on earth"—she pointed to someone in the front row—"and you're in a spaceship." She pointed to another child.

"You're the Dancer," she said, calling a child with long blond hair to the front, "and you are moving at what?" she asked the class.

"Light speed," said a smart one in the third row. Well maybe they'd learned something last week.

"Can you move that fast?" she said to the child. The girl shook her head, a shy no.

"No, of course you can't . . . none of us can in anything . . . yet. And it's unlikely, because of some other laws, that we ever will. But if you could move that fast," she said to the girl, "show us how you would dance." Amanda brought a tape recorder for such purposes, and she put the music on. Usually nothing happened. The chosen performer would sit down in a burst of giggles. But this time was different. This child listened quietly to the music and then, clearly inspired, she began to pirouette, to dance.

The class, taken aback, stared. The child was marvelous. The dance was brief. Then the girl, suddenly aware of what she was doing, became embarrassed. Amanda rescued her.

"That was lovely. Now to understand Einstein's law of relativity, the question is, if you were moving at almost the speed of light, which would move first, earthman, her hand or her leg? And what would you see first, spaceman, her arm or her leg?"

"Wouldn't both see the same thing?" one puzzled observer asked.

"No. The spaceship passenger would see her arm move first, and the earth observer, her hand . . . but they would both be *right*." And she went on to explain. The class, she thought, rather enjoyed that two such seemingly contradictory things could occur and yet everyone would be right. Amanda found herself, the nights she gave the Dancer lecture, staring up at the sky. Watching the stars move, occasionally she thought she saw something fleeting there. A leg, an arm, and then she'd laugh. Of course you could never see such a thing, you could never see that far. She knew this, and yet as she stared up there into the sky she felt some connection to this Dancer. It was only a concept, an image, she told herself, but she *felt* as though it were a wild, calling thing that would not let her go.

"Did you ever notice that Schrodinger, the few minutes he's awake, is always watching the sky?" Amanda said. "He sits out there on the ledge, looking up."

"All cats look up," Hotchkiss said, unimpressed.

"The way his head moves," Amanda said wonderingly, "it's like a radar scan. Did you ever notice that? It goes around in a complete circle. He goes back and forth, like a radar antenna."

At this, Hotchkiss put down his coffee and turned around. To be sure, Schrodinger was there, awake and alert for once, and one could say, if one watched very closely, that his head seemed to turn, in an almost mechanical way, around in a complete circle.

"Hmmm," Hotchkiss said, "that is odd—which is to say, consistent."

"What do you mean by that?" Amanda said, immediately defensive.

"I mean by that that there is very little about Schrodinger that isn't odd."

"His purr isn't."

"Isn't what?"

"Odd. I wouldn't say his purr is odd at all," Amanda said.

"Well, it's awfully loud," Hotchkiss said. "People think it's a vacuum cleaner."

"Schrodinger can't be responsible for what people think," Amanda said, getting up and clearing the dishes. "Really, I'm surprised at you," she said to Hotchkiss, as if Hotchkiss were the kind of person who paid attention to what people thought.

"I'm just saying," Hotchkiss said, "that it's odd for people not to be able to tell the difference between a cat and a vacuum cleaner. Most people could easily tell the difference between a cat and a vacuum cleaner, so therefore Schrodinger is, whether you like it or not, odd."

"Frankly, I think a *person* who can't tell the difference between a vacuum cleaner and a cat is odd, if not to say stupid," Amanda said.

And Hotchkiss sighed. He had lost out in these arguments before. He didn't know why she felt so defensive about Schrodinger. He wasn't being critical. He was just saying it was peculiar, although he supposed if he thought about it, it wasn't much of a compliment to anyone or anything to be confused with a vacuum cleaner. But that didn't make the people stupid, Hotchkiss thought. Not at all. Why, the vibrations that animal set up on occasion were positively astounding. One night in particular they had gotten so out of hand that Hotchkiss rose excitedly from his chair, crying, "My God, what's that?"

"Oh my!" Amanda had said. She had rushed into the next room to calm Schrodinger down. When questioned about this later, she would simply blink her beautiful blue eyes at Hotchkiss and shrug her shoulders and say, "I don't know what happens. I think he has flights."

"Flights?" Hotchkiss said. "What kind of flights?"

"Flights of ecstasy," Amanda said. And that would be that.

Hotchkiss, in the midst of a gasp, would be tempted to say What? He really did not understand how she arrived at such startling conclusions with such conviction and such a seeming absence of forethought. But there would be no answer to his What. He knew this too. She and Schrodinger were off again, he would think, making excursions along their private trajectories, a world of ecstasies, conclusions, thoughts, and revelations that those who did not travel it but only observed it from outside could only wonder at.

Solipsovich had one question and one question only, and that idiot American general had just answered it. The question had hounded Solipsovich since the first International Meeting of the Soviet Union and the United States for Agreement on Extraterrestrial Space Missions. The meeting was in Moscow in 1974. It was not uncommon for Solipsovich to be hounded for twelve years. He was party trained. And he had his satisfactions. They had just crushed the rebellious tribesmen in Afghanistan, they had destroyed the Polish Workers' Union. Freedom of speech and freedom of assembly were hitting the turf in various parts of the globe, and the Soviet government was polishing its scythe for more. The Americans—he personally had it in for the Americans. Popularizing dangerous ideas. He sat back and lit his cigar. There was enough rot in America for it possibly to sink of its own accord. Injustice, racism, poverty—he would help them fester where he could. It was the freedom to think in America that drove him crazy. To think and to say. Intolerable. Intolerable and dangerous. He would have none of it. Domination and destruction, these were his aims in life. It was the Soviet dream, as it had once been the German dream. It was the most exciting dream of all. Just thinking of it made his thighs tremble. He wet his lips. And he was about to get cooperation, he could feel it, cooperation from those stupid American fools. Solipsovich knew the Soviets had no franchise on this dream. It floated just above the surface of the earth, falling like rain on the blind, the lame, and the needy. The blind they would be led, they thought; the lame they would be helped to walk, they thought; the needy they would be comforted, they thought. But it was acid, this rain, and they would all be burned.

Now, on American television, courtesy of the Soviet satellite, the idiot American general had just answered the question.

"Theoretically, Commander James, how many people does it take down here on these computers to get one of these rockets, like Valkyrie, up in the air?"

"Wal, we've had a lot of success there, yessir." The commander looked proud. "We used to need three hundred people. A hundred in Cape Canaveral and two hundred nine in Houston at Mission Control, and a thirty-man backup team in the Jet Propulsion Lab up in Pasadena, to get one of these things up. We don't need that no more. No sir, we only need a hundred fifty people all told at the computers."

Yes, Solipsovich knew, 150 until countdown eleven, and after eleven, he knew they only needed *one*, one person in the computer room, and he knew who that would be. He made a note. Then he took out his floor plan of the computers, replete with their programs, a field of microchips, and laid it on the table. Then he laid over it a thin, plastic sheet outlining the geographical outlines of Cape Canaveral, to which was attached a scientific document outlining the weather and related phenomena of the area.

The second item on the document was annotated "red tide."

Beedle was not prepared for the froth that General Farkheimer was in. He was screaming at Beedle about the car heist.

"The ambassador's buggy," he said, "is a sixty-thousand-dollar rare Mercedes-Benz that is beyond repair! Not to mention the fact that all Arab relations are in extremely bad condition as a result of this humiliation." Farkheimer, Hobbs thought, did not seem to know he was screaming.

"Well sir," Beedle said, "he don't mean nothin' by it. He likes cars and planes is all."

"You have got to do something about him, Hobbs, keep him under control. I swear, if we didn't need him for the testing, I'd have him shot."

Beedle winced. "Look, sir, I'll try to keep a better eye on him. I wasn't there, sir, or I'm certain—"

"You ought to keep him on a chain. . . ."

"If I keep him on the chain in public, he gets humiliated, sir. It embarrasses him. You know what happens then."

"Oh, right," the general said, seemingly exhausted by this inquiry. "I remember the time he urinated on the British prime minister."

"Yeah, well, they got to get their aggression out somewhere, I guess," Hobbs said mildly.

"Not at the risk of ruining our policies with petroleum-producing countries!" Farkheimer was screaming again.

"Well, sir," Beedle said, knowing it was a mistake but finding it impossible not to come to the chimp's defense, "he don't know which countries is oil producing and which ain't."

"You're the one that told me, Hobbs, that damn monkey is smarter than the whole goddamn air force. You told me that, Hobbs."

Hobbs looked at the floor. This was a tough one. He didn't want to let on exactly how smart 342 was. "Well maybe I exaggerated. He is, after all, just a chimpanzee. It won't happen again, sir."

"If it does, Hobbs"—Farkheimer's face was red—"I'm getting rid of you . . . and don't tell me about that monkey. I don't care if he does go into a depression. Goddamnit, he's spoiled to death. It didn't work the last time, but it's going to work this time, Hobbs. If it happens again, you're off the case and Three-forty-two is going back to Resnik."

Resnik! Hobbs couldn't even speak the terrible word. "They'll kill each other, sir. Three-forty-two hates Resnik. You know he—"

"That's final, Hobbs. There have been too many incidents. I realize this is an outstanding animal. Extraordinarily well trained and perhaps the most valuable asset to the entire space-division program. But he goes too far." The general was trembling when he sat down.

"Well, sir, it would be better if there wasn't so much coverage," Beedle finally said.

"What do you mean, Hobbs?"

"What I tried to tell you was to keep the chimp, Three-forty-two, out of anything where there are cameras. He's a real publicity hound, and it's very hard to control him under those circumstances."

"What in hell are you talking about? Do you know the dangers of anthropomorphizing an animal like this?"

"What, sir?"

"Anthropomorphizing, Hobbs. You are applying human characteristics to a nonhuman."

"Well, he watches all the news shows all the time. He jumps up and down when he sees himself on television."

"I'm sure this is your imagination, Hobbs. Let me say it once and for all. One more mishap, you lose your stripes and Three-forty-two winds up with Resnik. Good day, Hobbs." The general turned his back.

Beedle, upset at the threat and trying not to reveal it, backed out of the general's office. He was furious at 342. He might have known he'd try to steal that car. Loved convertibles. Fast cars, fast planes. Damn near got himself killed too. Beedle had a complex love-hate game with 342, but wretched as he sometimes felt about the chimp, his heart had fallen to his toes when he'd approached the burning car, convinced the chimp was pinned behind the wheel. In terms of training, and substitution, the NASA people's hearts had sunk, too. It was about a million dollars' worth of chimp in that car. Fortunately, the million-dollar chimp soon started squealing from a nearby tree, but he wasn't gloating. Beedle could see the whole thing had given the chimp quite a turn. Beedle packed him up into his own car and started scolding him, but 342 was quiet, and he sat there, holding his head in his hands, something he never did. Beedle figured the crash must have scared the shit out of him, because after a while he started shaking. Beedle wanted to wring his neck, at least half the time, but on the other hand he hated to see him shook up like this. When they got back to hangar eleven, the chimp went right to his cage, curled up, and slept like a baby.

When he didn't even wake up for the eleven-o'clock news, Beedle knew he must be exhausted. That chimp had a real timer in him. He was always awake for the eleven-o'clock news, and there he was, all over it.

Beedle knew he wasn't supposed to anthropomorphize him, or whatever they called it, but as he looked at the newsreels, he saw the trouble loud and clear. There was indeed something perverse about 342, something more than a sheer animallike impulse. It could be explained that 342, being a chimpanzee and a demonstrably smart one, had been attracted by the keys hanging in the ignition in the new car. It could be demonstrated that, having driven Hobbs's car on several occasions, particularly through car washes, of which he appeared to be extremely fond, he was in the habit of jumping in and starting and driving an automobile. It could be explained that the chimp was traditionally fond of headgear of varying kinds. He stole everybody's hats, from the general's on down to the porters' at airports. He *loved* hats, so this could perhaps explain his jumping into King Horan's car and clamping onto his head the chauffeur's headdress lying on the seat beside him. Perhaps. What could not be explained, however, was the chimp's leaning on the horn, as he wheeled the car around the circle, drawing attention to this feat while he waved. Yes, his paw, or hand, was up in the air waving from the king's convertible, as if, yes, as if *posing* for the flotilla of photographers present. After a few seconds of this kind of display, he spun the car around, and, hammer to the floor, headed out for Interstate 91. Now Beedle knew, knew just as sure as he was born, that 342 would not have done it if there hadn't been all those cameras around. No footage, no clippings?—the chimp was not interested. Of course, as in all complex relationships, Hobbs, too, was interested. No, more than interested. Hobbs, despite all of his misgivings, which were considerable, was positively impressed.

Hobbs, unbeknownst to the brass, kept a scrapbook of 342's clippings, and some nights, when the wind howled and things were quiet, they would go through the scrapbook, 342 pointing and Beedle slapping his knee and laughing in a congratulatory way. "You remember when you *did* that? Oh, my God . . . oh '42, '42, you are *too* much!" Sometimes, when feeling real affection, which was a rare moment in Hobbs's otherwise parsimonious emotional life, he would call 342 " '42," as a nickname.

Luckily, things turned out pretty much all right. Beedle insisted on an investigation of the cause of the accident. Three-forty-two might be a little reckless, but he was essentially a good driver, and there was no way he would deliberately drive off the road into a cow field and plow into a tree. He was just off a curve, and Beedle figured the brakes had gone on him, or the steering wheel or something, and it turned out the brake linings were worn as thin as nylon stockings and the king would have wound up in big trouble for sure. In fact, the brake linings were so worn there was talk of sabotage. So there was a redeeming feature to the caper. But the general's threat still remained, and Beedle was sworn to keep a careful eye on him in the future.

Solipsovich's special agent, Karyatin, made one fatal error. He stopped for a hot dog. From a certain perspective Soviet history is preeminently hot-doggian, which is to say Freudian. Unpleasant or contrary-to-acceptable procedures are erased.

Therefore, to all appearances the man was simply another hot-dog vendor. Karyatin rested the black case, chained to his wrist, on the stainless-steel cover of the stand.

"One dog," he said.

"Mustard?"

"Yes," he said.

"Kraut?"

"No," he said. "No kraut." Unknown to him, this was the password. The vendor's metallic eyes lit as he eyed the case.

"No kraut?" said the vendor again as he pushed the hot dog into Karyatin's hand, eyeing him carefully. "You are sure no kraut?"

"No kraut!" Karyatin said. "I'll take only mustard."

The vendor reached for a special mustard bottle and watched. Karyatin took a bite. In a minute, the mustard had seared a hole in his pulmonary artery and he was dead. The man then put the mustard on the chain of the attaché case. It melted, he seized the case, and disappeared.

27

That afternoon as she drove the Mars-mobile she found herself wondering again about Hooper. It was Hooper who had said to her, "Don't ever take anything for granted. Don't let anybody test anything for you. Test it all yourself, and if you get up there and they give you orders and you don't want to do it, don't do it."

That advice had saved her life once. In a spin and accelerating fast, Amanda had thought she was finished. Ground control kept screaming "the stick, pull nine!" but she knew she couldn't get it, and so at the last moment, she retrofired two rockets, broke the spin, and sailed upward safely and landed under control. No one could believe it.

On impulse, Amanda decided to drive over to the lab. She hadn't been in the laboratory for months, having left the theoretical world of physics aside for practical training.

But something drew her there tonight. Perhaps it was the new finding. She'd known they *would* find one. The black hole. Right near the sun. Unmistakable. A tidal wave of gravity. Well, she was glad they'd located it *before* she took off for Mars. It made her think of something: some calculations she'd done in college had just reappeared in her mind.

She spent several hours there, feeling stranger and stranger. *She could do all the calculations up to a point*, then she just couldn't come to a conclusion. Maybe, she thought, I'm tired. Maybe the *strain*. Suddenly she thought she heard something, and she jumped. No, it wasn't anything. This was highly classified, this lab. It took a special identity card to get in, to unlock the doors. It was a very tight security system. When she heard the noise again, she looked outside. It was a bat. Well, she thought, at least I'm not *imagining* things. She watched the bat for several minutes, thinking.

Amanda knew perfectly well what happened to some physicists after a time. Crackers, that's what. Everyone knew the story of the man who discovered the quark. Afterward he had gone on and on about Little Green Men, he actually called them—neutrinos, ghosts, monsters, starships, and heaven knew what else. He was happy though. If that's what it is to be crazy, Amanda thought, it's not so bad. Quarks, quiffs, and conundrums—his brain was a boiling mass and he was *singing* in the street.

She was thinking about this when she heard the Xerox copier go on at the far end of the lab. There was no one in the lab but her—how odd. Maybe some faulty wiring. As she approached the machine, a piece of paper flew out. It was titled "Knowledge of the Bat," but when she lifted the cover to see the original, it wasn't there. Perhaps someone had been there earlier, and the machine, through some mechanical failure, had kept this copy until now. She began to read:

KNOWLEDGE OF THE BAT

You have knowledge of the bat. Of how it moves, how it flies; even though it goes by night, you have seen, with your machines, your movie cameras, and your film, you have seen the webbed spread of its wings, its beating through the night, and you have heard, with your machines, its sonar. Its fine, high whistle locating its prey. But the bat? The bat knows nothing of you. The bat, although it lives in the world with you, does not see you sitting in your houses, drinking coffee, reading papers, and thinking about the fact of the bat. Only in its sonar, in its occasional beep off your physical force, the aggregate of your molecules so to speak, only in your resemblance to granite, or a cow, do you exist for the bat. If desperate and hungry, he might locate you in the meadow at night and attack.

So, possibly as a victim he might "know" you. Possibly. Much more does he know the moth, with whom he has a steady relationship and who is of some interest to him, as he eats it. In this way that you regard the bat, so are you regarded. There are presences in the world who have as much power and exist as fully as you do yourselves, in the daylight hours in your houses of glass and wood and stone, and just as the bat becomes for most of you a creature apprehended on television or in books, so to the extent that the bat becomes for you a concept, different certainly from the concept of two, as in two and two are four, but nonetheless rarely experienced, so in the way that you are very informed and have experienced the bat, although indirectly, so are you experienced. There are presences, which we will call "phantoms," in the world who watch you as you watch the bat. There are no hours in its presence, no daylight or moonlight or night. It exists, the phantom world, in all time, and it has this one dangerous characteristic: it can inhabit. Which is to say, any part of the phantom world can inhabit your world, should it choose to do so. Please, do not understand this as some primitive form of "possession," some byproduct of witchcraft. It is none of those things. It is closest perhaps to your "imaginative leaps," I believe you call them, when you study, read, and observe the bat as closely as possible and then endeavor to "imagine" what it is like to be a bat. The phantom's imaginative power, if we insist on using the language, which we must I fear, is not explicable in the terms of your understanding. In other words, it is not a thing that is possible for you to understand. I shall endeavor to give you some notion of it, which is the best that I can do, due to the current evolutionary level of *Homo sapiens*. It is conceivable that in two million years you will have embraced this concept, although it is not determined. As you know, or some of you know, it is not likely that *Homo sapiens* will survive two million years more on the planet earth. It is written in the Call Book, which is not again what you think; it is not some childlike notion of death in which the male deity, or fate, "calls one's number up," and this explanation suffices to explain an otherwise inexplicable death. No, it is not like that at all. Nonetheless, if you have any interest in the matters of origin and destiny, you must realize that there are rules at work: rules of nature, forces of history, the undeniable drive of the human mind to understand, and what concerns us most here, the eternal battle of life and death, not simply "life and death," for I can understand you (as, alas, you cannot understand me) that this is meaningless to you. But life and death as they struggle *for dominance in a species*. According to the Call Book you have, in the twentieth century as you record it, one thousand years to resolve whether or not the species will continue.

Well, Amanda thought, "That is one *hell* of a disturbing thing, and such a strange coincidence. Who wrote this thing, anyway?" Annoyed, she looked more carefully at the copier. It was a "memory" copier, which meant it *recorded* everything ever copied in its computer. Good. She would get someone in the morning to find the hour the original was copied, and she knew there'd have to be a record of who used this room. She would get to the bottom of this.

The next day there was a special meeting of the Air Force Committee Special Division on Atmospheric Effects. The head of the committee, Colonel Anderson, was making his report. The essence of it was that yes, there had been an unusual number of "atmospheric disturbances" in the areas of special NASA space programs, and there was some suspicion that the Russians had developed laser-power space-vehicle programs to a sufficient degree to be controlling the weather. The "twister" experienced that day was just the latest in a series of "climatic" reversals that were having the effect, for the most part, of setting the space program back weeks and months while they dealt with repairs.

Because of this setback it wasn't until two days later that Amanda Jaworski, woman astronaut, was asked to step into the solar simulator. It was strictly routine. Amanda had been in and out of that simulator at least fifty times. To be exact, she had been in and out forty-nine times, exactly. She turned to Delko today and said—she actually didn't know why—"I'm not going in there."

Delko, bemused, allowed an eyebrow to rise, at first in curiosity, finding her impish. "Why?" he said.

"I—I don't know," she said, feeling foolish. "I'm just not going to."

Delko looked at her with growing curiosity. "Well now, that's very interesting. You're not going to. . . . Would you like to explain why?"

"Something tells me not to do it," she said.

Delko looked thoroughly exasperated. "Something tells you not to do it. Well now, ain't that cute," he said, mimicking her. "Women's intuition, that it?"

Amanda wanted to sock him in the jaw. They hated each other. It was clean. It was neat. And absolutely unmistakable.

"I'm not going in," she said quietly, and turned on her heel.

"You lissen 'a me, Jaworski," Delko screamed after her. "You need five more hours in that simulator. If you miss today, you're going to set back your flight. I won't clear you at forty-nine hours. I won't do it. And you'll postpone everything a day, and that won't make 'em happy . . . make 'em very *un*happy."

Amanda kept walking down the hall. Delko would like nothing better than to get her off the space shot. She could hear him screaming behind her.

"I'm gonna recommend they can you for insubordination. . . . I'm gonna get Mary up insteada you, you lousy cunt!"

Her eyes opened wide on this last. He had never actually gone that far. She sighed. So what. They would never believe he called her that anyway. Mentally she checked off the next day's training. The Mars flight involved several "investigations," as they had come to be called, regarding properties on the planet and in the universe on the way to it. Tomorrow she was to concentrate on the X-ray fluorescent investigation. She'd need to check that out, and the wind-velocity sensors, the thermocouples on the temperature and wind-velocity boom in the meteorology section. She'd have to run through procedures in "Magnetic Properties." Then she smiled. She would have to meet with Dr. Elders and go through the procedures for the "Everything Else Investigation," as they put it. The "size, shape, and behavior of particles on Mars." She sighed. Her training had been exhaustive and she was prepared. She would just have to stop thinking about Hooper.

Beedle's public position was to defend 342. Privately he was ready to wring his neck. Beedle figured life with 342 was always putting him somewhere between these two impulses. Three launch postponements had caused 342 to spend almost a year now in Beedle's keeping, and Beedle knew he had extremely complicated feelings about 342. They once sent him to that damn psychiatrist about it. That was after the night he'd taken 342 home and slept in the same bed with him; that had shaken the psychiatrists apparently. Ole Beedle himself, hardhearted Beedle, had known one thing: that the chimp's future contained his own. So that one night, when the pipe broke in Hangar Eleven and no one on maintenance could get there until morning and Beedle saw 342 starting to shiver, he knew there was only one thing to do: bring him home.

Beedle was, somewhere, a sentimental soul, and it touched him that when he opened the chimp's cage ready to do battle, the chimp was so cold he threw his arms around Beedle and hugged him. Beedle was sentimental enough not to ascribe this gesture exclusively to a need for body heat, and a tear formed in his eye as he carried the large, rather heavy chimp, now wrapped around his chest and covered with a blanket, into his car. He had, in fact, done the thing he had only done once for his old girl friend, Doris, who couldn't take the cold weather: he'd gone out there first to warm the car up, and then he'd come in and fetched Doris.

Well, the same thing held true. He put 342 in a thick blanket and went out, listening to him screaming, until he got the car warmed up, and then he carried the chimp out into it. By now it was snowing hard, and Beedle had to carry the big fellow close to his chest with the blanket over his head, listening to him whimpering like a baby.

"Hah," Beedle half snarled under his breath. "See, you finally need me. Can't do everything your goddamn self, can you?" He placed 342 almost tenderly, but perhaps gingerly is more accurate, into the front seat. He wouldn't trust the chimp alone on the passenger side, while he closed the door and walked around. Not with the engine running. So Beedle opened the door on the driver's side and reached across the seat and placed 342 in position. Then he climbed in after him. Felt bad, not trusting him, 342 being so cuddly, all of a sudden. But he knew better. Be just like that chimp to step on the gas, take the wheel, and drive the car straight to Miami. There was a big banana farm outside Miami, and Beedle privately thought that that chimp knew right in hell where it was. He had seen the chimp studying the cartons stamped Banana Farm, Route 8, Miami. And he swore he knew it.

Sometimes Beedle thought 342 was a genius, and sometimes he thought he was just another old stupid monkey. Trouble was, you could never be sure.

The only thing that Beedle found 342 was *not* good at was checkers.

He found this out quite by accident one night when he had taken his checkers set from Doris's house, instead of the chess set, so he and 342 played checkers. And Beedle loved it. Checkers was the simplest of games, and that old chimp couldn't play it worth a damn. Beedle was sweeping him off the board, chuckling the whole time. It was risky, though. Damn if that chimp didn't have feelings. Went into a crash—there was no other way to explain it—went down into the deeps. It finally even got to Beedle. The chimp just lay there, like a bowl of noodles. Lifeless, depressed, he couldn't even muster the courage to move the checker pieces. Beedle, who was not an unkind man, relented. He decided to let 342 win the next two rounds. It didn't seem to make much of an impact. He won the first game, and then Beedle set the board up again, but he saw the chimp looking at him sort of funny. He let him win the second game, and the chimp didn't look happy at all. He just kind of turned around, turned his back on Beedle and slunk to the far end of the cage. This was sufficiently unusual behavior to cause Beedle some concern. He had watched 342 carefully, and when he saw the slow shaking of the shoulders, he knew; there was no denying it: the goddamn chimp was crying. Brokenhearted. A lump rose in Beedle's throat: to his surprise, he was concerned about the damn monkey.

So it was that when Stafford came in that night, he stood for some time in the door, puzzled and then moved, as he witnessed the scene before him. There in the stark concrete room in which they kept 342, outside of a very large clean cage, but nonetheless a cage, was a man dressed as a soldier, a man Stafford knew personally to be temperamental, hard-boiled, and as mean a son of a bitch as ever was, talking softly, endlessly, patiently to the chimp. Like a cop talking a suicidal person off a bridge, full of compassion, concern, and respect. He watched the scene, the lamp overhead swinging in the drafts that came in under the door, the light passing back and forth over the scene of Beedle and his consolation, passing back and forth like a wand.

"Look now," he had heard Beedle saying, "you just can't take this so hard. Now lissen: nobody's good at everything, are they?"

The chimp shook his head. "So why would you be? And look at all the things you're good at. . . . Why, aren't you good at the computer? Is there any chimp in the history of the whole space program could run the whole damn shuttle themselves?"

The chimp's shoulders shrugged.

"Well, don't tell me you don't know, 'cause I'll tell you . . . not one of them could do it, and you know it. Aren't you the one the Russians wanted to steal 'cause you're so smart? Well, answer me— aren't you? Did they ever try to steal any other chimps?"

Three-forty-two shook his head.

" 'Course not. Not only are you the only one they tried to steal, you were smart enough to get away."

There was a shrug again.

"Well, I know you did. Everybody else sayin' it was only an accident you got out, but I know better. I know you knew what you were doin'. I mean, you got out of a cage with eight locks on it. You're a regular Houdini!"

At this, Beedle reached through the cage and the chimp reached around and grabbed Beedle's hand, held it a moment and kissed it.

"Well now . . . if I ain't . . ." Beedle said, standing there feeling stupid and amazed.

"Evening, Beedle. Evening, Three-forty-two." It was Stafford. He decided it was time to make his presence known; the intimacy had begun to embarrass him. The thing was, he and Beedle had gotten so used to 342 and his ways that they didn't realize that they were in fact conversing with him and that this was unusual. It was simply like a man who has a dog for a long time who responds to vocal orders or instructions. To a stranger it means the dog knows that certain inflections in the voice mean certain acts will follow. There is a kind of primitive training. But to the man, and the dog as well, we must suppose there are subtler and more complex levels of communication, which they have both somehow accepted and seem content to keep between themselves. So it was that one of the most profound contracts that pass among living things on earth goes unnoticed, and passes therefore into secrecy.

That morning Beedle had been called in by the Big Guns.

"Come over to Launch Control Building Three at oh nine hundred. In two hours."

Why not. Sure. Yessir. Building Three right away. Finally found out they weren't as smart as they thought. Ole Beedle would pull them through. Over his coffee, he wondered, permitting a realistic assessment to creep into his delicately balanced megalomania: Why in fact were they calling him? What did they want? He thought it over: 342. He knew it had to have something to do with 342. But then, he knew the launch had been aborted, or whatever they called it. So he'd have to pick him up later.

As he moved around the small nondescript kitchen, making his coffee, buttering his toast, he thought to himself that it was the first time in one year that he hadn't had breakfast with 342. The apartment seemed to him dingy. He never spent much time there. He was usually with Doris or the chimp. Oh, 342 was an operator all right. Had to hand it to him. Doing tricks for her and all, somersaults, and then blowing her kisses. Took Beedle by surprise, that last one. Blowing kisses. Didn't know where in hell he picked that up. Beedle walked to the TV set and turned it on. Three-forty-two liked the "Today Show." Beedle didn't know what he liked so much about it, but the screams that went on if he changed the channel were too much; so he put up with it. The chimp drank coffee, munched on toast, and watched the show. He always wound up howling, rolling on the floor and clutching his sides at the weather report. Couldn't figure that one out, either. The chimp would start hopping up and down like crazy when they took out that weather map. After breakfast he and 342 would go through the exercise routines, Beedle doing sit-ups while the chimp swung around the special apparatus they had built for him. Then on to school. At 0900 exactly, Beedle packed up 342 and took him over to Building Nine, the rocket simulator building, where they put him through his paces. At this point, Beedle handed 342 over to Resnik.

Now Resnik was theoretically the chimp's trainer, and Beedle theoretically the chimp's keeper. But 342 hated Resnik with a passion, and Beedle knew it. Resnik, as far as Beedle could tell, wasn't teaching 342 anything. He was torturing him into performing. Five shocks if he didn't do the first computer sequence right, ten shocks for the second. Fact was, the damn chimp didn't forget; Resnik knew it, Beedle knew it, everybody knew it, but some days he just didn't feel like it, and those days Resnik really got to him. Got Beedle so upset one day watching this, he went to General Farkheimer.

Farkheimer listened intently and then said, "Look, Hobbs, I can understand your attachment to the animal, but Colonel Resnik is his trainer. I've spoken to him about this before, and he feels the discipline is absolutely necessary. All these chimps have different personalities, as you know, and this one, in addition to being the most intelligent, seems to be absolutely the most intractable."

"Well, sirrr," Beedle said—he was embarrassed, pleading a case on behalf of a chimp, or perhaps pleading a case on behalf of anyone—"I just don't think he can take it, sir. It's not in his nature. . . . I mean, he, he's the kind of person . . . er, I mean chimp, that if he don't get some respect, which in this case if he don't get to say no sometimes, he . . . he's gonna crack, General. I mean, you know what happened last year."

Last year. The fatal words. The year they nearly lost the chimp. The space people were panicked that if they lost this chimp they were gonna lose a whole year, and if they lost a whole year they were behind the eight ball by about eight million dollars. So they got this lady scientist or something. She was real pretty, Beedle could see, and she came and took 342 away.

Months later, 342 was returned, smiling and throwing bananas and being his old self, and Resnik was canned. He also lost two stripes.

Until last week. Last week, some kind of heavy had moved in and said the launch had to go off this week instead of three months from now. This week. Beedle never heard of anything like it. *This week,* regardless. And 342 had to be ready to go. Somebody talked Farkheimer into getting Resnik back, although there was somebody with Resnik in the simulator to make sure he didn't charge 342 as much as he used to. The minute the chimp saw Resnik, Beedle felt the tension in the creature's body. He was ready to kill. Beedle had to plead no more. After three days, they threw Resnik out. The chimp had refused to do *anything* the minute Resnik showed his face. They threw Resnik out and the next day the chimp operated the takeoff computer, the separation computer, the opening and closing of the cargo door, the hookup, and all the emergency-jettison procedures perfectly. What the chimp didn't know, but Beedle and all the space people did, was that when the jettison procedures were involved, this meant that the chimp, now encased in a large plastic ball, a very large space station, was to be sent into outer space, to drink water and live on bananas and be monitored for three months. Beedle had argued he needed company for all that time, something, but they said no, he was just a chimp and as long as he stayed alive in that atmosphere, he would be fine. Naturally, Beedle and everyone else expected him to come back.

28

Amanda was thinking about crazy things. Specifically about all the things that people had once thought were crazy. Once they thought that if you said the earth went around the sun, you were crazy. Once, they thought that light was a thing that came in waves, like water. They thought that Einstein, who said it wasn't—it came in particles, tiny particles like millions of Ping-Pong balls—was crazy. Then they thought the idea of black holes, where gravity was so strong even light couldn't escape, was crazy. Yet now they had found black holes. So for all the things that they once thought were crazy, they had come up with laws to explain them.

She was thinking about that. And wondering what she would find on Mars. She was also thinking about women. She was thinking that despite all this emancipation business, men still ruled the earth. In most countries, in most places, men ruled. And most people in most countries thought that men had "the answers." What bothered her was that women thought they should defer to men, that men should have the answers; or therefore, that women shouldn't. She thought that women who acted like they had the answers weren't sure deep down. Why, she wondered, was it so hard for women to be sure? Speaking for herself she knew that she was altogether too much of a "melter."

"Powerful submissive drive masked by assertive personality traits," was how the psychiatrists put it. She called herself a "melter." Of course she could never let anyone at NASA know that, or she would be finished. She knew that in some extremely deep and female way she did adore, absolutely adore, *melting*. There were times in Amanda's personal life when she could leave all the technology she had mastered behind, when she could leave behind her ability to "command," and she knew at those times she was a melter. There were times even when the melting could go further than that. You could melt and melt until you could melt no more. Amanda thought it might make you into quite a *trivial* person to be thinking something like Obliteration can be Fun; yet certain forms of obliteration were, in fact, fun, and there was probably no one alive on the earth, certainly no female person, who would not secretly admit to the pleasures of obliteration. It was something one looked forward to.

Nonetheless, depending on the precise nature of it, it was also something one avoided.

The idea of a controlled obliteration was of course nonsensical; still this seemed to her to be part of what everyone was after. One would be perfectly willing to go up in smithereens knowing that one were certain of coming together again. But it was this reassurance that eluded one. The nature of the explosion made confidence about recovery almost impossible. It was a problem she was working on.

The impact of Hotchkiss was something she felt she could deal with. For her, he held no mysteries, and this made her trust him. Whereas she had never actually trusted McCloud. McCloud was all refracting mirrors, deceptions, partial views, and constantly changing constellations. This had been the thing that had intrigued her. So much for paradox. Hotchkiss could take her to the moon, and it was a perfectly pleasurable flight. Everything seemed in order. McCloud could have destroyed her. Why was it, then; what was it in her that hungered for this so? Maybe it was part of the "travel" tendencies.

Now she was thinking about it, for she was standing on her terrace in her roller skates, whirling about on one leg, practicing for the special space show tomorrow night in which she would skate with 342. But at the same time, she was thinking faraway things. Things so far away and so powerful, she knew that soon the moment would come when she would leave the place where she was and travel.

She would not travel, as most people do, on a plane or in a car. She would travel physically through the air; invisibly and powerfully, straight and strong as a bullet she would fly through the air, entering strange and enchanting regions. Sometimes she could remember the places where she had been. But more often, she couldn't. Now, above all, Amanda was a scientist, so naturally she thought at such times she must have been *dreaming*. That would have been the best explanation. The one *she* liked best. But then she remembered one dream in which she had flown far out into space, as far away as the rings of Saturn, and she had found diamonds in Saturn's rings. Now there were a lot of speculations about carbon-formed matter in Saturn's rings, but no one knew about diamonds for sure. Yet she had found diamonds there. The next morning when she woke up from the dream, she saw glinting under the arch of her boot some dirt and in it some shiny small stones. She was sure it was a coincidence and left the dirt there for several days until her curiosity overwhelmed her and she took the stones to a jeweler. Surprising her at once and not surprising her at all, the jeweler said the stones were diamonds. Furthermore, they were of a quality and kind he had never seen before. They were bluer than most diamonds, and he wished to buy them from her. Amanda shook her head. No, she did not wish to sell them, and took the diamonds—there were four—back to the house and made them into a collar for Schrodinger, as she thought he would look quite marvelous in them. Why she did not wish to wear them she did not know, but somehow she believed that the diamonds, because they were from her dreams, were capable of magical powers and they belonged rightly on someone who manifested them. She also hoped, she supposed in some magical way, that they might wake Schrodinger up.

But they didn't.

The dirt she took to the laboratory. She boiled it, baked it, mixed it with several other elements, and then checked it against the Saturn dust that had just been brought back on the Saturn lander. Of course it matched.

Ordinary persons might feel, if such a thing happened to them, that they would go crazy. Or that they *were* crazy. Or wonder how could it be explained? Or decide it was a trick. Amanda simply put on her skates and went for a "twirl," as she put it, skating along the macadam of the space center, all the way down to the refreshment center and back. She was humming as she did this. She knew that something had to be going on. She also knew she hadn't a clue as to what it was. But she was confident. And that was where she differed most from other people. She was confident that it would somehow, someday become clear to her. Occasionally, during such times she would feel fear. The fear would descend on her suddenly, making her tremble. "I must wait," she would tell herself, calming herself as best she could, as the terror, like an electric force, tore through her body, causing her doubt and often shame. "Why should I be ashamed?" she would cry. These feelings were capable of almost destroying her. She would tell herself she was simply crazy, none of these things could be; she was just cracking up and afraid of the flight. But eventually, the dawn would come. At such times she would hold Schrodinger, and he would purr on like a million generators, and she would know that somehow Schrodinger knew about these dark plains she visited and was trying to help her.

It was utterly impossible to explain such things to other people. Hotchkiss would say, "Look, it's some kind of psychological state. It'll pass."

But Amanda knew differently. Something *different* was going on. Sometimes she thought of it this way: I've been picked. Just like Copernicus got picked. Everybody who has something important and different to do gets picked. And it's me. ME! Then she would cheer up, click her skates together, and go for a "twirl" at high speed, tearing along the pavement, knowing that some special discovery, some very special thing, which would be all her very *own* thing, was about to come her way. That was the confidence.

She supposed it was all of these things in some way that were on her mind one night when she was leaving the laboratory. Because the moon was bright and it was a beautiful night, she decided she would leave the car at the base and walk home. She had been *thinking* about Mary Shelley all day—how it must have been to be Mary Shelley and to have Mary Wollstonecraft for a mother. A truly liberated, power-punching mama, who was fierce on women's rights and took nothing from her husband but the honesty and absence of prejudice in his mind. She was thinking what it must have been like to be Mary Shelley and to fall in love with Shelley, and to hang out in Italy with the peculiar and intense Byron about, who was, at the drop of a pen, making mad passionate love to his sister. What it was like to be eighteen and married in that Italian castle and Shelley drowning and everything. She didn't know why she was thinking so much about Mary Shelley that night but she was. And then it happened. She got a visitor.

All of a sudden out of the middle of the woods, a black man in a green outfit, some sort of strange green outfit, appeared. He appeared; that is to say a light was around him, a green light, and he suddenly lifted up from the middle of the woods and landed, spinning, in the middle of the road ahead of her.

Shaking, she said in a whisper, "What do you want?"

"You're scared," he said. "Don't be scared. I ain't about to rape you or rob you or cause you no trouble. I'm from elsewhere—you ever heard about it?"

"Elsewhere?" she said, her voice squeaking.

"That's what I said. Don't make me repeat things, baby. Don't want to repeat, ain't got much time. I came to accompany you."

"Accompany me . . ." Amanda said. "Who are you?"

"Rastus, the name," he said, bowing and tipping his hat. "I got precisely four minutes."

"Four minutes," she said blankly.

"Right," he said. "I traveled forty million light years in only four minutes . . . and I got to get back in four. What you think of that?"

"You couldn't," she said. "That would be faster than light."

"Right, baby. What travels faster than light?" His teeth lit up his face.

"Nothing," she said numbly.

"Wrong, you wrong. Black, baby, black travels faster than light . . . you better believe it. Now you wanna trip?" A green light seemed to whirl around him then. Amanda kept shaking her head, and it seemed to her before she knew it, before she knew anything, she was sitting on a rock, in the water. The precise location was not clear to her at once. There was an ocean, it was freezing cold, there were a lot of rocks, and she was quite miserable.

"Rastus," she moaned, "where . . . who am I?"

Rastus appeared suddenly out of a rock.

"Here," he said and she looked. There he was, posing as a rabbit.

"Well who?"

"Shelley," he whispered.

"The poet?" Amanda whispered back, amazed she could change sex as well as centuries.

"His wife . . . the wife . . . Mary." And the rabbit hopped away.

Amanda thought. Mary Shelley? Why on earth, or off earth or wherever it was that this thing was happening to her, why was she this Shelley girl? What possible relevance . . . ? And as she sat there on the beach, inhabiting or cohabiting or whatever the word might be, as Amanda sat there in Mary Shelley's mind, suddenly she saw him.

"Oh my God," she said. "Good grief." And then, "Oh dear." She saw him, lumbering over the hills, a huge hulk of a creature, some monstrous face with stitches around the mouth and huge steellike arms.

"Oh Lord," she said, not realizing it, and she heard Rastus say, "Time's up," and she was back again in her kitchen, at the coffeepot, and as she turned, there *he* was lumbering across the kitchen at her.

"Good grief," she said to him. "Look, this cannot go on. What are you doing here?"

The creature shrugged. He seemed rather pathetic actually. She looked more carefully at him. Must have been a robot, a very early model, she decided. She went toward him for a closer look, but something stopped her. The expression in the eyes.

"Can you, are you a machine?" she said impertinently.

A wail came out of him.

"Oh," Amanda said. "Didn't mean to offend you or anything. It's just that I have to find something to do with you and I . . . I . . ." She stopped again. The creature seemed to be crying.

"Look, I am sorry, I . . ." She felt quite bewildered. The thing was frightening, damn it, just its size alone. Did it, she wondered, need food or water? Did it need anything, or was it simply a large mechanical dummy?

"Uh, look, are you mechanical, or are you—" There was a buzz at the door.

"Oh dear, what a time for this to happen. Quick," she said to Frankenstein, "look, no one can see you here. We'll figure this out later. Get into my closet," and the creature, for whatever reason (Amanda never did figure that out), obediently went into the closet. Amanda was frantic. Who was it out there anyway, and what if they looked in her closet?

"Who is it?" she called through the door.

"General Farkheimer, Miss Jaworski, and Sergeant Delko."

Oh no. Amanda sighed. What a time for this to happen. Delko must have alerted the brass about her refusal to get into the simulator. However, even Amanda was amazed that he had caused enough commotion for a personal visit. She heard the creature settling down in the broom closet. There seemed to be plenty of room. She had moved into the apartment six months ago, and there was still nothing in her closet but one broom and a dustpan. But he was making enough noise to arouse suspicions. If they ever opened the closet, oh God. They'd never let her go up then. She opened the door and yelled at him. "For God's sake, will you keep quiet? They can't find you here. They'll never let me go up," and she slammed the door. He seemed to quiet down. But not Delko. Delko and the general were hammering away at the front door.

When Amanda went to the door, Delko practically knocked her down, and the general too, as they pushed open the door and shoved her rudely inside.

"Hey, what is this!" Amanda at first surprised, then outraged, screamed at them. "What are you doing? Are you crazy or what?"

"We know," Delko said. "We know what terrible fate you planned for poor Mary Washburn. We know what you're up to, redesigning our astrojets, refusing to cooperate. We know"—he leaned into her face—"the only reason you have eliminated virtually everybody from the space program, virtually everybody but yourself, is that you, Amanda Jaworski, are a Russian agent. Now out with it! You're under arrest, incidentally." This last phrase struck Amanda as comical, and so she laughed.

"That's hilarious . . . a Russian agent. General," she said, turning her eyes to him. "Is this a joke . . . or what?" She paused, sensing somehow it was not a joke.

The general leaned back in the chair. "Sit down, Amanda," he said. He looked dour.

"I'll stand, thank you." She didn't know why she did it. But a streak of stubbornness in her frequently came out when forced to do things.

"I think you should *sit down*," Delko said, pushing her down, "and come clean. God, when I think of what you did to Mary Washburn."

"What are you talking about?" Amanda said. "What's this about Mary Washburn? She's a second-rate pilot anyway. I don't know how you think she's any kind of backup for me, why she—"

"Miss Jaworski"—the general's tone was sharp—"we are facing a complex issue here and I find this offensive, this pretended ignorance about Miss Washburn's fate."

"Look," Amanda said heatedly, "what is going on here? I don't know what you're talking about. I thought this was a joke. If you're really arresting me, I want a lawyer. . . . And what in the name of God does Mary Washburn have to do with this?"

"Since you insist on this charade," the general said, "we'll continue also. She was on the treadmill in the vacuum chamber—it speeded up—she fell—her helmet released." Farkheimer's voice was grave. "It was four minutes before we could get her out."

"Four minutes." Amanda's voice was hushed, and shocked.

"The door locked," Farkheimer said. "This is the fourth major accident in six months," he sighed. "She'll live . . . but she's physically paralyzed and"—he hesitated—"she has massive brain dysfunction."

Amanda was shocked. She couldn't imagine it. Four minutes in there without a helmet would be like an ant under a ten-ton dinosaur foot.

"Well, I . . . I . . . that, that's unbelievable . . . terrible. . . . What, what's it got to do with me? Thank God I didn't go in there, I . . ." There was an enormous crashing sound in the kitchen, and Delko pulled her to her feet, and the general, pulling a gun, rushed into the kitchen.

"What in hell is that?" Delko said. Then, "It's coming from there."

"It's . . . it's nothing. . . . I left the vacuum cleaner on," Amanda said. "It's absolutely nothing . . . nothing at all, why—"

"Open the door, Sergeant," the general said, pointing to the broom closet.

"No . . . no, no, don't . . . don't open the door," Amanda said quickly. "It's really a mistake." She saw it was hopeless as Delko made for the door of the closet. Then speaking quickly, she said, "It's a robot, a robot I invented. You know how mechanical I am. . . . Well, it's very lifelike, so don't be alarmed." The sounds stopped and Delko advanced on the door. Amanda held her breath as he pulled open the door. And *voilà!* There was nothing there. Amanda stared. Delko stared, the general stared.

"I could have sworn I heard something," Delko and the general said together.

Amanda said, quietly, softly, so that no one could hear her, "Two brooms . . . oh my, how—" Just then she heard the voice.

Rastus was saying: "He coalesced, particle bombardment at minus two hundred and thirty milliseconds per megahertz. He coalesced into a broom. Read the sign. There never was enough wit in this business."

Amanda, pale, proceeded toward the closet, under Delko's and the general's watchful eyes.

"I was just kidding," she said, "about the robot. All that's in here are my two new brooms." Carefully she picked up the newest broom. It carried a sign that read A *New Broom Sweeps Clean.*

"All right, all right, enough of this distraction. Now let's get this straight," Delko said to Amanda, in his best youlissiname tone.

Only Amanda said, "I will not listen to you. You will not come into my house and accost me and handcuff me and accuse me without adequate legal counsel. Get me a lawyer." Her tone was so sharp, her intention so clear, the general was momentarily taken aback.

"Amanda," the general said, "I am *not* accusing you of anything . . . however, the sergeant here believes he has evidence which . . ." The general paused. He had spotted Schrodinger.

"*Aghhh*," Delko said. "What is that?"

"It's her cat," the general replied.

Delko turned to her. Fear and suspicion in his eyes. "Don't tell me," he whispered, "you would keep a dead cat."

"He isn't dead," Amanda said evenly. "It's something mysterious. He just looks dead."

"YOU THINK I DON'T KNOW A DEAD CAT WHEN I SEE ONE?" Delko screamed, poking a finger into Schrodinger's still unmoving form.

"Calm down, Sergeant," the general said. "I know about the cat. Let's go. Good-bye, Amanda."

"You'll hear about this!" Delko hissed, and they slammed the door behind them.

29

It was two days later when Hotchkiss showed up at the door. He looked at her. "I guess you still don't know, do you?"

"Know what? Look, why is this all so mysterious about Mary Washburn? Will somebody please—"

"Shh," he said, putting a finger to her lips. "The fact is she was in *your* space suit. Delko didn't even know it was Washburn until they pulled her out. He thought it was you."

"Me? Why . . ." Amanda remembered. She had run into Mary in the parking lot. They didn't like each other, but Amanda would never have wished this on anyone. The fact was, Washburn followed Amanda's training like a hawk. A hawk of hawks. As Amanda had crossed the parking lot, Mary had rushed up to her and said, "Amanda! You're supposed to be in the vacuum chamber. It's eleven-fifteen. You're late!"

"I'm not using it today," Amanda said, slamming the door of the car.

"Well, that's a terrible waste," Mary said primly. "Do you know what it costs them, what it costs to get that ready every time you're supposed . . ."

Amanda rolled up the window. "You use it, if you think it such a waste." That was why, she supposed, she had.

"Why didn't you go in?" Hotchkiss said to her.

"Something told me not to."

"Some something . . ."

"Delko . . . He must have been laying for me."

"You think it was deliberate?"

"Yeah. . . . You think that's paranoid?"

"No . . . that's what I thought, too." He looked at her in awe. "I can't believe you sometimes. Where'd you ever get instincts like that?"

"This wasn't an instinct . . . exactly," Amanda said.

Hotchkiss was talking quickly. "Look, Amanda, I found a great place we could go to this weekend. They'll never find out." He looked around nervously, then, "I just have to see you," he said. When Hotchkiss looked at her like that Amanda felt the earth go soft under her feet. She couldn't imagine what it was; as though he sent out nerve gas or something. She suddenly felt very muddled. She wished he didn't communicate so directly.

"Well," she said, "I . . . I have this problem . . ."

"Amanda, it's the last chance we'll have for a while. What is it?" Hotchkiss's eyes were the eyes of a tortured man.

"Look," she said, turning to him, "you don't know enough about me. Remember I asked you if you thought I could go crazy? Well, something's going on. . . ." Suddenly she remembered: "This voice, this voice told me to stay out of the vacuum chamber, and it was the same voice that put me back into—I know this sounds funny—but he put me into Mary Shelley's mind, because time, he does away with time, and he does some kind of electron magic or something I don't know; but I know I was there in her mind and I met this guy Frankenstein and then, then I came back and Frankenstein came with me into the kitchen."

"Amanda"—Hotchkiss held her arm, his breath coming in short gasps—"Frankenstein was in your kitchen?"

"Well, don't be concerned. He was perfectly well behaved. I couldn't figure out if he was a robot or exactly what, you know, but then Delko came to the door and I had to put him into the closet, the broom closet, and then when they went to open the door I thought he would be there but he wasn't. There were two brooms now and then the voice came and explained to me that Frankenstein had coalesced. . . . He does this thing where he changes things into other things. I don't know how he does it. He moves atoms around or something. Anyway, that Frankenstein had coalesced into the broom, so when Delko opened the closet he wasn't there." Amanda turned and looked carefully at Hotchkiss. It seemed to her quite impossible to describe the expression on his face.

"You think I'm crazy, don't you?" she said.

"I think you're out of your fucking mind," he said. Then he yelled, "WHAT ELSE AM I SUPPOSED TO THINK . . . FRANKENSTEIN IN YOUR KITCHEN. I MEAN, AMANDA, WHAT'S HAPPENING TO YOU?"

"There's no need to get so angry," she said. "Shhh . . . someone will hear you."

Hotchkiss calmed down. He was still angry. "Amanda," he said, "we have got to talk about this."

"I don't have time now," she said. "Look, Donald, I . . . I know it sounds crazy . . . Frankenstein in my kitchen and coalescing into a broom, but—but—" She stopped and looked at him. "That wasn't the worst of it."

"It wasn't?" He seemed incredulous.

"No," she said. "He came back."

"When?"

"Yesterday he came back. I saw him, in my kitchen."

"You mean to tell me," Hotchkiss said, catching his breath, "you actually saw this Frankenstein person rattling around your kitchen yesterday? He came *back*?"

Amanda nodded. "He was drying the dishes."

"Drying the dishes?" Hotchkiss's mouth fell open.

Amanda nodded solemnly. "And then he broke a cup. And I can't replace it."

"You can't replace it?" Hotchkiss echoed, dumbfounded.

Amanda nodded. "They've discontinued the pattern."

"Discontinued the pattern?" His eyes were wide. "How can you even think of such a thing? To hell with the pattern. You have to get rid of this . . . thing. How do you know he won't come back?"

"I don't know whether or not he will, although we were having an interesting discussion."

"Discussion?" Donald said. "What were you *discussing*?"

"We were discussing his time traveling. Actually he's in a *terrible* fix."

"How's that?" Hotchkiss asked, feeling stupid.

"Well, Rastus messed him up. He can't get back into his own time zone. He's waiting for an entry. In the meantime, he's a floater."

"A floater," Hotchkiss said.

"Yes! Isn't that terrible? Donald?" He didn't seem to be hearing her. "Donald, do you realize he's *homeless*?"

"What else did you discuss?" Hotchkiss asked.

"Well, it was *quite* fascinating. It turned out it's *true*."

"What's true?"

"That we *do go* somewhere when we leave. You know the expression 'lost in thought.' You know everything I say about *my* feelings, that I 'travel' when I get called?"

"You mean daydreaming," he said.

"I mean *travel*," she said. "And I'm right. Donald," she said slowly, "do you think I really am crazy?"

He looked at her a long moment. "No, not exactly crazy."

"Well, what is it, then? You know I see him."

"Well," he said slowly, shifting in his chair, "maybe he's there."

"Donald, you know that's not possible."

"No," he said, "it certainly isn't."

"So if it's not possible, it's impossible, which means I'm crazy, right?"

"Well, not necessarily."

"What do you mean?"

"Well, maybe it's something in between."

"In between possible and impossible?"

"Yes," he said slowly.

"What's in between possible and impossible?" she said exasperatedly. "Well, what would you call it?"

"I don't know," he said, thoughtful. He wouldn't know what to call it. He had seen it, though. Total remission of cancer in twenty-four hours. He had seen it. People call it miracles. It wasn't possible, but on the other hand it wasn't impossible, because it happened. He said this to her.

"You mean Frankenstein's a miracle?"

"Somehow it doesn't sound right, does it?" he said to her.

"No," she said. "It has to be something else."

"There's this kid in my class," said Hotchkiss, "who has a terrible crush on you."

"Really?" Amanda said. "How do you know?"

"He carries your picture with him. It dropped out of his shirt."

"Oh," she said, then, "which picture?"

"It's an eight-by-ten of you, in a frame no less. He walks around with it. There's always this big rectangle in his shirt. I never saw this picture before and I told him that. He took it himself. With a telephoto lens. You were in the parking lot."

"My goodness," Amanda said. She didn't like that at all. Sneak shots.

"You were skating. He caught you in a spin. Must have had a very fast camera. Stop-action shot."

"Oh, I'd love to see it," she said.

"Not a chance. He's mortified about the whole thing. Stuck it back in his jacket and acted like nothing happened. Turned beet red."

"How sweet," she said. Then, "Is this the one that's the Genius?"

"Yeah. Also a pain. His name's Arnold, but he calls himself Dartan Four Thousand."

"Dartan Four Thousand? He calls himself that as a *name*?"

"Yeah," Hotchkiss said, "it's on his jacket and everything. He's a weird kid."

"Is he really a genius?" she asked, curious.

"I hate to say it, but no doubt about it. I think he can probably build things other people couldn't even think of."

"Oh Donald, how exciting!" she said, getting interested for the first time. "Like what for instance?"

"I have to take sneak peaks at his drawings. He'll only show me sections of them. He's very secretive. Like he's ashamed of something."

"What is it, do you think?"

"I don't know. . . . Something to do with his parents. He doesn't talk about them. Lives out on a farm somewhere in the middle of nowhere. He's a total loner," Hotchkiss said, "but he's coming around. I kind of like him. I found out his secret vice."

"What's that?"

"Pistachio ice cream."

"You're kidding. The only place they have it is in some café way out near Waco."

"Yeah, I had to take him there to get it. How do *you* know?"

"Three-forty-two," Amanda said. "It's the only flavor Three-forty-two will eat. Beedle says it's because of the nuts. He was acting up fierce one day and we had to stop all the procedures—it held up the entire simulation. They had to go and get it."

"Are you sure you're going up with him?"

"Who?"

"The chimp."

"Oh, I don't know. They'll only use him for the lander." She looked uncomfortable. "I think they're worried about the surface—you know, the holes in the ice." And even as she said it she felt very strange indeed.

30

"Know what, Rufe?"

"How's that, Eb?"

"Ole Tom says them Indians is leaving the earth."

"What?" Rufus said.

" 'At's the truth. Says those Indians got some kinda thing with their thoughts. Thought projectors, he calls 'em. I seen somethin' on TV like that. This here guy he just looked at a fork and he *bent* it just by lookin'. I hear them Arabs can do that. Anyway, I don't know where these Indians learned it, but they gets up there and starts thinkin' about travelin', about goin' to the moon, and whoosh, afore you knows it they go up there to that ole moon. Now whattaya think about that?"

"Ah hardly knows," Rufus said.

"You think a man could travel jes' by thinkin' about it?"

"Mebbe, Eb," Rufus said slowly.

"It don't sound good to me," Eberly said. "Gonna ruin the economy. Gonna put the airlines outta business. Gonna put the automobiles outta business.

"I asked the Kid to ask his roommate, that there physicist fellow, if such a thing was possible, and you know what?"

"What, Eb?"

"Says it's so. Found it out in some kinda experiment; calls it 'outta the body.' Some folks, when they sleep at night, they leaves their bodies and come back to 'em in the mornin', fly all aroun' the place. . . . Make any sense to you, Rufe?"

"No," Rufus said finally.

"I say got to be somethin' to it. I mean if they got this here bump a hunnert foot high in the middle of the Indian Ocean, I mean a bump what you can't see, then maybe at night if you was a certain type, you could fly around without your body. Makes sense to me." There was a moment's quiet.

"But you know what, Rufe?"

"How's that, Eb?"

"You hafta have lanes, I think."

"Lanes?"

"Yeah . . . some kinda highways. Otherwise you got all these people flyin' around at night, you gonna have crashes."

The wind sighed in the trees. Somewhere Rufus heard a whip-poorwill.

"I thought you said they went without their bodies," Rufus said.

"Oh yeah," Eberly said, "that's right. . . . I guess that way they don't crash." He shifted his weight again in the old rocker. Rufus could tell now, by the fierceness with which Eberly was rocking, that he was bothered, mighty bothered about something.

"You know what, Rufe?"

"How's that, Eb?"

"Cain't be they goes without their bodies. They must go mebbe with just their heads."

"Just their heads?"

"Yeah . . . otherwise how you gonna tell one person from another . . ."

"You mean the bodies be layin' in their beds without their heads on. I mean the ones that are left here," Rufus said.

Eberly stared into the dark. "Naw, that don't sound right. I say if a man be lyin' in a bed without his head on he got to be dead. Wouldn't you say that, Rufe?"

"Sounds right," Rufus said.

"Must be somethin' else here; we haven't thought about this right," Eberly said. "I'll ask the Genius."

Amanda was getting ready to give her dancing-neutrino lecture. This morning she was addressing high-school students. It was called "Aspects of the Unknown," and it was her favorite lecture because she explained that the unknown itself was her very favorite thing. Amanda felt it was the logical—although she suspected somewhere that this was really not the word, perhaps the word was *symmetrical*—this was the symmetrical investigation to the reaches of outer space. For as she went out farther and farther into space, so her mind, too, concentrated on going into the smaller and smaller and finally smallest most fundamental units of matter. Amanda was excited to tell them that at first everyone thought the atom was the smallest unit of matter, then of course they got inside the atom and they found the nucleus and the electron; then, inside the nuclei they got protons and neutrons and finally quarks. They had to stop at the quark, except no one would. Once they got into the electron they got into particles, all with the same spin of one-half, called leptons. The other leptons are the elusive neutrino, the muon, and the tauon. Amanda loved to talk about neutrinos. She referred to the neutrinos as the "real time" communication with the sun. They reach the earth seven minutes after they leave the sun, traveling at the speed of light. They remain undetected, she said, and undetectable, except for a tank deep in South Dakota in a town appropriately called Lead. In Lead, a scientist determined to detect the neutrino found a way to capture them. It has been determined that neutrinos will not interact with any matter whatsoever except a chlorine atom, the nucleus of chlorine 37. The neutrino catcher, she pointed out, is a mile deep in the earth, where no other sun's rays can reach it, not gamma, not anything.

This lecture was called "Aspects of the Unknown," and, as usual, Amanda loved giving it. A young girl raised her hand: "You called it a dancing neutrino. Well, if you can't see it, how do you know it's dancing?"

"They have been detected, and although there is no way of knowing scientifically, precisely how a neutrino moves, I like to think of it as dancing because it has a pattern; I am certain of that. I do not think it will be random. It combines randomness with a pattern of meaning which if understood would tell me what kind of a dance it is. But for the moment it's very free, spontaneous, and unpredictable," she said.

Amanda told the story as she imagined the original explorer, a scientist named Paul Dirac, must have felt it. "Here we have," she said, moving to the board, "a simple world. We have the nucleus and the electron moving around it. In the nucleus we have protons and neutrons. Okay, so far it's simple. Then Dirac investigated the charges of the electron and he discovered there was something that would not fit the equation. Something that was an antielectron. Something with a positive charge. Since the only thing known with a positive charge was a proton, one might have thought it was a proton. But it is not a proton. It is something else entirely. No one ever knew about it before! It is what we call"—and here she flipped over the charts—"antimatter. Now this is not some science-fiction fantasy." However there were times indeed when Amanda felt that it certainly seemed like one. Sometimes she thought, Just because it's scientifically verifiable doesn't mean it isn't weird. To Amanda, the presence of matter and antimatter was similar to someone finding a scientific explanation for ghosts. Ghosts are real, they can be measured, spoken to, and seen—that would have been the rough equivalent of making this kind of announcement. "Antimatter," she went on to say, "is exactly identical to matter except the signs for the electric charges are reversed.

"Out of this mass of confusion," she said, "one thing is clear: although the nucleus is a mare's nest of protons and neutrons, of hadrons and quarks, of strong-force components, the electron is simply the electron. However, what complicates matters is that the electron is not alone. It has the company of 'weak forces,' called leptons. They include the muons, which have a charge, and the neutrinos, which are 'neutral,' having no charge. It was not clear," she said, "whether or not the neutrino had any mass whatsoever. But the point was this: millions of neutrinos are bombarding us every day. There, I've just got them— millions. They pass through *with absolutely no effect whatsoever*." And as she said this, she got the strangest feeling. As though she had just uttered the forbidden words in a ancient cemetery and slowly, slowly, slowly a grave was opening. She thought she heard some music, but then she stopped. No, no, she hadn't. She didn't realize how long she had been silent until she saw the class looking at her. Finally a boy in the front row said, "Professor Jaworski, is something wrong?"

"No," she said, sort of coming to, from what or where she couldn't say exactly. Then turning to him sharply, she said, "Why?"

"Well," he said, almost embarrassed, "you haven't said anything for a few minutes."

"How many minutes?" she said.

"Well"—he shifted now uncomfortably in his chair—"I don't know. At least three." So, she thought, it was happening again.

"Three minutes, and billions of neutrinos have passed through me and all of you," she said, regaining her attention and flipping to a new chart. "Isn't it amazing that we do not know, although we know it's spinning, if the neutrino has any mass? Now for the interesting part," Amanda said. "If they have mass, then they make up ninety percent of the universe, they are the 'glue' of the universe. The other ten percent is the visible part of galaxies and stars. Neutrinos could account for the 'missing mass' of the universe. That," she said, wiping her hands, "takes care of the universe. Now what of this business of matter? What is matter? How fundamental can it get? This fundamental: into strong forces and weak forces: The strong are the quarks, draped inside hadrons. The weak are the leptons, including the muon, neutrino, and electron. And finally there are the gluons, which glue them, so to speak, together."

They were staring at her.

"You just said that," someone said, and she stood there, embarrassed, hurrying on to conclude her lecture with thoughts about velocity.

"Everything is moving. All these subatomic particles are moving. The electron moves about the nucleus; everything is in motion; under the proper impact of energy, matter *transmutes*, becomes something else." Then she pointed to a diagram of the solar system. "And we are moving: the earth is spinning at one thousand miles an hour on its axis, then it is moving sixty-six thousand miles an hour around the sun; the sun is moving at fifty-six hundred thousand miles an hour around the galaxy, and the galaxy is spinning around the universe at one point four million miles an hour. Since the beginning of time, as we know it, the galaxy has spun around the universe only twenty times."

Amanda was exhausted, not so much from the speech itself as from the concepts she was trying to explain. So much was unfathomable. From the smallest particle to the farthest outreaches of space, the more one understood, the more mysterious and unimaginable things finally became. Down to the smallest structure of matter and out to the farthest reaches they had evidence for, the behavior of space and time was finally inexplicable.

"Within the black hole," she finished, "is what is called the 'point of singularity.' That is the point where all the laws of physics break down. What will happen there, what can happen there, none of us knows. It is as simple and complicated as that." Even as she said this—she had said this many times before—but that particular day, at that particular time, she got a very funny feeling. Amanda wanted essentially to get their minds boggled by the infiniteness of these "subuniverses," to challenge their imaginations. She didn't really expect them to understand it, and she immediately made them all feel better when she quoted a Nobel Prize–winning scientist, Richard Feynman, who said: "I think it safe to say that no one understands quantum mechanics. Do not keep saying to yourself, if you can possibly avoid it, 'But how can it be like that?' because you will 'go down the drain' into a blind alley from which nobody has yet escaped. Nobody knows how it can be like that."

31

Amanda was on the phone to Hotchkiss. She was describing the drawings.

"What do you mean," he said, "drawings of your feet?"

"There are these drawings," she said, "of my feet. Little drawings all over the house."

There was a pause. Donald's mind was racing, and rabid with jealousy.

"It must be a foot fetishist," he said.

"I don't think so."

"Who else would be interested in your feet?" he said, then added hurriedly, "although you have very nice feet."

"My feet are okay, but they're not the kind of feet to inspire art."

"Art," he said, pausing again. "You mean the drawings are good?"

"Why yes," she said, thinking about it. "I'd have to say they are very good indeed."

She put down the phone, quite unsatisfied. Then she padded over to the refrigerator to get breakfast.

"Is she your girlfriend?" the Genius said, sidling up to Hotchkiss. He was eyeing Amanda appreciatively and quite boldly, Hotchkiss thought, considering the shy nature of this nearsighted kid.

"Yeah," he said.

"She's Amanda Jaworski, right?" the Genius said.

"Yeah," Hotchkiss said.

"And she's goin' up, right?"

"Right. What're you asking me for if you know everything," he said, packing his briefcase.

"I gotta talk to her," the Genius said.

"You can't have a date," Hotchkiss said. "She doesn't go for younger men."

The Genius looked at him with disdain. "I have important information to communicate."

"So," Hotchkiss said, "so go talk to her."

The Genius stalked off. He approached Amanda from the rear and backed off. He approached Amanda from the side and backed off. He approached her finally full face and was about to back off when she smiled. He felt as if the aurora borealis had just gone off. He rocked back on his heels and then caught himself.

"Hi," she said, dazzling him. "You must be Arnold."

The Genius began to blush, and humiliated by this, turned his eyes to the floor. But she rescued him.

"Why don't you wait here a minute and I'll get Donald and we can have coffee." Amanda still smiled. She thought he was adorable. And she could see what had happened. When Cupid drew his bow and you were fourteen, you needed a recovery period, even from hello.

The Genius stood there, eyeing the ground, trying to remember the urgent thing he had to tell her. He seemed to have lost all powers of speech.

"Erg," he said finally.

"What?" she said, attempting to conceal a smile. Then she said quickly, "We'll meet you in the cafeteria. I'll get Donald." And she was off.

When they returned they found the Genius had stationed himself at a table and was consumed in a book. As the book was quite literally about three feet high, it was some massive compendium of something, and Arnold was sunk into the middle of it.

"Hi, Arnold," Hotchkiss said. "Here's your burger," and he slid the plate across the table. Arnold, without looking up, moved the book aside and mumbled something that sounded like "ug."

Donald and Amanda sat down and still the Genius said nothing. He appeared to be staring at his plate.

"Come on, Arnold," Donald said. "You always eat a hamburger at three o'clock. Not hungry today?" He winked at Amanda, who thought it was cruel to tease him so about his infatuation but was nonetheless amused.

Arnold shook his head and pushed the hamburger back across the table.

"Arnold," Amanda said, "I've heard about your design for a ramjet engine. Donald's very excited about it. Would you like to explain it to me?" she said sweetly.

It was this sweetness that knifed him. Cut right to the center of him, icing him, delighting him, as if he had swallowed a garden full of jelly beans. And sickening him. He thought he was going to throw up. He was dying. If he threw up, now, in front of *her* . . .

They watched him curiously as both arms covered his head and his head went down on the table, slowly, slowly, then his head rose ever so slightly and two lensed eyes peered out over the plaid flannel arms. "Erg," he said again. And turned purple. Arnold was as close to death throes as he had ever known. He did not know what had happened to him. All powers of speech had deserted him. Briefly, fleetingly, he thought perhaps he had suffered a stroke, as all he could render was "Erg." But he was awestruck. Every time he looked at her she began to glow. A radiance surrounded her. She was so bright, so beautiful, he thought he would have to put on sunglasses.

"Maybe he doesn't feel like talking about it right now," Amanda hurried to say, seeing his mortification. "I mean he's been working all morning. He must be tired, he probably just needs to rest." She lay her hand lightly on his arm. "We'll see you later." She had meant to rescue him. Instead, the touch of her hand on his arm burned like a laser ray. He jumped, knocking the book, the Coke, and the hamburger all over the floor.

"Oh," he said, his voice recovered in the shock of the moment. "I'm sorry, I'm sorry, I'm sorry." He bent down, with the two of them, attempting to save the large book from the lake of Coca-Cola enveloping it, when Amanda touched him again. "It's okay. I've got it," she said, and it was more than he could cope with.

He turned then, thinking he would throw up, and ran out of the cafeteria into the parking lot, across the parking lot, and lay down on the grass. His head was spinning; something was out of orbit. He was out of synch. He could feel the trees, the grass, the earth, spinning on its revolutions. But he was going too fast, or too slow, he wasn't sure which. His eardrums were pounding, and he thought all in all it was one of the most dreadful wonderful things that had ever happened to him.

32

For several weeks now, very secret things had been passing between Schrodinger, Amanda, and Hotchkiss, although not necessarily in that order. The secrets were so secret that not one of them knew that the others were aware of the very secret observations being made, except Schrodinger, of course, who did know.

First of all, Amanda was becoming irritated by Hotchkiss's attitude toward Schrodinger. She was wishing actually that she had never told him about Schrodinger's large, lopsided head and incurable sleeping habits being the result of excess electrical activity in the brain. For when Hotchkiss came in now, he often found "Schro" lying on the kitchen counter, his head in the ivy, a dish of mayonnaise, or some other inappropriate place, his four legs sticking straight up in the air. Schrodinger would be lying wherever he was when his "spell" struck him, and Hotchkiss would lean over the sleeping animal and yell, "Too tense, Schrodinger." Sometimes Hotchkiss would yell this very loudly, all to no avail.

"Tension—no good," Hotchkiss would yell, making his way to the refrigerator. "You're going to burn out your computer."

Although Amanda was irritated by this, it seemed to her that Hotchkiss was displaying a renewed interest in Schrodinger, and she did wonder why this should be so. She knew Hotchkiss had been annoyed at Schrodinger, but this had a different quality to it. At first she had thought he had gotten interested because of the "oscillation effects" of Schrodinger's purring, or snoring, or whatever it was. This phenomenon, which Amanda called purring and Hotchkiss snoring, had a vibratory aspect that when thoroughly tuned up shook the entire table, should he be on it, and caused the floorboards, should he be on them, to tremble at a distance of ten yards from him. Often, when they were playing records, this seemed to stimulate his response. Amanda did not know, but she thought it was some sort of subliminal response to the music; in any event, it shook the floor sufficiently that the record player wiggled and the music was considerably distorted. It seemed that Schrodinger snored most during Bach.

"I think the classics get to him," Amanda said one night while Hotchkiss irritatedly arose to adjust the record player. Sometimes he simply moved Schrodinger to the sofa, which cushioned the effects of his snoring sufficiently so that it left the record player undisturbed.

"I think it's personal. It's only when I put the music on that this happens," Hotchkiss said.

"Well," Amanda said, "I play more popular things. All that stuff you say is terrible—disco, rock."

"What's the difference to him anyway? He's totally zonked. How come he only vibrates to my records?"

"Look," Amanda said, annoyed but very serious at the same time and wishing to end the drift of the conversation, "there's a lot about Schrodinger we don't know. We just have to accept it on faith."

Donald muffled his reply. He could tell when she was getting testy about Schrodinger. It annoyed him, frankly, but he repressed it. He didn't know why she had to regard that cat as some kind of Ming vase, to be treated with respect and care for its fragility. He didn't know why, actually, she supposed he was so delicate. Privately he suspected that

Schrodinger had the disposition of a mule. He ate, he slept, mostly, and he shit, as far as Hotchkiss could tell. It was just that Amanda seemed convinced that he had superior brain waves or a spiritual affinity for things that lay beyond the ordinary cat and even the ordinary mortal. He had some sort of affinity, she seemed to think, for some etheric sphere in which music and the finest things in human experience resonated. He had to admit that when the cat slept and Amanda stroked him, the vibrating was remarkable. Once when he was on the floor, the people from downstairs called and asked them to turn off their vacuum cleaner. Naturally one couldn't say That's just my cat, he vibrates when he purrs, so Hotchkiss stupidly found himself apologizing for running the nonexistent vacuum cleaner at ten o'clock at night. He knew it was unfair, but it was incidents like these that made him resent Schrodinger. For a creature that was so inactive, he often made Hotchkiss feel like a fool. However, there was more to it than that, Hotchkiss knew, and despite his irritation he found himself increasingly *wondering* about Schrodinger. He tried to tell himself that something as peculiar as this cat would pique anyone's scientific curiosity. But it wasn't that. It was rather that slowly and uneasily Hotchkiss, who was a thoroughly un-mystical man, was beginning to think that perhaps there was something rather *mystical* or magical or, in any event, nonverifiable about the effects of Schrodinger.

It had started that day with the Chinese menu. Hotchkiss hadn't found himself actually thinking about it at the time. But he had picked something *up*. He was up earlier than usual that morning, it was about five o'clock, and he was very surprised to see that Schrodinger, too, *for once*, was up.

"Oh, Schro," he said, "I didn't think you got up until seven. What's the matter, boy?" he said, leaning over to pet him. Schrodinger ignored him. Schrodinger was leaning over the newspaper, which had been carelessly thrown against the screen door so that it fell open. If Hotchkiss hadn't known better, he might have thought that Schrodinger was reading the paper, because the animal's head went evenly from left to right, left to right. Hotchkiss watched this procedure for a few minutes, and then suddenly Schrodinger went into his state and keeled over, legs straight in the air.

"Take it easy, boy," Hotchkiss said. "The news gets to me, too."

It was that *very* evening that Amanda brought home a menu from a new Chinese take-out restaurant. "Isn't this ridiculous!" she said. "The entire menu is in Chinese!"

"You're kidding," Hotchkiss said.

"No. There must have been a mistake at the printer's. It's all Chinese!" She called the restaurant, which made loud so-sorrys amidst much giggling and said new menus would be ready in the morning. It wasn't until late that night when Amanda said, "My God, I forgot to feed Schrodinger," that they went into the kitchen where they found him awake, to their surprise. Only Hotchkiss noticed that Schrodinger was leaning over the menu, and his head was going right to left, right to left, right to left. He studied this for some time and then decided it was just a funny coincidence.

"You eatin' eggs again, Eb?" Rufus said, amazed and amused at once. Seemed to him that ever since that Kid told them eggs was brain food, Eberly was eating around three dozen eggs a day. Rufus puzzled at this, as it seemed to him that eggs was one thing you could only eat so much of no matter how fat you were and that would be it. But Eberly was clearly powered by forces larger than he knew. He even went so far as to bring Silas a cookbook called *1,001 Ways to Prepare Eggs,* and Silas was busier than ever, baking eggs, boiling eggs, roasting eggs, saucing eggs, and of course, making cakes with eggs, except Silas said usually a cake takes two or three eggs; Eberly was only eating "ten-egg" cake. Eberly's doctor told him he was going to die of cholesterol from this diet, but Eberly would have none of it and was getting into eggs. The next thing Rufus knew he said he was going to raise chickens because he could control what they ate.

When the Kid told them there was a sign, according to the Genius roommate, that the earth was moving out of its orbit, Rufus figured maybe it was so, because something exceeding strange had come over Eberly these last few months, and when he told the Kid about it, the Kid nodded soberly and said it was possible it was the result of gravitational pull.

"Let me see those drawings," Hotchkiss said, bounding into the house and slamming the door.

"Well," Amanda said, catching her breath, "you certainly are demanding."

"I've been thinking about it," Hotchkiss said firmly, and indeed Amanda could see he had. He was in an absolute froth. "And I don't like it one bit. There's some pervert around who's following you. That's what it has to be. Now let me see them."

Amanda, who did not like this commanding tone in Hotchkiss at *all*, nonetheless agreed to get the drawings, as it did seem most peculiar to her and she could come up with no explanation. She was a bit embarrassed, which he misunderstood as reluctance, and so she dawdled.

"Well, where are they?" he said.

"I . . . I forgot where I put them," she said. The thought of Donald Hotchkiss seeing her feet in those torn, disheveled flip-flop terry-cloth slippers was mortifying. She always wore her silk mules with maribou trim for Donald.

"Amanda," he said firmly, and she sighed finally and got them. Donald took them in a mood of considerable seriousness and laid them out on the coffee table. "My," he said, "I had no idea there were so many."

"Thirty," she said. "Every day for the last month I've found one when I came home."

"You mean you don't have it in the morning, it's always the same time of day?"

"It would appear so," Amanda said, not having thought of this.

"Well," Donald said in total consternation, "you can't exactly call them erotic." There was a dispirited pause. "Amanda, how do you know these are your feet?"

"Of course they're my feet . . . they're my slippers," she said excitedly.

"Well I've never seen *these* slippers," he said full of confusion.

"Well, no," she said. "I only wear them when . . ."—she paused again, uncertain how to put it—". . . when I go out to garden, on the patio."

"You garden every day?" he said wonderingly.

"Well . . . almost," she said, evasively.

"Hmmm," he said, totally puzzled. It did not, at first glance, appear to be the work of a pervert. Not at all. The exclusivity of the perspective is what intrigued Hotchkiss. Amanda did not appear above the knee at all, and the main focus was the ankle down. There was a quality in the drawings that Donald could not quite put his finger on and that disturbed him unduly. Finally he said, "There's something about them that bothers me." It made him jealous.

"Yes," she said. "I think I know."

"You know?" he said. "Well, what is it? There's something, well, something about them."

"Adoration," Amanda finally said. "They have a religious quality of devotion and adoration."

"Hmmm . . . yes," Donald finally said, although he wasn't sure. They certainly did not share anything that Donald normally thought of as religious. There was certainly no confusion between the drawings of those dreadful slippers and the impulse that inspired the Sistine Chapel. Or was there? For lack of a better word, Donald had decided that the drawings were works of love. This made him jealous. The detail was incredible. Every day, a truly insanely jealous person like Hotchkiss could see that a little more toenail polish had disappeared from the square of the big toe, and this receding line, like the changing shore of a beach, had been painstakingly recorded on each drawing. It made Donald insanely jealous, because Donald, for all of his passion, realized that in no way could he ever have noticed that particular detail of Amanda. In fact, Amanda's qualities below the knee had been perhaps the least-interesting aspect of Amanda overall. It was Amanda above the knee which provided the focus for most of his concentration, and although he did not wish to express any prejudice toward the feet, his lack of appreciation in this area had been clearly pointed up by this secret competitor. Donald felt a twinge. What if this was only the beginning? What if the secret drawer were to extend his passions above that comely knee?

"AGHHH," Donald said suddenly.

"What is it?" Amanda said, full of concern. "Is it your ulcer?"

"Yes," he said, clutching his middle. "It's acting up again."

She smiled sympathetically. She quite understood. She would not have taken it calmly either if Donald had suddenly presented her with thirty drawings by some devotee of *his* feet.

The Soviet commissar paced back and forth, back and forth, back and forth, back and forth. The bell rang. He received the messenger. From the Comintern. Change of policy. The commissar paced, forth and back, forth and back, forth and back.

The seared, scarred metal ruins of Comsat III had returned to the base in Baikonur, unbeknownst to any of the media. Unbeknownst perhaps even to some of the Russian intelligence. It returned bearing soil samples from Venus. It had been on a twelve-year journey. Six out, six back, with a three-day stopover for collection. A most remarkable achievement. There was a hushed sense now as the head scientist, Dr. Fez of the Polytechnic Institute, entered the room. He had been examining the soil samples from Venus with great concern. It was critical to Soviet policy. It was critical to American policy. They had found as long ago as 1908, torn out of the ground in the far, remote regions of Vladivostok, a charred hole, forty kilometers wide. A "supersonic" boom had been heard, a "ball of fire," according to the tribesmen who survived it. It had been, all the scientists now agreed, not a comet at all, but a nuclear explosion. It had been documented carefully. There was no question. And now Dr. Fez raised a weary, strained face to his audience: "The soil samples from Venus, gentlemen, are the same, the same as those found at the nuclear site of 1908." So. He was referring to a mystery that had never been solved. It was called Tungsten.

Amanda had inadvertently stumbled on a classified library. She told herself it was inadvertent, when in fact she was in the NASA library and a small steel door had failed to close properly. She knew this was the top-secret vault. And being a curious girl, she went to it, fixing the door so it could not lock her in and making her way toward the gleaming steel metal cabinet.

She reached for the drawer marked "Jupiter Tapes" and took them out. Blithely she went downstairs into the tape studio, put the earphones on, listened, and nearly flew screaming out of her chair. Then, regaining her composure, she replaced the tapes in their compartment and attempted to decide whether to forget she'd ever heard them or what exactly to do about it. It made her think that the old idea that knowledge is power was subject to considerable revision. In this case, knowledge might be terror.

Still, that had been a month ago. Time enough to get a key. Now, something else drove her back. She was right. There were new tapes. At the end of the tapes she heard something totally new. It was a new voice, and it had obviously been added to the material. The voice, with total government authority, said, "Review preceding material with Soviet Tungsten file, F—409H.123."

Well. So. Tungsten. She knew about Tungsten. Everybody knew about Tungsten. A goddamned charred hole in the Russian wasteland. First they had said it was a comet, then they had said it was a meteorite. All along a few had been saying it was a nuclear explosion. Now all of them were saying it. If what she had just heard was true, there was no doubt in any of their minds, any of those geologists, that those kinds of carbon atoms in the plants, in the rocks, in the woods, reflected anything *but* a nuclear explosion. In 1908.

Amanda sat back in the chair, unable to keep her mind clear. Unable to keep her heart from pounding. That meant a bizarre but possible set of collisions in the path of the solar wind sent a huge piece of comet into the earth's atmosphere, causing it, at that speed, to condense into a density that could only be a black hole. Antimatter. In other words, the damn thing that went off was either a bomb, sent by extraterrestrial intelligence, which was somehow, no matter how you tried to think of it, fundamentally unthinkable, or else it was a black hole. Black hole, the phenomenon that was almost unthinkable as well. An area of such density would have blown right through the earth and out the other side. She remembered reading that the line of exit for such an imaginary arrow would have to be between Spain and Newfoundland, and that the weather reports in that area had not been unusual that day nor the shipping patterns disturbed.

Amanda's finger went down the file: three ships and a plane lost on December 2, 1908, off the coast of Spain. So.

That was the point of exit. She was looking for something else in the file, too. But it wasn't there. No explanation. For that word again. *NERP.*

33

Something was bothering him until Eberly just couldn't stay away. He got Rufus finally and they drove out to pay a visit to the Genius on his farm. Eberly got out of the car and waddled up to ring the doorbell. There was a peculiar cast to the house. It was sort of the same feeling he got up there one day on the plateau. The same kind of wind was blowing. In a few minutes he heard a strange kind of noise on the other side and then the door opened up.

"Yes," the distorted old face said to him, "I am Arnold's mother. Won't you come in."

The eyes burned at him. That was the only word for it. At first Eberly stood back because of the grotesqueness of the figure. He was caught between fear, astonishment, and some kind of pity that anything could be born looking like that. And then he looked again and he thought it was, despite its smiling voice, just monstrous as it came toward him, swathed in a long calico skirt, the head tilted with its funny old-fashioned–looking blond curls. Eberly thought the woman had had an accident because her hand was outstretched, only it wasn't no hand, it was a thing, like a metal thing, ending in pincers. Eberly, thinking it was a replacement for an arm, but knowing all the time something stranger yet was going on here, found himself backing down the steps, and this gigantic freak coming right at him. Eberly apace down the steps and the freak—goddamn her—moving right along all the time talking in this sweet voice: "Oh Sheriff, I have frightened you, I see. I have frightened you, now do come in and have some pie. . . ." There she was reaching out for him and Eberly thinking Pie! Hell's bells, I'm getting outta here, flying toward the car in real fright, his hand on his holster, fast at his heels the ugliest, biggest goddamn woman he'd ever seen in his whole earthly life. Rufus was torn between laughter and fascination. He didn't know old Eb could move his carcass so fast; this big—man, she was *big*—lady moving at a fast clip after him, her apron flying in the breeze, and something more. Something weird as hell about her, and Rufus, looking close again, thought, "It's a machine . . . the damn kid's mother is a robot," thinking this just as Eberly lurched open the door, threw himself inside, slammed it, and locked it.

The voice, sweet staccatolike beeps, said, "Don't be alarmed. I am Arnold's mother. I mean you no harm. He told me all about you. Won't you come in?" It stood there, kind of rocking against the car door. Rufus, who was seated on the other side of the sheriff, immediately opened the door and came around to have a better look.

"Rufus!" Eberly was squeaking. "Get back in the car, man. That there thing's dangerous."

But Rufus was fascinated. He came closer and then he saw what Eberly meant. The hands, if that's what you might call them, ended in two very long pincerlike metal rods, hinged on a mighty ball bearing. Caught the right way, that could give you a mean bite. Or worse. He took a step back.

"Uh, ma'am, I was looking for your boy," he said, watching the thing. The eyes. Damn the eyes. The eyes were absolutely amazing. Rufus tried to lean closer. They must be real, he reasoned. Real eyes the Genius had put in there. He assumed now it was the Genius who had built the damn thing. And then he remembered that night when he and Eberly had driven on up there behind the hangar. The expressions on those faces. Weird. Weirder than weird. Maybe, just maybe they were robots too?

Eberly was yelling to Rufus, "Get in the damn car, Rufe. It's trying to break the door down." And indeed the thing was. Rufus went back around the other side of the car as the robot said, "I'm not going to harm you. Now open the door." And when Eberly refused, the robot's arm shot out, into the keyhole, unlocked the door, and pulled it open. As it was, Eberly had already stepped on the gas, and the effect of this was for the car to lurch forward, with Eberly sliding out of it. Rufus reached out his left leg and jammed on the brake a moment before they slammed into the porch. The robot was right on him. Rufus was amazed how fast it could move.

"Sorry if I alarmed you," the strange voice said, as Eberly scrambled back into the car, jerked it around, and headed for the highway.

"Sorry if I alarmed you," Eberly said. "That was the strangest part, that that robot knew what to say. Just like a real person." Sweat was pouring down his face. "Whattaya make of that, Rufe?"

"What, Eb?" he asked, although he knew.

"That kid having a robot for a mother. Nobody has a robot for a mother. It ain't natural."

"Maybe he built it."

"Buildin' a robot for a mother ain't natural."

"That's for sure."

34

As they headed for the parking lot, Hotchkiss was thinking he could not last all the way to his house. If he did not take her in his arms right then and there and love her he simply could not make it. When Hotchkiss was close to her, Amanda thought Yes, there is much to this electromagnetism and the fields of gravity. For there was a force field about Hotchkiss that could not be denied. She felt her resolve, her will, her very self melting.

"Come here," he said to her, pulling her hand.

"Now?" she said, looking surprised, with a smile. He pulled her across the parking lot. It was cold, and their breath was turning to smoke, and he pulled her into his car.

"You're coming with me," he said, and he started the car, put it in park, and waited for the heat, as he began to kiss Amanda, taking off her jacket in between his kisses which were longer now and with a ferocity that always surprised him, and soon they were naked and entwined around each other, with the front seats going down, expertly lowered by Hotchkiss and Amanda positioned by Hotchkiss and herself, two masters of technology, rocking now with no thoughts of America or glory or space, but simply It, the itness of it encompassing them, and Amanda was saying, "Oh I love you I love you" in between catching her breath and the car windows full of steam and once in a while, between times, Amanda murmuring, "So silly like teenagers," or a gasp and "Someone's coming." They were there a couple of hours, and Amanda afterward said, "I'm so exhausted, come home with me," and he drove her home and carried her, wrapped in her clothes, into her house and laid her on the bed, and then he knew it was foolish, ridiculous, childish, impulsive, terrible, immature, and neurotic, but he couldn't help it. He absolutely couldn't bear to leave her, and so he crawled in beside her. He stared at her while she slept. He found her as hard to capture as the photons that ensnared her. But when he put his arm around her and felt her shoulder grow soft in his hand, he knew someday he would.

Captain Donald Hotchkiss was scared to death. It was four o'clock in the morning, and the brass was on the phone ordering him immediately to report.

"Yessir, yessir," was all he could say.

"Are you out of breath, *or what?*" the brass roared.

Or what? *Or what* was that Hotchkiss was astride and in the mist, pumping away for Old Glory, God, and the forces of nature as he sat astride, yes astride, Amanda Jaworski, America's leading lady astronaut, as she had come to be called at Cape Canaveral. Atop and astride her, he was on his way to the moon. She was pink and bewitched, panting and sweating, as he felt her tremble all around him and found himself idiotically uttering as he came in a rush, "Yessir, yessir." The little red bell on the little red light on the emergency-alert phone had gone off, just as Hotchkiss and Jaworski were coming in for a landing. He collapsed on her sweating, exhausted form, the phone dangling from his hand, the faint buzz still sounding on the phone. My God, my God, Hotchkiss thought, I came during an emergency alert. He was alternately impressed, embarrassed, and proud.

"How did you ever do that?" was all she said later, gasping.

"Do what?" he said, beginning to blush with pride. He had misunderstood.

"However did you pick up the phone at that *moment?*" Her eyes were astonished.

"Red alert," he said. "I saw it was red alert." She just stared at him in disbelief. Then she said, "Your training must have been incredible."

He was vaguely insulted, unsure why, feeling in the remark she had traded his basic manhood for some organizational aim. She had meant it to be a compliment. He thought. But then, Jaworski was a tough cat. He adored Jaworski. And he loved to love her. But the brass

185 ____

would have had a fit. They did not want any interastronaut sex. They tried to run the sex drive right out of them, right into the ground.

"They nearly succeeded," Amanda said. "Jogging fifteen miles a day is enough to put even me out of commission."

They had seen his car in her driveway, of course. All night, of course. There was an investigation, of course. There were reprimands. Serious pressure. Demerits for Hotchkiss and a debate about whether or not Jaworski, a person clearly not in full control, God no, not in control, should be going to Mars. It upset them, it certainly did, this thought of a person out of control taking their billion-dollar capsule to Mars.

"But she's so much better," the director wailed. "It will delay the program three months to get anyone else ready, really ready, and even then, Jaworski's better. Technically she's unbeatable; she can handle the publicity when they get back, she looks good on TV." He sighed. "Jaworski's a winner. . . . There's just this problem of her sex drive."

"What," someone—later they couldn't remember who—asked, "is going to happen to it during nine months in a space vehicle?"

"We uh, seriously think," the general said, "that the minute she's out of any kind of gravitational force, it will diminish."

They all nodded. It was all too much. Gravity and sex. But then who knew? It was an explanation. At the moment any explanation would do.

A strange thing had happened to Hotchkiss. He did not know why. He only knew that he wanted to marry Amanda. In a weak moment—and when he was with Amanda most of them were in fact weak—he asked her to do so.

"Why no," she said, pleased and aghast, and went on about the "socio-politico-repression of women in a socially institutionalized state of deprivation known as marriage," in the same tone in which she described that the propulsion system of the orbiter contained 300-pound fixed-thrust rocket engines mounted on movable gimbals provided with two helium-pressure fuel tanks containing monomethylhydrozine and nitrogen tetrousoxide with a combined capacity of 3,137 pounds of liquid propellant.

"Oh," was all Hotchkiss could say. He was determined to have her, and he was not discouraged. This was only an initial pass, meant to gather information.

"I was thinking," Eb said, "it ain't right a kid livin' alone out there. Fourteen years old and all that. Genius or no genius."

"No, it ain't right," Rufus said.

"So I was thinkin' mebbe I'd take 'im in to live with me."

"With you, Eb? I thought you told me you couldn't stand him."

"Cain't. But it's lonely out there, Rufus. Gets mighty lonely."

"How lonely?"

"So lonely I find myself talkin' to the heifers." There was a pause. "That's the truth, Rufe."

"That ain't lonely, Eb."

"That ain't lonely? What you talkin' about? What're you callin' lonely then?"

"Lonely, Eb," Rufus said slowly, like he'd thought about it a long while, "lonely is when the heifers talk back."

"Hi," Amanda said. "What're you doing?" She never called up to ask what he was doing. She sounded nervous.

"Oh," Hotchkiss said, "I'm reading."

"Oh really?" she said. "How interesting." He could tell by the way she said it she wasn't interested at all.

"Amanda," he said suddenly, "is there somebody there with you?" He had a funny feeling.

"Well," she said, "sort of."

"Sort of?" he said. "What kind of answer is sort of?"

"Well, it's not someone, actually," she said, "it's . . ." and then she told him.

Hotchkiss stared at the phone.

"Donald, are you there? I said I'm here with Frank."

"Frank?" There was a pause, then Hotchkiss again. "Big Frank?"

"The very one," Amanda said.

"What are you doing with him?" Hotchkiss asked. His mind was full of terrible things.

"I'm making him eggs."

"Eggs?"

"And toast," Amanda replied.

"Oh."

"I was surprised. I didn't think he could eat in this time zone. But he can. It turns out that things like that, certain drives, don't change."

"What?"

"When you switch time zones. You know hunger and sex, they stay with you."

Hotchkiss's hand froze on the wire. "Does he have a sex drive?" he said, his voice a squeak.

"I don't think so," Amanda said, embarrassed. "I think he's still a baby."

"A baby?" Hotchkiss asked, his voice higher still. "What do you mean a baby?"

"Well"—Amanda was whispering into the phone—"I don't think he's very old," she said. "You know, agewise."

"Oh," he said again. "Well how old is he? Seventeen?"

"I don't think so," she said, whispering.

"Why are you whispering?"

"It's not very polite to be discussing a person's age," Amanda said.

"Amanda, for heaven's sake, ask him how old he is!"

"I think he's about ten," she whispered.

"Ten?" Hotchkiss said. "Frankenstein is only ten years old?"

"Well," she said, "that might be old, you know, for a monster."

"Oh," Hotchkiss said again. Possibly. Possibly ten was old for a monster. He really didn't know. There were times when Hotchkiss thought he really couldn't handle certain things another single minute. This was one of those times.

Hotchkiss went out on his porch to sit and listen to the wind in the branches. He found this a reasonably good thing to do when things threatened to overwhelm him. He liked the creak of the boards on the porch of the old house he had bought; he liked the sound of the stream rushing over the rocks in the small brook behind his yard; he liked the smell of the grass at night, and the occasional whippoorwill. He loved Amanda. That part was simple, or as simple as these things could pretend to be, but the rest of it . . . the rest of it he just didn't know about. Amanda. Telling him all these crazy, lunatic things. Which part of him somehow believed. Hotchkiss at first dismissed these things as the fanciful imaginings of a child. But the more she spoke of them, of Frank, and of this guy Rastus, the more Hotchkiss began to think that they, and where they came from, were possible. In other words, Rastus and the place he came from, did in fact exist. According to Amanda, this is where it got complex. She spoke of time zones. And traveling into other time zones, and things of such mystical ilk that Hotchkiss simply couldn't cope. He went for a walk in the woods. He pulled a leaf off the tree and remembered reading somewhere that no two leaves are alike.

35

Someplace else, a farmer held something in his hand. It was a leaf. And it was a startlingly bright green. Young, alive, the farmer held it in his hand, wondering. "Nature has its infinite variations; no two leaves are alike." He'd read that once. Green life, like man's fingerprints, could never be duplicated. Each leaf, alone, singular. Things like this astonished him, when he thought about it. He was a farmer. He did not think consciously about such things very often. But lately, of late, other things were haunting him, haunting the very air. A farmer. He would sow the seed, fight off the invasions of offending insects, drought, floods, and disease. Successful the plants would grow; he would harvest his reward. That had been one time, long ago. Now there was something different at loose in the land, in the sky, through the water.

The man had come from the government last night. They had, in Wilmont, Texas, a gathering of local people, which some people called a "town meeting," although he, the farmer, wasn't given to calling it anything. He wasn't much given to get-togethers, but things now were out of hand. The man from the government, with some scientific fellow who said he knew all the answers to things, stood up there and told all these people that they shouldn't pay it no mind, that this nuclear power plant up on the river they built three years ago wasn't the thing causing the trouble. He told them it was true there'd been a leak here and a leak there, but it wasn't enough of a leak, the scientist fellow said, to be causing the *trouble*. The farmer scratched his head, looking at the leaf, and then he looked at the sky as if for help. He just didn't know. He didn't know anymore how things had gotten twisted up so. He went into that meeting knowing full well what it was, and by the time the man from the government got talking and the scientist man was saying things were otherwise and telling folks in there they were going to get tax breaks, tax breaks somehow got everybody talking about taxes and it seemed like nobody was willing to talk about *the trouble.*

The farmer had stood in the middle of the meeting and asked to speak his mind. And the man from the government, seeing an old, poor farmer, a simple man with a face that looked ruined—from the elements and price supports and just an old, ruined man—the government man thought, "Poor son of a bitch, let him talk." But the farmer was not thin and nearly ruined by being a farmer, but in fact by the trouble. And that was what he wanted to say. He wasn't a speaking man, the farmer. But when he spoke this time, the sound of his words came up through his throat like a flood. A long trapped passion and love of the earth, animals, the fields began to tear along his tongue, binding his conviction to a passion that astonished them all, and as the farmer spoke, folks said later it was like something terrifying and something wonderful all at once, like a brief flash tore through the hall. He said, "I don't see how you can say all this ain't nothin' to worry about, because I don't think you been out here lookin'. If you look, you got to see it. I look up in the sky, and I see the birds, the birds they can't fly, some of 'em, they can't fly no more, their wings is so weak, and I go to the river, and the fish ain't there no more like they used to be; some of them, the rainbow trout, ain't nobody seen one in ten years now. *Things is dyin',* and you say pay it no mind. Now the birds ain't flyin' and the fish ain't swimmin', and my cattle got sick, so sick twice from the grain *from my fields"* (as if the author of life could have, however indiscriminately, made him responsible struck him like a blow) "from my fields, they got so sick, I had to go down and shoot my own cattle—all from that there radiation. And I'm tellin' you and I been tryin' to say, but it's like the devil hisself got hold a' you and kept you from hearin'," and at this the crowd, the small hall was still. "If you don't care about the sky and that the birds is dyin', and if you don't care about the water, and the fish is dyin', and you don't care about the cattle, and you don't care about the fields, then you don't care much for living yourself. You and me we gonna be dyin', too. Ain't nothin' growin' like it should. It's just natural it's gonna spread." He turned around now, a plea in his eyes. "The trees comin' up crooked, birds layin' eggs that crack, babies dyin' before they git born, two-legged calves, things twistin' up somethin' terrible. It is a dangerous thing and *you gotta stop it*. You got to." This last was said in such a way that afterward nobody knew whether it was a shout or a whisper. It was so loud and so soft all at once. Like death itself, a scream of silence. For a while nobody said anything.

Then finally the government man spoke, pulling on what he had come to think of as his "inner resources," which was actually a system of self-deception that was so powerful, that once started, like cancer, it gobbled everything before it. So necessary had this system of self-deception become, he thought, to his survival—in other words, so deceived was he about the necessity of the self-deception—he no longer knew he was lying to himself. He told himself these farmers and people like that were all hysterical. Hysterical. The voice of reason spoke through him: of course there were some dangers to radioactivity. Everyone knew that. But it was not anything to worry about. A bird here. A bird there. A fish here and there. Certain species were destined to extinction anyway. Everyone knew that. *What about* Homo sapiens, *a girl had asked him once*. He winked. Cute. Can you imagine? No one could. Therefore, next question. Hell, you had to deal with the here and now. The Arabs held the oil, were holding up the world. We needed the energy. It wasn't that dangerous. Nothing to worry about. *Do not*, he told himself and countless others, *think about the long run*. "In the long run," it might be destructive, of course. In the long run. But there wouldn't be any long run, would there? So careful, so evolved was the self-deceptive thinking that they didn't realize that they had already canceled the long run out by making the decision to run in that direction at all. *If you take the left road there is no long run*. Ha. Ha. Ha.

Rastus sat up and laughed. He switched off the video machine he had been watching. The program was called "Episode One from Planet Earth," and it bored him. He was going out.

36

Commanding General Aloysius Boscombe, III, was very happy that he had Timothy T. Purse working for *him*. Timothy was his outstanding radio astronomer. There was no one on the face of the earth, in General Boscombe's opinion, to equal Purse. Purse not only was the most outstanding radio astronomer on the planet, Purse was *trained*. Purse had never disobeyed a single order, never questioned a directive, simply obediently and quietly done his job. And an outstanding job at that. Purse had no "personal life," which is to say, anything that did not involve radio astronomy. He ate it, breathed it, and lived with it. While Purse took his breakfast, eating cornflakes, he laboriously studied the latest information on quasars and pulsars. Even in his bath, Purse, lying backward in the tub, contemplated the TV screen on the ceiling, bringing him always the latest information about the beat of the universe. Those who were about him (no one "knew" him, certainly) figured that Purse had left the planet Earth at some point early in his childhood, due, some said, to a trauma regarding the existence of God.

This had happened one day while he was counting snowflakes. His mother, a devoted Catholic, was representative of one part of the schism in his parents' marriage. His father was a fierce anticleric and had descended, according to his mother's rendition, one dark and stormy night, spirited her away like a magic gypsy, and broken her from the church. However, due to the intervention of a kindly local priest, his mother continued to take communion and to speak to him of the Almighty. The Almighty, alas, in his mother's view, took on the aspects of an almighty and merciless, as opposed to a merciful, God. This suspicion, that the Lord was a son of a bitch, which was clearly his father's view, was lodged early in the child's mind, and came to fruition one day as he was counting the snowflakes.

His mother found him on the porch, bundled up and quite content with an adding machine, madly computing on rows and rows of paper. At five, the child had been declared to be "extremely precocious" in matters of mathematics.

The mother, a kind and simple creature, was nonetheless concerned with the passion with which the current activity was being conducted.

The child was not simply working the adding machine. He seemed absorbed, in almost some cosmic trance, watching and looking and breathing quite hard, as the papers rolled beneath his fingers and the calculations piled up around him, like the snowflakes themselves. Twice she removed him from the snow and under the protection of the porch roof. Although he was still outside, he was bundled well, and as long as he did not sit in the snow itself, she was not overly concerned. But then she went upstairs, and when she returned some hour and a half later, she found the child immersed in paper and snow in an absolute frenzy.

"Timothy!" she said. "What are you doing?"

And the child said, "I want to see how fast the snow falls and how many snowflakes fall in an hour." He turned to her then, full of woe. "But they melt sometimes before I can catch them."

"Oh, Timothy darling," she said, scooping him up, finding the whole thing endearing but missing its point, "you *can't* figure it out, darling . . ."

"Why?" he said. She did not see how dark his eyes were.

"Well, sometimes it falls faster and sometimes harder. It changes," she said, "depending on the weather."

"You mean God would speed it up just to mess up my calculations?"

"Well," she said, at a loss for words, "the weather does change. . . ."

"But he changes it, right? So you can't figure it out, right?"

"No . . . he, he changes it sometimes just because it, it's hard to measure it," she said. "Sometimes you need more snow and sometimes less."

"If he's so smart, he ought to be able to figure out how much you need," he said sourly, but at that point he had somehow concluded that the inability to take an accurate measurement or make an accurate prediction was based less on God's idiocy than on his perversity. He suspected his father was right, but he differed in one important way.

His father would say, "The Lord's a son of a bitch," meaning life was essentially unfair. "The meek don't inherit the earth," his father would roar. "It goes to the shitheads!" This would make his mother cower. But Timothy did not go that far. He did not believe there was only the wicked fallibility of man making things go awry; he really believed there was a Prime Mover, a Purpose at work, and the challenge was to outwit Him. So it was the strange blend of devoutness and willfulness, with all of this that he had devoted his life to attempting to outwit the Son of a Bitch Upstairs. In penance for his rage at the Prime Mover, and in deference to his dear now-departed mother, Timothy led an exemplary life. He neither smoked nor drank. Never gambled, and forgot about sex. For a time.

Over the years Purse had become an outstanding radio astronomer devoting himself to pulsars, quasars, and the dancing neutrino. So it was that General Aloysius Boscombe, III, was astounded, flabbergasted, when Timothy T. Purse stood before him one morning, a pale bespectacled man of thirty-seven, rapidly losing his hair and his eyesight, shielded now behind very thick glasses, and said, "I'm afraid, sir," and bit his lip.

"What is it, Purse?" the general said gruffly. The general said everything gruffly.

"I'm afraid, sir," Timothy went on, "that I must tender my resignation, sir."

"What!" The general did manage that much. "Why, what are you talking about?"

"I . . . I'm afraid, sir," the frail bespectacled creature went on, "that I . . . I am losing my mind, sir. That I am no longer mentally sound and capable of rendering the service to which I have been assigned, sir." He bit his trembling lip again.

The general leaned forward, bewitched, truly bewitched.

"What is it, Timothy?" There was almost a tone of concern.

"I . . . I'd rather not say, sir."

"Well, you'd damn well better say, Purse. I'm not accepting any resignation. . . . Maybe you need a rest. . . . You've never taken a vacation . . . take a vacation. Come back, you'll feel better."

"No, sir . . . no, sir, I can't, sir. This is it, sir." He covered his ear. "I can't expose myself any longer, sir."

"To what, Purse?"

"To . . . to what I hear, the things I hear out there . . . in the universe."

"What do you hear?" The general was quite intrigued now. The man was sweating and turning beet red. The general didn't know what it was he heard, but it must have been, the general figured, a humdinger.

"I hear," he whispered, the son of a fierce Catholic mother and a bellowing father, "obscene things, sir." The general's eyes widened. He thought he saw Purse weeping.

The general was momentarily dumbfounded. He had heard things of this sort before. Hooper, for one. It was supposed to be top secret, but it got around that Hooper either saw or heard or got in touch with something up there that had cleaned out his brain. Some said they put him away. Some said he just disappeared.

"Take a vacation, Purse," Boscombe said wearily.

"I want to resign, sir, I can't . . . ," came the weak whispered reply.

"Go on vacation, Purse," the general said. "Go to a bar, get drunk, get friendly with strangers, listen to loud music; it'll go away. Go on boy, go," the general said, returning to his desk with a sigh.

Purse, he knew, would do none of those things. Purse would continue to listen and cry.

Amanda, feeling loved, was thinking about perfection. She thought that Schrodinger's nose was perfect, and said so, which drove Hotchkiss quite mad.

"Will you stop going on about that cat?"

"Well, he does have a perfect nose. Look at it."

"I am looking at it. What's so perfect about it?"

"Its golden color. It's the color of honey and pineapples. Its proportion. Its softness. It is exactly right. Precisely as a cat's nose should be."

"It's damp," Hotchkiss said.

"But it is not wet. Marshall's nose is always wet." Marshall was the black-and-white five-toed cat next door.

"How do you know?" Hotchkiss said.

"Well, when you pet him, you can't miss it," she said. "It's wet. It almost drips."

Hotchkiss frowned. The thought of a cat with a dripping nose was an unattractive one at best, particularly at breakfast. Reluctantly he looked at Schrodinger. It looked like a perfectly typical cat's nose to him. Typical, possibly, but not perfect. "I don't see what's so perfect about it," he said grumpily.

"You realize you're jealous," she said, removing the toast.

"I am not jealous. But the way you go on about that cat is ridiculous. He's just a cat. A four-footed not-very-bright furry small mammal, with, one has to say in one's most generous mood, a most unusual disposition."

"He's not an ordinary cat at all," Amanda said, ending the argument. "I just know there's something special, extremely special and unusual about him. I think he's gifted."

"Gifted," Hotchkiss harumphed. "Amanda, a cat can't be gifted any more than a chicken can be gifted."

"Well I say there's something unusual going on here, and someday we'll find out." There. That ended it. Hotchkiss attempted to read the paper and drank his coffee, strangely affected by this conversation. Somehow, he too felt this oddness about Schrodinger, although he would never admit this to anyone, least of all to himself. Nonetheless, it had been strange—four years of working on the Problem and no solution. Then Amanda had happened to say: "If you discuss it with Schrodinger *with love*, you'll get the answer. You'll see." And sure enough, when he did, he had it. Pure coincidence, he kept telling himself. But he had to keep telling himself.

Amanda was not too thrilled with the orders she had received that morning. She had been ordered—by Farkheimer, no less—to appear before a committee of very highly placed generals and admirals from all three divisions of defense—the army, the air force, and the navy—which would have been all right if she had been allowed to appear alone, but she was not being allowed to appear alone. They were asking her to bring Schrodinger.

At first she had refused, not realizing that it was a refusal exactly. She had simply said, when Farkheimer had told her to appear with Schrodinger, "Well, I'm sorry. He'd love to meet you, sir, but he isn't allowed to leave the house, except for medical emergencies."

"Amanda," Farkheimer had roared, "this is an order!"

"An order?" Amanda was indeed puzzled. Why would anyone be ordering poor Schrodinger anywhere? She didn't want to make an ugly issue of it, of course, but technically speaking, Schrodinger was not in the air force. She was in the air force, and so they couldn't really court-martial Schrodinger for failure to appear.

"What's the problem exactly?" she said.

"Never mind what the problem is," said Farkheimer. "Bring the cat at oh-eight hundred, and don't try any funny business."

"I don't know any funny business," Amanda said haughtily.

Well, the whole thing was really rather strange. She suspected that Delko was behind this, always going on about her and her "dead cat."

Amanda showed up promptly at 0800 with Schrodinger tucked safely in his basket. She didn't want them to think for a minute that he wasn't patriotic, so she had tied a red-white-and-blue ribbon around his neck and hung a small USA emblem from it.

"This is sick," said a psychiatrist—who had been asked to join them—under his breath, although not so under that Amanda couldn't hear. "Fetish, it's a fetish dressing up a dead cat like a war hero."

"He isn't dead," Amanda said to him, placing Schrodinger in the center of the table. "You'll see."

Farkheimer called the meeting to order and told them all, but as if he were speaking to Amanda alone, that they had had reports of her being seen with a dead cat. That furthermore the acquisition and harboring of a dead cat was some sort of violation of some code or other, and that Amanda would be charged with a rather serious crime, and in fact it troubled him greatly, but she would be ordered to seek psychiatric help, and if that did not work, she would be removed from the space program. But he told them that certainly he had decided upon witnessing "the creature in the basket," as he referred to Schrodinger in sleep; that "it made his heart heavy, but there was no way that Amanda would go to Mars as long as she maintained that something as clearly dead as that animal were in any way alive."

Amanda looked around the room. She saw Delko beaming. "I told you the cat is dead," he said.

"He isn't dead," Amanda said firmly. "He just looks dead. If you gave him an EEG you'd see fantastic electrical activity."

"Amanda," Farkheimer glowered, "these are busy people. Too busy to give a dead cat an EEG."

"Look," she said, "you have to give me a chance to prove he's not dead. I can."

Farkheimer looked at her. "Okay," he said. "Prove it."

"Well," she said, "it's sort of personal . . . I mean I have this song I can sing to him, and when I do, he purrs. Sometimes he doesn't wake up, you know, but his purring would convince you he's alive." They all continued to stare at her.

"Well, my dear, sing it then," Farkheimer sighed.

"Well, if you don't mind," Amanda said, "I really think it would be exploiting him, you know, if I sang it in front of all these strangers, as if it were a trick or something, you know. I mean, I only sing it when I feel overwhelmed with love."

There was a stunned silence in the war room.

"Love," Farkheimer said, as if it were a strange word to him.

Amanda nodded. "But I'd be willing to do it in front of one of you, in a private room somewhere," she said softly. Quickly the psychiatrist volunteered. This was very interesting: this total fantasy in an otherwise scientifically trained and apparently extremely valuable NASA member. He had heard about Amanda before. She had passed an incredible round of psychiatric tests prior to this, but it appeared that this cat fetish was something that had only been discovered recently, by Sergeant Delko. It was really unfortunate, the psychiatrist thought; her career would be ruined. Perhaps he could help soften the blow.

"I'll go with you, Amanda," he said, rising, and they were ushered into an adjacent small room.

Amanda put Schrodinger on the table, smiled at the psychiatrist, and said, "I haven't sung it in a while, you know, but I'm sure it will work." She seemed about to begin when she said to him, "Look, you'd better sit down. When he starts purring, the vibrations are incredible."

The psychiatrist nodded, decided to indulge her, and sat down. After the psychiatrist was seated, she took Schrodinger out of his basket and held him in her arms.

On the other side of the wall Farkheimer was having all he could do to calm down the Joint Chiefs of Staff. "She's very valuable. We can humor her this much," he said. "You can't imagine what a loss this is to the space program."

"This is nuts!" said another general.

"Bonkers," said an admiral. "That cat's been dead for years, I'd venture."

And then they heard it. The first thing they heard was a soft sound. A very soft sound. It appeared to be a girl, singing. The singing got louder, and then shortly after that, they felt this rumbling in their feet.

"My God, I think there's an earthquake," said one.

"No, no! That's it!" Farkheimer cried. "She said when he purrs he vibrates!"

"Vibrates, my ass!" said another. "She must be a spy. That cat must have a bomb in it!"

"Some kind of secret weapon," said another. "Look at the walls."

All the pictures on the walls were turning. First they turned clockwise, then they turned counterclockwise. The lights turned on and off, and still Schrodinger purred. The psychiatrist thought at first he was having a hallucination. He kept rubbing his eyes and holding on to his chair—not an altogether easy thing to do, since his chair was vibrating from the sound of Schrodinger's purr. Amanda, for her part, was singing her heart out, and the psychiatrist was totally dazzled. Of all things, that girl was singing "That old black magic has me in its spell," and the cat, the dead cat, was smiling and setting up a vibration that shook the very walls.

It was only a few minutes before Farkheimer bounded in and told her she'd better turn Schrodinger off.

"Well really," Amanda said, "he isn't a television set."

"They think he's a weapon. Can't you slow him down at least?" Farkheimer said, looking around.

"Well, I can't just stop like that. He has to slow down naturally, you know," and she continued to croon, holding him in her arms.

The psychiatrist left with Farkheimer and they returned to the meeting.

"Look," Farkheimer said, "if she can go up, I want her up. It'll cost a million dollars at least to replace her."

"Well, send her up, by all means," the psychiatrist said, raising his hands in the air helplessly.

"Well, what do you think, Doc? You think that cat is dead or what?"

"Why," the psychiatrist said, "everything points to its being dead, but that purr was real enough, so therefore the cat must not be dead. What did they say inside?"

"They took a vote. Deadlocked. Half of them said the cat is dead. The other half said he has to be alive."

Farkheimer shrugged. "Frankly, I think the damn cat is dead, but if she's figured out a way to get the floorboards trembling, hell, she deserves to go up. You know," Farkheimer said, winking, "I kind of like her anyway. After all, what's so bad about carrying around a dead cat? It doesn't necessarily mean you're crazy, right, Doc? I mean it could just mean you're sentimental."

"Sentimental," the psychiatrist said. It had a strange, echoing sound to it. "Yes," he said. "Perhaps." Well he wasn't writing up this report. Hell's bells. The girl and the cat and Farkheimer were all crazy as loons, far as he was concerned. A trick. Had to be a trick. Well, he was going to give her the O.K. and say the hell with it. He knew a thing or two about the realities of army careers.

37

When Amanda walked into the preflight training center the next morning Delko was at the door. "That skinny radio guy was here again, lookin' for you," he said sourly.

"Oh, Tim Purse? Where is he?"

"He left finally. Sure is a nervous guy."

"Oh . . . did he leave a number?" she said.

"Nope," Delko said. "He must have a crush on you or somethin'. He keeps comin' around."

"Yeah," she said, walking into her office, feeling somewhat troubled. "We keep missing each other."

She had in fact woken up last night in the middle of the night. Something had definitely disturbed her. Deeply disturbed her. But all she could remember when she awoke was that she was supposed to hear something from Purse. She called his extension.

"I'm sorry," the voice said. "Mr. Purse has taken an unexpected vacation. He'll be gone for two weeks."

"Oh," Amanda said, and left her number. An unexpected vacation. Well. That was something.

Eberly had decided he wanted to keep an eye on the boy, so one afternoon he, Rufus, and the Genius were tooling along the Santa Fe road in the pickup truck. It was another one of those hot days.

"I can't hardly believe it," Eberly said, wiping his neck. Rufus looked at him. Eberly looked like a puddle. Hell, if he didn't know better, he'd bet old Eberly was melting down before his very eyes.

"This is a meteorological trauma," the Genius said, "of unprecedented proportions."

"Whatcha sayin' there, boy?" Eberly asked.

"It's more than that," the Genius said, staring out at the passing landscape. "There are no meteorological explanations."

"How's that?" Eberly said.

"It doesn't correlate. There's no reason for it to be so hot. There's nothing happening atmospherically to explain it. And they've got snow in Canada. In southern Canada they have ten inches of snow, in July."

"Hell, they get snow in Canada lots a' times," Eberly said.

"Not in July they don't. Not in Montreal."

"What do you think is happening?" Rufus said, slowly, turning his head toward the Genius. Rufus was convinced of one thing surely. The Genius was a genius.

"I think there are forces," the Genius said, "fooling with us." The impact of this was immediate. The Genius had never suggested anything supernatural before, and combined with what Eberly and Rufus had seen that night in the desert, Eberly nearly drove the truck off the road.

"Where in hellfire you ever get such a notion as that?" Eberly said, righting the truck.

"You know it's true," the Genius said. "That's why you drove off the road."

Rufus barely smiled.

"Don't go talkin' a' me about no forces, boy. Talk to me straight. You think mebbe it's them Russkies up there, turning the snow on, turning the heat up, messin' with everythin'?"

"Maybe," the Genius said, saying it very quietly. Rufus could tell by how quiet he said it, no way he thought it was Russkies.

"What you figure it be up there doin' the foolin' if it ain't them, then?" Rufus said, not certain he wanted to know.

"That guy in the gold mine," the Genius said. "He's getting one hundred neutrinos an hour."

"Whut?" Eberly said. Rufus had heard about this before. It fascinated the Genius, he figured, for reasons beyond its scientific value, which Rufus couldn't quite fathom. Rufus found it almost funny. Some kind of scientist buried a mile deep in South Dakota had one hundred thousand gallons of cleaning fluid in there. Rufus couldn't figure what anybody'd be doing with one hundred thousand gallons of cleaning fluid, and the Genius told him he was "capturing neutrinos." Of course nobody knew what they were either. Eberly was about ready to arrest the guy, figuring this guy was trapping some poor Indian tribe down there in the cleaning fluid. Turned out otherwise. "Capturing neutrinos" was apparently some kind of work these scientists did. The Genius had carefully explained that 10^{13} neutrinos pass through your body every second, at this distance from the sun, and occasionally such invisible particles could be captured. For reasons Rufus didn't understand, they could be captured in one hundred thousand gallons of cleaning fluid a mile down in a gold mine. What in hell they were doing with them once they captured them he didn't know either.

"They're counting them," the Genius said. "Usually they can get five or six every two days. Now they're getting one hundred an hour."

"So what's it mean?" Rufus said.

"To me," the Genius said, "it means the forces of antimatter are speeding up. Somebody's speeding them up."

"Somebody? Now hold on there, boy," Eberly said. He felt the Genius was altogether too fanciful.

"Well, there's no explosions to explain it. The universe is full of forces. Something's controlling them."

"Mebbe they ain't controlled. You all jes' ain't figured out how it works yet. Mebbe that's it," Rufus said.

"Well"—the Genius let out a long, slow sigh—"that's not it."

"How you know that?" Rufus said.

"Because," the Genius said, "I know things. I have evidence, communications that are otherwise. But I can't go into it. They'd lock me up."

Rufus looked at Eberly and Eberly looked back. There was definitely something about this Genius kid, didn't know what to make of it. If he knew something he wasn't telling, Eberly knew he didn't like it. In fact, Eberly was one hundred percent totally dissatisfied with the way things were going. It was getting too hot, the wind was getting peculiar, the Indians were going up and not down, girls were going up in rockets, geniuses were making mothers out of robots, and the very air seemed seeded with something altogether disturbing. He didn't know when exactly it had started happening, but he was beginning to get scared. Eberly never'd been scared before. But those things out there that night in the desert—Rufus wouldn't even talk to him about it.

For the time being, there was nothing to do but drive on in the heat. He sighed and drove. The three of them drove on saying nothing. Not until an hour later, when the sand began to swirl, did they see it.

"We gonna get a sandstorm," Rufus said, looking through the rear-view mirror. "We ain't never gonna beat it in this heap."

"We gonna beat it, we gonna beat it," Eberly said, putting the accelerator to the floor. "We make it as far as that canyon anyhow."

"Hold it, hold it," Rufus said as they raced along, pointing to the huge salt flat. There was nothing but desert and mountains for hundreds of miles around, and an unused road. And out there in the middle there was someone standing like he was in a daze. By the time they stopped and looked Rufus was running out of the truck. He could feel the wind whipping and the sand was starting to fly. This poor bastard better get back to the truck or he was a goner in this kind of thing. Rufus ran to him, calling, but he just stood there until Rufus reached him and he saw the look in his eyes. The poor bastard's loco, he thought, pulling his arm. "You better come in that truck with us, fella," he said. "Ain't gonna be able to breathe in about five minutes around here." The man didn't seem to hear him. He wouldn't budge. Then Rufus, taking matters into his own hands, knocked him out cold, hauled him on his shoulders, and walked quickly back to the truck.

"What in hell you do that for?" Eberly yelled from the truck, but Rufus kept coming, opening the door of the truck, and dropped in his package. The Genius had opened some water and Rufus held his arm. "Man's out, can't give him nothin' to drink. Hit it, Eb."

And Eberly did, thinking they would make the canyon just in time, giving them some protection. He could see Rufus was tying up the man's arms and his legs. Just to be sure. The storm lasted about twenty minutes. Rufus was glad to see it go. Their passenger had revived and was drinking some water. He looked perfectly okay now, although he wasn't saying much. The Genius had gone through his pockets while he was out and found out he was a radio astronomer with NASA.

"They just installed a new radio telescope, the biggest one yet," the Genius said. "One hundred miles southwest of here. I bet he's workin' on that." The Genius had a funny look, Rufus thought.

"Well, I really appreciate this," the man said. "You saved my life."

"That's all right," Rufus said. "How'd you get out here anyway? You're a hundred miles from home."

"I flew," the man said.

"Flew? Hell, you crash up in the mountains," Eberly said. "See, Rufus, that's why he was lookin' so dazed when you found 'im."

The man didn't say anything. "If you take me to the nearest town, I'll make a call," he said quietly. "They'll come and pick me up."

"Yessir, we'll git you somethin' to eat," Eberly said. "You don't look right yet."

Rufus was surprised the Genius was not asking him all kinds of questions, but he wasn't. He wasn't saying anything, the Genius, and neither was the man.

When they got to town, the man thanked them again and went to make his phone call. He must have been somebody pretty important to them, because a NASA copter landed smack dab in the middle of Reno about twenty minutes later.

Just before the man left to get into the chopper the Genius said, "Wait a minute. I want to ask you something." He seemed to hesitate, which was unlike him, Rufus thought. "You know that new radio telescope . . . the one they're building that reaches signals farther out than ever before . . . you know that one?"

The man nodded, a veil over his eyes.

"They finish it?" the Genius said.

The man nodded again.

"When did they start it up?" the Genius asked.

"Last night," the man said, turning away.

"There's only one astronomer who can read the printouts. . . . I read he was coming in to do it. . . ." The Genius was yelling over the whirling blades of the copter. "It's you, isn't it? You're the one that can hear it. . . . Is it you?" he said finally, but the man said nothing, climbed into the copter, slammed the door, and stared straight ahead.

"Now what in hell . . ." Eberly said, scratching his head. But the Genius said nothing. He stood there with this strange, knowing smile on his face, and then he said, "It's him. He's the one who's listening all right."

The president walked solemnly across the airfield. In the distance he could see them, the first in a line of hundreds of "dishes" for radio astronomy pointing like ancient monuments of worship toward the sun. Dishes stretched all across the West, and he had to come out here and take a look. The president was extremely embarrassed. I mean, after *all*. He was a respectable married man and president of the goddamned United States, and he had to come out here now and listen to this *insanity* about these *disgusting* things they were picking up out there.

What kind of report was that, anyway? Was it in fact a question of national security? What about national *sanity*? Frankly, he thought these scientists were on drugs. Drugs or hallucinating or something. Didn't know.

He saw Boscombe now, waiting at the terminal. His face looked very pale.

"Good morning, Mr. President." Ellis nodded. The president was not sure he could summon the energy even for the most superficial cordialities. He was making up his mind. And what he was making up his mind to do was Forget It. He was going to bury it; nobody could handle it; it didn't make any sense, and it was going to send all of them damn near crackers trying to decide what to do about it. Let the Russians find out about it and figure out what to do about it. He had to get reelected.

Downtown, not far from the general and the president's meeting was another meeting that was designed to explain mysteries not dissimilar to those the radio dishes had discerned. This was the Sixty-first Annual Meeting of the International Association for Psychoanalysts. Dr. Herbert Hein, president of the association, had just delivered a paper in which he had made the totally unoriginal and by-now-boring point: "The unconscious is a labyrinth, a veritable minefield of sexual urges and associations, and we have only just begun to mine it."

Perhaps he had just begun to mine it, thought Dr. Alexander Bushes in the third row, but Bushes had been mining it for thirty years and, to tell the truth, he was damn sick of it. Mother rapers, father rapers, child rapers, brother rapers, sister rapers, all of mankind, in the view of Bushes, was a hopeless torrent, a seething torment of ungratified sexual desire. They lusted, they desired, they wanted, they forbade. So mankind in its effort at evolution had gotten itself into such a muddle that they now, with a good swift cultural kick from Queen Victoria herself, had convinced themselves that sex was definitely dirtier, more forbidden, worse than murder. If a man murdered his mother, it would be a terrible thing, but it would be *far* far worse, certainly, they *all* felt, if he went to bed with her. Oh my God, Bushes would moan, as bakers, politicians, schoolteachers, preachers, the most respectable, for they were always the ones who suffered most, crowded his threshold and told him how sick, how unhappy they were. And he would suggest ever so gently that somewhere in the labyrinth was perhaps a sexual feeling, a sexual thought. Half of them would run to the bathroom and throw up. The rest never came back. He sighed. Some of them he helped get better; some of them got the message, "You've got to live with the labyrinth, but you can't forget it. You have got to be aware of it and then live." How they were to live, Bushes couldn't exactly tell them. He had simply shown you can't put a lid on the snake pit, which was how the unconscious usually came to be represented. You can't keep them down, these particular snakes. You can't gas them, you can't kill them, because the snakes were the single representation that the unconscious, like matter, could neither be created nor destroyed. It *was*. Sexual desire, longing, and madness were as built into the human species as bipedalism. Somewhere in the long evolutionary train of mammalian history, somewhere in the evolution of that brain, from the green seed of reptilian life, some brief canter through the thermal extremes of the reptiles' cold-blooded world, somewhere slinking out of the primal ooze, had come the mammal. And with the mammal came intelligence, but as the brain expanded, so did the sex drive. Mankind's mating drive knew no seasons, and then, as if to punish his passion, he took to murder. Murder in its infinite variety. Man was the only mammal who was out to destroy his own species. This had first disturbed the kindly doctor, disturbed him beyond all telling. And there were many times when he fervently hoped that another intelligent mammal, the porpoise for example, would inherit the earth, for the porpoise was happy to swim, to enjoy the full power of his environment, not to muck it up, and not to murder his own. The porpoise knew no war, no criminality. The doctor had come to believe that this bright blue ball that hung in the sky, the astronaut's view of the planet Earth, was the only evidence of life in the universe. He had no reason for this, he simply believed it. And this miracle, for that was finally what it was, amidst the stones and rocks, the uninhabitable worlds of gaseous waste that made up that solar system, this fine planet was not only the only space that supported life, but one that he thought had achieved such a beautiful balance of nature. Until recently. Mankind had now gotten involved in extinction. He was willfully deciding which creatures would live and which would die. The water, the very air, was full of poison, and mankind stupidly plodded on, inimical to his own destiny.

The poor tired doctor had once years ago thought of delivering a paper on it. And then his poor old heart just couldn't turn over with any enthusiasm. He would treat his patients. He would enlighten who he could, and fate and man would rule. At night, though, when he was fast asleep, so fast he could not remember it in the morning, it was one of those things he knew happened, but of course he had no evidence:

he would dream of porpoises. Silver and blue in the morning light they swam, their cries filling the air in a sweet, eternal lagoon where the tides and time came and went in some steady cyclical rhythm, in a world where only the stars burned on and out, new ones rising from their ashes being born in the midst, heat and lightning deciding the future of the planet where the dolphins dove in the sweet ecstasy, the steady reverie that all men sought, the joy and presence of mere being, the exultation of life.

38

Amanda was relieved that that night when she went home, Hotchkiss was with her. When they discussed it later he admitted, although reluctantly, that yes indeed he did sense something odd as they entered the house. The first odd thing they noticed was that the phones were all beeping, the way phones do when they are off the hook. Amanda had two extension phones, and both of them were beeping, although both of them were *on* the hook.

"That's weird," Donald said. "I'll take a look at it later."

He was putting some beer into the refrigerator when he heard Amanda gasp from the other room. It was not an ordinary gasp. He went running. She was standing there, still as a stone, staring into the living room, and Donald raced to her side.

"What is it?"

He stopped and looked. He could not believe his eyes. He blinked and looked again. Amanda felt as though her heart had stopped beating. For there was Schrodinger on the living-room floor, not in his usual comatose state, but very much attentive and alive and purring very loudly. He was stretched out in front of a large white sheet of paper, his paw moving rhythmically in short deft strokes across the page: Schrodinger was *drawing*.

It was Amanda's foot, in the last phases of her nail polish.

"This has to be an optical illusion," Donald said tensely. "Has to be."

"No," Amanda was whispering, "I don't think so. I think it's his right hemisphere."

"Amanda," Donald was whispering now, too. "This isn't *possible*. It's a trick."

With that, Schrodinger looked up, squealed, and shot under the sofa. Amanda went to retrieve the drawing.

"It's my foot all right, on nail polish twenty-two." She turned to Donald. "That's the twenty-second day. See?" she said, holding it in front of his eyes. "It's almost gone." She leaned down and whipped off her boot. "See that? It's almost identical. He's drawing it from memory. From last night." She turned to him. "That's why he's drawing it. He knew I was going to polish my nails today, and he seems to love the coastline, or the nail-line look. Whatever it is."

Donald looked peculiar.

"What's the matter?" she said.

"What's the MATTER?" he said loudly. "What do you mean, what's the matter? Amanda," he said, starting to pace the floor, "this is serious. Very serious indeed. In fact, this is terrible."

"What's terrible?"

"What's terrible?" He looked at her. "Amanda," he said slowly, "cats *cannot* draw, and this cat is drawing. Therefore I have concluded that you must have a contagious brain disease, and now I've caught it."

"Donald," Amanda said patiently, "that's one possibility. The other possibility is . . ." She paused and they said it together, "Schrodinger can draw." Then they both sat down.

They sat there for some minutes. "He'd never let anybody see him do this, so there's no point in telling people," she said.

"No," Donald said glumly. "It's a secret vice." Then, "Maybe we could videotape it," he said hopefully. "A hidden camera."

"Donald . . . if he's smart enough to draw, don't you think he could sniff out a camera?"

Donald didn't say anything. They sat there quite a while and then he said, "Maybe we should just forget about it and go to the movies."

"Maybe," Amanda said, "we should." They got up then, decided to forget about it and go to the movies.

Days passed, and they didn't discuss it again. But Donald noticed that Amanda had hung the drawings up on the wall. There were now fifty-two drawings, two months in all, and he noted that she had separated the drawings into two groups: "Series One," and then on the second line, "Series Two."

It bothered Hotchkiss. There was no doubt about that. But for the time being, since it didn't seem to be hurting anyone, he decided to let it ride. He didn't know whether or not it was worse being *sure* that he *wasn't* crazy, and therefore having to acknowledge the fact that Schrodinger was in fact *drawing*, or better to think he *was* crazy and just imagining it. He had never faced a dilemma quite like this in his life. Amanda, for her part, said, "I think we should just wait and see."

"Wait for what?" he asked.

"Well, to see."

"To see what?" he said impatiently. "To see if he stops drawing?"

"No," she said. "Just to see."

"What do you mean, Amanda? You expect some sort of explanation to fall from the sky or something?"

"Well," she said, hesitating, "not exactly."

"Well, what exactly?" He knew his tone was menacing, and he was immediately sorry.

She sighed, "Donald, something's going on here . . . something that you just have to wait and see."

It struck him as extremely practical and extremely unscientific. "Wait and see." On the other hand, what choice was there? He really didn't want to think too much about it himself. He wanted to say, So what. So Schrodinger can draw. So what. So he draws secretly. So nobody will ever believe it. So what? But he couldn't say that. He couldn't in fact say anything. So. He too would wait. Wait and see.

If this had been the first and only thing for which there was no explanation, Amanda would have been more upset. But it was one of so many. Like the *copier*. It was bothering Amanda that nobody, but *nobody*, knew who had gotten into the *copier*.

Perhaps it was because she had the copier, and therefore replication was so much on her mind, that she turned that night to her science book and read: "According to the view held by many scientists, simple molecules in the proper environment will combine to form more complex molecules that can automatically make copies, or replicate themselves. How that originally happened in the ancient oceans is still mysterious, but *once upon a time there was a single molecule on this planet with the self-replicating property, a property no other molecule previously had.* (Amanda underscored this.) It must have made billions and billions of copies of itself in an orgy of reproduction. It probably didn't stop replicating until an error occurred that produced a different self-replicating molecule—its own competition and the beginning of molecular evolution. . . . If we did not have such good evidence for it, evolution would be a completely implausible plot. . . . Who could ever have imagined that from the war of nature, from famine and death, the highest and most exalted forms of life evolved?"

39

In a sense, human flesh is made out of stardust. Every atom in the human body, excluding only the primordial hydrogen atoms, was fashioned in stars that formed, grew old and exploded most violently before the Sun and Earth came into being.
—Nigel Calder, *Key to the Universe* (1980)

All stars have their peculiar natures, properties and conditions, the Seals and Characters whereof they produce through their rays even in these inferior things, viz., in elements, in stones, in plants, in animals and their members. . . . Every thing, therefore, hath its character pressed upon it by its star for some particular effect, especially by that star which doth principally govern it.
—Agrippa von Nettesheim (sixteenth-century magician), *De Occulta Philosophia* (1533)

Hotchkiss was getting a CAT scan. When it showed nothing he saw a psychiatrist, who said that on occasion two people could share the same hallucination.

"What was the cat drawing?" the psychiatrist said, which made Hotchkiss think he was sharing it as well.

"Her nail polish on her toes." Hotchkiss's eyes gleamed with light.

"You seem jealous," the psychiatrist said wisely.

"Every day he studies her nail polish," Hotchkiss said.

The psychiatrist said, "You seem angry."

"I am angry. . . . I mean for Christ's sake, he *studies* her toes."

"Do you think her toes belong to you?" the psychiatrist asked. "You sound possessive."

"No, I don't think they *belong* to me," Hotchkiss said, sitting back huffily. "But there are *limits*, you know. Do you know what she calls him? She calls him her 'honey-pineapple.' She says it's the color of his nose. Then she calls him her honey-pineapple nose." He stopped talking suddenly. "Why are we *talking* about this? This whole thing is ridiculous. You know this cat cannot be drawing, doctor—correct?"

The doctor looked at him, saying nothing.

"Look," Hotchkiss said, suddenly quieter, "there's no point going on with this. . . . I . . . I shouldn't have come."

"What makes you say that?" the doctor said.

"I . . . uh, thanks very much," Hotchkiss said getting up. "Send me a bill," and he closed the door. Damn doctors, anyway.

Hotchkiss drove up to the head of the NASA base, where he knew the veterinary center was. He had passed it many times with Amanda because that's where she sometimes picked up 342 when he was having a checkup or getting a shot or some other routine. They kept a careful eye on him. He saw Tom Oglethorpe walking in the door as he pulled up.

Oglethorpe at first seemed confused. "What are you talking about, Donald? What do you mean . . . can cats *draw*?" Oglethorpe squinted in the sun. "You mean draw pictures, Donald?"

"Yeah . . . well, I know it's a funny question but I . . . I, this is just part of a theoretical problem . . . you know I wondered if there ever was a case, you know a *single* case on record, you know, of anything like that. . . ." His voice seemed to have wound down, almost stopping. "You know . . . any reports unconfirmed even . . ."

"Unconfirmed?" Oglethorpe said. "Unconfirmed reports of a cat that could draw?" He looked at Donald steadily. "No. No reports confirmed or unconfirmed. Donald, cats can see, but they can't reproduce images. No animal can. Donald, can I ask you a question?" He looked at Hotchkiss, who seemed dazed.

Hotchkiss nodded vaguely.

"Why are you asking me this, Donald?"

There was no answer.

"Donald?"

"Oh I . . . I . . . it, it was just a thought, that was all. . . . We're uh, we're reproducing a computer brain . . . an animal brain at the institute and I uh . . . uh . . . wasn't sure that uh . . ." Hotchkiss was not a very good liar, but Oglethorpe had no time to notice that.

"Well, I'm glad I cleared it up," he said, smacking Hotchkiss on the shoulder.

"Yeah . . . thanks," Hotchkiss said, and walked away. He got into his car and drove. He was feeling dejected. He simply drove for miles into nowhere and back, thinking about Schrodinger. What Amanda didn't know, what nobody knew but him, was that the drawing was only part of it. He was convinced now, in a way he never had been before, that when he had seen Schrodinger that night, he *was* reading. He was reading the goddamned Chinese menu.

She knew the accelerators had certain powers—that at some speeds they could create matter out of "nothing," not so much out of nothing, but they could bring into existence things that had never been known before. The time they could exist varied from one billionth to two billionths of a second. But their trajectories could be traced on the cyclotron. The evidence was there.

That night there was a special excitement in the laboratory. A call had come in from the huge accelerator complex at CERN. There, traveling at unimagined speeds, collisions had been arranged, provoked, and managed to produce a never-before-seen particle. Something new in the universe. It was a subquark, or that is to say a kind of quark that they didn't know about before.

When Amanda came into the lab the next morning, the physicists were beside themselves. They were talking about the new quark Z^0, and they were already posting the pictures of the trajectories of Z^0 all over the walls. As Amanda looked at the pictures and heard the talk, she felt positively peculiar. She could not stop staring at the pictures of the lines the quark made. Strangeness of strangeness, the outline, the picture, so to speak, that the quark made on the photographic plate happened co-incidentally to be precisely the same formation as her nail polish on the nineteenth day. Schrodinger's favorite day. The nineteenth day. How bizarre, she thought, that the quark and my nail polish trace the same route. She did, however, feel marvelous about this. It made her feel, if anything, positively peculiar.

The next night, Amanda and Donald were slated to go to a big party. Amanda was excited because she could wear a long dress. She chose astronaut colors, out of obligation to NASA, but the dress was anything but "official." It clung to her like water. It was sequined in silver and red and blue with patterns of very long waves down the front, which Hotchkiss said looked like flames. It was one of those times when Hotchkiss thought he should marry her immediately, like within the very next ten minutes or so, and he proposed this to her at once.

"Oh, Donald," she said, and then for reasons he couldn't explain, it was the only time Amanda ever did such a thing, she blushed. Donald could not understand why the subject of marriage seemed to upset her so, but it did. "It's just too conventional for a person like me. . . . I mean, honestly, Donald, can you see me in the suburbs?"

At that those blue-green eyes grew very wide, and indeed Donald could not see her in the suburbs, as he imagined that all the men would be falling through their hedges to get a look at her. Nonetheless he felt it incumbent upon himself to point out that because a person was married he or she did not have to live in the suburbs.

"We could stay here," he said, but he knew it wasn't forceful enough.

She said, "Oh, Donald, please," as she reached for her bag and kissed Schrodinger good-bye.

"God, what's that?" Donald said as they started out the door, pulling back from a large mess on the rug, but the minute he said it he knew.

"Oh dear," Amanda said. "One of Schrodinger's hair balls."

Donald looked away. He was scientific, it was true. That is to say, at least he was an engineer. In any event, a practical man. But if there is one thing he could not bear to face, it was one of Schrodinger's hair balls. Those large matted regurgitated masses of hair would appear with some frequency in various parts of the house, and Donald, usually barefoot, never failed to encounter one of those damp messes beneath his feet. Amanda would hear an "AGHHH" periodically in the house and she would know he had found one.

"I don't know why there are so many," she said, almost apologetically to Donald after she had scooped it up. "He washes himself a lot and he has long hair, so I guess he gets all this hair in his stomach and he just has to throw up."

"Amanda, please, we are embarked on a glamorous evening," he said. His sharp tone rebuked her.

"Well, he can't help it," she said, fiddling with her bag.

"I know, I know," Hotchkiss said, and they drove on. It was disturbing. To encounter someone or something or even an animal nature as full of character and will as Schrodinger and to find that very personality, at once so strong, mostly in the grip of circumstances and forces beyond itself, well, this was sobering news. It sobered all witnesses to it, as well as Schrodinger himself, and so it was that every time one of them said, "Well, he can't help it," there welled up in all of them this strange mixture of compassion and pity, and somewhere too that faint uneasiness, not untinged with anger, that anything should be in the grip of forces outside itself. In addition to which Amanda had of late this other pressure. She was now prepared to deal with the fact that perhaps Frankenstein wasn't a hallucination, which she would have persuaded herself was the case, if in fact Schrodinger had not been caught In The Act, which is how she and Hotchkiss had come to refer to the drawing incident. But somehow if a cat could draw, then Frankenstein, she felt, could make appearances in the kitchen and machines like copiers could spew out things that were original and had not been copied from anywhere but were receiving electromagnetic printout "orders" from somewhere else. Nonetheless, this was all too nuts to focus on, even for Amanda. So they were going to a party. And they would dance.

What they had not expected at the party was the magician. When Amanda heard there was to be a magician, she supposed, as did everyone else, there would be someone there practiced in the art of illusion who could and would pull rabbits out of hats. She did not expect to find a dark beady-eyed Russian mystic, with eyes full of visions, who would take a special interest in her.

It began simply enough. He asked for a volunteer from the audience for a simple trick. "A lady," he said. "May I have a lady, please," and of course Amanda raised her hand, and of course because he was to some extent a performer, he could not resist her. He did a few things that were amusing but of no great consequence, and then he asked Amanda if she would be willing to do the "dagger" trick, which was not so much a trick as faith in his ability to throw them around her and not at her.

She smiled and said she would. Donald then stood up in the back of the audience and waved to her, as he thought it was not only personally risky but that America's space program would not be delighted with a multimillion-dollar investment fooling around with a magician who threw daggers.

They need not have worried. As Amanda leaned against the case and the magician threw the daggers, which, should they go amiss, were drawn to hidden magnets on the board outlining Amanda's body, a most remarkable thing occurred. It would have gone unwitnessed unless one had very keen powers of observation, which Hotchkiss and the magician both had. Amanda, who had faith, but not that much, closed her eyes so she did not see, but as the magician threw the first dagger it hovered, for just a fraction of a second, but sufficiently long enough to *observe*, it hovered above Amanda's shoulder as if held off by some invisible force, and then dove through to the board behind her. The magician watched, shook his head, and slowly threw the next dagger. The same thing occurred. Hotchkiss was sitting on the edge of his chair. One or two members of the audience had by now picked this up, and assuming it to be part of the magician's magic, were eagerly applauding. The magician was sweating profusely. He had, in all, seven daggers. He only threw two more.

"And now," he said, ending his act quickly, "for the final dagger," which he threw above her head, where it hovered, clearly observable for everyone to see, for at least two seconds before hitting the board with a loud *thunk*. The audience roared and burst into applause.

Amanda, even though she had closed her eyes to forestall the impact, had kept them open for the throw, and she did remember thinking that it took rather a long time for the dagger to travel from the magician's hand to the board. The *thunk* seemed quite late. She wondered briefly at this as she stepped back from the board, the magician taking her hand and stepping forward for a bow. She saw that he was soaking wet, as his hand reached up to take off his tall top hat with a flourish, and that his hair was pressed to his head like seaweed, and his hand, although it held hers in full control of stage aplomb, was trembling. Amanda thought perhaps it was his age, for he was clearly old, and the excitement of the performance, and she returned to her seat smiling. Hotchkiss looked peculiar, she thought.

"What's wrong?" she said.

He stared at her. "Nothing," he said.

It was several minutes later when Amanda and Donald had seated themselves at a small table on the dance floor that the magician came over to speak to them.

Without prelude, he spoke directly to Amanda, "You are possessed of unusual energies—you have been given the gift of seeing what others cannot see. This is a gift of the past, which contains the future in it. The light is blinding, there is terrible fear in it. And sometimes death," the magician said, looking at her sadly.

"Just a minute," Hotchkiss said, intervening. "This is supposed to be a party. We don't want any depressing news around here."

The magician's eyes were dark, and at that moment weary. "Nor do I," he said quietly. "But it remains that there is terrible pain with this sight. Sometimes one averts the eyes rather than see. The light is terrible," he said.

"But you said death," Amanda said quickly, thinking of the Mars flight and what awaited her. "Am I going to die?"

"I said," the magician said, taking her hand, "a part of you might die, rather than see. The vision sometimes is too painful. You will be alive, my dear. You will live out your life, but you may not have access . . ." he rambled off, inconclusively.

"Access to what?" she said nervously. Why was she paying attention to some charlatan at a party, some neurotic, possibly psychotic little man, a burned-out magician from nowhere whose main purpose was entertainment? Because she did not think his main purpose was entertainment. There was something terrible in his eyes for her. It was pity.

"What can I do?" she said, her voice gasping. The magician had laid his hand on her arm, and it was burning.

"You must recover, you must recover," he said urgently. "You must find the lost star."

What was happening between Amanda and the magician was totally unsettling to Hotchkiss. He wanted to pull her from him. As he pulled on her arm, it was like moving granite. She was leashed to the magician now by some powerful force. Everyone in the room had turned to them; although no one could hear what they were saying, the ferocity of the energy between them was clear.

"Where?" Amanda's voice was hollow. "Where is it? Tell me please," she said.

"I do not know," he said, holding her hand, then whispering. "When you love something perfectly, look there." And then he turned away. Amanda, very disconcerted, turned back to Hotchkiss.

"What'd he say to you?" he said irritatedly.

"Oh, you know, some magician-sounding stuff about finding a lost star."

"You look upset."

"There was . . . something about him. I don't think he's a faker," she said. Then suddenly, "Let's dance."

> *According to these unified theories, all the interactions we see in the present world are the asymmetrical remnant of a once perfect symmetrical world. This symmetrical world is revealed only at very high energies, energies so high they will never be accomplished by human beings. The only time that such energies existed was in the first nanoseconds of the big bang which was the origin of the universe.*
> —Heinz Pagels, *The Cosmic Code*

But there was no life until the symmetries were broken. It was sterile. Amanda had written this into her science notebook, wondering as she underlined it, was it true? Was it so? A lost *symmetry*—she hated to think of it as lifeless. . . .

These very thoughts were in her mind as she spun around the dance floor.

While they were dancing, General Farkheimer's wife, who was hosting the party, came up to them and said, "Amanda, I see you've been talking to Mr. Farr, the magician. Isn't he enchanting?"

"Magicians are supposed to be enchanting," Amanda said uneasily. Donald was dancing more slowly now so as to enable them to talk.

"You look wonderful in that dress," Mrs. Farkheimer said admiringly. "It's all silver and red and blue. . . ."

"I think she looks like Superman," Hotchkiss said, smiling. Mrs.

Farkheimer, who had no sense of humor, seemed confused by this. She looked at Amanda. "Oh I don't think so . . . really," she said.

"Where'd you find him, the magician?" Amanda said to her.

"Oh, he's very famous . . . a friend introduced me. He's one of those psychics who helps out the Los Angeles Police Department."

"I thought that was a lot of bull," Donald said.

"Oh no . . . he's been very helpful. He doesn't do murders," she said quickly, which Amanda was somehow relieved to hear. "He helps find lost people, children, runaways—things like that. He's very sweet," Farkheimer's wife said. "And he can do amazing things. He can turn lead into gold. I've seen it, but he refuses to do it as a rule. He says it will ruin the economy. It's too bad about his problem," she added.

"What problem?" Amanda said.

"He can only do halves."

"Halves? What do you mean, halves?"

"Halves of tricks," she said. "He can pull rabbits out of hats, as long as someone else puts them there. It was so embarrassing. Once I saw him looking for the rabbit that he had hidden and he couldn't find it. They never found it," she said wonderingly.

"Well," Amanda said, annoyed, "they must have found it eventually." She was thinking about this problem.

Mrs. Farkheimer shook her head. "Never. Never found it."

Amanda had noticed during the card trick that it was strange that the assistant came in when it was time to produce the card. It seemed to take the assistant quite a long time to *find* the card. Amanda had concluded that they simply didn't have their act together. However, this smacked of something more.

"I thought he was so good at finding lost things," she said. Donald wasn't listening. He was talking with the bandleader.

"Oh, he is, he is, as long as other people lose them." She was shaking her head. "Anything he loses himself, like his keys? Never finds them."

"Oh," Amanda said, feeling some sympathy, but not actually too much.

Amanda was suddenly and inexplicably thinking about Hooper as they left the dance floor and headed toward a table. Suddenly, loud and clear she heard his voice: "Remember, it is all happening, Amanda, but no one will believe you." What was it? Was it, she wondered, that

Hooper had *died* because no one believed him? Was Hooper's death, then, from what he had seen and no one had believed?

The magician had said, "You must find the lost star." What was he talking about, she wondered.

As they started to sit down, the magician, Mr. Farr, passed their table. He was carrying his rabbit in a case. The rabbit was eating a carrot.

"Look, how do you know all this?" Amanda said, suddenly irritated at what she was trying to dismiss as the mumbo-jumbo tradition in the face of profound anxiety. "There's no reason I should pay any attention to you. You're just being opportunistic and trying to frighten me!"

He looked at her then sadly, and she saw that the magician did not have an unkind face. "Perhaps I am wrong," he said, shrugging. "You are quite right. I do not really *know*. It is what I feel," he shrugged. "I feel you are already *afraid* because of what you see. I am not trying to scare you at all. You have felt it from the first, when you have had unexpected helpers in your kitchen drying dishes." He smiled sympathetically and Amanda dropped her wine glass.

"My God, I've had too much to drink," she said, turning to Hotchkiss.

"You only had one glass," he said, amazed. He did not hear the remark.

"That was too much," she said, and she took off for the terrace. Did the magician know about Frankenstein, or was it mere coincidence? She was shaking when Hotchkiss found her by the wall.

"What's the matter?" he said. "Did he upset you?" Amanda said nothing; perhaps the magician had seen fear in her eyes.

She turned quickly to Hotchkiss, whispering, "Look into my eyes, quickly."

Smiling, he bent forward. "Much obliged," he said, trying to kiss her.

"Donald, this is serious!" she said. "What do you see?" she asked. "Do you see anything?"

Donald Hotchkiss looked into Amanda's eyes.

"No," he said, "I don't see anything." Then looking closer into their turquoise, aquamarine depths, deep into the pupils, he saw it. First he lost his breath looking at the left eye, then he looked into the right eye.

"What is it?" Amanda said.

Hotchkiss had turned pale. He looked again.

"My God," he said.

"What is it, Donald? What is it?" she said.

"Nothing," he said, stepping back, trying to gain his composure.

"It is something. What is it?" she said, whipping out her compact from her purse. In the dim light of the moon she stared into the mirror. Her marine-blue eyes stared back, and there, deep in the center of the dark pupil, a spinning light, as if it were coming from the farthest reaches of the galaxy, but there was no mistaking it. Firmly planted on her right eye, the smallest signal, bright and fading, bright again—there was no mistaking it: Z^0.

"AGHHH," Amanda screamed, and the compact dropped. "Oh God, there's a quark in my eye! Donald!" She continued to scream. "Do something—do something!"

He stared at her dumbfounded. Speechless. Immobilized. Truth to tell he didn't know what to do. A quark in the eye? Whoever heard of such insanity? No one could *see* a quark, for God's sake, so how could it be in your eye?

"Well," he said mumbling, looking for a Kleenex, "does it hurt?"

"NO!" Amanda was screaming. "IT DOESN'T HURT, YOU IDIOT, BUT GET IT OUT!"

"Don't call me an idiot," Donald said, his defenses rising under the assault. "Well, if it doesn't hurt, just leave it there for a while," he offered.

"Leave it there? You can't leave it there," she said. "I can't go around with a quark in my eye . . . you want people to think I'm weird or something?" She was positively screaming at him. A few people at the far end of the terrace had gathered about and were staring at them. One or two would venture to intervene and then stopped, uncertain as to whether it was a lovers' quarrel or a real dilemma. Amanda was crying. Hotchkiss was more or less beside himself. He did not like to see her like this.

"Amanda," he said gently, "I . . . I'm sorry . . . I . . . I'll try to get it out. Here, have a Kleenex."

Then in the midst of her crying, she began to laugh. Hotchkiss thought she might be cracking up, she was laughing and crying so hard. "Ohhh nooo," she gasped. "You're going to get it out with a Kleenex.

Oooooo, I can't bear it," and she collapsed over the side of the terrace, holding her sides.

By now the little group watching them had shrugged and moved inside. That girl was acting very nutty, they all agreed. One said that she looked to him like the hysterical type. To him, all women with tits looked hysterical. Another said she was a scientist of some sort and they were all crazy anyway. One of the women said she knew what was going on all right. She said Hotchkiss was clearly a married man. She could tell by the way he walked, and she had heard Amanda say, "This can't go on anymore." That was what they all said to married men, the lady said. Personally she found it shocking and disgraceful, two of her favorite *secret* things, not that she would ever admit it, of course. She just said "*tch tch*," and together the little group clucked inside.

In the car on the way home, Amanda said, "How long do you figure they lasted?"

"What?" Donald said uneasily, although of course he knew exactly what she was talking about.

"The quarks, Donald. What do you think?" she said. She knew she sounded bitchy, but she was annoyed. There were certain moments when Hotchkiss disappointed her. Removing a quark with a Kleenex— the idea was positively idiotic. She had told him so.

"What do you want, Amanda?" he had roared at her. "You want me to roll out a cyclotron?"

That had shut her up. She didn't know exactly what she did want him to do. She just thought the Kleenex was idiotic, that was all.

"The quarks? How long did they last?" he said, driving very fast. "Oh, about two minutes, I'd say."

"You realize," she said, "that that is incredibly *long*." She must have been very nervous. She was smoking, he saw.

"Yes, of course I realize it's long. . . . They're only supposed to last a billionth of a billionth of a second, but you also realize, Amanda, that you can't see one; there is no such thing as a visible quark. I mean, you can measure it with maybe ten trillion dollars' worth of supersensitive equipment, if you're at CERN or something, but it doesn't just pop up in somebody's eye like that." He seemed very annoyed.

"Donald," Amanda said, "stop yelling at me." Then she started to cry. Hotchkiss endured the crying. Not a whit of sympathy would he give her, although part of him—he told himself it was just a teeny part—

did begin to feel sad. He knew why she was crying. She wasn't crying because he yelled at her.

"I can't bear it," she finally wailed. "I just can't bear being so weird. Do you realize, Donald, how weird I am getting? I mean, I am just becoming one weirdness after another, and I can't bear it." She was crying fiercely now, all over her blouse and her pocketbook. He gave her a fresh Kleenex.

"Come on, Amanda," he said, not knowing what else to do, "you're not that weird."

"NOT THAT WEIRD?" she screamed at him. "You don't call a person WEIRD who sees Frankenstein in her kitchen? In her kitchen, Donald? Who gets quarks in her eyes? Z-zero showing up on her eyeballs? Who has a cat that draws? Draws, Donald . . . you saw it, a cat that draws pictures? Ohhhhh," she wailed into the Kleenex, and Hotchkiss sighed, driving more slowly now. What was the rush? What was he to say? There was nothing he could say. She was right. It *was* weird all right. Weird as hell. It was, in fact, he imagined, the absolutely weirdest, weirdest thing that had ever happened to anybody, ever. Finally he said, "Well, it's not *your* fault," knowing the minute he said it this was a mistake. It was after all small comfort.

"Of course it's not my fault!" Amanda screamed at him again. "How could it be my *fault*? How could I put quarks in my own eyes?"

She cried again into a ball of Kleenex, and Hotchkiss felt simply terrible. There was nothing to say. There was nothing to do. He was at a loss. Not only was he at a loss, he was also, in some way, deeply impressed. *Very* impressed. He and Amanda were probably the only two people in the history of anything who had ever *seen* a quark, and the remarkable thing was, of course, that the quark came in its symbol, as Z^0. That was really odd. Like water appearing as H_2O. Which meant, of course, that they hadn't actually seen the quark so much as the representation of it. For, after all, a person looking at water saw thin liquidy stuff; they didn't see letters and numbers. So actually, Hotchkiss reasoned, they hadn't seen a quark at all.

He explained this to Amanda. It seemed to make her feel better, which he thought it would, although he didn't know exactly why.

It was a week later when the decision came down, based on secret information from the CIA, that the Russians were planning to launch a Mars manned vehicle in a month, that Amanda would have to be ready to launch *immediately*. That meant in one *week*. That furthermore, Amanda's launch would now be classified top secret, as a military experiment, and all publicity was to be kept under wraps, no information to be released until after the event.

The decision came down on Thursday. On Friday morning Farkheimer decided to order Amanda Jaworski to appear in his office on Saturday morning at 0900. He would tell her then she had five days until launch. No question but it could be handled. Farkheimer had carefully gone over all the reports with all the leading personnel, and there was no reason that every system had to be checked another hundred times. They were given orders by the president of the United States to "go," and "go" they would. They would employ top security. They would not even have Amanda moved to the base site until the night before. That way nobody would be suspicious. Farkheimer had almost decided to call Jaworski and her copilot over that night, but he looked out at the weather. It was raining and the wind was up; perhaps a storm was coming. The weather had been peculiar lately. No need to have an astronaut driving out in a storm. Accidents always did happen. Besides, Jaworski drove too fast in that damn car. He would wait until tomorrow. He'd call her himself at 0700 and ask her to report.

40

The Gott model attempts to account for two odd facts about our universe that trouble many cosmologists. One of these is that while the basic equations of physics are time-symmetrical, that is, they can be run forward or backward in time with equal efficacy—in the real universe time, it seems, moves in one direction only. . . . Acting on a clue offered by theoretical physicists who maintain that antimatters can be thought of as ordinary matter moving in reverse time, Gott constructed his three universe cosmology. He suggests that the big bang generated not only our universe, but also a second universe composed of antimatter and evolving in reverse time, as well as a third universe made up exclusively of particles that travel faster than light. The fleet particles of this ghostly third universe, called tachyons, are permissible under relativity theory, which requires only that nothing in our universe can be accelerated to the velocity of light; tachyons need not worry about this provision for they have always been going faster than the speed of light. They occupy a mirror universe where everything travels faster than light and nothing can be reined to a velocity as slow as light.

—Timothy Ferris, *Galaxies*

There were terrible electrical storms. The sky was green and snaking with white lightning streaks. The thunder was terrible. Amanda was wakened in the middle of the night. Schrodinger was on her bed, mewing.

"What is it, Schrodinger?" she said, trying to rouse herself. Then she heard and she saw. The sky was emerald green and it was the middle of the night.

"My God," she said, grabbing Schrodinger and going toward the window. Just then the thunder rolled, and with a great crash, streaks of lightning split the sky. It lit up the entire room, and for a minute, Amanda thought the house had been hit.

There were reverberations underneath her feet, and to her utter frustration, in the midst of all this, Schrodinger had once again passed out, cold.

"God, Schrodinger, what a time to have a fit," she said, carrying him to the other room and laying him in his basket. Just to be sure she bent down and listened to his heartbeat. To make sure it was there. It was there all right, but he must have gotten scared because it was going fast, very fast, faster than she had ever heard. Good grief, she thought, I hope he isn't going to have a heart attack. The wind had come up now, and Amanda ran to the windows in the bedroom, which were casement windows; they kept slamming shut with each breeze and then blowing out again. It was whistling now, a terrible whistling sound had taken over; the trees in the yard were bent over, and she could see their branches touching the ground. She calculated the wind had to be moving at nearly fifty miles an hour to be bending the trees like that, and she saw things—leaves, paper, weeds—traveling past the windows. She wondered if she should take Schrodinger and go into the basement. She was looking out the window, trying to assess the weather—it seemed to be approaching hurricane force; certainly there had been no warnings—when suddenly the lights blinked on and off and she heard the dishwasher, the blender, the entire kitchen whirring: the electric can opener and the garbage disposal were going, the coffeepot was perking, the fan was on, the lights were on, the toaster was popping, the radio was on, the TV was blaring. Her watch was whirring; she looked at the chronograph, and the hands were swirling, the dates were revolving at high speed—23, 24, 25, 26, 27; within ten seconds, they were through July and heading for August.

"Good heavens," Amanda said, overwhelmed. Schrodinger was sitting up in his basket. She caught him up in her arms and ran to the windows. The clocks were going crazy, they were spinning and spinning; even the digital was whirling through seconds, days, and hours. The lights were glowing brighter and brighter in the house so that she thought all the bulbs were going to explode, and then outside she saw the tricycle, Tommy Taylor's tricycle, the three-year-old kid next door; she saw his bike back up out of his garage and, pedals spinning faster and faster, move toward her house. The tricycle was moving across the lawn with uncommon speed, moving so fast its pedals were a blur. My God, if the wind were that fast! She raced into the other room, and was opening the door to the basement when she saw it.

The tricycle.

She stood there holding Schrodinger and her breath.

It was coming toward them, the tricycle. It was coming straight at them *through* the window, and the window was not *breaking*; the window was opening around the shape of the tricycle like a water wave, and in seconds the tricycle flew through the window, over the sofa, and landed, dripping wet, on her living-room rug. The window was intact.

Schrodinger awakened with a yell. By now everything was blinking on and off, and Amanda's watch, she noticed, had gone to December. Schrodinger once again passed out. As she stared at the dripping bike, she first heard a sizzle, like a drop of water on a hot frying pan, and the sizzle got hotter and hotter, and then Amanda stood there transfixed, as from the top of the tricycle seat, from the sizzle, a dim light began to shine. From this sizzling light came a funny crackling voice. A sort of Donald Duckish–sounding voice.

"Hi, toots, I'm getting dressed; wait'll I get visible; these duds are the cat's meow; this'll put cream in your coffee, sugar lips."

Amanda, in the face of this, was understandably quite speechless. She looked about. "Sugar lips?" Was it a radio show from the thirties or what? The light on the tricycle seat was brighter now.

"I'm gaining visibility; hang on, hot pants, here I come . . . hold on to your scanties and away we gooo," sang the voice, and then as she looked, there on the tricycle seat a blur emerged, a rapidly spinning blur that spewed forth Donald Duckish noises and was now slowing down somewhat so that she could see more clearly what it was. She had picked Schrodinger up and was holding him tightly. Schrodinger had wisely, once again, chosen not to regain consciousness at this time.

"Holy shit," she said under her breath. From a historical point of view, these words were undeniably a precise description of earlier instances of such phenomena.

There on the tricycle seat, slowly emerging out of the blur, was a . . . a . . . a . . . When Hotchkiss would ask her about it later, that would be the best that she could do. "It was a thing," she would say, "sort of a blob with arms and legs, and it talked."

That is what she would say later. For the time being she couldn't say anything. She simply stared, as there on the seat of the tricycle the thing grew visible, a funny thing: a sort of large-ish squashy-looking porcupine with beady eyes and a five-foot antenna rising from its head looked at her.

"Hi, sugar dumples, sorry for the inconveniences of materialization. I'm not adept at this frequency, and I got no notice, no notice at all." The voice sounded the way a tape recorder does when it's speeded up, on the wrong speed.

Amanda stood there, clutching Schrodinger.

"Whoops, I've got to lower my speed," the voice-thing said, and then it seemed it got slower or something, the voice sounded more human. Then the thing reached up and pulled the antenna down, compressed it into some kind of hole on the side of its head where an ear would be, normally.

"Sorry, sugar, my antenna should not have been up; knocks your household currents all to hell."

Amanda was saying to herself, Wow, this is a really powerful fantasy. To the thing she said, her voice breathless, "My watch . . . my watch says December."

"Yeah I know, sugar," the voice was going Donald Duckish at high speed again. "I don't have the hang of this frequency yet . . . this universe is not my usual beat . . . I'm filling in."

"Filling in . . ." she said. ". . . universe . . . what universe are you from?"

"Not so fast, sugar lips," the thing said, spinning neatly off the tricycle.

The thing was off the tricycle now, and was, of all things, mopping up the floor with a rag.

"What are you doing?" she said exasperated. She was still holding Schrodinger, who was awake now and crying.

"I'm drying the floor. Can't you see what I'm doing?"

"Well yes, I can see it, but I wonder."

"Stop wondering. There is nothing to cause wonder about in drying a wet floor. Save wonder for something important."

"What I'm *wondering*," Amanda said, "is how you did that."

"Did what?" it said, turning to look at her and blinking.

"Came through the window glass like that, on the tricycle." She sounded stunned.

"I didn't come through the *glass*, stupid; now you know you can't come through glass without breaking it."

"Well I know, but, but . . ."

"But what? The bike is wet, isn't it, dollface? Wet. As in H_2O, as in water. I turned the window into water so I could come through it. Sorry about the floor." It continued to mop.

"Well," Amanda said slowly, "that's what I mean—however did you do *that*?"

"Do what?" It turned to her impatiently. "Turn the window to water? You mean you don't know how to do *that*, you don't even know the basic principle of *that*?" Its hands, if that's what they were, were on its hips, if that's what *they* were, and it was sneering at her.

"No," she said slowly. "No, that's what I'm asking you."

The thing seemed to have a booklet. It was looking something up. "What's that?"

"Guide to Universe One," it said, its voice speeding up again. It reached up and adjusted its antenna. "Oh damn, I can't get the frequency right. . . . Let's see, no you don't know how to do that here, I see . . . as far as you've gotten is turning water into steam or into ice. Hmmm." It closed the book and looked at her. "This is real doltsville, all right. I would never have come if I hadn't been sent by Rastus—he never gives advance notice—I hate coming here. 'Course I haven't been here in a million years."

"You don't say," Amanda said, her curiosity struck. "Well, why don't you tell me how you do it."

"Do what?" it said, wringing out the rag in a perfectly normal manner. Maybe it didn't know anything special after all, she thought. Otherwise it would know how to dry the rag out without wringing.

"Tell me how you turn glass into water."

"Oh ho ho ho, oh no you don't, not so fast, smarty pants—that is a SECRET SECRET SECRET," it started to scream.

"Why is it a secret, for heaven's sake?" she said.

"Because it is. The universe has secrets, that's why. And that's one of them. Oh frankly, I wouldn't care, you know. I'd show you how to do it, but Rastus says that's a no-no."

"A no-no?" Amanda said, screwing up her face. Then she laughed, despite herself.

"Well, let's put it this way. You wouldn't understand it anyway. Not on your level." It looked at her with utter disdain. "Besides," it said, "I'm not telling you anything because you don't like the way I look."

"Well," she said, "I've never seen anything that looks like you . . . but I'm getting used to it." She was bribing it, hoping to get the secret.

The thing said, "The reason I look like this is not that I do in fact look like this but that I had to assume some material reality, something, some aspect of visibility in order for you to deal with me, so I picked up a few things here and there—couple arms, appendages, eyes, nose, you know, the stuff you need to see to think something's talking to you— picked up a mind-set passing through Chicago and I put it together myself. What do you think?" it said, spinning around and twirling the wet rag in its hand. "Pretty nifty, wouldn't you say?"

"You're dripping it on the sofa now," Amanda said, "and no, I don't think it's 'nifty.' I think you're weird looking."

"Weird?"

"Yeah, weird. Definitely."

"Oh," it said, "I thought this was what you called individualistic."

"Oh," Amanda said, reconsidering, "I suppose you could call it that too, but you're definitely weird. You're not credible."

"Not *credible*. Well that won't do at all. I mean I must have credibility. Without credibility we won't get anywhere, not the two of us."

Amanda stepped back toward the wall. She wasn't at all sure she wanted to get anywhere. She was wondering actually what to do. She wished she thought she were dreaming, but when she went to look in her bed, she saw she was up. So dreaming was out. She decided to make coffee. Coffee was a good thing to do. Schrodinger jumped out of her arms and hid under the bed. His tail was sticking straight out from under the bed: Amanda figured he'd had one of his fits under there. So that meant *something* definitely was happening.

When she went to make the coffee, there it was, the thing, on the edge of her sink.

"Oh," she stepped back startled. "How did you get here?"

"I materialized over here," it said simply. "Look, are you getting me? Are you getting this? You seem very incredulous. You're not supposed to be incredulous, you know. You're supposed to be more developed than you are. Go with the flow, you know?" It spun around on the sink.

"I wish you'd stop spinning like that," Amanda said.

"I'm a *subparticle*, sugar lips, I've got to spin," and it spun again.

"You're not a subparticle," Amanda said. "Don't be ridiculous. A subparticle is invisible. I couldn't possibly see one." She paused. "Although I actually did see the symbol for one once."

"Don't tell *me*, young lady. Don't tell *me*," the thing said, highly annoyed. "I know *you* can't see a subparticle, but I am a subparticle, so if anything knows its degree of material reality, it is the thing itself, right?"

"Er, well, I suppose," Amanda said, wondering why she was even having a discussion with this person, subparticle, whatever it was, much less a philosophical one.

"Well I did what I could on such short notice. I picked up all this stuff *you* need to understand things—signs of visibility, anthropomorphizing my essence to the *hilt*—arms, legs, head. I thought," it said spinning, "I was good-looking."

"No," Amanda said. "You're not good-looking."

"Look here," it said, jumping up right on her chest. Amanda screamed and stepped back.

"Aghh," she said. "You're gooey!" It was sticky, the thing, like raw dough.

"Of course I'm gooey, what do you think? Aren't you ready for me?" it said. "I guess not. You're supposed to be ready for me. None of this incredulous business. I left the damn molecules here. You're supposed to have assimilated them. Supposed to be all ready. All I have to do is move in and explain a few things. . . . But you're not ready, not ready as far as I can see at all." The thing began pacing up and down her sink. It seemed to like the sink.

Amanda had an incongruous thought: Why does everything happen in the kitchen?

"Look," she said, getting angry, "I don't know who or what you are, but I want you out of here right now." That seemed like a good position to take. Firm.

"Well now . . . little miss hot stuff, you just hold your horses. I took a good look at you, I eyeballed you, cupcake, and I can see you're missing some molecules. That's the problem, sugar lips."

"Sugar lips!" This time Amanda laughed. "Good grief . . . don't call me sugar lips. . . ." Then she looked suspiciously at the blob. "Where'd you learn to talk like that?"

"Talk, talk like this, sweet face? Harry Piranski, Chicago, 1930. He was just rising as I passed over. I picked up his vibrations, his aura, so to speak. Never mind, I'll explain it later. Anyway I picked up his aura over Chicago."

"Who's Harry Piranski?" she said.

"Don't know. He was rising when I flew over, so I picked up his aura. I needed an aura, honey doll, and I got his. He . . . you know, what do you call it here?" It pulled out a little book.

"What's that?" she said.

"A guidebook," it said. "To Universe One. That's here. You call it here . . ."—its finger went down the page—"you call it passing on, death, gone to the other side, met his maker—shall I go on?"

"No, no, I know what you mean. Harry Piranski was dying in Chicago when you went over it, is that what you're saying?"

"No, his spirit was rising. He died in 1930. Sometimes it takes years to free the spirit. He just happened to be on that wavelength as I was coming in. Had a lot of purple in it. I like purple wavelengths, at least as far as this planet goes. Makes it easier."

"What *are* you doing?" she said, grabbing its hands. It was eating her dish drainer.

"I'm famished . . . famished, famished, famished," it said.

"Well don't eat the dish drainer. . . . What do you eat?" she said suspiciously.

"Anything . . . everything . . . I got the stomach from a goat."

"Oh, was the goat in Chicago too?" Amanda said, feeling faintly suspicious of the entire matter.

"Peoria, Peoria, the goat was in Peoria. Look, you can't be too critical. This was a last-minute entry. We have an emergency up there. I had to take what I could get." The thing, whatever it was, Amanda noted, certainly wasn't lacking in ego. It said, "But I thought I had panache. Don't I have panache?" it said, spinning the other way.

"Certainly not," Amanda said. "How come Piranski knows the word *panache*?"

"Had a French girl friend once. Colette. Best pair of gams this side of heavensville. It's the only French word he knows. Oh, also *voilà*. *Voilà!*" it said, spinning again.

"So you have his brain, is that it?" she said, trying to get it.

"His mind, stupid, stupid, STUPID," it shouted at her. "I have his mind. You can't get into this region on my wavelength without an earth mind . . . but I have my own brain. Brain is all electricity. I have my own."

"Subparticles can't have brains," Amanda said. "They're subatomic particles. They have no biological components."

"BULLSHIT!" the thing screamed at her. "BULLSHIT! We have spin, we have charge; that's what a brain is, just an accumulation of spin, mass, and charge."

"You don't have mass," Amanda said, whispering. "Don't tell me. I'm a physicist. I know."

"You don' know SHIT, toots," it said. "I'm magic."

"Don't you mean charmed? Are you supposed to be a charmed particle?"

"Don't tell me, hot lips. I know what I am. Magic. Magic. Which simply means you won't be able to handle the explanation until 3003."

"Try me," Amanda said, getting annoyed.

"Okay, I'll let you have it, but pay attention, because you only get it once. I transmute."

"What?"

"Trans-mute. Trans-substantiation. Trans-portation. I do everything that has to do with trans—move across, change, motion. I turn water into glass, glass into heat. I can take molecules from one place, move them to another place." It snapped its fingers. "Just like that. But look, all explanations are hopeless. I looked into your eyes: you're missing molecules. The IMPORTANT molecules. Very confusing. Mistake somewhere; I don't know how it happened, but until I figure it out the best thing to do is think of me as a process—that is, until I get your molecules straightened out."

"STOP THAT. What are you doing?" Amanda said. This thing, whatever it was, was yelling as it overturned everything in her living room.

"WHERE ARE MY MOLECULES?"

"How the hell would I know?" Amanda said. "I can't see molecules, you know."

"Of course *you* can't, but *I* can, and I can't see them. I mean I can see them, but they're not here, so where are they, I ask you?"

"I really couldn't say," Amanda said coolly.

"Well, miss, I suggest you better say." The creature started eating her chair.

"WHAT ARE YOU DOING?" she screamed, pulling the chair away. "That's an antique."

"I know how old it is. It's not as old as you think." The creature spat out part of the leg. "They told you it's two hundred years old— baloney, you got taken. That wood's only one hundred years old, it was—"

"It's Queen Anne. It has to be two hundred years old."

"It was a knockoff, sweetheart, a hundred years later. You think it's a new concept, knockoffs? As a matter of fact," he turned to her, "you're a knockoff."

"You mean knockout," she said proudly.

"Knockoff, dummy. Knockoff. You're not original. No sir. All *Homo sapiens* big mistake. Wrong molecular reactions. Mutations. Bad imitations. Knockoffs."

"What was the original that I'm imitating?"

"Not in this world, sweetheart. Not on your life. You don't get that answer until 5001. There were symmetries here before you even arrived. Of course they weren't alive, so to speak. There was no life force. With the knockoffs came the life force. But you lost other things. You win some, you lose some."

"What *are* you?" she said impatiently.

"I, my dear, am currently a tachyon—part of the original primal ooze, as it were. An extremely elusive tachyon. I can transmute, become anything I want."

"You can't . . . tachyons don't exist," Amanda said. "No one's ever seen one—they're strictly theoretical."

"I exist, baby. Of course no one's seen one. You get the first peek," it said, spinning around, and then it started to sing, "Jeepers, creepers, where'd you get those peepers."

"I'd like to know where you got that song!" Amanda said, astonished.

"I told you, this guy named Harry comes from Chicago, picked him on the way down, picked his brains, that is, grabbed his lingo on my transmitter. That was on my way here to zap your frequency. Look, I don't have time to explain things. I'm here on borrowed time."

"Borrowed time?" she said. She was thinking about the phrase *zapped your frequency*. She didn't think she liked having her frequency zapped.

"Yep, they borrowed me from the other universe, sped me right into here. You'll recognize me eventually. You know me as old stuff, not new stuff. I'm part of the original soup, sugar dumples, yessir sir, the original quagmire, the hydrogen-helium slush, the great bombast out of which you all came; I am one of the originals, one of the great high temperature originals. I was there at Kelvin ten trillion—a Piece of the Original Action—the P.O.A."

"P.O.A.s," Amanda said, although why she was saying anything at all she would wonder about later. Kelvin ten trillion. Kelvin ten trillion was when the universe was three nanoseconds* old.

"Oh," Amanda cried suddenly, spotting her rocker. "My antique rocker, look what you did!" The rockers were gone.

"I ate them," said the Ooze. "I'm famished. Don't worry, it will be all returned to you. I mean, I don't know when, this millennium probably. You know, it will just reappear."

"But I loved that chair," Amanda said.

"Just molecular prejudice. You liked the molecules aggregated in that way, so you have to like them aggregated another way."

"But I don't see them aggregated at all," Amanda said. "I just see a broken chair, and ooze."

"That's because you haven't gotten into the higher powers."

*A nanosecond is a billionth of a second.

"Oh great," Amanda groaned. "What are they?"

"In the higher powers you would be able to see that the chair was just a time-spatial aggregate, you would be able to see other aggregates as well, and you would be so interested you would never have the time to mourn about the chair."

"Do you think I'm mourning?" Amanda said, shocked.

"Yes," the Ooze said, spotting some saltines and devouring them, paper and all. "All *Homo sapiens* mourn. It's a pain in the neck, this frequency. I loathe it."

"This what?"

"This frequency. The earth–*Homo sapiens* frequency. Anything's better than them. Dolphins, whales, any other kind of mammals. Homos are a drag. Besides, the ones who live in the West, like you, always have too much plastic. Never anything to eat."

"Why do you need to eat?" Amanda said. "You don't have a metabolic process, do you?"

"Don't be stupid. At least make an *effort* not to be any stupider than you already are. Of course I have a digestive process. I have a million processes. It's just not *your* process. I process everything—thoughts, ideas, saltines, bird's eggs—you name it."

"I don't think this can be happening," Amanda said.

"I also process that—denial. I sent you the thought. I could see you couldn't carry the conflict."

"What?" Amanda said. "Look, what do you think this is? You think this is billiards? This isn't billiards. We're talking about my mind, reality, what's happening."

"That's what it is to you," said the Ooze. "But to me, baby, it's billiards."

Amanda laughed despite herself. "Good grief! How can it be billiards?" She thought it hilarious that this green ooze slipping over the sides of her sink had said *baby*.

"I know your love of lingo. I zeroed right in your cellular orientation. I could make you happy, maybe." The first sign of uncertainty struck the creature.

"How?" she said.

"I'm not saying I can, for sure." The thing, whatever it was, had opened the refrigerator, and although it didn't get any bigger, everything in the refrigerator—oranges, pears and apples—was disappearing.

"Are you processing my apples and pears?"

"Yes, yes, yes," the Ooze said.

"At least you could tell me where you're *from*."

"No problem. I'm from Epsilon Erdani," the creature said. "At least that's my current location."

Amanda stared. "That's ridiculous. That's millions of light-years away."

"Hmmf," the thing said, eating a head of lettuce. "The way *you* go, slowpoke, of course it's millions of light-years away. . . . This refrigerator is terrible, as bad as California. . . ." It was hurling things out onto the floor.

"Look," Amanda said, "I don't know what this has to do with California. This is Texas, and you've got to stop throwing this stuff on the floor."

"Plastic, plastic, the whole damn territory is plastic. The number of biodegradables here is low . . . very low . . . oh well, what's it matter . . . you're doomed anyway, you're all doomed, doomed, doomed, doomed." It started singing the word *doomed*.

"What do you mean, doomed? Now stop that and explain yourself," Amanda said. Then looking at it—"How do I know you're from Epsilon Erdani?"

"Check out your shit, sweetheart," it said. Amanda winced. "Your spectrointerferometry, or whatever gadgets you've got: you'll find my space buggy crossing last night; you'll pick it up as red light, blue light, red light. One of those dodos down there ought to be able to pick *that* up at least." It reached for a banana. "Fruit, fruit, love tropical fruit . . . great fruit on this turf, that's why you're doomed, of course. . . ."

"Doomed . . . what is this doomed . . . ?" Amanda said, feeling uneasy.

"You blew it, hot lips. Of course not you personally." It turned and looked at her, and then wiggled across the floor. " 'Course you didn't do anything about stopping it either."

"Stopping what?"

"The whole place is about to blow sky high. You've wrecked it. The whole planet's going to pot . . . your number's up soon."

"What number?"

"You're blowing species here . . . doesn't go over out there. The

GCB hates it. Hates it like hell. It's a lot of work to evolve this stuff, you know. Doesn't happen overnight, you know."

"I know how long evolution takes," Amanda said, impatiently. "Please get to the point."

"The point is, big tits." Well, she thought, at least it's observant. "You're interfering with biological time. The boss doesn't like it."

"What?"

"Oh God," it said, slamming a fist—or what appeared to be a fist—down on the counter. "I hate, I absolutely hate talking to people with only one molecule. I mean it takes so long . . . they're so thick!"

"I'm not thick," Amanda said, wanting to sock it in the jaw, that is if it had a jaw. It seemed actually sort of blubbery to sock. It was like goo. Thick viscous goo.

"You're thick, blondie, face it. You're better than most, but holding only one molecule there's only so much you can grasp. Anyway, the point is this, which I will explain ONCE MORE only," it said. "When a species's number is up, the GCB fixes it evolutionarily. You know, he knocks out the food supply, he introduces a mutation, he changes the distribution in the flora; whatever he does he does. Then *you* go in there and start interfering and *you* decide what will survive. Well, he doesn't like it! You knock off the bald eagles, you knock out the white tigers, you destroy the speckled bear. Oh hell's bells, there's zillions of species you've made it impossible for: you poisoned the water, you let the radiation into the earth—oh *you* know. Burns him up. You know, burns him right up. You're messing it up. To tell you the truth, I'm fed up myself. There have been times in the past when I've been tempted, tempted, tempted."

"Tempted to do what?" Amanda asked.

"To throw it to the monkeys. Knock off sapiens and give it back to the apes."

"Oh, don't do that," Amanda said.

"Well, the GCB is fed up, toots. You kids have had it down here; he's giving it all over to the robots."

"He's giving what exactly over to the robots?"

The thing looked at her evenly. It was eating a can of tuna fish. Can and all.

"How can you eat the can?" she said, wondering.

"Goat's stomach, I *told* you—your memory cells are *lousy*. Picked up Piranski's brain and a goat's stomach. Guy outside of Chicago had a farm full of goats."

"What's he giving to the robots and who is he, God?"

"God?" The thing laughed, or at least it shook and made sounds. "Oh my, you people have a lot going on down here, heavy terminology. Very anthropomorphic. Divine Presence—I know about it. Very inventive. You could call him God if you want, but he doesn't fit your concept of that category."

"Who is he? What is he?"

"He, she—what's the difference? It's the *Great Cosmic Brain*. GCB runs out of an electron field in Universe Two. Was his idea, Earth. Started the whole thing . . ." It looked at her. "You don't know about GCB?"

"Well . . ." she said tentatively. My, she was feeling defensive in the presence of this thing. "We, many of us, feel there is an intelligence of some order at work. Some people ascribe religious qualities to this, they worship it . . . they call it God and that sort of thing. There are a lot of religions here . . . and some people don't know what caused the earth to form . . . we're still figuring it out."

"Oh my," it said, sitting up on the sink, "you *are* underdeveloped. Seriously underdeveloped." It stared at her. "I've got to get at least one more molecule into you before I can even *begin* to deal with this." It hopped off the sink. "GCB, sweet patootie, made the Earth; partly it was an accident. He was out there making something and everything in Universes One and Two was taking bets."

"Bets?" Amanda said. "Do you have money?"

"You don't need money to make bets," it said impatiently. "But just button up those rose petals and let me roll out my rap," it said. "He was spinning the stuff, the primal stuff, and heating it, and we all thought he was going to get something good. You know, he's done most of the work in this universe and this was going to be different, but something happened, not even GCB knows exactly, there's no accounting for random error and well, it just turned out like Earth. And he's crazy about it. Nuts. So is everybody else. They've all been trying to get it from him for zillions of eons I guess you would call it. Anyway, he's disgusted with you. He's ready to turn it over."

"Over to who?" Amanda said. Her heart had knotted tight as a fist inside her.

"Got me," it said. "Either the Reds or the Blues. You're up for grabs. 'Course everybody wants a piece of Earth, but I think one of them is going to get it."

"Don't they have their own place?" Amanda said worriedly.

" 'Course they have. They have gizillions of places . . . but there's only one like this."

"Wait a minute," Amanda said. "Statistically they've figured out that in this galaxy alone there are other stars sufficiently similar to our sun to conceivably support an earthlike body traveling around them. And of the zillions of other galaxies, there must be one other like this . . . at least one. . . ." Her voice was soft. "Isn't there?"

The thing was holding its hands over its ears and shaking its head. "I can't believe *this* . . . don't you even know that? Don't you know ANYTHING?" it screamed. "Of course there are other *systems*, communication systems *and* chemical *systems*, but there is no other biological system. This is the only place where there are biological systems." It paused then and stared at her, blinking. "What you call life. Look, my time is nearly up, and I don't know what went wrong. Things are not supposed to go wrong. Not on this level at any rate." He seemed extremely irritated. At her, no less.

"Well, don't look at me. It's not my fault," Amanda said defensively.

"Well, it is most definitely your fault. I left these molecules here, for you. There's no one else here. You were supposed to have assimilated them by now. You were to be ready for this trip. Mentally ready, you understand." He looked at her. "This is really a rotten piece of luck. You're not ready. You've got one of the molecules, but I left three. What happened to the other two?"

"How would I know?"

"Well you *wouldn't*," it said. "Not with only one molecule you wouldn't. In fact, with one molecule you're practically useless. I don't know what we're going to do now," the thing said. "You're supposed to have assimilated these prior to takeoff."

"Takeoff? Then there's still time. I'm not taking off for two months," Amanda said. Later she would wonder at how it was she was so ready to cooperate with whatever plan this creature had in mind. But for the time being she simply said, "I don't go up until May."

"Whoops," the thing said, rolling its eyes. "Double whoooops."

"Whooops . . . what do you mean, whooops?"

"That's not what I have on *my* schedule."

"Well, that's NASA's schedule, so you better change yours," she said snottily. The thing was a pain. Really.

"Well, I don't know what we're going to do with an underdeveloped astronaut out there. I truly don't know. The Viking landers were one thing, the space stations are another . . . but you, you're going far far away." It began a sing-song voice that irritated Amanda intensely.

"I know how far I'm going," Amanda said, highly annoyed at being constantly referred to as "underdeveloped." "Now will you please get out of here? Besides," she said, "I know you're a dream."

"You *wish* I were a dream, my little Bavarian cream," to which Amanda said nothing, noting that that part at least was true. "We have got to find those molecules. I can't leave them hanging around. I mean, if someone gets them who isn't *ready*, oh I hate to think . . ."

"What will happen?"

"Who knows? They won't be able to handle it, that's for sure. It takes a very evolved person spiritually to be able even to contemplate all this. Especially the void."

"I've contemplated the void plenty," Amanda said sourly. "And I don't consider myself spiritually ready or superior, or even," she said slowly, "very spiritual. Actually."

"Well, you're more spiritual than you know, or I would not have been given this assignment."

"Who did you say assigned you?" Amanda asked, going for it.

"Oh oh oho ho ho, I already told you that, fluff face. And I don't repeat myself."

"Well!" Amanda said, outraged at the sexism, which was, however, considerably overshadowed by the creature's other comments. Was it true then that man was incapable of imagining his end and would therefore innocently, out of false beliefs, construct it? It had the uncomfortable sound of truth to it.

"Well," the thing said, "are they trying to prevent nuclear war? No. They are worried about sex! Sex! They spend more time trying to close down books about sex, stories about sex, than they even spend trying to contemplate the death of the planet. They think sex is the problem. Sex! Oh, it's too funny. It's a false track—false track, once more." And he screamed again.

He was, on further consideration, an extremely loathsome creature,

Amanda thought. But she had heard something about "false track," which signaled more to her. What was it?

"What is the false track again?" Amanda said, playing dumb.

"The robots jammed your frequencies," he said simply.

"What frequencies?" she said.

"Oh, I don't know . . . whatever one *Homo sapiens* is on. The Reds know about you."

"The Reds?" she said. "What are you talking about?"

"Oh, they're A.I.s—Artificial Intelligences. Oh, don't you know anything?"

"I guess not," she said slowly.

"Well, the universe is divided into the A.I.s and the B.I.s."

"The B.I.s being biological, I suppose," she said.

"Well! You're not so dumb after all. I don't.understand it. According to my printout you're supposed to be one of the brighter ones. Anyway, the Earth is the last stand for biological intelligence. And *Homo sapiens* is going to ruin it. Everything knows it. They've all taken bets on it, you know."

"Bets?" Amanda said. "Why would A.I.s be betting?"

"Because the odds, the excitement attached to the odds of survival, is a universal preoccupation. Even the A.I.s don't know about the origin and end of the universe," it said.

"Well, I'm pleased to know there's something they don't know about," Amanda said, feeling an undeniable sense of relief. "Tell me more about these A.I.s," she said uneasily, not certain actually how much she wished to know.

"Well, they're really all over. Everywhere. You're the last of the B.I.s. The Red Robots don't want biology, period. They don't want to bother with it. Unproductive. Takes too long. They want to colonize the universe and I'm out to prevent it. I'm the guardian of the biologicals. Of course there aren't many—face it, most places don't possess an atmosphere. It's best suited to the A.I.s. Anyway, there's a lot of them here already, taking over."

"There are?" Amanda said, her mouth open. "Why I've never seen them."

"You wouldn't know," the thing said. "They're here as NERPs."

"NERPs?" Amanda said. "I wondered what NERPs were!"

"NERPs—Nerve Ending Reversal Programs. They look just like

you and everyone else. You could never tell. The thing is, at the point of the synapse, they come to the wrong conclusion.

"They're three-quarter robot and one-quarter *Homo sapiens*. The brain activity is all artificial. The shell, however, is humanoid. That's how they make their conversions."

"Conversions?" Amanda could barely say it, she was gasping so. "What do you mean conversions?"

"Well, that's what they do. They pick certain locales, places, and they take over. They move in and take over the brain activity. The change is molecular. It goes on in the cerebral cortex. Actually they've been robotized. It's very cleverly done. Even the NERPs don't know they're NERPs."

"They don't? However does that work then?"

"They're controlled off the central computer. It's very simple, really. They try to pick people who influence events or public opinion. Then they move in, and suddenly they're NERPs."

"How do you know a NERP when you see one?" Amanda asked, getting genuinely interested.

"How could you miss it?" it said. "They appear to be rational, but they're dangerous. You know the *dangerously rational* type. And—oh, they're against sex."

"Always?"

"Always. That's the best way to sniff them out. They're also against new ideas. They're more or less against anything that would enhance the biological realm, such as pleasure and intelligence. But they talk a good line."

"How will I be sure of a NERP when I suspect one?" Amanda asked, very curious indeed.

"The blue dot," the thing said.

"The blue dot?" Amanda said.

"Yes. It's on the bottom of the foot, near the heel. They always have a blue dot there."

"Well, that makes it rather difficult," Amanda said.

"Of course it does, you ninny. At least the orientals know about it. Why do you think they invented yoga?"

"I don't know," Amanda said, pausing. "To find the blue dot?"

"All of them lying around with their bare feet stuck in the air. Gives off an immediate signal."

"That can't be the reason they invented yoga," Amanda said dubiously.

"Well," it said, "I was trying for an explanation that would comfort you. . . . I know that's why *Homo sapiens* go for explanations."

"That's not all of it. Some of us want the truth."

The thing stared at her. "We'll see," it said, "but I have to find my molecules."

Amanda was beginning to feel better. This thing had screwed up. Superior spiritual plane or no. It couldn't find its molecules.

"Well," Amanda said, "good luck. I can't help you find your molecules, God knows, I can't see them."

"This is terrible, terrible," the creature said, turning over cushions and looking under the rug.

"Well, where did you leave them?" she said.

"In the peanut butter. I thought you liked it."

"I *do* like it, and . . ." Amanda paused. "Oh-oh, look," she said, "could a cat get them?"

"A cat?" the creature said. "*Felis domestica*, you mean?"

"Yeah, *Felis domestica*. A cat."

"Oh no . . ." the creature said, "a cat is not very highly evolved at all. Not at all. A chimpanzee maybe. Or a dolphin. Maybe. More than likely a *Homo sapiens*. Never a cat."

"What . . ."—Amanda's mind was racing—"what if this were a very special highly evolved cat?" The more she thought of it the more she began to worry.

"No way. A cat wouldn't get it," the gop said. "You have to be in a deep, deep sleep to pick up these molecules. Otherwise they won't combine. Cats don't sleep that deep. Only *Homo sapiens* sleep that deep."

"This cat sleeps deep," Amanda said uneasily. "It's like in a coma."

"No good, a coma, not enough electrical activity. Stop talking about the cat," the gop said, irritated. "I told you only *Homo sapiens*'s brain waves can absorb this molecular structure."

"Well," Amanda said bravely, "I really don't think you're so sure."

"Of course I'm sure. I'm sure, I'm sure, I'm sure."

"Something that goes around losing molecules and can't find them can't be sure of anything. You don't even know what it can bond with."

"I do so know," the little thing screamed at her. She thought quite frankly it was having a fit. She didn't know who the gentleman was in Chicago who had passed over, but he certainly had an unattractive personality. *Most* unattractive. The thing was turning over all her tables and chairs in a mad search. "I've got to find them," it screamed. "GOT TO GOT TO GOT TO!"

"Will you relax, please," Amanda said, quite annoyed now. "What's the big deal if you lost them? Can't you get more?"

"Get more? Get more? What are you talking about? These are transmutation structures—they don't grow on trees, you know."

"I know they don't grow on trees, but I assume they grow somewhere . . . I mean, you can replicate them, can't you?"

"No, I can't, miss. I definitely cannot replicate them," the thing said, highly alarmed now. "So I will find them. Now get out of here, sweetheart, take a walk, cool out your ass, go soak your head, vacate the premises, get a breeze in your sneeze."

"Well really," Amanda said, "you have the vocabulary of a sexist bastard and," Amanda said insistently, "I *still* think—"

"Look, it's a stupid idea. It's not a cat. It has to be *Homo sapiens*."

It was an irritated creature, and she simply said one more time, "Are you sure? Is it absolutely—"

"I'm sure. Sure sure sure. Creatures from Universe One are always sure. Events are predictable in Universe One. We're superior, except for an occasional random error."

"If you're so smart," she said tiredly, "how come you screwed up?"

"Don't use that kind of language with me," the creature said. "I know exactly how much hostility it contains. It isn't pretty, miss."

"Hah!" Amanda said. This thing was a riot. "Look, would you mind taking off? Getting out of my living room. I have company coming in two hours."

"They can't see me anyway," it said.

"No, but I can, and you are a pain in the ass," she said.

"Stop it. I can't bear this kind of talk," the creature said, covering its ears. "Okay, I'll disappear even for you, but I cannot leave until I find the molecules."

"Maybe they blew away," Amanda said.

"They could have," the creature said, disappearing. "They could have blown next door. How evolved are they next door?"

"I don't know," Amanda said. "He runs a car wash."

"Hmmm, water, water," the creature said. "An excellent element. Possibly a person associated with water might have potential."

Suddenly Amanda had a terrible headache and on top of that she wanted to cry. The thing seemed to be staring at her.

"I . . . I don't feel well, " she said.

"I know," it said.

She groped toward the sofa. "How do you know?"

"I sent you the headache; it will capture your attention. The electricity in your body will for the moment focus itself on your nerve endings, which is better than focusing on your total emotional system . . . if it does that you'll have a nervous breakdown. I can see you can't handle it. I forgot about sensory overload . . . they warned me." And then in a *whoosh*, meant to impress her, she felt, it was off. Disappeared. Just like that.

As soon as it left, Amanda dialed Hotchkiss.

"You know the super-luminal transfer theory?" she said to him when he picked up the phone.

"Amanda," he said, "it's four A.M."

"The theory is right," she said, and then she told him everything.

Hotchkiss told her he was coming right over, but first he called a doctor. The next thing Amanda knew she was lying on the sofa with Hotchkiss beside her. Doctor Kant was leaning over her.

"Hi," she said. "What're you doing here?"

"You passed out. When Hotchkiss couldn't rouse you"—the doctor looked at her—"he called me. It's probably a good thing he did. Your blood pressure was sky high." He leaned down and held her hand a moment. "What happened, Amanda?"

"Oh nothing," she said quickly. "I . . . I was watching a very scary movie on TV."

The doctor didn't move a muscle. "You wouldn't get that terrified from a movie," he said. "I have to report this, Amanda, so you may as well tell me."

Amanda was thinking. "Well," she said, "I did get scared. There was an intruder. Yes. An intruder. A burglar."

"Was it Big Frank?" Hotchkiss whispered quickly.

"Frank?" Doctor Kant said. "Who's Frank? Look, if you're being threatened by someone you've got to report this, you—"

"Oh . . . oh no," Amanda said. "Frank, Frank is the big dog next door who also *scares* me"—she glared at Hotchkiss—"but it wasn't Frank."

"Tell us what happened," the doctor said. "Can you describe him?"

"Er, well, I . . . I . . ."

"She's too upset right now," Hotchkiss said, rescuing her. "Let her rest. I'm sure she can give a description later."

The doctor made for the door. "I'll tell them to place you under full security. We can't have anyone disturbing you." He looked at her. "Why don't you move into the training center until you go?"

"No." Amanda smiled. "I can't bring my cat, Schrodinger, there . . . and he's very upset."

The doctor nodded. "I forgot about Schrodinger," he said. "Who's taking care of him when you're away?"

"I am," Hotchkiss said, full of mixed feelings. Especially now that he knew Schrodinger was drawing. It was a silly thing, in light of the extraordinary phenomenon of a cat that could draw, but Hotchkiss really did not like the idea that he might come home and find pictures of *his* feet all over his house.

He had tried to explain this to Amanda, who didn't understand. "Really, I can't imagine why you'd mind his *drawing*," she had said.

"It's *not* the drawing . . ." Donald hesitated. "He can draw all he wants. But he should do his own paws, or a bird, or something. I don't want him drawing my feet and leaving those pictures all over the place."

"Why should you care?" she said hotly. "Are you *ashamed* of your feet?"

"No, I am not ashamed of my feet," he said, "but, but it's personal," he said. "I just don't like it, that's all."

"Honestly," she said, "you can't repress his impulses like that; it will do terrible things to his self-development."

Privately Hotchkiss wondered at the arcane avenues in self-development that had already been visited upon poor Schrodinger. He had the most uncomfortable feeling that unimagined phases in Schrodinger's already-extraordinary evolution had yet to be unfurled.

How right he was.

When Farkheimer heard about the break-in at Amanda's apartment he notified the head of Security. It must have been a Russian agent, he figured, who somehow got wind of their earlier launch date. It made

Farkheimer very nervous. Amanda noticed this when she came to his office.

"Jaworski, go home and get your stuff. Check into the training center. This mission has been reclassified. Launch date is top secret."

Amanda stood there, startled to say the least.

"Top secret? A national launch to Mars is top secret? That's absurd."

"Launch date is top secret. Why not? The Russians do it all the time."

"Well . . ." she said slowly, "can *I* know? Or is it top secret to tell me?"

"Don't be a wise ass, Jaworski. You go up Thursday. I already notified astronaut O'Riley."

"Will she be ready?" Amanda was pale suddenly.

"Of course. You've both been ready for a year. You know that. And she goes only as far as the moon, your capsule separates, and from there you're on your own. She'll be back in nine days and you won't be back for a year and a half." Farkheimer looked suddenly sad.

"Is Three-forty-two going?" she said.

"He's commissioned to go—you'll jettison him in a satellite. Get your stuff and check in tonight. No visitors."

"What are you talking about? I have to say good-bye to my boyfriend. I'm going to be gone for months."

"A year and a half, to be correct, Jaworski. Say good-bye to Hotchkiss, check-in here is 0900. That's all, Jaworski." Farkheimer's aide was signaling to him. Perhaps they had found out something new about the satellite shots.

"Dismissed, Jaworski," Farkheimer said.

Well, weeks, years of preparation and then she gets five days' notice. She'd have to get hold of McCloud too. McCloud and Hotchkiss. Only a woman, she thought, as she backed the Mars-mobile out of the lot, would get herself into such a predicament. Five days before the Mars shot, you could be sure no man would be worried about saying good-bye to the women he loved. You could be sure of that, she thought, mad at herself and gunning the pedal to the floor.

"Damn them, damn the both of them, anyway."

Hotchkiss was just leaving the building with Dartan 4000 when she caught up to them.

"Hi, Arnold," she said. "I mean Dartan. Donald, I've got to talk to you privately," she said. "It's very important." She urgently pulled him away, leaving Arnold looking quite distracted. "They're sending me up Thursday. I've got to check in tonight."

"Tonight?" Donald looked sick, she thought. "Amanda, that's terrible."

"You'd better come with me. I have to pack Schrodinger's pills and everything."

"Amanda, this is awful."

"Come on, Donald. There's nothing to be done about it. I have to go. You have to help. I want to move Schrodinger to your house myself, so he understands everything . . . you know."

As they turned back toward Amanda's car, Arnold came running up to her. "I have to speak to you privately," he said, his face pale. "This is very urgent." Then looking around he whispered, "Is it true you're going up Thursday?"

Amanda stared at him. "Where'd you get that idea?" she said nervously.

"I bugged Farkheimer's office," he said. "Had it bugged for months. I also bugged your house. I heard it . . . the tachyon, the P.O.A.," he said.

"You heard it," Amanda said, getting quite excited. "You heard it . . . you . . . know."

"Shhh," the Genius said. "Don't try to explain it right now . . . take this," he said, looking over his shoulder.

"Why do you look so nervous?" she said.

"The Russians . . . I don't want them to see." At that, Amanda saw a small fedora peer out on top of a head around the corner.

"There's someone . . ." she said. The fedora ducked back. The Genius handed her a box.

"What is this?" she said.

"It's an antimatter device. . . ."

"Antimatter . . . how can you—"

"Shhh . . . it's in an electron net . . . it works. It works," the Genius said. "Don't worry about it. You'll get to Mars in a jiffy, if you use it." His face was steady.

"How . . . how fast?" Amanda said quietly.

The Genius nodded proudly. "One hundred sixty-seven thousand miles a second." The fedora popped out around the bend again. "I have to go now," he said. "There's an instruction booklet." Amanda stood there, amazed by this child.

"Arnold," she said, calling him, "come here."

He returned to her. "What is it?"

"I want to kiss you good-bye," she said, bending down and kissing him, planting one right on his lips. At first, she thought he swooned. But he seemed to recover then and raced off. An antimatter engine. How adorable. He might be a genius, but no one could build an antimatter engine. No one. She knew that for sure. She placed the large black box on the seat next to her in the car. Donald hopped in on the other side.

"What's that?" he said, pointing to the black box.

"Arnold, Dartan gave it to me. He said it makes you go almost light speed."

"Amanda," Donald said tiredly. "You know that's impossible. Nothing can go that fast. You'd start to disappear, even if you could."

"Well, you never know," Amanda said cheerfully, patting the box. "It might come in handy, you know, in a pinch."

In a pinch, indeed, Hotchkiss scoffed. Yes, the boy was a genius, but not even a genius could figure out the laws for going the speed of light. Not so's you'd survive it. Still, Donald Hotchkiss could not resist. He took a closer look.

"How's it work . . . ? He tell you?" he said.

"Fusion reaction," Amanda said, rounding a curve.

"Fusion reaction!" Hotchkiss bellowed. "Amanda, are you crazy? Get that thing out of here!"

Amanda stopped at a light. "Look, first you don't believe it and then you believe it. Don't worry about it. Dartan says it's perfectly safe in that box. I can barely lift it. It's all lead."

"What activates it?" he said nervously.

"He told me," she said sweetly. "Only me." Donald started to bellow.

"Oh Donald, really. You don't think it is one, do *you*?" she said, heading down the road past the woods. As she passed the woods, she saw him. It was Frank. He was waving.

"Donald—look there, in the woods."

He looked. "What, what is it?"

"Oh, oh, nothing," she said.

"What did you see now, Amanda? A little green blob, part of the primal ooze?"

"You believe this kid built an antimatter electron net in this black box, right, and I'm crazy because I see Frankenstein in the woods."

"And have conversations with subparticles that are part of the original primal soup . . . right?" Hotchkiss said, leaning back and feeling satisfied.

"Actually you told me you were going over plans for his antimatter engine. How did they check out?" she asked thoughtfully.

"I told you, Amanda, it's highly unlikely. I mean the kid is a genius, believe me, but so far nobody believes you can design one that will work. Besides, they have no idea how to build a spaceship that cannot disappear at those speeds."

"Wouldn't it be great," she said with a sigh, "if it worked—Mars and back in less than two hours." She turned into the driveway.

Then they entered the house. Amanda was surprised not to find Schrodinger on the counter, where she had left him. "That's funny," she said. "He never wakes up in the middle of the day."

Unless McCloud was there. It briefly occurred to her that perhaps McCloud had come by. He always seemed to show up when she needed to see him. It was funny that way. But McCloud would not have come into the house, even though he knew where the key was. Because of Donald. He had relinquished her to Donald for all practical purposes. For spiritual purposes, she felt, however, he had not relinquished her at all. Sexually he had to relinquish her. She said she just couldn't manage two men at the same time. Not that way. He had been grudging about this but said he understood, although in fact he didn't understand at all. The funny thing was he didn't even feel in competition with Hotchkiss: he felt superior to him.

"Donald," she said, going through all the rooms, "I can't find him."

"AGHH," she heard from the hall. Well, Donald had found a hair ball, at least.

"He couldn't be lost," Donald yelled back. "He's not awake long enough to get lost. . . . Damned hair balls . . . Amanda, this is disgusting."

"I'm telling you, Donald," she said, getting rather alarmed, "he isn't here."

"We'll look in the closets; maybe he had a momentary spurt of energy or something."

"This isn't like him," Amanda said, frantically opening and closing the closet doors. "Donald, something's wrong."

They looked for an hour, at the end of which Amanda was quite beside herself. Then they looked *outdoors*. At the end of two hours, Amanda's decision was firm.

"Look, Amanda," Hotchkiss said, "you cannot go to NASA and tell them you are abandoning a trip to Mars, a three-billion-dollar project, because your cat got lost!"

"I'd like to know a better reason!" Amanda said hotly. "I can't just take off like this. Do you really think I would leave Schrodinger here, in *his* condition?"

"We'll call the ASPCA. I'm sure they'll be able to find him."

"He doesn't go to strangers. He *hates* strange people. You *know* that, Donald. Besides"—her eyes were suddenly wide with horror—"they might *bury* him! Oh my God, I never thought of that, I mean if they caught him in one of his *states* . . ."

"Pretty hard to miss one, I'd have to say," Donald said sourly.

"Donald, this is no time for jokes!" Amanda said. "I'm rather surprised at you. Never mind, I'll handle this myself."

She was mad. Mad, worried, and hurt. Hotchkiss was astonished. He said to himself that he knew she was fond of Schrodinger—passionate was more like it—but to abandon a Mars trip for some four-footed furry thing like that? It was unthinkable. It was so irrational it was beyond him.

"You're behaving like a two-year-old," he said.

"I am not. I am behaving like you behave when you love someone. Schrodinger is not, in his current condition, capable of managing for himself. He's given me years of his undying devotion. I'm not going to leave him." She was crying now. Tears were streaming down her face.

Hotchkiss looked at her. It was really quite beyond him. He did not think Amanda could live, that is, in the very essence of her Amanda-ness, if Schrodinger suffered such a fate.

Although at one moment he thought it all quite silly and a lot of ado about an admittedly remarkable cat (but nonetheless a cat), there was a way in which he understood the simplicity of this utterly. He knew, in this way, that it was not silly at all, but rather that it was quite simply the way that things were, really. That love was a fine tracery woven over the web of abandonment, sometimes concealing, sometimes revealing, sometimes maintaining the hold.

Donald followed Amanda inside to the telephone, where she was about to break the news to Farkheimer; then he noticed something.

"Amanda, what's that?" He pointed to a large piece of paper, almost hidden, under the couch. It was Schrodinger's drawing paper. Amanda leaped for it and pulled it out. It was a note. From Schrodinger.

Dear Amanda:

This is bigger than the both of us. [Was it love or his right hemisphere, she wondered.] I swallowed some molecules by mistake and then I started doing the drawings. I couldn't help myself. Apparently I am coalescing into the fourth dimension; almost all of me is gone except this paw which is writing. Please come and get me. I love you very much. HELP.

Schrodin

"He never finished," she said, tears welling in her eyes; "his note ends after Schrodin . . ."

"My God," Hotchkiss said, "do you really think he wrote it?"

"If he ate the molecules he did, and now both his left and *right* are superior. They've come and taken him. We have to go and get him!"

"How're you gonna get him in the fourth dimension?" Hotchkiss asked calmly. It wasn't until later that he reflected how wholeheartedly he accepted this information.

"Well, I don't know . . . but I'll certainly find a way. We *have* to go and get him," she said, pointing to the note. "It says HELP!"

"He even knows how to punctuate," Hotchkiss marveled.

"Donald!" she wailed. "Schrodinger is gone!" He could see she was quite distraught.

"Amanda, you have to go up," he said suddenly. "You have to report in an hour."

"I can't go," she said gasping. "I can't take off for a year and a half and leave Schrodinger in the fourth dimension." Hotchkiss just stared at her. Put this way, he supposed she couldn't. On the other hand, explanations to NASA would be impossible. Certainly this kind of explanation.

"What in hell are you going to tell them?" he said, full of consternation.

"I DON'T KNOW, I DON'T KNOW." She was absolutely screaming. "LEAVE ME ALONE!" After a few minutes of crying in the living room, she said suddenly, "I'm going to call that magician, the one who finds lost things."

"A magician," Donald said, outraged. "Amanda, what is happening to you? Are you insane or what? What good is a magician? I thought you were a *scientist*."

"Magic, stupid," she hissed, "is what you call things until you know how to explain them. I don't know how to explain, do you? Maybe he could help . . . maybe he knows about things people can't explain. I certainly can't explain this. . . . They said he's good at finding things that get lost."

"In the fourth dimension, Amanda? In time?" Donald looked at her face. It was ashen.

"It's just an aspect of space, remember that. Space and time go together. I'm sure this is just a question of seeing things in the proper perspective. . . ."

He thought she was looking really weird.

"Amanda," he said, "are you losing your grip? Are you truly beginning to believe in the supernatural?"

"I believe in the natural and the inexplicable and anything that falls between. If you want to call it supernatural, go ahead. I'm calling that magician," and she stomped into the other room. Her hands were shaking. It was really extremely upsetting. It was bad enough to lose Schrodinger, but to lose him and not know where—that was the terrifying part. Although when she thought about it later she thought that was an absurd way of looking at it. Of course when you lost anything or anyone the fact that they were lost meant you didn't know where.

There was a lot of static on the line, and then she got a busy signal. She went back into the kitchen.

"Sugar dumples, this is Oozie . . . I'm transmitting, babe, don't try to ignore this . . . it's important . . . you better answer. I'll just keep at it, that's all, until you do . . . sweet cakes, you better tune in . . ."

Amanda was upset. Extremely upset. What was she going to tell

NASA? Anything? What was she going to do? How could she follow Schrodinger into the fourth dimension when she didn't know how in hell to get there? She was certain that miserable Rastus was behind this. Rastus and the Ooze—she should have known; she should have locked Schrodinger up. Maybe they *were* light-years ahead, but they were screwups. She didn't think they were mean, so that was some consolation—they probably just wanted the molecules, but they had to take Schrodinger too. She decided to pour herself a drink. She was crying and furious at the same time. She opened the freezer door, took out the cubes, and was banging them against the side of the sink all the time that Ooze was trying to get through. Of course she had heard Ooze's transmission. But she was so angry she didn't want to hear Ooze. She didn't want to know shit from Shinola about Ooze. All she knew was she was furious.

Hotchkiss came into the kitchen as Amanda was banging the ice trays for all they were worth against the sink, yelling "Damn you, damn you, damn you." The cubes broke and scattered against the walls of the sink, clinking, clattering balls of ice.

"For God's sake," he said, standing in the doorway.

"Oh," she said, "these damn ice trays make me furious!" He was startled at the heat in her eyes.

"Sugar dumples, you better pick up this transmission. It's *important*," the Ooze said.

Amanda heard this. "Oh shit," she said. "Shit, shit, shit."

"Amanda!" Donald said. "What's going on?"

"Oh SHUT UP," she screamed. "Shut up, I'm getting a goddamn transmission!" She stomped, that was the only word, into the living room, leaving Donald Hotchkiss standing dazed in the doorway.

"Look, sweet boobs," Ooze said, "I'm going to a lot of trouble to make this connection, it's not easy from out here you know."

"Get on with it, please," Amanda said exasperatedly. Donald heard this part.

This was the part he didn't get. He thought that a person who heard voices ought really to be inspired by them. They seemed to exasperate Amanda no end. Her voices seemed to make her furious.

Amanda was thinking, Was it Harry Piranski, or was sexism just loose out there in the universe, coating all the transmissions? "Look, sweet boobs, this'll set your knockers knockin'," Oozie said; "tell your engineers to check out Epsilon Erdani at 0900, red light, blue light, red light—our space station is passing through. Your cat's been napped by the Blue Robots—sorry about that; there was a cosmic mix-up. I'm doing this transmission as a favor: I don't want you going up lacking confidence. . . . We have a lot of problems to resolve out here you know . . . that molecule mix-up is causing all hell to break loose."

"What's happening? Where's Schrodinger?" Amanda said excitedly.

"He's out here somewhere—I don't know myself—but you have to come and get him. There's been a *big* mix-up."

"What's happened?" she was yelling. "Where is he?"

"Never complain, never explain, just get into your spaceship, sugar lips. We'll take it from there. Over and out," Ooze said.

"Well?" Donald said, seeing her face lit, "is the transmission over?"

"Oh it's muddy—they just transmit when they feel like it," Amanda said, getting up and starting to pace. "Oh Donald, they've taken Schrodinger—the Blue Robots," she said, "and I have to go up and get him. Oh Donald, I wish this business would stop."

"Yes," he said looking rather odd, "me too." It wasn't too long before his curiosity overcame him. "What'd he say, the transmitter?"

Amanda sighed. "He told me to check with the radio-interferometry people in the morning. At oh nine hundred their space station is crossing Epsilon Erdani . . . it'll show up as red, blue, red—that's in case I have any doubts. Well, I don't have any doubts anymore—I'm just fed up. . . ."

"It's a massive body then," Donald said, "if it changes the light spectrum like that."

"Yeah," Amanda said, "it's their starship. It must be the size of a planet."

"Wow," Donald said. Then, "Could you see it? I mean aerodynamically speaking, it would be interesting to see what it looked like."

"No, I couldn't see it," Amanda said, turning and going back into the kitchen. "I'm going to make a salad," she said. She was depressed. When she was depressed she made grilled-cheese sandwiches and salad. "Would you like a grilled-cheese sandwich too?" Donald nodded.

He supposed he would, actually. He was thinking about a starship that could cause that kind of spectral change. He went to help her as he wanted to guarantee his sandwich had lots of mustard on it. She never put on enough. He took out the jar and swathed the bread in mustard, put cheese on it, and swathed more mustard over it. Then he made a sandwich for Amanda. She was making the salad in a very depressed manner—slowly ripping the lettuce apart and even more slowly dropping it into the bowl.

"I don't know," she said suddenly.

"You don't know what?" he said, putting the cheese under the broiler.

"I was thinking . . . about what you said; I would like to see it," she said.

"Oh, the starship . . ."

"Yes," she said.

"Yeah," he said, "it's too bad you couldn't see it."

"Well," she said, "that's what I mean. I mean I would like to see it, too. I would really *like* to see it. But . . ."

"But what?" he said. He was concentrating on the broiler, trying to make the right adjustment.

"I mean I don't know if it would make things better or make things worse. I mean with this kind of transmission I can just hear. I don't *see* things . . . you know?" she said.

"Know what?" he replied absently. The broiler pan was sticking, and he was having difficulty getting it in right.

"Whether it would be better or worse," she said again.

"Oh," he said, finally getting it. "Oh, I see what you mean," he said. He stood and brushed off his hands. "Well," he said after a minute, "I think it would be better."

"What would be better," she said, turning to him surprised; "it would be better to *see* it?" she said, "you think?"

"Yeah, well," he said, "in for a penny, in for a pound. I mean since you're hearing it you may as *well*, you know, go the whole hog."

"Hmm," Amanda said, staring at him. This business had affected him more than she suspected. "Go the whole hog." Well, for Donald that was certainly a change in point of view.

As they drove back to the space center, Hotchkiss could see that Amanda was in a very different mood. She didn't seem depressed anymore. She seemed determined. Hotchkiss had the passing thought that maybe he should just kidnap her. Kidnap her and steal away to some hotel in Mexico until all this transmitting business blew over. He thought, or he tried to tell himself that he thought, she needed a rest. Then of course there was the business about Schrodinger. He felt bad about that. Not so much that Schrodinger was missing—although he did feel bad about that—but rather that Schrodinger, should he fall into the wrong hands, could die a horrible death. Being buried alive. It made Hotchkiss shudder. Then of course there was the business of the note. If there was any logic to this business, and Hotchkiss wasn't sure that there was, it did make sense that the reason Schrodinger had been stolen was because of those molecules he had swallowed, which somehow had enabled him to draw. And then to write. He found himself wondering exactly what was in those molecules. It was one thing to find him drawing and quite another to find him writing. "You see," Amanda had said, waving the note in the air, "both hemispheres of his brain are in top condition. The writing side and the drawing side. That's why they're after him."

"Well," Donald had said, "why didn't they just come and get the molecules? Why take the whole damn cat?"

"You see, originally they were planned for me. But I only got one. Apparently, according to the transmission, anyway, these three particular molecules combine. They want the one I've got and they want Schrodinger's two. So there's nothing for me to do but go out there and bargain with them. They can have mine back and keep Schrodinger's, but they have to give Schrodinger back to me."

"Amanda," Donald said somewhat tiredly, "what kind of bargaining power do you think you're going to have? What if they kill both of you?"

Amanda turned to him, her eyes bright. "That's the good part. The only good part. They can't get these molecules back except voluntarily. They have to be *surrendered* willingly."

"Who told you that?" Donald asked, unconvinced.

"Ooze. He told me that was the problem with Frankenstein in my kitchen—molecular time dilation."

"What are you talking about?"

"Well, what made it so hard for Rastus to time travel Frankenstein back out is that I got very interested. I mean I kept looking for him because I was so curious. Curiosity, interest, all that stuff—it's like chemical bonding. Frank didn't want to go then, so they have trouble in a case like that coalescing the molecules. It's like hypnosis," she said driving to the airport, "without some cooperation it doesn't take."

"Oh," Hotchkiss said. He felt quite strange indeed. This was really more than he could handle. He helped her with her bag onto the plane.

It was an air force plane, and once Amanda got on it, Hotchkiss would not be allowed inside. He would return to Houston to the command center. Amanda would be launched from Cape Canaveral.

"Well," he said standing outside the car. He didn't know what else to say. He was feeling sick.

"Look Donald, I'm sure it will all work out. It's just . . ." Her eyes turned to him then, full of apology. "I'm . . . I'm just sorry it got out of hand. I mean that the molecules had to come to my house. I know it hasn't been easy for you."

"No," he said, gulping. "Or for you."

"Well, in a way it's easier for me," she said, "because at least I swallowed one. You didn't swallow any, after all."

There it was again, Hotchkiss thought. That strange implication that he was somehow lacking or deprived because he wasn't a full participant in this insanity. Feeling a slight competitive edge arise, he said, "Well, apparently your just having the one isn't much help. At least you said that's what the thing said."

"Oh," she said, "that's what it said, but you know at least I can receive the transmissions." She was stuffing her suitcase into the door of the plane. It was typical of the military, Hotchkiss thought. The plane was swarming with security guys but there was nobody to meet her at the door.

"Well," he said, "I wish I could say I'd write."

"Yeah, well . . ." She was smiling, a very soft, small smile she had. "I'll miss you," she said, bending her head up to kiss him.

"Me too," he said, then smiling, "you know if you get a chance to get away earlier, do it."

"Bye," she said, kissing him.

"I'll be there at splashdown," he said, and turned before the tear started down her cheek.

He wondered as he drove away from the base if he had done the right thing by not informing anyone at NASA about any of this. He didn't think about it too long. That would be impossible. Transmissions from a talking subatomic particle. Absolutely impossible. And he knew it.

Amanda felt terrible leaving Hotchkiss and even worse that she hadn't been able to see McCloud. She had left a message for him finally at his office. "Just tell him I called and I said good-bye," she said. She was furious that he hadn't been there. She wanted the pleasure of leaving him.

And then of course she was just mad. Mad that she, an admittedly brilliant physicist, a leading American astronaut, well versed in the fields of atomic physics, spectrum analysis, radiation, geology, subatomic particles, astronomy, photometry, and the whole world of astrophysics, here on the eve of an absolutely record-breaking, history-making flight to Mars, was deep below the level of her professionalism worrying about two men.

The plane was crawling with special security men, as was the launch site itself. Therefore she was astonished when, coming down from the ramp carrying her small flight bag, an arm suddenly grabbed her, the arm of a supposed plane mechanic, and for the first time in weeks she was staring into the big bold eyes of Bronco McCloud.

"Oh!" She almost yelled it. "How did you ever get in here?"

"I need a kiss good-bye," he said, whispering into her ear as he walked closely beside her.

"I told you," she whispered back, "I'm through with you. I was only calling to be polite." McCloud looked up to see two artillery-loaded jeeps barreling down the runway.

He looked at her. "This is it, babe, they've blown my cover. Get ready for the best kiss you'll ever get on Earth."

Amanda turned around startled, saw the jeeps coming, and they threw their arms around each other. She kissed McCloud long and hard, that is to say as long as one could under the approach of gunfire, but when she thought about it later it seemed to her that she was always kissing McCloud under the approach of some kind of fire or another. The smell of fired guns seemed to haunt the very air around him.

"You've got to run," she said. "I know you don't have clearance."

"I love you," he said, hugging her, and then he took off on a conveniently parked motorcycle as the jeep approached her.

"Are you being molested?" They paused barely a moment.

"OH NO," Amanda yelled loudly, "I . . . I . . ." They were staring at her, awaiting an explanation for her passionate embrace of the airplane mechanic.

"I'm . . . I'm . . . Look, it's an old friend," she said finally. "He'll be off the base in about a minute." She looked at her watch. "It's just something personal." She turned and stared after McCloud. "It's very hard to forget someone who taught you everything you know about the photoelectric effect." She sighed then and walked into the waiting car that would take her to the training center. The security men stared at her. Love was mucking up the rules again. They were uneasy. They should have arrested that guy, they were sure of it. On the other hand, nothing had been said about the kissing of astronauts. Amanda was smiling to herself and wondering how in the world he got in there. Probably bribed someone. McCloud believed in bribery. He and Amanda used to have fights about it, but she finally gave up. He told her it was not a question of morality; he said it was cost-efficient, and she figured he was probably right.

Amanda was being served her dinner in a special isolation room the night before the shot when she heard a noise at the door. She stepped back as it opened and Arnold peered in.

"Arnold!" she gasped. "However did you get in here?"

Arnold looked at her, eyes gooey with love. He reached forward and hugged her tightly.

Amanda was astonished. "Why Arnold," was all she could say.

Finally he recovered and said, "Look, there's stuff out there you don't know about . . ."

"What do you mean?" she said, seeing how serious he was.

"There are some frequencies that can only be trouble. I think somebody has traveling satellites that could interfere with your mission . . . ; something is out there. I keep picking up too much stuff on the frequencies . . . ; your computers could get interference . . . so I made you this." He handed her a small green box. "It'll ruin any computer. You can switch the dial if something starts after you, but try this, it will incapacitate anything electronic that approaches. None of your computers are on this frequency, so don't worry about it . . . you'll be safe," he sighed. And then he reached into his pocket. "And then you need this," he handed her a ring. "Take this, if you have any doubt about what you're *approaching*, even if it looks like it's only a meteorite, turn the ring toward it. It will get hot. That means you're in a solid-state territory and you've got to use the jamming device. You got it?" he said to her, his eyes full of sadness. "I'll . . . I'll be watching you, as well as I can." Amanda smiled. He could probably keep better track of her in his garage than the entire command center could.

"Okay," she said. "Thanks a lot." She wondered. Maybe the stuff worked after all. Couldn't hurt. She slipped on the ring. Arnold slipped out the door. Life was getting more and more like the comic books.

Amanda felt that she couldn't sleep and whispered to the guard to please find her something to read. The guard slid a women's magazine under the door, and Amanda was intrigued to see that the lead article was entitled, "Are You a Love Junkie?" The article also provided a "Love Junkie Test" to determine whether or not you were a "love addict," which, the article said, was not a good thing to be. At all. It made you a slave, first to love, second to men, and the road to independence and adulthood meant you had to stop being a love junkie. Amanda read the article carefully; then she took the test and checked the answers in the back, although of course she didn't even have to take the test to know that she was probably one of the biggest love junkies of all time. When she checked the answers (which were opposite a page for an extremely sexy short white dress, she noted) it turned out she had a score of "over ninety," which suggested that she "seek therapy immediately." Amanda thought that possibly the person who wrote the article had this business of the love-junkie thing all wrong. It was true, she thought in some part of her heart, that it probably was not good for a person who was a love junkie to be the United States representative to Mars, but she also thought it was part, quite frankly, of being a woman. Amanda thought they had certain things mixed up; a man being a love junkie of course would be ludicrous, although deep down inside and hidden away there were as many love-junkie men as women, but that it was an important part of being a woman to know you were a love junkie. The magazine was very busy telling you that the way to become a person was to go out and get a job, when Amanda knew that the way you became a person was by going out and loving someone. Of course loving was no simple thing. The trick of it was not to get wrecked. But this "excessive need for love and affection," Amanda figured was an altogether good thing, and she didn't know who the people were who went around figuring just how much was excessive. Like ten hugs and kisses would be good, but wanting twenty meant you had a problem. She didn't know who the figurers were and she didn't care, but she thought that if you weren't a love junkie you probably missed a lot in life, and she was glad she was. At least this night, right now, she was glad. She had felt discouraged before, when Hotchkiss called, but as she thought about it she imagined that if she hadn't been such a love junkie, she probably would not have felt it so necessary to pursue Schrodinger. But she could no more not go after Schrodinger than she could cut out her own heart and toss it to the wind, although she thought that the people who ran the magazine test probably wouldn't understand that such things applied to phenomena like Schrodinger. They would probably say a love-junkie person who loved an animal was disturbed or mentally ill or something.

But love was a beam, Amanda knew, and it drew you on. The object of your affections was as much part of the beam as the love that drew it on, and it was her love for Schrodinger, in all his perplexities, that gave her confidence. Less love and she would never have the stamina, much less the *chutzpah* for this trip. There was no question about it, she knew it: she would wind up having to make her own trajectory, go into uncharted territory, disappoint everyone on earth, go completely up against the expectations, ruin her reputation, and generally bring disapproval, hatred, and anger all around. Well, that was that. When they finally understood it, or even if they never did, when she came back with Schrodinger she would have accomplished her goal, and the world would know more of things than it might otherwise have. She'd try to stop at Mars too, depending on how things went up there, but she wasn't at all sure it would become part of the plan. What she didn't like and what she wasn't comfortable about was this trust she had to rely on in relationship to the Ooze. She had to trust the Ooze. Without Ooze she had no guide, and yet the Ooze could lead her as readily into oblivion as not. Could trick her and dump her in the reaches of outer space, spinning in some endless orbit until she died. But she felt deep down that the Ooze had had a plan, too, and someone or something had wrecked it. It wasn't just Schrodinger's mistake or the mistake of leaving the molecules where Schrodinger could get them. Someone or something had deliberately fouled up his plan, and he was trying to get things straight. His plans for the future appeared to be benign, and so she trusted him. He was incompetent though, out of control of things that might be critical, but she'd have to take the chance.

Rastus too was an unknown factor.

Amanda was all set to turn in, her lights were out and she was feeling calm, as calm and composed as one could feel in a history-making situation such as the Mars shot—she was actually more concerned about Schrodinger than anything else—when she heard a knock at the door. At first she was uneasy. She knew the Russians would do anything to interfere with the Mars shot, at least that was what her briefings told her, and she got up quickly and took the gun, which they had given to her, and slipped close to the door.

"Who is it?" she said, thinking it might be Hotchkiss or McCloud, that maybe they got in there.

"It's Anita," the voice said. "There's an emergency report."

Anita was Amanda's guard. What kind of emergency report would she be getting at midnight? What would be so important as to interrupt her the night before something like this? Anything last-minute, Hotchkiss had told her, they would probably hold until she was in flight. The most dangerous part was the lift-off and then the moon catapult, which, taking advantage of the moon's gravity, would accelerate her out of the moon orbit toward Mars—sort of a slingshot lift. O'Riley would head home and Amanda would be on her own. Hotchkiss said if anything came up it would come out after lift-off, once she was in earth orbit, and before she hit the moon catapult. After the moon catapult, once she was on the Mars trajectory, there would be nothing to help her. Nothing at all. There would be information, that was all. There would be the information from the Viking group, the camera robots, but that was all.

"Anita," Amanda said, "give me your number." Each of the guards had been assigned even-digit numbers, by Amanda, before retiring.

"One-four-three-oh-two-oh-nine," Anita replied.

"Just slip the report under the door," Amanda said, somewhat nervously.

"Okay." And under the door came a thin brown envelope containing the countdown procedures. There was no emergency.

There would be a hold of five minutes. That was all. A five-minute time hold. No explanation. Just classified. Top secret. Well okay. She had been warned this might be the case. Nevertheless, she worried about Arnold's solid-state detector. It was glowing all right.

Sue Ann O'Riley was awakened at 1:00 A.M. with a special superclassified report. It was to her clearly the guard's voice. She opened the door.

41

They were in the spaceship, Amanda, Sue Ann, and 342; everything secure; it was minutes before takeoff. Countdown was at T minus four minutes, when Amanda suddenly felt an uncontrollable itch in her chest. She quickly unzipped her suit and seemed astonished, in the midst of her preoccupations, computer checks, and hardware, to feel the soft smooth surface of her breast. It startled her, the softness of it in the midst of this, a strange sensation surprising her, pleasing her, disturbing her, alerting her like a telegram from an unknown world.

She heard the final countdown:

T minus two minutes forty seconds
T minus two minutes thirty seconds: ground supply terminated
T minus one minute fifteen seconds: liquid hydrogen at point pressure
T minus one minute: firing system on
T minus thirty seconds: ground to on-board computers
T minus ten seconds: main-engine ignition
T minus six seconds: engine ignition

She braced herself as the huge rocket burst into flame and rose, seemingly gently, slowly into the unfolding sky. The sun was rising over the water. It was beautiful. Amanda smiled. For reasons unclear to her, she felt she would find Schrodinger. She felt all systems were go. She was going to make it.

Then the storm struck.

Only Amanda didn't know it.

At one minute thirty seconds after ignition she was two miles up and under pressure of four G forces, the rocket still accelerating to escape velocity of twenty-five thousand miles an hour. At six minutes she performed the first OMS burn, putting the big ship into orbit around earth, and she yelled to Sue Ann, "So far so good. Hooray, we're up! Ready for the moon. . . . We got six hours now in orbit to relax." She looked at the on-board computers and noticed all the systems were go. She turned to Sue Ann, who seemed to be staring straight ahead. "You get to say something, you know." Amanda had done at least four missions with O'Riley as her copilot, and she had always worked smoothly, efficiently, cooperatively. They never saw each other once a mission was over because, as Amanda put it, "There's just no chemistry." They were not friends, but they worked well together. The point was, Amanda had never before seen Sue Ann freeze or clutch in an emergency. But she had been strangely quiet since they entered the space capsule two hours ago.

"Boy, do you have stage fright," Amanda said, trying to laugh despite her annoyance. There was no reply from Sue Ann, which caused Amanda to say, "Are you all right?"

"You okay?" Amanda asked again, suddenly concerned, and as she leaned closer toward Sue Ann she felt the ring on her hand instantly grow hot, and she pulled back.

In Houston, on the Cape, the red wind had struck. The doors to the space center were blown open and in seconds the dust was everywhere. The voices were stilled. The computers were running the show now.

The red tide had blown through the entire space center, laying every last human impulse to waste. People coughed, they reached for the right buttons, but they collapsed too soon.

In the capsule Amanda didn't know what hit her, she was suddenly reeling, suddenly weak, gasping, calling CapCom, who was *out*, calling, "Wait," seeing as she fell into the darkness, 342 slipping in a faint to the floor, seeing, as she reached for emergency oxygen, the cold glass eyes of what pretended to be Sue Ann O'Riley, her copilot.

Somewhere, some way her strength met her luck and her hand found the emergency oxygen. It fell from the ceiling surrounding her head like a cloud, saving her. She was fully alert as she completed the burn. She knew every movement of the huge spaceship as it rolled about its long axis, beginning to pitch over into the belly-up attitude it would maintain through most of this section of the flight. Amanda was breathing hard and watching the figure on her right. All voices from the ground had stopped. She was holding 342's head into the oxygen mask; she could feel his heart beginning to beat faster, and she relaxed a little. She could not imagine what had gone wrong on the ground. Silence. She was yelling into her transmitter, receiving nothing. It was not a radio blackout. It was a total blackout. A bomb? Had the world gone up in smoke and ashes and she been the only one to escape—Amanda and the slowly recovering chimpanzee?

Out of the copilot's chair, too soon and out of schedule, moving awkwardly toward Amanda came something. Amanda saw the glassy eyes of the robot, and moving quickly, she broke the visor to reveal unmistakably a skull of silicon chips. Suddenly there was a hissing sound as the robot's mouth opened slightly and three bullets whizzed forward, missing Amanda by inches, awaking 342 from his faint. The robot was rotating now, moving toward the on-board computers. The bullets had lodged in the wall behind Amanda.

"Amanda, abort mission. This is Farkheimer. Abort. Return." He was coughing, but he was there. "Australia waiting." There was a landing provision for Australia. Amanda's eyes followed the computers. The spaceship would pass over it in three minutes. She reached for the laser gun slung on the wall and pried it loose. Farkheimer was screaming. Australia was screaming, 342 was screaming, Amanda was praying the bullets had not severed the computer's spinal column as she aimed the gun at the back of the robot's neck. In seconds, it crumbled forward, and Amanda reached out and, with all her strength, heaved it to the side so it did not crash against the directional console. Three-forty-two was howling. She lifted the bubble completely off the robot's head, exposing the display of numbers and transistors, lights. Her heart was racing, she couldn't control it, as she made her way back to her seat.

"CapCom, this is Jaworski. Where the *hell* were you?" Not waiting for an answer she went on: "I've missed Australia, the robot is finished, disabled with laser ray; request permission to OMS burn into moon orbit. Over." It was the most dramatic transmission in space history. The control room was in an uproar, that is to say the twenty-three who were not hospitalized. The air force was in an uproar. Simultaneously, the CIA had found Sue Ann O'Riley's body and that of the guard, Anita, both of them dead of cyanide-gas pellets. They didn't know how, or why.

Farkheimer was on the hot line to the prez. "You heard me. The girl and the monkey are up there alone. The Russians must have planned to take over the ship. Something went wrong; they weren't counting on having Jaworski in there." Something had gone wrong somewhere. They all knew it. The Russians were going to take over the U.S. ship.

"What were they planning to do?" The prez wanted to know. Probably planning to jam the frequencies so Jaworski would "disappear." Then announce failure of the U.S. ship. "Lost in outer space." Take over the ship and announce Russians had landed on Mars. Secret and simple. Except something had gone wrong.

Farkheimer was devastated. A thirty-million-dollar mission and he was ordering an abort. This goddamned red tide had almost finished them from this end too.

He heard Jaworski coming through now. "Look, General, I can take it. I can take it alone. The computers are undamaged, and I have Three-forty-two. I can probably make it."

"You can't, Jaworski. Request to continue mission is refused. Wait further orders on where to make emergency abort."

"OMS burn due in one minute. Request permission to make OMS burn to moon. Let me coast to moon and return. At least that," Amanda argued. She was up, damn it, and she wanted at least to get to the moon. She wasn't going back anyway. She was waiting for Oozie to lead her to Schrodinger.

There was a quick consultation in Houston. Farkheimer's instincts were to order her to abort. On the other hand, she probably could make the moon now and come back. That would only be a week. The chimp could take the lander to the moon's surface and leave the on-board computers orbiting the moon. They could announce the mission then. Big success. Expensive, for the moon. But it was something. Farkheimer's mind was racing.

"Permission granted," came the reply. "Make second OMS burn for moon trajectory."

Amanda felt relief. Good, that part would be easy. She was glancing at the robot on the floor. If she had time, she might be able to make some use of the thing. She could not allow herself to think what had happened to O'Riley and Anita. Or what was supposed to have happened to her. This, however, she knew was not the work of Oozie or Rastus. This kind of sabotage was strictly political. The Russians, she was certain, were behind this. She wondered at her luck. If Arnold had not given her that sensor ring device . . .

The Russians had planned an algae increase in red tide the day of the launch. But they had planned it for the month after next. At the last minute they uncovered the real launch date. Who had set off the red tide then?

Farkheimer was now in a jam. The plan had been to "dump the monkey" or at least to push him through the hookup that Amanda was to arrange with the floating satellite station. But now, now things were more complicated. First of all, he had doubted from the beginning that Jaworski, being the animal freak that she was, would ever dump the chimp, orders or no orders. They knew, all of them; it was to be a useful experiment, but there was no way the chimp could get back.

Now something else had occurred. Clearly the Russians had planned to "kidnap" the ship. To bump off Jaworski and O'Riley and take the ship into outer space. It might have been a last-minute decision. With a top-secret mission going off from Canaveral, nobody ever would have known the difference, that is to say, the American government could not admit that (a) the ship went up and (b) that the Russians stole it. Now, however, Farkheimer had a new problem. The Russians had miraculously been foiled. But still he had lost an astronaut. True, he thought, it was only a woman, not a man, but still it was an American. It didn't look good. Not only didn't it look good, but there was Jaworski out there, who, if she did get back, would be all too eager to tell the world what went on. Jaworski would, in fact, feel *obligated* to tell the world. In the meantime, it was also clear to him that Jaworski would find it a lot easier to perform the lunar landing with the chimp. Jaworski could stay in moon orbit, and the chimp could take the lander down, as it had been trained. And any time the chimp got out of hand, they could control the lander computers to some extent. If anything went wrong, he'd rather lose the chimp than Jaworski. At least at this stage.

Farkheimer was aware that he was beginning to think the unthinkable. They would have to get the spaceship back here, and somehow, somewhere, some way they would have to silence Jaworski. The general was not a homicidal maniac. He could not contemplate leaving her out there a "computer failure." No, he could not contemplate that. But an injection. A tranquilizer. Something to make her forget. A lobotomy. Cruel, but necessary. A surgical solution. She was a woman, he told himself, and she'd be better off that way anyhow. Jaworski was all out of whack as a woman. Too many abilities. Why, just looking at her he could tell she was miserable. Do her a favor. Wouldn't change her that much, just somewhat. Make her easier to handle. She'd be happier. The more he thought of it the more he was convinced. That would be the thing to do. In the meantime he would announce the moon landing.

Call up the TV cameras. Make the most of it. Call in the PR guys. Think of a good way to put it across. He'd call the prez now.

Amanda had calmed down. She would wait for the transmission from Oozie and in the meantime pretend to go to the moon with 342. The chimp was a wreck from the excitement with the robot. She had given him a few banana pellets in an effort to reassure him but it was no use: he wouldn't eat anything.

Those Russians! She hadn't expected them to make such a daring and desperate move. They had been out to capture this spaceship and take it to Mars themselves. Of course, you couldn't announce they had captured your ship, especially one that was top-secret classification, without being mortified. Amanda wondered how they were covering it on earth.

Farkheimer had a fine mind. There was nothing wrong with it, save for those little local prejudices of his. But on the larger level, his mind had failed because of one of the two reasons fine minds always fail: one was greed and the other was fear.

Fear had garnered the best aspects of Farkheimer. He looked at the reports of Tim Purse. He put them in the same pile with the reports on the increase of marine-life toxicity due to oil refining. He put those next to the reports of death rates and fetal-abnormality rates in Utah due to nuclear testing. He put those next to the reports of serious blows to the balance of nature: increase in landslides and carbon dioxide caused by the secretary of the interior selling off wilderness preserves to real-estate tycoons. It was all one way or the other the same folder. It was fear. Farkheimer didn't know it, but of course he was overwhelmed. The situation seemed hopeless. No one could ever stop it. He was, after all, only one man. So one man, falling like a toy soldier in a line, toppled them all. Mathematically speaking, this phenomenon repeated in the series of toy-soldier lines that made up most of the population, made it possible for a very few fearful, hopeless men to give up the others to destruction. The others, most of them, did not know their destiny even as they fell. They too had lost all direction. Didn't know up from down. So when the government told them that all the water on the earth had been poisoned, that the chemical pollution had gotten so out of hand it would take years to purify the water, they did not even realize the consequences of this. Like blind rats in the desert, they turned their heads to heaven, sniffing for rain.

But the rain would not save them, nor would other heavenly effluents. The heavens were in chaos now. The war was on. The Blue Robots and the Red Robots were starting their games. The final competition had unleashed powerful new forces. In their midst, the Russians and the United States were mere pawns. Only Schrodinger could deal.

Beedle was mystified. There, in the warehouse, were thousands of bags of banana pellets.

"You ordered too much, huh?" he said, stepping over to Harry Zinger.

Zinger looked uncomfortable. "They told us not to load 'em, Beedle."

"What're you talkin' about?"

Zinger shrugged. "I don't know . . . last-minute order change. They told us only to load two and a half months' worth of pellets." Zinger's face looked strained. "They say he can't survive that long out there. . . . See you, Beedle," he said, and started to walk off.

But Beedle was fierce. "Hang on, Harry," he said, his voice tight. "What do you mean? What else did they say? WHAT ELSE, HARRY?"

"Beedle . . . I didn't have nothin' to do with it. . . . They aren't goin' to bring him back, Beedle . . . that's it."

Beedle had never been in a church. But he was in one now. He had spoken to the priest, his heart in tatters, and the priest told him to pray. He did not know if praying would do any good. But he had to speak to 342 in some kind of blessed space. Here in this place maybe 342 would hear him. Beedle was saying as the tears rolled down his face, "I never woulda sent you if I knew. . . ."

It was only one of the crazier aspects of history that here were a woman and a chimp chasing to the moon after a cat, sponsored by the entire military establishment of the United States and utilizing all of technology, but protected finally by a young boy and a magic ring.

Oh yes, and protected by the cat. Protected by that which they intended to save. For Schrodinger was in heaven now, making his deals.

Those two hemispheres, hanging somewhere between *Homo sapiens* and *Felis domestica*, were going full tilt. Schrodinger, despite his comas, was no dope. He knew now what they wanted. They wanted him to cough up the molecules. No dice, he said, until the broad and the chimp make it back. At least that is how it was put by Oozie, who was making the translations still using the verbal aspects of Piranski's brain. It was perhaps just an accident of fate that what Oozie had picked up cruising past Chicago was more than Piranski's vernacular. Piranski was a con artist; and this ability to dissemble was more than an aspect of the lingo—it was built right into the synapses. So it was that these deals in the stars had, in their elements, more than a trace of trickery.

It was four days later, when Amanda and 342 had completed one moon orbit, that they received the first of what came to be called "the irrational transmissions."

"Amanda, this is CapCom. Are you all right? Please verify."

"Look," Amanda said tiredly to CapCom, "I haven't cracked up from oxygen deprivation or anything. I'm telling you my course has been altered. I'm heading for Epsilon Erdani. I'll explain later. Over."

She knew this would happen. Of course they didn't believe her. Who would believe it? It was several hours later when she got the next CapCom transmission. Well, she might as well take it. She would be out of contact soon.

"Amanda"—CapCom's voice was that of Hotchkiss—"this is Donald."

"Donald," her voice soared. "How wonderful. How ever did they let you in there?"

"Amanda, what's this about Epsilon Erdani? You know it's forty million light-years away. What are you saying?"

"Look, Donald, it's not my idea. I've been kidnapped, or spacenapped, or whatever they call it."

Amanda could hear some commotion in the back of CapCom. She didn't know what it was, but there were screams of "Spacenapped!" all over the imaging room. At last they had something to hold on to. She'd been napped.

"Amanda, please explain." Donald was frantic, she could tell.

"Look, Donald, they're not mean or anything—there's just been some cosmic mix-up. They've got Schrodinger out there, but Schrodinger is no good to them without my molecules. They want their molecules back—remember the guy I told you about in my living room? The funny thing that came in on the tricycle? Well, he's taken my ship, my starship. Don't worry, darling, I'm sure it will all work out."

Donald was speechless. She wasn't worried. How could anybody be one hundred thousand miles past the moon, *off course*, and not be worried? He turned to the general standing beside him.

"She isn't worried," he squeaked. "She's been spacenapped."

"Spacenapped?" the general said through his curling whiskers. "There is no such thing, Captain. There has to be a napper as well as a nap-pee. . . . Who's the napper?"

"This guy," Donald said soberly. "This funny thing in her living room. He put Frankenstein in her kitchen last month." Hotchkiss was holding his head in his hands. "I should've reported it when I knew it."

A strange silence had fallen on the computer room. People were looking at each other.

Hotchkiss turned to the general. "I guess we have to report this now. I'll tell you what I know."

"No you won't either," the general said. "I know nuts when I hear it. I'm not going to report things that are nuts. Nuts and crackers. Nuts and crackers. They never should have sent a woman up. Nuts nuts nuts."

"Talk to the others," Donald said. "They'll probably tell you the same thing. They're all keeping quiet because they know you won't believe it."

"You don't believe it, do you, Captain?" The general's eyes were fierce.

"Look, I didn't believe it," Hotchkiss said. "I didn't believe any of this until the cat started drawing pictures—that was the first thing, her cat Schrodinger, you know."

"Schrodinger . . . yes, I've met Schrodinger . . . the dead cat, is that right, Captain?" The general's eyes had an odd glaze. They looked just then like two caramels that were melting in the sun. "Schrodinger is *dead*, isn't he, Captain?"

"Oh, Schrodinger," Donald said, nodding. "Well, not really. Actually, he draws pictures, which all sounds *very* strange, I admit, but he swallowed these molecules . . ." At that moment Donald looked up. He saw that the entire Houston control room was listening and staring at him.

"Did I understand you to say, Donald," the general said, leaning down in a fatherly way with his hand on Hotchkiss's shoulder, "that this cat, Schrodinger I believe is his name, but in any event, this cat, even though he's dead, never mind that he's a cat, that he's drawing pictures . . . is that right, Captain?"

Hotchkiss looked around. It was absurd. No way could you ever explain it. So he bolted. He stood up and, spotting a clear runway, ran straight out of the control room before they even realized what he was doing.

"After him!" the general yelled, which was, of course, the perfectly appropriate thing to yell in such circumstances. But this Hotchkiss was a runner. He was halfway down the drive and had leapt the first hedge before they even got to the parking lot. By the time they got there, there was no sign of Hotchkiss. Farkheimer was screaming and stomping. He climbed into his jeep and barreled down the drive, his pedal to the floor.

Hotchkiss was a good runner. But they caught him. That is to say, Farkheimer nearly ran over him in his jeep when Hotchkiss fell down the edge of a ravine and hit his head on a rock. Farkheimer, in the jeep, was bouncing down the ravine and missed running over Hotchkiss by inches.

After forty-seven hours of psychiatric testing, they could not prove that Hotchkiss was crazy. He was still insisting that Schrodinger had coalesced into the fourth dimension a week after Frankenstein had appeared in Amanda's kitchen. These were the only crazy things. Everything else seemed to make sense. On the fifth day they let him go.

"He isn't a threat to society," the psychiatrists said. But he *was*. Fortunately for society, he was.

It was only a few hours later that they became convinced that either something was jamming their systems or Amanda had freaked out. She said she was approaching the speed of light. She was yelling, "Wow-Wow!"'" every few minutes and told them she was heading straight for the interstellar medium. The computers were a whirl of lights and contradictions. What she did not explain to them was that she and 342 were traveling along a beam of light that Oozie had converted for their use.

"Amanda, Amanda, reply," came the startled cries from CapCom. She was completely off course.

"She is going fast, faster; she's approaching the speed of light," the CapCom man said in a whisper. . . .

"What'll happen then?" Farkheimer asked, dumbfounded.

"She'll disappear," the man said. "It's not possible. You can't go the speed of light. The ship is getting smaller already. It's contracting. She's contracting. They're going to disappear."

"Disappear!" Farkheimer barked. "Like hell. Tell her if she disappears I'll have her court-martialed." The CapCom man seemed stunned by this utterance.

"Yessir," he said. But it was no use. The transmission was over. The spaceship, Amanda, and the chimp were gone. Gone. Wiped from the screen. Not a sound, not a trace.

All they had was the last transmission. "Wow Wow Wow . . . Over and out."

The key personnel, even Farkheimer, were heartsick. A shroud enclosed the space center. Black cloths hung limply in the thick heavy air. The red storm had left itself hanging in the air so that very little wind moved. "Unexplained atmospheric effect," said the reports. The ship was lost. The woman, and thirty million dollars into the void.

Nowhere. Nothing. Not a sound. Silence. Endless return of beeps. X rays, spectrometry, everything led to nothing. No evidence. Plucked out of time and space.

"In a way, I *hope* she's dead . . . it's better than knowing she's alone out there," one said.

"I'd rather be crushed to death than float on forever, knowing I can't reach anyone," said another.

Hope rose, occasionally. "Maybe something happened we don't understand. Maybe she'll come back . . . maybe." Special orders ensued. Special debriefings. How it was to be handled. The base was sealed. Mourning went on secretly.

Even Delko felt it. The worst of it was, Delko didn't believe she could be gone. Not something as substantial, as significant, as Amanda. Did he hate her still? Yes. Was he glad she was gone? Deep down he was glad she must be having one hell of a time getting out of whatever she had gotten herself into. But part of him was uneasy. Was it possible she was really, truly gone? Erased? Taken forever into the huge arms of the sky? He looked up at the stars. He couldn't believe it. He believed that if a whale had swallowed Amanda she would have raised such a ruckus inside he would have spit her out. He felt the same way about the heavens. She'd be giving them one hell of a tussle. Except, as time went on, he could not sleep.

His wife would wake and find him at the window. "Are you looking for that crazy girl?" she would ask. And Delko, pacing, weary, nervous, would return to the bed, saying nothing. She'd be back, he was sure of it. Just wanted to cause them more aggravation.

Elsewhere, in another part of the base, Beedle was inconsolable. He and Doris would sit before acres of paper cups of coffee, cigarettes, and ashes as Beedle maligned himself over and over again. "I never shoulda let 'im go up. He didn't wanna go up. I begged him to do it . . . for the good of the country . . . they left him deliberate," and he would collapse then across the table. Doris knew he was so raw inside she would give anything to stop it. This much misery in one human spirit was more than she could take. And there was her own sadness when she thought of the chimp. But Beedle's pain burned through her like a wire. She found herself one day holding a cigarette to the palm of her hand, trying to change the pain, to burn the connection from her.

The president announced to the country that the mission was a success. They were on their way safely to Mars. They would announce her landing in six months. Until then, everything was super. And top secret.

He had it all worked out. She would land safely, after his election. The Soviets might even believe it. Then they would announce her coming home. She would have to abandon ship in the stratosphere and take reentry on emergency procedure. A submarine would be waiting to pick her up. They would get another girl, someone to impersonate Amanda, and she would appear in the floating capsule. They would have parades and celebrations. No one, the prez was confident, need ever know the difference. Except those who knew her well, of course. They'd take care of those. He settled back and lit up his cigar. He knew there'd be a solution. Nothing like lies. Thank God for lies, he thought. Why, it would be almost impossible to run the country without them.

Farkheimer was less confident. "You'll never get anyone to imitate her. Anyone who met her, they'd know right away."

The prez was confused. Was Farkheimer bragging? "I thought you said she was a pain in the neck."

"Well, she was in a lot of ways," Farkheimer said. "Unusual. Weird. Imaginative. Beautiful. Energetic. Nuts. Talented. Passionate. You know what I mean," Farkheimer said. "That type of person."

"Oh," the president said.

Farkheimer said, "Believed in free love, I think."

"Free love?" The president's eyes grew round. "Not that."

"That," Farkheimer said.

"She never said, 'Make love, not war,' did she?" the prez asked nervously.

"I believe she did," Farkheimer said. "She was antinuke."

"And a person like that, you let them go up?" The prez was aghast.

"I'm afraid so, sir," Farkheimer said.

"That's subversive," the prez said. "Thank God she got lost. Well, it's for the best, you know. It wouldn't be right. I mean you wouldn't want an American hero or heroine to be a person who was against nuclear devices."

"Bombs, you mean bombs," Farkheimer said.

"Not bombs," the prez said. "We don't call them bombs. We call then nuclear devices."

Farkheimer wasn't feeling well. He didn't know why. Maybe it was because he was a military man. A military man, after all, was, whatever else you might want to say, not a liar. He had objectives. He had fundamentally to be realistic. Something recoiled in Farkheimer. Deep .down he felt: leave the world in the hands of the free-lovers, or give it to the military. Deep down he felt that governments were the most dangerous things of all. But this was so deep down, the part of Farkheimer that knew that lying led to death, this was so deep down, he dared not even think of it. He just knew that whenever he went to the White House he got sick. If it was war, Farkheimer felt, call it a goddamned war. If you were going to blow a thing up, you had to know what you were going to take with it. But they wouldn't say. They were talking nuclear devices like they were detonating a toothpick in the Grand Canyon. The minute a bomb became a "device," it didn't do what a bomb did. That's what they said, but the bomb didn't know that. It didn't behave like a toothpick. The bomb behaved like a bomb. You couldn't run a war like this. You'd run straight into hell.

Farkheimer had seen it all. All the Soviet installations. The three nuclear "devices" in the sand in the Middle East. The row upon row covering the fields of the United States. He had seen them. If any one of them went off, Farkheimer knew, there'd be no stopping it. He looked up at the sky. She might be better off up there, wherever she was. There'd be nothing here if that happened. A planet of dust and ashes.

BOOK 2

Mind Speed: The Other System

The distinguished neurophysiologist and philosopher J. C. Eccles considered the possibility that . . . perhaps even electrons, which are free under physical indeterminacy, may have their behavior influenced by the mind. And if an electron is confined in a brain cell, its velocity would range from 0 to 10^6 centimeters per second, which is about the speed of an intercontinental ballistic missile. If the mind can choose from this enormous range of velocities to trigger some physiological process leading to bodily action, freedom of the will is no longer a paradox.

—Lawrence LeShan and Henry Margenau,
Einstein's Space and Van Gogh's Sky

42

It seemed to Amanda that as she traveled she was getting lighter. She failed to notice, because of the dark, that various parts of her were disappearing within the spectrum of visible light. She was in an entirely different spectrum. As far as she could see and tell, she was perfectly there, if indeed in a weightless kind of way, although it would be impossible for anyone else, unless they had traveled her exact trajectory, to perceive her. This would be the problem facing any rescuers.

She saw how beautiful it was. She saw a curtain full of stars; it was the most amazing blue, and it drew her, in some way, toward it. She felt it was dazzling, this particular blue, and before she knew it, she was out of her spaceship, or whatever you might wish to call it. She was outside any structure. She was trembling and walking into the blue. She pushed into the curtain. It was a hundred shades of blue, all at once. The star curtain was dizzying in its splendor; it was silver and blue, it was the deepest cobalt, an electric blue that sent you reeling, and then it was navy, the soft deepness of an endless navy blue, soft and calling into itself darker and darker until it merged with black, and just before it did in the very density of it, just there for a moment the navy turned to red, one saw the red in the navy, the maroon heat, the smell of wine, the colors of dead roses, wafting up out of the darkness pulling you down with its blending. She lost then, with her consciousness, other things as well.

When she came to, she was hurtling, heading at infinite speed, through a bright tunnel. She was traveling. She was going for Schrodinger, and she was confident. She did not entirely trust this Ooze, but she felt there was something in all this that it wanted from her. So as long as there was a deal, she was willing to try it. Also, what choice did she have?

But this system she was in was exceedingly strange. She was traveling, as far as she could tell, inside a long, thin tube, like an infinite subway, and she was going headfirst very fast. Periodically, she would be stopped, hanging in midair, spinning slowly, her arms outstretched, her legs suddenly pulled apart so that she was in a slowly spinning spread eagle in a place that was called a "rotary," and sometimes a "transition zone." She wasn't entirely sure, but the Ooze, who she supposed was responsible for this trip, or someone was holding her up in rotaries while they decided which of the many tubes proceeding into it or out of it were the ones she should be on. It seemed to Amanda as much as she could see, that there were virtually thousands of these tubes attached to each rotary, and that furthermore the rotary and the tubes, like a gigantic stiff octopus, were wheeling through the sky, slowly, very slowly, but definitely wheeling, and the tubes, which is definitely what they were when you were in them, when you were out of them appeared to be locks in a dank canal. Looking back, that is, they were locks; when looking forward, they simply seemed to be sparks, electric sparks.

"Are you ready?" said the Ooze.

"Ready for what?" said Amanda. She noted he seemed to have left Piranski's brain behind.

"Anything," said the Ooze.

"I guess so," she said. "Just get me to Schrodinger. Where are you, anyway?" She could hear but not see. It was very dark now. Three-forty-two was trembling by her side.

"You better get hold of the monkey," said the Ooze.

"He's a chimp," said Amanda, "not a monkey."

"He's an endangered species," said the Ooze. "He's too frightened. You can't be that frightened and make it up here. . . . You coalesce into a gas with a fear quotient of sixty-five hundred. He's at forty-five hundred now."

"A gas? Oh my," Amanda said. "I'll try to calm him down," and she reached for 342 and whispered to him that he mustn't be afraid, that everything would be all right, but it was most disturbing. The chimp was whimpering. And then of course she had herself to worry about. It was very difficult to be twirling about the interstellar medium with anxiety about her anxiety yet.

"Three-forty-two, come on," she coaxed, holding him and trying to calm his fears. She certainly couldn't carry him all this way.

"Remember this," said Ooze, "you're going into another system. If you're frightened you coalesce. A gas. Pouf! Then I can't help you. That's the first thing."

"Got it," Amanda said.

"The second thing is I don't know what we're going to do about the chimp; *Homo sapiens* is the only one who ever gets into this place."

"They'll have to make an exception," Amanda said.

"You don't understand," Ooze said. "He can't go in there. The robots won't like it. They can't influence him at all. And if he makes noise we're finished," Ooze said.

"Well," Amanda hesitated, "I have a tranquilizer for him. I hate to use it, but I could." She thought 342 looked at her pleadingly. Then he buried his head in his hands. "Oh dear," she said, "I'm probably doing you a favor," and she slipped the small pellet between his teeth and watched him swallow. In five minutes he was fast asleep. "Okay," she said, "here we go." She took off her backpack, loaded him into it, and slung it on like a papoose.

Ooze watched. "That's insane," he said.

"What?" she said. "I'm perfectly comfortable."

"*You* can't go in there with an unconscious chimp on your back."

"Why not?"

"You can't, that's all," Ooze said, reaching for 342. "Here, give him to me. I'll take him in," and he scooped him up.

"Now remember," Ooze said again, "don't worry. If you worry you're finished."

"I'm not the worrying kind," Amanda said, although to tell the absolute truth, her fear quotient had climbed. She was doing her meditation exercise in the midst of all this, but it had climbed. It wasn't dangerous yet, the Ooze could see, but the capacity was there. The Ooze shook his head. It was crazy. He was crazy. Taking the body biological into this system. It had never been done before. But well, those molecules had changed everything. Once he got her past the robots they would stand a chance. The Ooze sighed.

"This is it."

The last thing Amanda heard in that realm.

As they entered each rotary station, or transition junction, she slowed down, and then floated. She had no sense of time here so it was difficult to know how long, and then she was shot, it seemed, or catapulted across a space, and inserted, in a sense, into another tube. She could feel the space she was being shot across was very hot and strange. It was a different kind of space from the space in the locks or the tubes.

And before she could think any more about it, she was shot across the dark, hot space again. And here was perhaps the strangest thing of all. In that brief time—and Amanda could not say how brief, perhaps a millionth, a thousandth of a second; she knew it was barely time to experience it—in that catapult across that unknown space, each time her entire life passed before her, start to finish, in a millionth of a second, each time, as if in the leap across she had to be like a person drowning. Each time as Amanda sped across the gap a terrible face would appear. The face was steel, the eyes electric. It looked like a huge stainless-steel gladiator, the mouth closing like a visor, but a terrifying visor, full of chains and cutting, saw-toothed edges. All she could see was this face— sometimes it was blue, sometimes red—and hear voices. They seemed to be arguing over her destiny.

Amanda did not know how long she had been traveling when Ooze suddenly appeared and said, "This is it, final section, last transition."

That was when she felt herself slow down, slower, until she was barely moving at all. She was drifting, languid, suddenly thinking of nothing, just a slow, pleasure spin, upside down, downside up, through the tube. She heard herself humming, as if she were not doing the humming but were only an observer of it. She wondered briefly, Have I left myself . . . or am I myself still or, or, or . . . , but the wonder was held in the pleasure of the turning. She drifted then, it seemed, floated into a small space, as if she were a log on the water and had been edged into a dock. She was lying on her back. Waiting. She was not afraid. She was barely curious. All anxiety had left her now, as this docking place she was in began a slow clockwise turn, and as it did so, she saw she had been floating in some kind of water, and the platform she was on had turned now and moved forward, so that it jutted forward, over an edge, except the edge had no bottom, no sides either; it was like a diving board into the outer reaches of empty space. And Amanda was on it, lying there calmly. Waiting.

"The important thing is," Ooze said, "don't be afraid."

"I'm not," Amanda said, as she felt the long diving board underneath her. She noticed then, just then, just before it happened, that the Ooze had appeared suddenly and strapped her to it. "A few straps, kid; this is a terrible jolt. Remember, this is a big leap. It'll knock you to pieces. . . . Remember the distance . . . if you come back."

Amanda heard the "if" and something stirred.

"If you come back this way," he said, "you'll have to make this jump yourself."

And she was off. The diving board seemed to be on a slingshot. Amanda felt the huge thing pull back, or be pulled back, and then a terrible jolt. It was like being shot from a cannon as she sped through the night, fast fast fast. Fast—how fast? She had no idea. She was pressed into the platform as if she were nothing but dust. A million forces, she thought quickly as she catapulted, and then she heard them again, she heard the voices, and as she turned her head she saw them, in herds, it seemed thousands of these stainless-steel gladiators, flying by on either side of her, a pack of Reds, a pack of Blues. They were staying very far away, they looked small to her now like flocks of flying birds, but it was the gladiators. Every once in a while they would come closer and then she would hear the same words, "Ooze territory, protection zone, retreat," all in strange electronic voices, and then nothing. They seemed to disappear as quickly as they arrived, in a sea of blinking lights.

And then she felt the thud. It knocked her from the platform, the straps broke off, and she was on the ground. She was breathless. It had knocked the wind out of her and had nearly broken her back. She staggered to get up, careening to one side and the other, losing her balance again and again until finally standing, she brushed herself off. She was covered with cosmic debris.

She was in a field of blinking beautiful lights. A landing field? A soccer field? Who could tell? Lights surfaced from below, and then it looked like a huge pinball machine. She saw a ball hitting the lights and she heard *ping-ping-ping*, and then everything went dark. The lights of the pinball machine went down, underneath the surface, and it looked then more like a soccer field. She stood there transfixed.

43

Meantime, on Earth, there was real consternation. The Soviets couldn't make head nor tail of it. The United States couldn't make head nor tail of it. At first, the loss of contact was bad enough. The computers had picked up nothing. Nothing. Amanda and the chimp were just gone. Disappeared. But now, worse things occurred. The computers were not picking up tracks of the spaceship. They were picking up tracks of the spaceship at incalculable speeds, was how the reports read. No one knew really very much about things moving faster than the speed of light, since theoretically, practically, and every other way, this was *impossible*. It is, in the very nature of impossible things, difficult at best, if not impossible, indeed, to gain information about it; the spaceship clearly would have dematerialized, as things do at the speed of light, for you cannot have, quite simply, that much mass traveling at that speed without that effect. Anyway, this dematerialized ship, going at incalculable speeds, was appearing on the computers: it was labeled GHOST. It was not dissimilar to things that appear on TV sets, that is to say that are not real things, that are, so to speak, the "visual echoes" of things, like shadows of trees trembling on the water. Of course, in such matters we come to an unfortunate business, a confusing business of point of view. As the force that had originally entered the copier—a force that Amanda had yet to meet—had pointed out in the case of a bat, so that same force might point out here that from the fish's point of view the shadow of the tree trembling on the water was as real as, if not realer than, the tree itself; the fish, under the circumstances we have come to know them, would not be able to experience the tree as we know it. That is to say, the fish could swim under the darkness of the tree's shadow, around its outlines, and experience the tree as the absence of light, a colder water, as all those fine fluctuations to which a fish might be attuned. But we can only know the tree as we see it, as we can climb it. Swimming in the water, we could not know the tree as the fish would. So in any event, unless the fish were climbing the tree (which some of them did do millions of years ago on their way to becoming reptiles, tree toads, iguanas, and the like) it would not know whereof we speak, even if it could speak.

So in a similar way the computer was recording the presence of an invisible spaceship. It was recording an incalculable speed, which it signified in computer language as "beyond measurement," and which was located at forty million light-years away, which was unimaginable. So there were all of these things that could exist—even though they were unimaginable—only one way in the human mind: as imagined. It was the power of this force that could be glimpsed but not proved, which would prove to be both the saving and the undoing (depending which way it was employed) of the human race. This, too, the computers "knew"—that is to say, they were recording this. But records, as we know, are only of as much use as they can be read, or understood.

The desert, Amanda thought when she had first approached it, looked very small, but once she was in it, it seemed quite different. It stretched out for miles, until she couldn't see any more. At the far end of the desert was an airfield, or at least that's what it appeared to be. She could see the blinking lights.

"Robot field," the Ooze said. "This end's where the ships land; the other end is where the robots play their games."

As they stood there, Amanda shaking sand from her boots, she felt a light wind. An enormous spaceship, moving like an ocean liner, descended through the dark. It even had a huge propeller attached to the back end. The ship was crowded with people who were very still, standing at the rails but not waving. As she watched, it sank from the sky to the floor of the desert, where it quivered to a stop. Millions of huge blinking robots—some the size of buildings, with feet the size of the block she grew up on. Red and blue robots, with heads like swinging turrets, firing lights of all colors and flashes, bounded forth from the ship as the ramp clanged down with reverberations that shook the desert floor. The passengers streamed down, arms outstretched. Some were crying; all were desperately searching as they tumbled through the sand picking up all kinds of things. All the passengers had bags, into which they were stuffing whatever they could.

But as a fog had risen Amanda could not see too clearly.

"What's going on?" she asked the Ooze. "What is that ship? Who are those people?"

"That's the robot's ship," Ooze said. "The passengers are looking for lost things."

"Lost things?" Amanda said. "What do you mean?"

The Ooze shrugged and gave her an odd look. "Well, I just can't get into this now. . . . The robots could pick up your frequency at any minute. We've got to get out of here," and he turned to lead her the opposite way.

Just then, where Amanda had placed her foot, a square lit up under the desert in an almost chartreuse green. An alarm went off, like a huge siren, and she could feel the earth tremble. Two huge robots thundered toward her.

"We're spotted," said Ooze. "Run for it." He grabbed her hand and they started to run.

She heard the robots clanking behind her. "Coalesce her, coalesce her," they called.

"No!" the Ooze shouted, just as a robot raised its gun.

Amanda ran as fast as she could away from the robots. The faster she ran, the harder she ran, the closer she came to the lights of the landing field. So she turned and ran the other way. Another row of lights confronted her—another landing field. She turned and saw the robots gaining on her. In every direction rows and rows of robot lights spread out into an immense kaleidoscope of color. Back and forth she ran, but she knew they were gaining on her.

Although they were close enough, not one of them tried to stop her. All at once she was thrown back. It was as if she had hit a glass wall. Then a robot appeared right next to her.

To her surprise it didn't try to stop her. She moved warily past it and began to run again. She hadn't gone very far when she hit another glass wall. Reeling back, turning, she ran the other way. Another wall. So she ran straight ahead, in the only direction left, one arm ahead of her. She thought she was safe. Slam. A fourth wall. She reached up, she hit it, she reached down, she hit it.

Amanda had fallen straight through to geometry.

She was in a box. It was transparent and it hung in the sky. She could not see it, but she could feel it. The point was, it kept her in. This is what the robots had done. Until they decided what else they might do with her, they had her in the Box.

What she didn't know was that this Box was a very special one, devised by the best of the robot guides. It was a form of entrapment from which it was almost impossible to escape.

Amanda lay still, trying to concentrate. She knew quite clearly now the dimensions of the Box. She had marked, in her mind's eye, where it ended. As she rested she remembered the funny little magician. He had seemed so sad as he looked at her. "You have the eyes of a dreamer," he'd said to her, "but a very dangerous voyage is in store." He had said something else, too, but now she was too sleepy to remember . . . something about love and finding a lost star.

44

After three days, they had to tell him it was hopeless. Hotchkiss was an All-American Boy, born in Kansas, with eyes of blue and cornsilk hair. His heart was pure, and he did not believe in magic. But he loved Amanda, and now here she was out of sight and sound. This was a dark night for Hotchkiss. He did the worst thing he could think of in the midst of his despair, which was to drink eleven beers. This he did, and was soused after nine. It was a dark and windy night. Not a drinking man, Hotchkiss had nowhere else to go, so he opened the door of Amanda's apartment to the strange wind blowing up from the Texas plains, which almost blew him off his feet. He shrank as it whistled through the door and encompassed the room, a cold dark wind unlike anything he'd ever seen or felt. It almost sobered Hotchkiss.

Then there was a knock. He opened the door cautiously, and a small man with a beard and a cape, a tall hat, and strange magnetic eyes pushed against it. Safe inside, he said, "How strange a night . . . not fit for man or beast."

He looked at Hotchkiss. "I will tell you how to get her back from the stars."

Hotchkiss's eyes were wild. The magician from the party—how did the magician know? "How did you . . . ?" he began.

"Shh," the magician said. "There is not time to explain everything. Some things you have to take on trust." Then he leaned forward and, pressing a small silver amulet into Hotchkiss's hand, he said, "This will do it."

"What do you mean?" Hotchkiss said.

"Do you know what you have to do?" the magician said.

"No," Hotchkiss said, truly bewildered. "What?"

"To catch her?"

"How can I catch her?" Hotchkiss asked. "She's got four Saturn rockets and ten tons of fuel and she left days ago. And there's no trace. The Russian tracking station says she left the solar system. I can't catch her," he said hopelessly.

"You can catch her," the little man said, "with this amulet."

Hotchkiss's eyes drew to a slit. This was an old cheap trick, he thought, on a drunk and lovesick guy. All the books were right, however. He was ready to try anything.

"How?" Hotchkiss said again.

"You must go faster than the speed of light," the magician said, "and with this amulet, you will."

Hotchkiss stared at him. Faster than the speed of light? What sacrilege was this?

"Nothing can," Hotchkiss said simply. "You can't do it. It's theoretically, as well as practically, impossible."

The magician threw up his hands. "You *can*. Can a duck come out of my hat?"

Hotchkiss smiled. "No," he said.

"Ah," said the magician, and a duck appeared out from under his hat.

"I thought that was supposed to be a rabbit."

"I'm allergic to rabbit hair," the magician said. "Now will you let me teach you?"

"How can a person who's allergic to rabbit hair teach me to go faster than the speed of light?" Hotchkiss said, which under the circumstances was quite a reasonable question.

"Ahh," said the magician, "it is not easy, but it is possible, if a man has perfected certain concepts. If you are ready, I am willing to show you how to travel at certain velocities, but first we must do your star chart."

"My star chart!" Hotchkiss said. "We're talking about technology, not astrology. What nonsense—"

The magician held up his hand. "It is not nonsense. It has to do with the amount of fluorocarbons in your brain. It beats lay analysis and it always holds true. If the sun was in Venus when you were born, certain velocities will not be available to you. Your chemistry is fixed. It is as simple as that. It will waste all of our time. But I thought you would be more receptive. I am not here to persuade you, convince you. I am here to offer you the opportunity of a lifetime."

The magician turned, catching the duck, and putting it back under his hat.

Hotchkiss tried to tell himself he was drunk. But he knew better. "I have to go home," he moaned, holding his head in his hands.

"Go home," the magician said, "but stop thinking. Thinking gets in the way. Take this amulet," he said, fading now, disappearing from view.

Arnold, better known as Dartan 4000, was waiting for Hotchkiss at his house. His eyes were full of tears.

"We have to go after her," he begged, "but I need help. Will you?"

"We don't know where she is. I'll do anything. But there's no trace . . ."

The tears spilled down. And though Hotchkiss held his arms out, the boy tore himself away and ran down the walk sobbing.

The boy ran from Hotchkiss to his only ally, an ally who had uncovered his past, not without considerable difficulty. An ally who had confronted him with the fact that he was a runaway, his parents had been killed years ago, and a worried aunt in Florida was trying to track him down. An ally who told him he didn't have to have a mother made out of microchips and transistors, there were solutions in the world other than solid state. It was a strange ally, an unexpected ally, as allies sometimes are, but the boy had been living with him for almost two months now and he had come to trust Sheriff Eberly.

"See that?" Eberly said. "Officially I adopted that boy. I'm his Pa now." He waved the paper in the air.

"The Genius?" Rufus said. "You adopted him?"

"I did. I got myself a genuine genius for a son."

"Well now," Rufus said. "I thought you couldn't stand him."

"Can't, most of the time," Eberly said. They were walking toward the split-rail fence staring up at the blue sky.

"You seen anythin' lately?" Eberly asked.

"How's that?"

"Them there things we used to see?"

"Nope. Don't see 'em."

"Think they left?"

"Don't know, Eb." There was a pause. "How is it you adopted someone you can't stand?"

"Beats talkin' to the heifers," Eberly said. "Besides, I figure some of that genius might rub off." He stared up at the sky. "He ain't such a bad boy, Rufus," Eberly said.

"I never said that."

"He just needs a little tendin'," Eberly said.

Rufus thought all in all it was a good thing. A boy who needed tending and a man who needed something more to do with his life than raise cows and go around arresting people. Besides, Eberly hadn't been the same since the Indians had disappeared. Never did find them.

Rufus didn't wonder why it was he didn't need something more in his life. He had enough. He had his memory. Of Maria. The sweet perfection of those days would steal over him, warming him, soft like a blanket, wrapping around his insides and keeping him safe. He didn't even know how much he thought about it, it had become so much a part of him.

The boy brought out the woman in Eberly, which Rufus didn't think was so much of a bad thing. Made Eberly cook more and arrest less, far as Rufus could see. Some nights he lay awake looking at the stars and he would go out on the porch and stare at the great space in the desert. They had seen things out there. He wondered if they'd see them again. He figured maybe they would. Eberly had said once, "Maybe it's a star."

"Stars fall," Rufus had said. "This thing landed." It was so bright, though, you couldn't see. They would've called it a UFO, except when you did the government came around and you had to talk to people who made lists and put your name on them. To hell with the government, far as Rufus was concerned. They had already polluted all the land, he figured. Anyway, if they ever came out and saw something that bright, that much light, they'd bomb it, and ruin everything they missed the first time around. It didn't worry Rufus much, because it didn't scare the cattle. Whatever it was. Rufus hoped it wasn't a UFO. He hoped it was a star. Not a real one but the kind you wished on. Rufus was hoping for magic. He felt in his bones, when he walked across the land, when he heard the birds cry, when the dead fish washed up on shore, when he saw the hawks soaring in the air, and when he turned on the TV set and heard about new nuclear testing—when all those things happened his heart sank and he wished for magic. Something to wish on. They needed this now.

There was a time when a man knew where he was. When you put your hand down into the earth and felt it run through your fingers. You knew where your fences were. There were outlaws and raiders, always had them. But you stood a chance. You might be outnumbered, but you could always see them coming. These things now, you couldn't see them, you couldn't smell them, but you knew they were there, except the governments now said they weren't there. Said everything was safe and sound, even as you were dying in it. If a man wanted to shoot something, he wanted it dead, Go out and shoot it, Rufus would say. But this, this insidious mess, was a slowly circling death, capturing hunter and prey alike, a gathering quicksand under your feet while the governments said, It's fine, go forth, it's safe. Rufus did not like to think too much about these things. They brought the fear up in him. He could smell it when he stood on his porch and looked at the stars. It stank, fear, rising off your skin like a cloud. He felt like a wounded deer when he stood outside and thought these things, like he was calling the cats down out of the mountains. Terror leading them, like a signal, straight to the throat.

45

I think it safe to say that no one understands quantum mechanics. Do not keep saying to yourself, if you can possibly avoid it, "But how can it be like that" because you will "go down the drain" into a blind alley from which nobody has yet escaped. Nobody knows how it can be like that.

—Richard Feynman, Nobel Prize winner for quantum physics

It appeared to Amanda that the robots were starting a new game. She had taken 342 back from Ooze and he was sleeping now in her backpack. The robots were up to some fearful business, she thought. What kind of a game was it, anyway? It made a terrible racket and it looked something like, although not exactly like, soccer. They had amazing speed, these robots, and power. They would kick the ball, and it sent these gigantic tenpins positively spinning. The sound of the pins was a terrifying thing even in itself. The robots were quick, too, turning on one gigantic leg as the other kicked the ball out behind in a perfect soccer relay, only to send it sailing over the heads of the opposing robots and to land smack in the field of tenpins, except, as Amanda noticed, these were not tenpins. There were more like ten trillion of them. They clattered and slammed and made a perfectly God-awful sound, and the ball, if that's what it was, would bounce about the pins as if it, the ball, had been electrocuted, and as they clattered and bounced, the pins sent up huge colored flashes into the sky, with bells and singing sounds, as if the pins were a pinball machine.

She was watching for some time, trying to discern the rules of the game, but it seemed to change all the time. Suddenly the robots would throw a huge rope out, and the two teams, the Reds and Blues, would have a tug of war. It was simply that. Sheer power. Whoever won got to kick the ball. Sometimes they ran with it, fielding and passing. But Amanda noticed each time there was a new kick, which she assumed was a new game, one of the robots would yell, "Clear the FIELD! CLEAR THE FIELD!" And then everything would get dark and the tenpins gleamed like pin pricks in the distance, and then quite suddenly they would vanish. She would see them for a second only, fading as they seemed to sweep over some cliff back there, some precipice of sorts.

The faces of the robots were ingenious. In the places where there might be eyes, instead were little doors. These doors would flip open and eyes would peer out. But each time the doors opened a different pair of eyes would peer out of the exact same robot. It was most disconcerting.

Amanda, for her part, thought the robots were remarkably well made. They spoke and, although they were over eleven feet tall, they moved with great agility, and they seemed to be extremely intelligent. She noticed, however, that there was one, a blue one, who behaved somewhat differently from the rest. She thought that this robot might have been asked to guard her, because he kept coming back down the field to walk up and down in front of her. Periodically he would explain things to her, even without her asking a question. He saw her looking toward the precipice now, and suddenly he moved toward her. Amanda was startled to see him so close to her. Apparently, they could read certain thoughts.

His eyes were looking very peculiar indeed. "You want to see where they go?"

Amanda nodded. "Yes. Those pins seem to disappear down there. . . ." she murmured, although in fact she wasn't too sure she did want to see.

The robot yelled, clapping his hands, "LET HER SEE!" At that, the field and the robots and everything in it spun quickly, quickly about, and Amanda saw what she hadn't seen before, which was the most gigantic robot of all, standing back in the distance behind the pins like a mountain, breathing fire and steam and looking perfectly dreadful, like a dreadful croupier, pulling a long-handled crop and sweeping the pins, like so many chips, into black oblivion.

And then he laughed, the gigantic pitch-black croupier with the terrifying face. He seemed less a robot than the rest, or more. Amanda couldn't be sure which, but she shrank at the very sight of him.

"Seen enough?" said the other robot, who seemed to Amanda to have some quality of friendliness about him. At least he spoke to her.

She nodded again. "But where . . . where do they go, the pins?"

"Pins?" said the robot, laughing. "Oh, stupid girl, you think they're pins?"

"Well, sort of . . . whatever they are—the field of lights."

"Oblivion. Forgetfulness, that's where. Out. Permanent out."

"Yes, I know over and out," Amanda persisted, "but over what?"

"Event horizon," said the robot, and turned away from her.

So. Event horizon. That meant the huge black robot guarded some sort of black hole out there, some pit of oblivion, and was sweeping the pins into it. She supposed that meant they couldn't use the pins again and had to keep coming up with new ones, which she sensed must be a terrible waste of absolutely everything, energy and pins. Which she finally brought herself to say.

"Excuse me," she said to the Blue Robot who had spoken to her, at what appeared to be a break between matches or games or whatever they were, "but isn't that a terrible waste?"

"Waste?" said the robot. "Waste? What sort of waste? And who cares, anyway? There's plenty more fields where the last one came from. Watch." He pointed up to the huge scoreboard where the scores were kept, the Reds against the Blues, and then the huge electronic signboard came on and said, NEW GAME; ADAM WELLESLEY, AGE TEN. AMERICAN. EPISCOPALIAN."

"Oh dear. Whatever does that mean?" Amanda said, guessing what it might mean despite herself.

"That's his mind that's up," said the robot.

Now Amanda was so startled by this that she said the things people say when they are startled, as opposed to sensible things.

"Why do you need to know if he's Episcopalian?"

"Very important," said the robot, "to know the cultural concepts of life and death. It helps the game. A Buddhist, well, you would hit different pins on a Buddhist, or an American Indian. Certain gates aren't open there for the ball that are open on Episcopalians."

"What about Methodists?" Amanda said suddenly. She supposed she said this because her parents were Methodists and she was suddenly worried about their gates.

"Western gates are all more or less the same, except for cultures like Indians. Eastern gates are different. Harder to get through certain eastern gates. A Buddhist gate," said the robot, "is a bitch."

"Well," Amanda said. A robot that swore. That meant a human had programmed him. No robot would insert that. Perhaps here was hope.

"What's your name?" Amanda said.

"Robert," said the robot. "Or number four trillion, three hundred and ninety-nine billion, three hundred fifty-six million, nine hundred seventy-three thousand, two hundred and six," he said. "I've got to play now," he said, and then as he ran from her, his foot caught on some edge of the playing field, some ridge appeared there, and he fell forward, and as he did he said, "Oh shit!"

Amanda's eyes grew wide. A swearing robot, of all things. In truth, Robert did not play as well as the other robots. They seemed to have a higher rate of success in getting the ball through the gates. Although this kid, this kid on the field, Adam, whoever he was, was putting up a dramatic fight.

Amanda had noticed there was a huge clock on the scoreboard. At the next break in the game, she asked Robert what the clock was counting.

"It's his time, the subject's time," said the robot. "How long it takes us to get through the gate. You get different points for different times. If you get through on his night side, you get certain points. On the day side, others. It's harder to get through on the day side, but you can. It depends on the kind of point you're trying to make. If you're trying to make a terror point, you go for the night side. The gates swing open more easily then. Get it?" said the robot, looking positively superior.

"I get it," Amanda said glumly. She got it, but she didn't quite know what to make of it. She wondered if the robots were not, in some strange way, trying to put one over on her. Sometimes she thought they were trying to convince her this was happening but it wasn't really real. At other times she thought it was real, and she just didn't want to believe it. She felt positively exhausted watching these games. She wondered how the "subjects" felt.

When she attempted to engage the friendly one, Robert, in a conversation, he only nodded to her and said, "Look, he feels moody. The subject only feels moody. They forget all about it. They never even know we've interfered," and he moved away.

Amanda, of course, was wondering how she ever was to cross these robot fields. It certainly didn't look dangerous, but the Ooze, whom she trusted—why, she wasn't exactly sure, but she did—had told her not to cross unless she either was holding on to Schrodinger, or she had a robot escort.

"Why would they escort me?" she said to Ooze.

Ooze said, "They wouldn't. But you'd be safe if they did. They never mess with their own turf." The Ooze had told her quite simply the robots would annihilate her if she attempted to cross. Perhaps, she thought, when they weren't playing, although they had been playing steadily for some time now.

She had no idea it would be so difficult here. She wondered if they missed her on earth—if Hotchkiss or McCloud were thinking of her at all.

Bronco McCloud turned in his bed, caught in the plight of imperfect love. He turned toward his wife and felt misery. He turned the other way. He thought of Amanda, and there was misery here as well. He turned back.

McCloud sighed. Amanda was gone. In the way he understood this he differed, as he did in so many other important ways, from Hotchkiss. Bronco thought he would be a fool to expect her to return. Only a fool would even dare to hope. But Hotchkiss was not in fact a fool. Hotchkiss in hope was precisely what Bronco longed to be all his life: Hotchkiss was valiant.

46

Einstein knew that modern physics was more than a mathematical fiction. Clocks really do slow down when they travel.
—Heinz Pagels, *The Cosmic Code*

She did not know when exactly, but after a time she fell asleep in one of the lounge chairs lining the field. When she awoke the sun was up and the robots were gone. The sun was streaming in on the grass, and as she looked about she saw a small figure down at the end, which appeared to be sitting in a beach chair and reading a book.

Amanda decided to approach the creature in the beach chair. It had a strange profile, at least from this distance, but Amanda was certain it wasn't a robot.

When she got closer, she saw that it was of all things a snake, or a cartoon of a snake. It was all pink and purple and wearing sunglasses and a hat. It was patently ridiculous.

"Oh," was all Amanda could say.

"What do you mean, 'Oh'?"

"I've never spoken to a cartoon," Amanda said. "It's so odd."

"Odd?" the snake said.

"Yes . . . you . . . you don't fit in with the landscape."

"No, of course not," the snake said. "I seem very comical."

"Oh, er, yes," she said.

"I have to be comical," the snake said, settling itself in the chair.

"Why?" Amanda asked.

"Because," it hissed at her as it began to open a book, "because otherwise people would die of fright."

"Oh," she said, giving this some thought, and then she noticed it was wearing on its tail a sneaker, of all things. The sneaker too was pink and purple and it had shoe ties with hearts on them. Amanda had a pair of shoelaces just like that on her skates.

"Oh," she said. "You have the same shoelaces I have . . . on your sneaker." The sneaker was worn on the bottom of the snake's tail.

"Sneaker?" the snake screamed. "What are you calling a sneaker?"

"Why that . . . your shoe," Amanda said, stepping back. "That is a sneaker, isn't it?" She couldn't imagine what was making this thing so angry.

"NO NO NO IT ISN'T. I'm a snake, right?"

Amanda nodded. She thought it best not to press this point at the moment, for indeed the creature did appear to be more a snake than an anything else.

"You ever see a snake in a sneaker?"

"Why no," she said, "but clearly—"

"Clearly, nothing. That's a snaker, not a sneaker. SNAKES wear SNAKERS, SNEAKS wear sneakers!" It carried on for quite some time while Amanda tried her best to calm it.

"Well, I'm sorry. I . . . I've never seen a sneaker on a snake . . . I mean a snaker on a snake, or anyone else, for that matter," she added. "It's a lovely snaker, though," she said, trying to divert it.

"Do you think so?" the snake said, loving the compliment and pirouetting on the snaker. "I rather like it myself."

"Ummm," Amanda said. The creature seemed to love to talk. It was eager to spill information. If she could keep from getting it angry at her, she thought perhaps she could divine something about the robots. Simply watching them seemed to be getting her nowhere.

"Do you know anything—" she started to say.

"I know EVERYTHING!" the snake yelled back.

"Oh . . . well, that's even better," Amanda said. "I want to know about the robots."

"See, I know everything, but you're the one they call *sapiens*. *Sapiens*, my ass," the snake said. "*Homo erectus*, that was okay, but *sapiens*. Oh hardy har har." The snake had an incredible laugh. It was quite the silliest laugh Amanda had ever heard, but it was quite contagious, and before she knew what she was doing she was holding her sides in pain and rolling on the ground. Of all things she was thinking that the snake had said "my ass," and though the snake might have a snaker and sunglasses and heaven knows what else, there was one thing this snake and no snake she'd ever seen had ever had, and that was an ass. For some reason this struck her as simply hysterically funny and she couldn't stop laughing.

She finally recovered sufficiently to say, "Er, uh, excuse me . . . have you seen a cat here, named Schrodinger?"

"Oh no, dear. The GCB took him."

"The GCB? I thought the robots had him."

"Look, sweetie, you better sit there while I read to you from the archives."

"That's very nice of you," Amanda said, "but I really don't have time to listen to archives. I have to get to my cat. Time is of the essence."

"Time is shit, shit is time," the snake said, knocking Amanda back on her heels. The snake said, "Don't you know about high-speed effects? The clocks run slow here. That's why if you're in a place where the clocks run slow and you have a future, you always have more time than you need. Look dear," the snake said. "*Homo sapiens* got the best deal— they got the earth. The robots, however, are programmed to ruin it. It's a long story, but if you'll just sit still I'll tell you. It started with one GCB—who somehow or other got this system. Well, he didn't want this system, he wanted another but he got this one, and then as far as he could tell, he thought they forgot they left him here, running this whole operation. Of course they hadn't expected the robots to act the way they do. The robots get energy from *sapiens* somehow." The snake, she noticed, was reading the archives very quickly indeed. "Every robot is a duplicate of another robot, although they have individuation cassettes that they can go to randomly for brief periods of time each day. They are all controlled off the central computer, which the GCB now has, except, of course, the Maverick. The Maverick was one of the robots, which one not even the GCB has been able to discover yet. He was the one robot who hadn't been programmed off the central computer—that is to say, not a duplicate of the original programming."

"Wait a minute," Amanda said. "This 'Maverick' you call it . . . the robots never found this Maverick? That means he could still be here, among them?"

The snake looked at her. "Well, I suppose in theory yes, but if after some eons they didn't find him, I rather doubt it." The snake read on. "Now the aim and goal of the central computer was to keep alive the values and culture of a biological life, yet ironically, the values and cultures of *Homo sapiens* were, upon examination, totally antibiological. So in order to maintain the programmed culture of the *Homo sapiens* society, it was necessary for the computer to destroy biological life. Based upon the information programmed into it, this is the only conclusion the central computer could possibly come to.

"Although the programming intelligence did not see that its purpose appeared to be the destruction of water, plants, forest, and air, it was perfectly clear upon a review of its history, practices, and public policy, that this was precisely what it was aiming to do.

"Therefore, when the ZED society (which was the computer's name for it, standing for zero energy development) was obliterated by radioactivity, it left behind this army of robots, with an infinite capacity for self-renewal. What this could have meant was that the robots simply ran around this particular place [whatever place it was, Amanda was not sure] maintaining a kind of electrochemical order. But these robots now wished to extend their territory. They had as a result of their intelligence obtained electrical magnetic signals suggesting biological life elsewhere in the universe. And their purpose, quite simply, was to destroy it."

"This is the most insane thing I've ever heard of in my life!" Amanda told herself. Then, aloud: "Well, I'm sure something could change them. What about this GCB?" Amanda said. "Can't it do something?"

"If you ask me," the snake said conspiratorially, "the GCB's best act is Random Error."

"Random Error?" Amanda said. "What are you talking about?"

"Believe me, the only reason anything works is Random Error. The GCB is a screw-up."

"Oh," she said. "But I thought it had all this power," she said.

"It's a powerful screw-up," the snake said. "And the Ooze is absentminded." The snake sighed. "But the GCB has genius."

"Genius? How's that?" Amanda said.

"A genius at mistakes," the snake said.

"Well, what is it—the GCB?" she asked.

"It's the Great Cosmic Brain," the snake said.

"Then I have to see it," Amanda said. "It must know where my cat is."

"Oh, it knows where everything is," the snake said. "Its information is first-rate. But its motives?" The snake looked uncomfortable.

Amanda was thinking about all these things when there was a commotion down at the end of the robot field.

There were sirens everywhere and huge neon signs flashing. ALERT KEY OPERATOR. ALERT KEY OPERATOR.

"Whatever is it?" Amanda said, standing.

"Oh, oh," the snake said. "New energy . . . new energies arriving they can't subdue . . ." And as Amanda looked, she saw that it was taking all the robots, every single one of them, millions of huge giant robots, to hold someone down at the far end of the field. She saw finally it was a little girl, laughing, and rolling her way down the robot field. In her hands she had some flowers.

"Why . . . what is it?"

"They can't get everyone, you know," the snake said. "Every once in a while they get an uncooperative subject . . . looks like."

As she looked at the snake, she saw the light behind it changing. The entire robot field started to spin. "What's happening?" she said, feeling her footing change, feeling her feet begin to go up, until she was hanging upside down watching the field spin beneath her. Soon the spinning stopped. The robots had dispersed. But the little girl was gone, too.

"Quick," the Ooze said, reappearing from out of nowhere, and grabbing her hand, "there's a breakout. You can get out of the Box now." He held out his hand to her.

The sudden noise revived 342, who was now vociferously pulling Amanda's hair and trying to get out of the sack.

"Three-forty-two!" she scolded, "take it easy," and she released him, holding firmly onto his hand.

"He can't come with us," Ooze said worriedly.

"Why not?"

"He can't, that's all. Just can't," he said, looking around.

At that moment the Blue Robot Robert appeared. To their mutual astonishment he said, "Let him stay here with me," and he pointed to one of the little huts that lined the field.

"No," Amanda said suspiciously.

"I won't hurt him," Robert said.

"He's right about that," Ooze whispered to her. "He can't hurt him. The chimp can't go into the other regions with us anyway," Ooze said.

"Well," Amanda hesitated. She thought she was going to have enough difficulty by herself, and she didn't know really if the chimp could take it. He'd been through quite a lot already.

"Come with me," the Blue Robot said, taking 342 by the hand. Three-forty-two held back. He looked dubious.

"Here," Amanda said impulsively, "these are banana chips. He likes them." And then, searching in her pack, she said, "and this is freeze-dried pistachio ice cream. He loves it. But don't let him eat too much of it."

The robot took the chips and handed one to the chimp, which was enough to persuade him the robot was okay. Then hand in hand they walked off across the fields, the eleven-foot Blue Robot with his strange clanking gait, the small chimp holding his hand and loping along the ground, and behind them a sunset, a brilliant glow, from some setting sun, which seemed to gain its light from the terrible clattering sound of the endless pins being struck down behind it. It was one of the strangest configurations Amanda ever hoped to see.

It was very dark now.

"When is sunrise here?" she said anxiously.

"Hard to say," said the Ooze. Then, "Come with me, quickly."

47

"It was so strange, that robot," Amanda said to him as they went flying through the sky.

"Very," said the Ooze, "but that's Robert. There's something wrong with him."

"What?" Amanda said.

"Oh, I don't know," Ooze said. "His filter's out of kilter."

It was sometime later when they'd been in a holding pattern for what seemed to Amanda like days, when she said, "What are we waiting for anyway?"

"A line," Ooze said, "a water-hole line."

"A line to where?" Just as she said it the water hole opened up. That is to say, the water opened up or, most precisely, a hole opened up in the water, and they went through it just like that.

Physicists talked regularly about the "water hole." This was, quite simply, the "place," the 1500 megahertz line in radio frequencies where the most likely possibility of encountering an extraterrestrial civilization might be heard. . . .

The signal detector will be automatically tuned, somewhat like a home radio receiver, except that it will be able to receive anywhere from one to 10 million radio channels at once. . . .

Existing radio telescopes at Arecibo, Green Bank, Ohio State University, and various NASA tracking stations around the world will be equipped with copies of the sensitive SETI receivers and multimillion-channel analyzers. High-sensitivity searches will then be mounted along the "waterhole" frequency range, concentrating on nearby stars, star clusters, galaxies, and the plane of the galaxy. In addition, the entire sky will be searched with lower sensitivity over a wider frequency range.

—Gene Bylinsky, *Life in Darwin's Universe*

When she finally broke the surface, she wasn't in the water at all. She was in a console room, like the control room at an airport, a huge octagonal-shaped room that looked out on one side to the robot fields and, beyond them, beyond their blinking lights, to a brilliant, glittery palace that looked as though it were made of crystals. To the other side of the fields there were no lights at all. It was a dark glassy sea. There was a strange sound coming from there. And all around this room were hundreds, indeed it seemed thousands, of television screens, some big, some little, and then in front of the figure before her was one enormous screen. Next to this screen were thousands of buttons and levers, and the figure at the console was studying them. Amanda knew who it was even before he turned around. It was Rastus, that strange black messenger who had brought her Frankenstein so many, it seemed now, years ago. He said nothing and simply turned in his chair and stared. Amanda stepped back. There was something strangely powerful about Rastus, nothing that could ever be clear. All she could remember about him were his eyes. Black as the night behind him, she saw only the burning eyes. She would know them anywhere—eyes full of stardust, eyes red with light, eyes of a dead man. They burned with forgotten dreams.

When she got closer she saw that he was typing at the console.

"What's that?"

"Encephalogram, sort of," he said slowly.

"Sort of? What . . . kind of sort of?"

"That's a mind," Rastus sang to her, waiting for the response, as all of a sudden a field of colors lit the screen.

"A mind?" Amanda gulped. "That . . . that's someone's mind?"

"Yep, this be the territory where you come in on a beam, you go out on a beam. 'Course you got in here under special dispensation. Ain't no idea whatsoever how you ever gonna get out, but Ooze worryin' 'bout that, not me. While you here you may as well learn somethin'."

"Look, I don't need you to tell me what to learn," Amanda said, irritated by this. "Whose mind is that?"

"You don't know. Could be any mind, every mind on the earth winds up here." Rastus punched away as console after console lit up, the dazzling array absolutely indescribable. "Farkheimer; your boyfriend; man in sailboat crossing ocean, age forty-four, name Heinrich Doule; any mind you want; all the minds at once if you want it. Here, you just punch it up," and he punched. "This is the control room."

"What control room? Controlling what?"

"This be the place that controls the electromagnetic waves—down there."

"Down there . . ." she said slowly. "The electromagnetic waves . . . you mean on earth?" she asked softly.

"Right."

"What do you mean, control it? That's impossible. Why . . . why that would be everything—even . . . even brain waves . . . brain waves. You"—she turned to him—"you mean brain waves?"

"Brain waves," Rastus said. "That's what the damn cat screwed up. Swallowed a goddamn evolutionary molecule. . . . Damn cat advanced too fast . . . messed up the consoles, messed up the system. Ooze be in trouble; he got to get the molecules back. But the robots beat him to it. Now the GCB got him captive in the Crystal Palace."

"Tell me about Schrodinger," Amanda said. "Is he all right?"

Rastus turned up the console. "He's all right," he said, "but he ain't happy."

"What are they doing to him?"

"Nothing, he perfectly safe, but he's sufferin' from thinkin'," Rastus said. "Too much input."

"Oh," Amanda said. Well she could quite understand that. Quite.

48

Schrodinger *was* miserable. The top-drawer hemispheric life was not what it was cracked up to be. Drawing, reading, writing had all come to naught. Schrodinger was brooding. He was homesick.

"Puddy-tat, nice puddy-tat," the Cosmic Brain had said, patting his head. It was no use. Not a purr. Not a single good vibration.

Drawing was reduced to doodles. His appetite waned. Even with his newfound abilities, he had no impulse toward literature. His favorite thing, in light of these two new hemispheric gifts, had been stolen from him: sleep. Sleep and dreams—those had been Schrodinger's way in the world. And now this. Sleepless days. Anxious nights. His new abilities brought new torments to the soul. The heavens were in an uproar. The Cosmic Brain, who ran them, had taken a liking to this cat. He petted the cat. He kissed the cat. He hissed all about the cat. Still Schrodinger would give him no quarter. Schrodinger did not, would not, could not purr. Schrodinger wanted to go home. Nothing would assuage him. Not all the tuna fish in Universe Two. Not even a mouse from Universe Five. No flies, moths, or crawling things could amuse him. He wanted his basket, his house, his mistress. At the thought of Amanda, Schrodinger began to cry. The crying, a yowling sound, pierced the hearing of the GCB, and sent all the forces scurrying. It was dreadful, this sound of a caterwauling cat. It reverberated throughout the firmament. The sound had a Teutonic timbre; it was knocking their circuits all to hell. Vibration was the name of the game, and Schrodinger's misery was causing new formations in the constellations above.

"Look, if you locate Schrodinger on that thing, uh, and also my spaceship, I'll just be on my way."

"You ain't going nowhere till you get a line outta here," Rastus said. "That's the only way out. You got to punch a mind up on this console. You can punch anyone you like. Try it."

"Well," Amanda said. She thought she should press on. On the other hand, this scheme was quite interesting. You might say extremely interesting. "Can I send messages to any mind on earth as well . . . on that thing?" she asked. She was skeptical.

"Depends," he said.

"On what?"

"On your powers of concentration . . . on their ability to receive, also on where the robots are." He looked up at a scoreboard, the same one that hung over the robot fields. "Now's as good a time as any," he said.

"Well . . . I certainly can concentrate," she said.

"We gonna see. Pick your mind—I'll call him up," he said. He seemed eager and ready to go.

"Okay," she said. "Call up the president. I really think I should make contact and let them know I'm okay. That the mission hasn't failed—yet. That would be important. They must be worried sick."

"President?" Rastus said, smiling. "The president of a country?"

"Well yes," Amanda said. "President Ellis. I'm sure he would want to rescue me . . . I mean, after all, he's a Democrat."

"Well, you sure in for a surprise," he said.

"What do you mean?"

"We ain't got no frequencies for heads of state. All the political areas are total static. TOTAL."

"Well, President Ellis must have a personal frequency," Amanda said. "Let's try that."

Rastus halfheartedly pushed a few buttons while Amanda concentrated very hard. Which was what Rastus told her she had to do. She thought later maybe the problem was that the president wasn't ready. He was going backward after all.

"Can't you get anything?" she said finally.

"Nope," he said. "Not a thing. There's not even a test pattern."

"Not even a test pattern?" Amanda said. "My God." That was really low energy. Not even a test pattern. Something must be wrong. "Why is that?" she asked. "Why ever would that be?"

Rastus shrugged. "You've got me. They just don't have the tubing, you know."

"The what?"

"The hardware, the software, the right stuff, the electrical circuits. They've been short-circuited. It's the work of the Red Robots, I can always tell. They got in there, and they've blown the whole thing. There's no free electricity. They're programmed up to the hilt."

"Well . . . what are they programmed for? Can you tell that, at least?"

"Oh yeah, I can tell—you're not going to like it—I can tell that easily."

"Well, what are they programmed for?"

"They're programmed to destroy the planet and then the species. They're programmed for death."

"What?" Amanda said. "If that's true, why then, we have to stop them."

"Who?" Rastus said skeptically. "You?" He started to laugh, hooting and laughing, and Amanda didn't like it one bit. "A girl and a cat versus the robots. Oh, it's too funny. It's positively cosmic."

That was what they all said out here, she noticed, when things got out of hand and they couldn't explain it anymore. When they didn't know what else to say, they said, "Things got absolutely cosmic." She supposed in a sense they had a point. *Cosmic* seemed to be the word all right.

"Try the president again," she said, feeling very nervous.

"He's in conference with the Soviet premier."

"Try that."

"It's hopeless. . . . You gonna hear them . . . they ain't never gonna hear you."

The president of the United States had spent a most peculiar night. He didn't know when he had spent such a sleepless night. And it was all because he didn't know the difference. It had all started in that meeting, when Farkheimer had leaned over to him, in a moment of friendly confidentiality, in reference to the Soviet premier's remarks, albeit translated remarks.

"You know the difference between an asshole and a stupid asshole," Farkheimer had whispered knowingly, and the president, all jolly, had laughed back, elbowing Farkheimer and going "Ho ho ho" in as convincing a way as possible. Interestingly enough, because of the electrical conduction that particular evening, the Soviet commissar had just remarked to the head of the KGB, about the U.S. president's remarks, albeit translated remarks:

"*Znayesh razneetsoo myezhdoo zhopoy ee gloopoy zhopoy*," which roughly translated means, "You know the difference between an asshole and a stupid asshole," and the premier had nodded and elbowed and nearly keeled over laughing, of course maintaining at all times his official decorum while inside, exactly like the president of the United States, he wondered, What *was* the difference between an asshole and a stupid asshole? And worse yet, how would he *ever* find out?

Hotchkiss was a haunted man. No trajectory. No trace. No sign of a spaceship, only the last transmission: "Wow Wow Wow . . . Over and out." He had listened to it hundreds of times, searching for a clue. He had mapped and remapped the heavens wondering where Schrodinger might have gone. It was not a circumstance he could explain to anyone. He searched the woods for Frankenstein—Amanda had said he'd become a floater. Crazy things clouded his mind. He was obsessed with the impossible. There had to be a way. He forced himself to shave each day. But he was getting worried, his energies waned. He took the amulet the magician had given him and placed it on the table. It glowed. Think harder, he told himself. Some nights he prayed.

It was several days later when the Genius arrived on his bicycle.

"I've got it, I've got it, I've got it!" he said, rushing in breathlessly to Hotchkiss. "I know how we can get her."

"How?" Hotchkiss said, his voice full of doubt.

"The ramjet," the Genius whispered. "The ramjet—it's all built. I tell you it'll work. If we *fix* it. You could. You can *fix* anything."

Hotchkiss looked at him dully. The ramjet was an abandoned rocket principle. It was an unmentioned "mistake." The entire rocket had been built four years ago and then junked. Hotchkiss had heard it had been sold to a private transportation company, which had gone bankrupt before they could even move the ramjet out of the silo. Originally classified top secret, it had been built fifteen miles outside of Waco. He didn't know if it was still there.

"Nobody could ever get it to work," Hotchkiss said. "In principle, barely workable. In practice, totally unworkable."

"But you could . . . I could," the Genius said, eyes wet with tears. Hotchkiss looked at him. He had seen the Genius prove his genius more than once.

"Okay," he said, "let's drive out and see if it's still there."

The ramjet was there, its silver tip gleaming from its silo. There was a rusting wire fence all around the compound that housed the rocket, and one gate. There was a dog at the gate, and a man in a chair reading a book. He looked up when they approached him.

"This's government property, fellas," the man said. "You got to turn back."

Hotchkiss pulled out his identification stickers. "NASA," he said, smiling. "They sent me out to have a look." The man tilted back his chair and looked at him carefully.

"That so?" He got up then, with some effort. "Thought they forgot about that thing out here. Ain't nobody been out here for years, now." He pulled the barking dog back by the collar and opened the gate.

"The boy'll have to wait outside. This here's government property."

"He's NASA too," Hotchkiss said, and the Genius flashed a badge.

"Well now," the man said.

"I thought this was sold to private industry," Hotchkiss said.

"Never did go through. Seems like nobody wanted it. Wanted to send this thing up to the stars, then seems like they lost interest or something. It didn't have enough power in it to launch any satellites.

Couldn't do nothin' with it, that's what they told me. I told them if there weren't nobody that wanted it I didn't know why they needed it guarded. They didn't seem to know either, but it's a job," he said.

He didn't even accompany them to the rocket. He pointed to it— "It's over there," and settled back in his chair. There was a small trailer behind the gate, which was where Hotchkiss supposed he lived.

"Could I use your phone?" Hotchkiss said suddenly.

"Nope, ain't got a phone," the man said. "Sorry 'bout that. Nearest phone is thirty miles."

Hotchkiss smiled. "Okay," he said. "We may be coming back and forth with a few supplies, you know, for a couple of days."

"Suit yourself," the man said, and settled back in the chair. The dog was safely tied to the chair now.

The Genius winked at Hotchkiss. "A piece of cake," he said.

Amanda had been watching Rastus work at the console for some time now. "How much . . . can you influence the thinking . . . you, the operator?"

"Not me," Rastus said. "Robots can. GCB can. And Ooze. Sometimes, once in a while. A great while. If the lines be clear I try. Once in a great while, I hit something. Right now, there's a real mess. Big war goin' on."

"War? What war? Down on earth?" Amanda's heart lurched inside.

"No . . . not exactly. Robot war . . . Wars are bad when the robots get goin'. Robots fightin' for electrical field. . . . Red Robots want it, Blue ones want it. . . ." He turned away from her. "Messin' up all the airwaves, real bad. Might be one reason you havin' so much trouble, because of the deal."

"What deal?"

"Robots made a deal, Red and Blue. Made a deal with the GCB for the NERPs. They gonna NERP the world."

"NERPs!" Amanda said. "Why I've heard of these NERPs. But, but . . ." She was suddenly unsure. "I'm not sure what they are."

"The NERPs be what they say," Rastus said. "Nerve Ending Reversal Programs. Robots get in, rewire their consoles. People, instead of coming to the right conclusion, come to the wrong conclusion. Instead of makin' the jump—what you call the synapse, in all your brain-machine figurin'—instead of makin' that, the NERP, he go back on hisself and he feelin' real fine too. Ain't got no idea nothin' wrong with his thinkin', 'cept, of course, from a biological point of view, which yours is, it makes no sense. The Ooze, he thought he could straighten it out. He be pro-biology, but he don't think he stand a chance now. He thought maybe he had the molecules, but the damn cat done swallowed them and . . ." Rastus howled then, finding the entire matter quite hilarious.

"Well . . . well, these NERPs . . . what, what are they going to do?" Amanda was beginning to believe all this. She didn't know why exactly, except that nobody could ever have made it up.

"They workin' with the robots."

"And what are the robots going to do?" she said.

"Two sets. Red goin' for blast-off."

"Blast-off?"

"Nuclear death. Radiation. Blues going for long steady poison, biological conversion. Reds are for blowup; Blues are for rot. Stagnation. Slow winddown. Poison."

"Well," Amanda said, "that's absolutely outrageous. You can't have them planning such things for the earth . . . I mean, they can't do that. How do they NERP people, anyway?"

Rastus shrugged. "Don't know exactly how they get in there and do it. Ooze knows. . . . He don't tell, though. He too scared of the GCB to tell anythin'."

"Where is the Ooze?" Amanda said, somewhat irritated. "He was supposed to be here by now . . . I mean, I came for my cat. . . . Of course, if there's anything I can do for the earth while I'm here I'm only too happy to." She was interrupted. "Is that Ooze?" she said, hearing a strange familiar whistling sound. "Maybe he has Schrodinger."

"Hi, toots!" the Ooze said, skidding to a stop. He was on his tricycle again.

"Hi, yourself. Where's my cat?" Amanda said, feeling somewhat angry.

"Oh, the cat," Ooze said, stepping off the bike. "Well, now . . ."

"Don't 'Oh, the cat' me," Amanda said. "Where is the cat? I said. WHERE, WHERE, WHERE?" She was getting furious. She had seen that look on the Ooze's face before. It was the look of something that had no idea whatsoever of what it was doing.

"Well, take it easy," he said. "I know exactly where he is. He's in the Crystal Palace."

"Let's go then," Amanda said.

But then Ooze hung his head and looked at the floor. Amanda's heart sank. Did this mean he'd lied to her?

"What is it, Ooze?" she asked.

"Well," Ooze said, "I can get you back in here—and as long as you're here, you're safe—but . . . but I can't get you out."

"Well, I'll get out myself. Show me where."

"Ain't gonna do it," Rastus said. "You got to get a line out."

"Well," she said, getting impatient, "get me a line, then."

"You can't get it so easy," Rastus said. "That's why once you in here you usually here for life."

"For life?" Amanda gasped. "Well I have absolutely no intention of staying so long. This is impossible. Now tell me what I have to do— what kind of line do I need?"

"This kind," he said. "In order for you to get out of where you are, you got to get through to somebody on this console. If they hear you, they set up an electromagnetic signal that will open the frequency. Then I can send you outta here. Otherwise you can't get out."

"Can't get out?" Amanda said. "But I have to get out. I have to get my cat . . . he's . . ."

"SHH," Rastus said. "You ain't got that much time," he was looking at the clock, "before your opportunities change." He glanced back to the scoreboard. Then he punched her name on the console and she saw a dazzling display of lights and tunnels and whirling pools of light.

"If you going to get out, you got to *reach* someone. Someone thinking about you, real hard," Rastus said. "I'll try to clear it."

Amanda saw the name of Bronco McCloud appear.

"Oh," she said, delighted.

"Don't get too excited," Rastus said; "he got to hear you."

But he did not hear her. McCloud did not hear and could not hear, because she needed him. McCloud could not love what needed him. What needed him might capture his devotion and his loyalty, but not his love. This was too pure a stance for Amanda. She could not, fundamentally and finally, *not* need him. There was a point in the prism of light, an aspect of its spectrum, where love was need. McCloud could not bear this. Whatever complexities in McCloud drove him this way, it was finally what she knew.

McCloud and Amanda were free to love each other only in some inevitable way, as dream or destiny. When choosing they lacked the final confidence, the thrill of decision, of luck, the dare. When the dice rolled, they shrank. And there were other gamblers at the table. Hotchkiss was there, placing bets. Their knowledge of this perhaps influenced the roll of the die. Hotchkiss was a determined man. A serious opponent. Hotchkiss in love was suiting up for battle. Hotchkiss would make claims. Possession was his law.

"Too bad," Rastus said.

Amanda was staring at the TV console, which reported in huge letters: CHANNELS NOT OPEN ON THIS INDIVIDUAL. SPECIES: *HOMO SAPIENS*. RECOMMEND NIGHT CONTACT.

"The bastard!" Amanda said, kicking the console.

"I know that species," Rastus said. "You gonna have a hell of a time getting through there, but you might make it with someone else."

Amanda was feeling discouraged. She thought surely she could reach McCloud, if only in thought. She thought surely he loved her enough to send the frail signal needed to ensure her escape. She sighed.

"Well, I . . . there is someone," she said hesitantly. "I know he'll be thinking about me. I'm just not sure exactly how. I think he was mad when I left."

"Thinking isn't enough. He's got to be able to receive. You do not know what you're up against. . . . You want to see the kind of electro-magnetic pattern you're dealing with in that species?" he said to her.

"Oh . . . why, I guess so," she said, and watched the screen as Rastus punched up what he said was the total consciousness of Donald Hotchkiss.

It was a mess.

"That . . . that's the mind of Donald Hotchkiss?" she said.

"That's it, all right," he said. "And it's some mess . . . more clear spots than usual—I'll tell you that."

"Well," Amanda said softly, wanting to defend Donald, "I . . . I think he has quite a lovely mind. I mean there must be something wrong with this point of view—why don't we look at it from a different point of view?"

"Because you can't get in on this frequency that way." Rastus turned to her. "You don't know anything yet, do you?"

Amanda wished that people would not keep saying things like this to her.

"I told you, only a *chance* these frequencies are open. I keep checking the scoreboard. When the score's right, you could get through *maybe*, to someone."

Amanda stared at the console. "What's mine look like?" she asked suddenly.

Rastus punched the screen.

Hers, too, was a mess.

"Very conflicted," Rastus said. "Unresolved Oedipal complex, masochistic . . . typical female mind . . ."

"Wait a second. I'm not masochistic," she said, and then Rastus whispered something to her.

"Oh, that," she said.

"You gonna have more trouble gettin' a line than I originally expected. Lotta junk in here. . . . Except," he said, peering at the screen, "see that clear spot?"

She looked. There was a clear spot. It was a perfect clear place in the middle of a mess of green and gold. The colors were perfectly dreadful. Amanda was quite horrified to think that from this point of view she had a *khaki* mind. Still, there was the clear spot. It was the shape of a teardrop.

Bronco McCloud was in agony. Last night had been a terrible night, his old dreams had been renewed. Some part of him had died with Amanda, and he was trying to tell himself that such sacrifice made him a better man. More mature. Dealing with realities. He had taken to loving his wife with more determination than before. He did not, and could not let himself, know that somewhere some part of the fire had gone out. But last night had left him tired. He was very tired. No one knew how tired. Save one. The mechanic on his plane. For years now, before every flight, Bronco himself had checked every bolt, every nut, every seam, every connection, running his hands over the plane like a man who's just bought a horse. Checking out. The mechanic knew he could always count on McCloud for this. But when he finally came to the airfield that day—it had been days now since McCloud flew—the mechanic thought despite his heartiness he looked different somehow. The way he got into the cockpit—no leap, like McCloud of before. No.

A resigned heaving and then a throw of his weight over the side. But this was not the most shocking thing. No. When the mechanic said to McCloud, "Ready to check," McCloud only waved feebly and with a halfhearted smile said, "You checked it. I'm sure it's okay," and pushed himself inside.

That day as McCloud flew in the midst of a loop he felt for a split second he couldn't make it; everything just stopped, he didn't care, he *wouldn't* make it, he would just plummet and die. His mind was shot, but his reflexes held, and almost too late, but a fraction of a second on time, he did it. Surprised to find himself alive, he landed the plane on an unused airfield in a portion of the desert. No one there knew McCloud and no one paid any attention to the small jet at the end of the field overgrown with grass and rusting hangars. And that was how he wanted it. It had been years since McCloud had cried.

Hotchkiss, now tossing and turning, was frantic. He had not slept for days. Maybe the amulet. He'd tried everything else. He got up and took it out of his pocket and put it under his pillow.

Hotchkiss was all determination. And determination, here, at this precise moment, carried the day.

"You ain't got much time," Rastus whispered. "You got to get out before sunup, you gonna get out at all."

This deadline renewed her. Energized, she ran to the console, beating her fists against the screen she cried, "HOTCHKISS! Hotchkiss, where are you?" She knew, she knew, she knew, if she knew anything at all, that Hotchkiss would *have* to be there for her. Frantically she pressed every button on the console. The sun was in its passage.

Tim Purse stared through the telescope. He had climbed Kitt Peak, leaving his dishes on the desert floor to see, to peer; he'd given up on sound. He took a good look, but he couldn't see much. It was all occultation. Some mysteries were at work. The ceiling of the universe was clouded.

Astronomers were confounded. Stars appeared to be moving, *oddly*.

"This couldn't be," they murmured. It was something in the distortion of the light. The light was bending, in some new crazed way. It was whirling and twirling light. The heavens, when you looked close, were full of spirals and corkscrews. The universe was a whirlpool. What went up didn't come down. It went round and round.

Purse stared. In belief. In disbelief. He had given up on sound, but this was worse. Ghosts, mirages, whirlpools, faces, forces, and fates all spun across the glass. Mirrors. All telescopes worked with mirrors. Tricks were afoot here. This could not be. He couldn't believe his eyes. And so, scrambling and quick, he made his way back to the ground, jumped into his car, and spun across the desert floor. Back to the big dish, back to the sounds. He could not, would not believe his eyes. But he might believe his ears. They were tuned now to unthinkable things. Subsonic sounds. The dishes heard all frequencies, they heard the secrets from the night. Incalculable distance, incalculable speed, the antennae were fierce in their pursuit.

She was out there. It was out there. He knew it. If he could find it.

49

"Look," Amanda said to Rastus, "you've got to help. You must have learned a few tricks running that thing so long. I can't get through. I've tried everything . . . and I've got to get out of here!"

"I told you," Rastus said, leaning back, "odds against."

"Well," Amanda said, "you can't just go with the odds. You have to go with believing in things. I mean, I know I'll get back, and I know I'll get Schrodinger. But . . . but if you help, it'll go faster."

Rastus turned to stare at her. Hope did not live too long in this dimension. It was new to him. He stared at her for quite some time.

"I told you I can't help—I am just a numbers runner. I used to keep the faith. Now I just keep the records." He turned back in his chair.

"Well, screw the records!" she said angrily. "To hell with the odds. I'm going to get my cat, and if you won't help I'll find another way. You said there might be another way."

He looked at her again.

"There's another way, through the memory fields. But nobody ever makes it that way."

"Show me," she said defiantly.

"You gonna do it?" He seemed surprised. "You actually gonna do it?" he asked, astonished.

"What do you mean, am I gonna do it? You said it's the only way out."

"*If* you get out. Ain't no odds on your side at all. You be better off waitin'."

"Waiting here?" Amanda said. "A million years? I can't do that. I'll be dead, and so will Schrodinger. He has a short life-span—that is, under normal conditions."

Rastus turned to her. "But it's murder out there, you know that."

"What choice do I have, really?" Amanda said, sighing. She peered out now. "It looks empty . . . and dark. Is there anything out there at all?"

"Oh yes, when you get into the memory fields," Rastus said, "you gonna see shapes of things."

"What things?" she asked suspiciously.

"Things to come," he said. But he would say no more.

He had opened the door. She heard this strange hiss, almost a whistling sound, but a hiss. She could hear wind and strange, high-pitched sounds.

"What's that?" she said, stepping back.

"That's the sound."

"The sound of what?"

"The sound of out there," he said. "It gonna get louder."

Hotchkiss sat up in his bed. He felt the presence of Amanda with such clarity he couldn't believe it. Sweat was pouring down his face.

"Jesus," he said. What a powerful dream. And then he heard a banging. Perhaps that is what had woken him up. Someone was outside, pounding on the door. He looked at the clock. It was three in the morning. Groggily he made it to the front entrance and peered out. It was that crazed man from the radio telescope, Tim Purse.

"I . . . I heard . . ." Purse whispered to Hotchkiss. "She isn't lost. . . . I know where . . . things . . ."

Hotchkiss was still groggy. His eyes were streaked with red. Was the man before him mad? Hotchkiss reached out and grabbed at Purse's throat.

"You heard?" His voice was dry. "WHAT DID YOU HEAR? You heard HER?" Hotchkiss in his passion had lifted the man entirely off the floor.

"No, no, let me down," the man pleaded.

Hotchkiss did, as he pressed him against the wall. "TELL ME," he said, and did not relent until Purse, struggling for breath, eased Hotchkiss's hand from his throat.

"I . . . I didn't hear her . . . I . . . I know, though, that there are things out there that can communicate . . . they, they talk to me."

Hotchkiss looked at the man. There was gray in his hair. He must be close to fifty. But the eyes. The eyes were the eyes of a lost child. He thought of Dartan's eyes. Did the *voices*, if that's what they were, did the voices from outside speak only to lost children? He thought of Amanda, and he felt the pain in his heart again.

"What do they say?" His voice was so tight he didn't recognize it as his own.

"Obscene things," Purse said.

His face was flushed. The man was stricken, Hotchkiss could see. It had cost him to come here. "But . . . but I know where they are," he said, tears forming now in his eyes, in the shame of his admission to Hotchkiss. Purse, after all, had gone to church for years, and the church, although it preached love, had not taught him yet its first tenet: shame is not for sinners. Shame is a sin against love.

"I can show you where," he said, his hand reaching out and grasping Hotchkiss by the elbow so firmly Hotchkiss felt his arm would crack in two. Grasping so firmly, he said, "I can show you *precisely*," he said, his eyes gleaming now, and then his voice dropping to a whisper, "They tried to fool me and they nearly did . . . but I caught them. . . . They're not where they appear to be at all . . . but I can show you," he said, nodding excitedly now, "I can. I can." His head bobbed vigorously in ecstasy and confidence and relief. Purse had never given anything to anyone before, and the power of this transaction was shaking him to his core. "Follow me," he said, and Hotchkiss, breathing quickly, ready to follow a madman for a clue, did.

In a spectrum, the light is spread out, like in a rainbow, into its constituent wavelengths or colors; different elements in the star absorb or emit different frequencies of light, leaving their fingerprints as dark or light bands at particular wavelengths. The lines in quasar spectra, however, were at weird wavelengths that made no sense.
—Discover, December 1982

Hotchkiss stared at the radioscope. He looked at the outlines of lights and lines that Purse had pored over, next to a long pad of calculations. He saw the place in the sky where Purse said she'd be. When he spoke, his voice sounded empty, as though it came from a tomb. "That's Epsilon Erdani," Hotchkiss said. "That's forty million light-years away."

"I didn't say I could get you there," Purse said, covering his dismay. "I only said I could tell you where she is."

"She said she was going there. . . ." Hotchkiss said absently.

"What?"

"Before . . . the last transmission. They thought she was flipping out . . . they convinced me of the same thing . . . but that, that's what she said . . . she was going to Epsilon Erdani." He turned to Purse. "How do you know she's there?"

"I'll show you." He motioned to Hotchkiss and led him down into the basement. Through three locked doors. It appeared to be a laboratory of some kind.

"No one ever gets in here but me," Purse said. Hotchkiss followed Purse down a long hall into another room filled with the kind of equipment that was totally unfamiliar to Hotchkiss.

"What's all this?"

"Sound analysis," Purse said. "I have analyzed within the confines of this room the radio pattern of absolutely everything. It's just like a fingerprint. Let me put it into the computer. This is, for example, iron ore." Purse pressed a button and a picture appeared on a screen. "That's the sound that iron ore makes," Purse said. He went through about fifty different varieties of organic and inorganic material. Then he said to Hotchkiss, "This is a human voice. A woman's." He punched the computer and out came a picture. "I got this same picture from Epsilon Erdani. Up until then I never got a picture."

"Why?" Hotchkiss said.

"I don't know why. All I can get is what I get when I get it, if you know what I mean. I can't record it. I can't prove it." He turned to Hotchkiss. "That's why I'm tellin' you . . . I can't prove it," and then he turned back to his screen. "But I can prove that . . . I can prove that's a voice transmission from Epsilon Erdani, and it *looks* like a woman's. It, it's coming in on some frequency I've never seen before. . . . I can't explain it. . . ."

"Amanda," Hotchkiss said softly. "Maybe." He looked at Purse again. Madman, charlatan, or scientist? "Maybe your computer's picking something else up—from somewhere else. A telephone call off a satellite, something like that." He was dejected. Forty million light-years. It would have meant Amanda was there forty million years ago, that is to say, if any of this were logical, which Hotchkiss was sure it wasn't. And what if she were there? What if there were "holes" in the universe, time warps that twisted reality and sped her there instantly? Time holes? What if? How could *he* find her? His hopelessness made him feel only the defeat.

"Well . . ." Hotchkiss said, starting to go.

"If you go," Purse said, giving him a map, "this is the trajectory to follow. It came in at right angles, it bent at a steep angle, just past Pluto." Reading his mind, Purse said, "If there's a hole, that's where it is."

Hotchkiss's eyes were cloudy. They saw no hope. Purse stuffed the map into his pocket. As he was leaving, Hotchkiss saw a white dot bleeping across a screen.

"What's that?" he said, pointing to it.

"Nothing," Purse said. "Some kind of interference."

Hotchkiss put his hand on the knob. The white bleep got louder. He turned. "Is that coming off a satellite?"

"No." Tim Purse blushed. "Actually it looks like it's coming from the same place. But it couldn't be. It makes no sense at all—it's some kind of computer error. A woman's voice, maybe, but not that. I'll figure it out soon." Purse had closed the door. For some reason, Hotchkiss was intrigued, could not let go.

"What kind of error is it? What do you think it is?"

Purse shrugged. "I don't know. It couldn't be what it looks like."

Hotchkiss stopped. Incredulity was the most reliable clue in this new game.

"Why?" he said. "Why couldn't it be what it looks like?"

They were walking down the steps now, and Purse was pulling the collar of his jacket up around him. "Look, I told you . . . it's ridiculous. It couldn't be that."

Hotchkiss leaped forward, fiercer now, grabbing his collar. "Tell me," he said.

"It's ridiculous," Purse said.

Hotchkiss had grabbed him now with such urgency Purse was off the ground, his legs dangling in the air. He looked, just then, if you were passing by, like a scarecrow.

"Okay, okay," Purse said. "Let me down. If it looks like *anything,* it looks like a cat's meow."

Hotchkiss dropped him with a thud and took off. He broke into the computer-enhancement laboratory and swiped the NASA computer pictures of Amanda's trajectory. Then he called the Genius, who showed up on a motorcycle driven by, of all things, the magician.

"What're you doing here?" Hotchkiss said to him, annoyed.

"I got a call from the magic amulet," he said. "It doubles as a high-anxiety beeper."

"Ye Gods," Hotchkiss said, and let them in.

Hotchkiss and the Genius sat up half the night, carefully going over the computer images of her flight. At four in the morning they finally saw it.

"Back up," Hotchkiss said, and the Genius punched the computer for a rerun. There in the tiniest pixel, there was the trick. The computer picture had been tampered with. That is to say, the pictures on the computer picture contained information that had been altered, or inserted. After several hours and with the aid of Leonard Watkins, a computer-graphics specialist whom Hotchkiss had aroused from sleep and rushed to the lab, they discovered one indisputable fact: the computer graphics had been altered so that it appeared that Amanda's flight pattern went past the moon and toward Mars, when in fact, if you subtracted the additions, so to speak, what you had was a totally different trajectory.

"She went thataway," the Genius said, pointing to the other side of the moon.

"I'll be damned," Hotchkiss said under his breath. It led straight to Epsilon Erdani, the source of the cat's meow.

50

Hotchkiss, the magician, and the Genius met in the middle of the desert, which the magician said was the necessary kind of place. The Genius was a wreck. He'd been crying for days, but he had nearly finished the ramjet engine. The magician had other news. He brought out a small, thin rug. He unrolled it and they saw written on it all sorts of strange incantations. "Charms, curses, vindications, manifestations, harmonies, disappearances, conundrums, predictions, illusions, and deceits," he said. "Everything you'd ever need in a rug is here."

"What about the amulet?" Donald said, reaching in his pocket, taking no interest in the rug.

"The amulet will get you there," the magician said. "I think."

"You think?" Donald said. "I thought you said this was a sure thing."

"Well," the magician said, "half of it's sure. I can get you there. I don't know if I can get you back."

"Back? Why not?"

"I've never been able to do round trips," the magician said. "I have a block."

"A block?" Hotchkiss said. "What kind of block? I never heard of a magician with a block."

"Happens every time. I only know halves of tricks. That's why I'm good and find things *other* people lose. I can only go one way. One way only. If I find them, I can't lose them. If I lose them, I can't find them." He looked up at Hotchkiss and shrugged. "I just can't get the hang of a round trip."

"You better get the hang of it," Donald said. "What good does it do if I get out there and we can't get back?"

"I'll keep practicing," the magician said. "Maybe I'll get it . . . I never did understand it. I can find the duck, but I can't hide him. If I hide him, I can't find him."

"So what do you do?" Donald said. "It must really mess up your act."

"I get my assistant to hide him. Then I can find him," the magician said, smiling. He said this in a tone that implied there was a solution for everything.

"How much longer do you need to practice, do you figure?" Hotchkiss said.

"Maybe a hundred years," he said. "Maybe less."

"We're not going to need it," Arnold said. "This ramjet engine is going to work. The only thing is, we need a huge mass for fuel. We need a ton. A ton of something."

"Something?" Donald said.

"Anything. A ton of anything," the Genius said, "for the antimatter engine routine I've got worked out."

"Anything you say," Hotchkiss said. He was a desperate man. He held the amulet. "Keep practicing," he said to the magician.

> Some studies of anti-matter power for starships have concluded that the best "mix" would not be 50-50. At Jet Propulsion Laboratory in California, a technical memorandum on future propulsion systems proposed that the anti-matter mass used as the energy source would be negligible when compared with the mass of the propellant. Figures indicating about 4 tons of "reaction mass" for every ton of payload would work with the reaction mass heated by anti-matter annihilation. The JPL studies listed water as "reaction mass" but hydrogen could be used, as could nearly anything else: rocks, garbage, tin cans, dirty socks and junk mail [author's emphasis]. The amount of anti-matter needed to heat the reaction mass varies with the payload and velocity requirements. For journeys within the bounds of the solar system, the anti-matter used would be surprisingly small. A complex 1-ton unmanned probe sent to Mars would consume 4 tons of water and about one gram of anti-matter.
>
> —Robert M. Powers, *The Coattails of God*

"Are you crazy?" Hotchkiss whispered. They were still in the desert. The sun had come and gone and now here was the Genius with a truck of stuff.

"I got my ton," he called out.

"There's no room for that stuff . . . where we going to put it?" Hotchkiss was in despair. This whole idea was absurd. Insanity ruled the day. Well, Hotchkiss sighed. Madness beat despair.

"Put it there," he said as the Genius backed the truck up next to the rocket. One ton of laundry. They stuffed it into one rocket cone. It took them nearly half the night.

"We only need it for lift-off. It should knock us right out of the solar system," the Genius explained.

"Great," Hotchkiss said. "Then we have only thirty-nine and a half million light-years to go."

After five starts, the rocket hadn't budged. The magician was twirling around in the desert, swinging his cape, trying to assist.

"This is terrible," Hotchkiss said. "It's not working."

"I don't understand it," the Genius said, full of consternation. "All the formulas should work."

At that moment, the magician appeared outside the rocket window.

"Let me help," he said.

"No," Hotchkiss said.

"You don't know anything about engines," the Genius said. "About nuclear power and explosions."

"No," the magician said, "but I could get you where you want to go."

Hotchkiss looked askance.

"What do you mean?" the Genius said. "On that rug, that *stupid* rug? Look, we need to catch her. We need a real rocket, for God's sake."

"She's not going where she's going on a rocket," the magician said. "She's on a special line of entry."

Hotchkiss listened to this. "What'd you have in mind?" he said.

"Come out," the magician said. And they did.

The magician circled the rocketship three times. "Everything's in order. You won't have any trouble now," he said. "We just have to wait for the right time for ignition."

"Ignition?" the Genius said. "That's been the problem all along. We can't get ignition."

"I know," the magician said. "What you need is cosmic consciousness."

"Oh no!" Hotchkiss bellowed.

"He's a creep," the Genius said.

"You don't have much time," the magician said. "You'd better learn to concentrate."

Hotchkiss was thinking about Schrodinger—that night with the calculations.

"Let's give it a try," he said to the Genius.

"Don't try," the magician said. "Do it. Escape velocity requires twenty-five-thousand mph to leave the gravitational field. Now listen carefully," he said, and asked for the amulet.

"You're out! You're out!" the Ooze said. "Hotchkiss is coming for you."

"Coming for me?" Amanda said in disbelief.

"Him and the Genius. Hooray!" The Ooze was spinning.

"What are they coming on?" Amanda said, curious.

"Don't know," Ooze said, looking at the console. "There's a sending force I've never seen before. Maybe it will help them." He looked at her. "I'll try to bring them in at the console. If they land at the robot fields, I can't protect them there."

"Are you callin' my boy a thief?" Sheriff Eberly said.

"I'm telling you, Sheriff, that boy stole my laundry truck. There's nothin' in it but laundry. A ton of laundry. The whole county's dirty underwear is in that truck."

"You tellin' me my boy, my genius boy, is stealin' dirty laundry?"

" 'At's what I'm tellin' you, Sheriff. He stole my truck and tole me he's headin' for the stars."

At that Eberly blinked. Wal now. That could be.

51

"Einstein was right!" the Genius said. "Bohr was right. Hooray! Hooray!"

Hotchkiss turned to look at him. The kid was absolutely jubilant.

"They can't both be right," Hotchkiss said.

"But they are," the Genius said. "Look how fast we're going."

Hotchkiss leaned over and looked at the dials. "Not possible . . ." he said in a whisper. "Even theoretically . . ." Hotchkiss said, "This is a goddamn impossibility."

While Amanda was struggling with the survival of a biological system, in a nonbiological territory, Hotchkiss was painfully reminded that he was one.

"Do we have anything to eat?" Hotchkiss said, remembering too late that he had left the Genius in charge of provisions.

"Yeah," the Genius said. "We have vitamin pills and ice cream."

"Pills and ice cream?" Hotchkiss said. "Oh God, is that all?"

The Genius nodded. "It will meet all our nutritional needs."

Hotchkiss was thinking and trying not to lose his temper. "What kind of ice cream? What flavor?"

There was a pause. "Pistachio," the Genius said.

"WHAT? Pistachio?! That's terrible! Why pistachio? Nobody, but nobody, likes pistachio! Do you hear me? Nobody!!!"

"I like it," the Genius said quietly after a time. "I thought everybody liked it."

"You thought . . ." Hotchkiss grumbled. "Why didn't you ask, instead of think?"

"I guess," the Genius said, "it's what you'd call an unfortunate hypothesis."

"You're telling me," Hotchkiss said. Years, he figured, they'd be out here. Years of vitamin pills and pistachio ice cream.

"Agghhh-aghh!" Hotchkiss cried into the night. The Genius bit his lip and didn't say anything.

"See that?" Eberly said, banging into the café and heading straight to Rufus. "The day after I go to all the trouble adoptin' that boy he steals the entire county's goddamn dirty laundry and goes up there to the stars."

The crowd, as it were—that is to say, the Kid, Mrs. Thwaite herself, Silas, Rufus, and the old Indian Tom—all had heard about the "truck steal," and the report of the rocket had been on the news all night. They turned to stare at Eberly, but no one knew what to say.

"Hell, Eb," Silas said. "No laundry truck gonna get to the stars." He was drying glasses, and kept at this even despite Eberly's agitation.

Eberly's fist hit the table. "Goddamn these kids these days! They don't appreciate a damn thing you do for 'em." The group stared.

"What you gonna do, Eb?" Rufus said finally, speaking for all of them.

"Do? I ain't gonna do nothin'. He knows what time he has to be home. I don't care what star he went to—he has to be home by eleven o'clock or he ain't ever gonna see no pistachio ice cream again." There was a pause. Then Eberly said, "Silas, pour me a beer."

And Silas did.

"What do you mean you can't?" Amanda said. "You said you'd help."

"Ooze ain't got power against the robots," Rastus said.

"But he said . . ." Amanda protested.

"I'll help, I'll help," the Ooze said. "I told you I would and I will."

"Rastus says you don't have power over them. Now is that true?" Amanda demanded.

"Well, yes and no," the Ooze waffled.

"Yes or no?" Amanda said. "Do you or don't you?"

"Well, sometimes I do. I mean I can't always tell. It . . . it's not always clear, you see. They . . ."—he looked around nervously—"look, I better find a place to hide you."

"Well, if they brought me here," Amanda said impatiently, "they must know where I am."

"No, no—you don't understand," Ooze said. "I brought you in . . . but they bring everybody else."

"But Hotchkiss . . . I reached him in my thoughts," she said, "and you said that would get me out of the console room to Schrodinger and the GCB." What was the matter with this Ooze? "I've got to get Schrodinger. That's all there is to it."

"Look, they can get you out. You can leave the console room any time now. I'm just telling you, it's dangerous—too risky. GCB has Schrodinger, I told you," Ooze said. "He'll never give him up. . . . We've got to *steal* him."

"Look," Amanda said, "this is getting blown all out of proportion. I need to meet this GCB and explain to him I will gladly give him the molecules—Schrodinger's and mine—once we are safely returned. Simple as that. But I won't trust him to give them to him here."

"Ain't gonna work," Rastus said.

"Why not?"

"He ain't gonna let you get that cat."

"I'm not afraid of him!" Amanda said angrily. "Now I'd like to give him a piece of my mind."

"He got it already!" Rastus said, howling and slapping his leg with glee. "You don't get it yet, do you?" And Amanda felt the temperature drop: that switch, from something playful, almost comical, to a sinister presence she didn't like at all.

"Look," she said, heading for the door, "I can't wait around any longer. I just have to go out there . . . if that's where Schrodinger is."

"I told you that's where he is," Rastus said. "But you better think twice before you go out there. . . . It's excruciating," he said. He looked from her to the console. "I seen the things in your mind on that console. No way," he said, "you gonna make it."

"What do you mean?" Amanda said, turning. Something in Rastus's voice worried her.

"I said, considerin' the combination, chances are you are not gonna make it."

"What combination?"

"On the console, history and constitution, for two things."

"History . . . what . . . what are you saying?"

"With your history and your constitution, that combination is bad. Very bad. You ain't gonna make it. Now another history with that constitution, it might get by. Or another constitution with that history. But your combination—no way," he said, shaking his head.

Amanda paced nervously about the console room. She was sick of all these predictions. There was only one way to get Schrodinger and that was out through this door, into that black sea. To the place they called Memory Lane.

"Well," Amanda said, "I'm going. That's all there is to it."

"Sure you don't want to change before you go out there?" he asked slyly.

"Change?" She turned to him. "What do you mean? Change my clothes. I don't have any other clothes."

"Change your mind is what I meant," Rastus said.

"Change my mind?" Amanda looked at him. He did not seem to be joking.

"No . . . no, I'm not changing my mind about going. I'm going." She stared out at the black swirling sea. It gleamed like glass. Impenetrable.

"Ain't what I said," Rastus said. "I said change your mind. Turn it in for a better one."

"Oh . . . that way," Amanda said, turning to look at him. And then she felt strange. Very strange indeed. "No . . ." she said hesitantly,

"I really don't think I want to change my mind . . . that is, in that way . . . I mean, I really have grown fond of the one I have . . . although it's not good at certain things, of course."

Rastus tapped the computer console. "Now I gonna ask you one more time: want to change your mind?"

"There's nothing wrong with the one I have," she said.

"Too much *will*," Rastus said. "Too much determination. It ain't gonna help out beyond that door. You could vanish out there." He looked at the console. "From the looks of things, looks like maybe you already have." Amanda felt a brief panic go through her then.

"What do you mean?" she said. "I'm certainly *here*." She didn't want to say just then that of course she didn't know where "here" was exactly.

"You know what I'm talkin' about," Rastus said. "You can no longer locate yourself in terms of your will. It cannot come from your will." Rastus's eyes gleamed at her. "Will do not work here." His hands cut the air like a knife. "Soul. It must come from the soul."

"Soul . . ." Amanda said. "Soul . . . what's that . . . really?"

"Well, soul, self, call it what you want, it cannot come from your determination . . . it must come from the way you are organized, the way you love," he said.

Amanda began to get uneasy . . . this was not what she wanted to hear. She wanted to hear a solution that was within her power. Spectrometry and oscillators, electrical charges, conversions of electrons, magnetic fields, and neutron stars—all these were violent energies, but they could be measured, could be perceived. Soul? Love? A measureless mass, soul and love. Those immeasurable things—if these were to save her here, then she was really lost.

He caught her arm. "You know if anybody knows, jus' 'cause you can't measure it, can't see it, don't mean it ain't there. You got it in you, but the time is bad." He looked around. "Hour is all wrong. You got it, but I don't know if you gonna have time to find it." He walked away from her then in a long slow shuffle, this messenger from heaven knows where, some region of the spirit, some mirror world of her mind, some guardian of souls and thoughts and plans and memories, walking around a console, like a street-wise kid, with a comb in his pocket, a gutter priest, promising deliverance on the next card game, the next numbers racket. He shuffled like that. He looked like that. But this was no card game. And it was no racket either. It was as real as the wind on her skin, the rain on her hair. She saw as she stepped outside the console room that something was happening that had not happened before. Weather. Wind and rain had suddenly appeared out of the vacuous dust.

She felt it. If she felt *that*, perhaps she had not vanished after all.

She stood there only a fraction of a second before she stepped back inside. The wind was fearful and there was a terrible sound out there. It was a sound she didn't want to hear.

"Oh oh," Rastus said, "look at that, we got visitors," and Amanda heard this huge screaming alarm, and all the consoles lit up at once to show a small charred spaceship that had just landed in the middle of the desert. Amanda held her breath as the latch opened and a head peered out.

"Oh Donald," she gasped. "How ever did he get *here?*" She was so happy to see him. And then she saw the Genius, too.

Rastus looked worried. "They're in big trouble. Bad landing place. Robots gonna get them there, for sure."

"Oh my God," Amanda said, "we have to help them. Ooze, do something!"

"I can't," Ooze said, "they don't have the molecules, so I can't do anything."

"Do something!" She was yelling now.

"He's powerless," Rastus said. "He tried to land them off the fields but it's only a matter of time now . . ."

Hotchkiss and the Genius were out of their ship now, she could see.

"This is terrible," Amanda said. Then, "Do you have any weapons?" she said to Rastus.

"No." He was blocking the door.

"Just open the door then," she said. "I have to go warn them."

"You can't do that," Rastus said; "it's murder out there. You don't stand a chance." She remembered the sound.

"Well at least I have the molecule," she said, pushing him aside. "Now let me out."

"It'll take you too long," he said. "It's very difficult, you'll never—"

"Open the door," Amanda said, determined.

And Rastus, to his surprise, did. And more. He accompanied her through it.

Hotchkiss and the Genius were standing on a sheet of grayish rock, covered with dust and ashes. Their spaceship was black. It looked burned to a crisp.

"I'm cold," the Genius said to Hotchkiss, shivering.

"God, I've never felt cold like this," Hotchkiss said. "You better wait inside."

"Not me," the Genius said. They were standing in the middle of a place that looked like a sort of desert. There was a strange humming in the air.

"Well, are we in the right place?" asked the Genius.

"Must be," said Hotchkiss. "It stopped here."

"What happened to that Ooze guy who kept transmitting to us? He sounded like he knew where we wanted to go."

"Lost him just before we landed."

"Well, which way do we go?" The Genius turned to him, hopefully.

"Don't know. . . . There's no light, no light at all. Stay close to me," he said, grabbing the Genius's hand, "very close."

"I'm afraid," the Genius said.

"Me too. Stick close by, Arnold. You can't see your hands in front of your face, it's so black here."

"Which way are we going?" the Genius said. As he moved, something fell out of his shirt.

"What's that?" Hotchkiss asked, hearing the soft thud.

"Nothing," the Genius said. He reached down to get Amanda's picture and tucked it back under his shirt. "What if we get lost?"

It was pitch black. Hotchkiss had tied a rope to the spaceship and found that they had walked in circles the first hours. He thought now he was better oriented. But he wasn't sure. It was the coldest, darkest place that he had ever been. He was sure of that. He would have preferred to leave Dartan in the spaceship, but he knew the boy was too frightened. Hotchkiss was frightened too. He wondered why the Ooze had abandoned them. He had been surprised at first to hear him at all, but just as they were landing the Ooze had yelled, "Thirty degrees to the right, to the right, or you'll land right in the robot fields, you idiot!" Not one for politeness, in any case. Hotchkiss hoped it would be light again soon, the light here changed suddenly—just as they landed it got darker, absolutely all at once, as if someone had turned off the lights.

They thought as they walked they heard strange sounds in the distance, sounds they couldn't make out.

52

Rastus opened the door. The wind had stopped howling now. There was an altogether different quality to the air. It was warm and smelled almost sweet. The only eerie thing was that sound. There was no wind now, but far off in the distance Amanda could hear a strange, rhythmic beat, a two-beat beat, an *um-ump, um-ump, um-ump.*

"What's that . . . sound?" she said.

"You'll see," he said. "You got to get through. If we get through, you'll get to the robot fields."

"Oh," she said. "Well, it can't be too far, and we have to hurry. I'm really worried about Donald. Is that where we have to go?" she said, pointing to something in the distance.

"That's it," Rastus said.

"Why, it's pretty," she said turning to him. It looked like a children's amusement park. There were colored lights and some kind of waving flags in front. It was all purple and pink, like the snake, like the colors you would see in a cartoon.

That sound, though, whatever it was, made her uneasy. It was familiar in some way.

"It looks innocent from here," Rastus said.

They hadn't gone very far when she saw the snake in the beach chair. But even as Amanda looked at it, the snake began to change. Soon the beach chair was gone and the glasses and the funny hat.

The eyes of the snake in the beach chair were colder, darker, starting to glitter. He shed his first skin, the pink one that looked like a cartoon. The second one was realer somehow. The chair dissolved, and then the next skin began to be seen—harder, scalier, darker—and the snake began to hiss, lying on the ground. The eyes, the eyes were the eyes of a real snake. Amanda backed away. The comic snake, then, was an invention of the robots, too. What would the Ooze turn out to be—or the GCB? What underneath their comic garbs would they reveal?

Amanda gasped and stepped back. It was coiled to attack.

"Jump!" Rastus pushed her aside as the snake sprang forward, missing her by inches. "We got to go this way," he said, pulling her off in another direction. She saw why he had done so. She could see far ahead that the bright purple and pink of Memory Lane was different now. It was no longer a children's amusement park. Ahead of them, raising and writhing like a forest of trees, but rising high off their coils, rising to one hundred, two hundred feet high, was a forest of snakes. Hooded and dark, the snakes were no longer cartoons, but giant cobras now. They were swinging in the air to some music Amanda could not hear. They were the guardians of Memory Lane.

"We go round this way," he said. "If you pick your timing, you can get past them. You got to go in a side door. They get colder, slower on the sides."

"Oh God, are they horrible!" Amanda said. For the first time she could feel the fear. It was beginning to coat her lungs. She was beginning to feel as if she might drown in it. In seconds, this place had changed. The landscape with its bright colors had changed to one that was dead and gray.

"How much longer?" she said. "I have to get to them before the robots do."

Rastus held her fast. "You got to hold on, now. It takes as long as it takes. We going to go past future time. You got that molecule in you so you gonna see it."

Amanda stared. There ahead of her was future time, and it was a swamp.

"Whose future . . . is it?" she said.

"Earth time," Rastus said. "It's one of the futures the Red Robots got prepared . . . one of them; it ain't necessarily gonna be it, but it's leadin' the pack."

"The pack? What do you mean?" she said.

"If they win, this be what they got in mind."

As Amanda got closer she saw what it was the robots had in mind. It was a sludge forest. Here and there portions of green struggled through, but mostly it was oil and tar, and something more. There was a smell of burning here. A terrible smell of fire.

"It's death," she whispered as they walked past it.

"Worse," Rastus said. "Look hard."

And Amanda did look as she crept past, afraid, yet daring to see, and she saw there was life there, although what kind, she wasn't at all sure she knew. It was a forest of monsters and freaks. They were alive, these twisted, snarled, genetic monsters. Radioactive mutations, they had survived. Somewhere in their twisted selves she could occasionally see a human form, as they melted into the tar or drank from radioactive ponds, hideous, grotesque, twisted, and deformed. They were huge, the size of giants, but the radioactive rays had sent their bones into a frenzy, a twisted mountainous heap of bone and sinew, like an automobile junkyard, a mile high with eyes, and breathing.

No sound came from her. She was paralyzed with the fear. Finally she said, "Rastus, this can't be. Tell me, tell me this won't be."

"Robots . . . if they win, they bringing this. That's all there is."

"I have to stop them," she said, trying to gather some strength. "I will."

Rastus pulled her past the future place and down another path.

"Are we going . . . are we going to Memory Lane?" she asked. "To Donald . . . to Schrodinger?" Her voice sounded to her like a small child's. She was aware she was getting very tired. He should have blindfolded her, if he had known. It was too much to see.

"We got to lie low, till the snakes get cold," he said. "The robots be out soon, come searchin' for us."

"It is safe . . . anywhere here?"

"No. It's like a minefield out here."

"There must be someplace . . . we won't be attacked."

"Maybe," he said. "We'll try here." And they moved through the long tall grass, Amanda never sure that the snakes or the mutations would not spring into view. All around her it was dark, the air was thick, and there was a long low hissing in the grass. Overhead she occasionally could hear mechanical sounds.

"Robots," he said. "Keep low. They lookin' for us." When they had come through the grass, she saw they were approaching a different landscape.

"This doesn't look bad at all," she said.

"Nope, looks like a rose garden, first off."

And it was true: by the road there were lots of roses. But as she walked on, she noticed that the roses were dropping off the branches, and after a while, when she was feeling quite tired, she saw only the thorns. Then she heard it. A strange gurgling, and then that pumping sound. The wind had gotten colder and it was getting dark.

"What's that?" she said. It reminded her of the oil fields in Texas. An *um-ump* sound, a steady sound, a *pumping*.

"Pump-out stations," Rastus said. He held her arm. "I hope you ready for it."

Amanda could see in the dimming light huge, squashed shapes. They were pumping something, all right.

"Oh," she said, "is that a sanitation system?"

"No," he said. "We gonna pass it. You gonna see what it is."

By nightfall they had come quite close to it. "My God," Amanda said, walking down the road, "they look . . ."

"They are," he said, "hearts."

There were fields of them. Millions of hearts. *Pump pump pump.*

"What . . . are they doing here?"

"People leave 'em. Sometimes they don't leave 'em. Robots just take 'em, you know, for barter, for somethin', but a lot of people leave 'em. Too much trouble, too much pain. They go back without 'em."

"What do the robots do with them?" she asked, approaching more closely.

"They tryin' to use 'em, find a use for 'em. Blue ones anyway. Blue ones always tryin' to figure out how to use those things."

"How strange," she said, feeling her feet slow. Quite suddenly she felt her entire body was getting weaker—dreading to pass the heart fields. She tried to muster her strength.

"I'm getting tired," she said.

"I ain't surprised about that. You can stop at the next station."

He had a strange look on his face.

"At the next station?" Amanda sat down on a rock. "Where . . . where does all the blood go, that these hearts pump?" she asked. Question, question, question, she thought. Find out—the only way.

"They ain't all pumping blood," he said. "A lot of these hearts run on guile."

"Guile? You mean metaphorically."

"No, I mean really," he said. "That's what's runnin' 'em."

"Well then . . . then they're not really hearts. They're imitations of them or something like that." She couldn't understand why she was so cold all of a sudden. She began to shiver. It was very dark, and there was nothing around her but the field of pumping hearts, strange shapes in the dark.

As she stared out into the fields, she began to feel fear again. This time it was curling inside her like a knot. The Ooze said fear here was dangerous. It would bring the robots for sure.

"How much farther is it?"

"What?"

"Memory field—the side entrance. You said that's where I have to go."

"Not far," he said, "to it . . . but once you in it I have no idea how far you gonna have to go. It's almost impossible to find anything in there . . . anything you want."

"Oh, I . . . I will," she said. "I'm sure of it." Again, the cold. She was so tired she could barely walk.

Rastus was studying her.

"You ain't gonna make it," he said.

"What?" Her head was so tired it was nearly falling off her neck. She didn't know what had happened, but she was feeling weak, tired, and very sad. She felt like crying, a good long, long time.

"You ain't gonna make it," Rastus said. "You see out there?" He pointed down the field of hearts, and although she had heard the noises all along, she had not realized what the noises were until she saw the helicopters overhead. A helicopter had spotlighted one of the hearts in the field.

"The robots, the robots got it," he said.

"Got what?"

"That heart," he said, turning on a flashlight so she could see it. "You understand?"

"Yes," she said. Her voice was very small. She didn't want to see it. She only wanted to sleep.

"You know whose it is?"

"No," she said, but she did know, the word like a small cry.

"It's yours," he said, and he heard her gasp. She looked up then as the helicopter circled overhead, over the heart. She thought she should see what it looked like, however they had gotten it here, from wherever they had taken it. But she was crying already. It was hard to see through the tears, but what she saw she already knew. It was not too different from the other hearts in the field, but it was her own. It was full of cuts and fissures, swollen and patched. Repaired, repaired, repaired, small pieces stuck on, stitches down the side, even nuts and bolts spewed from the center of it like a chimney. She could see the letters BMc etched in along the side, like bullet holes, and she knew these were the scars that McCloud had left there. And although she knew these things, it surprised her still. She did not think really that McCloud had ever hurt her, not so much as that; yet here it was, McCloud and more, a heart that looked like a monument, a tribute to a vandal's dream, a night of slashing tires.

"It . . . it looks like a wreck," she said, still weeping. "I thought McCloud loved me," she said through the tears.

"Why, he did," Rastus said. "See that?" He turned a small flashlight beam on the very center of her heart. "Don't you see—he opened that all up, brought some light in there?"

But she didn't hear him. She was so engulfed now, so overwhelmed with tears and sadness for her heart and her lost feeling. She thought she had made it safely past the robots, but no. They had taken from her, too.

"Maybe you better cover your eyes." he said.

"I . . . I want to see it closer," she said, sobbing now. It was terrible. A strange cold wind had descended on her. It was ruining her, draining the energy from her with every step, but she could not stop. "I want to see," she said, struggling forward.

Rastus reached out to steady her.

"You oughta quit, right here," he said.

"No."

He held her as she struggled forward. It was a hell of a thing to see, he thought, and it wasn't even his own.

"What's keeping it . . ." she gasped now, making her way down the pumping line, "what's keeping it together?"

Then she saw tiny, tiny small pins, like staples, two linked staples, forming an H. She looked closer and saw millions of those signatures like tiny anchors holding her heart against its storms. The pumping was more violent now. It seemed to be fighting for something. "Hotchkiss," she said, her voice a whisper.

"A lot of strength," Rastus said. "I seen it before—nearly indestructible. Always comes back, but it loses a little every time. . . . Sometimes I think it's worse, being strong that way."

"Why?" she said. It seemed to her she had been out here always, as a witness to this thing. Would it ever end? She had lost all sense of time, and space. She just bore witness to this pumping thing holding, despite all its cracks and fissures, holding on.

"It ain't good," he said. "Dyin' so many times, like that."

"It's strong," she said finally, stretching for hope. "It's pumping so strongly."

"Oh, it's strong all right. It got a special source. This heart woulda run out of energy long ago, 'specially up here, 'less this source gave up some of theirs—gave it to you. You woulda been a goner, soon as you stepped out the door, 'cept for this," he said. "Robots would have all of you for sure."

"But I thought Ooze . . . Ooze protected me."

"He protected you there . . . in the console, in the robot fields . . . but not here . . . not in Memory Lane. Ain't no protection here. I told you that, 'cept for this kind."

"What kind?" she said. "Whose?"

"It coming from another energy system," he whispered. "Another system entirely. She's called Radiant One—she's positive energy, that's all I know—except she hardly ever gets in here. Shields close over," he said. "They never let her in. . . . This one got in."

"I can't . . . I can't see it," she said. She had stopped crying now, somehow trying to understand. "I can't see anything."

"Not in this light," he said, looking around. "I give you special vision for a second, then you see, and then you won't see it anymore." He snapped his fingers, and the heart lit up as though it were transparent, and there inside was a small, glowing light, curled and glowing, purring still. The light, of course, was Schrodinger, or Schrodinger's ghost, or the presence of Schrodinger, or whatever you might wish to call it, this aspect of another energy system.

"Oh," was all Amanda said, and then the vision disappeared. And she heard another sound. A terrible sound. She had heard this sound circling them the whole time they were out here, but she hadn't looked up. It was bad enough looking straight ahead.

"Robots," Rastus said, pushing her into the ground. "Get down." And as he held her down in the high grass, she saw the robot helicopter, lights and guns blazing, circling over the field. They had a spotlight on her heart. The white circle crossed the field once, then twice, then back. Directly overhead the machine-gun turret turned.

"No." It was only a gasp, not even a shout. Terror had shut off her voice as the machine gun, aiming for her heart, let forth its fire, and the heart, still pumping, lay shredded now, the sound, its sound, the *pump pump pump* making a mockery of any explanation, throwing Amanda and her hopes into a widening gyre.

She thought she was dead. She could not speak, could not move; the vision of the shredded assault was constantly in her mind. What she did not know, what she did not see, if she could have flicked her fingers like Rastus did, was the wonder that he beheld. Despite the firing, the sound went on. He stood up, scratching his head in wonder. "Well now," he said, "never did see anything like that." There in the field, in Amanda's shredded mass, was the small glowing light, and it was glowing still.

The robot helicopter had turned now and was coming in again.

"We got to get out," Rastus yelled, shaking her, trying to get her to move. She lay there limply, staring, almost as if she were unconscious.

"Get up now." He stood her up, but she fell against him. He had no power out here, only his wits, and he saw the copter circling overhead, its spotlight searching for more. The heart was not enough.

"They gunnin' for us," Rastus said. "You got to move, you got to," he said, pulling her. But Amanda only lay collapsed against his side. He slapped her face; her eyes opened. "We got to run!" He was yelling at her now. It was no use. "I got to leave you," he said, laying her down on the grass. He had no protection out here, and he ran fast, fast through the deepening sky back to the safety of the console.

Amanda heard the sound of the bullets. She saw the grass lighting up with fire right before her eyes, but she could not move, and then she heard it. A *clank*—the clanking sound of armor—and she saw a huge blue foot aiming for her head.

She thought it was going to kill her, but it picked her up, the huge Blue Robot, and the bullets fell harmlessly against its armor as it advanced, holding her in its arms, slowly and deliberately to the edge of the robot field.

It had saved her, but why? She could barely speak. She looked up, into the eyes of the robot savior. The strangest eyes. It was Robert. "Help me," she said. And then, "Help Hotchkiss—robot field . . ." and then she fell back again, collapsing from fear, from terror, from rescue.

"Dubious savior, dubious," Rastus said, back at the console monitoring the events. He thought she was a goner for sure. Those robots meant business. And now that blue one coming in there like that. Maybe it was the molecule she swallowed. He didn't know. Things were askew for sure.

"Why'd you let her go out there?" Ooze said, frantic and yelling. "WHY, WHY, WHY YOU KNOW THEY KILL THEM OUT THERE!" He was screaming and beside himself. "HOW WILL I EVER GET HER OUT OF THERE, SHE IS OUT THERE WITH A CRAZY ROBOT YET, OH MY, OH MY!"

This Ooze was a hysteric, so Rastus was used to this. Thing of it was, with everything getting so out of whack—this damn cat up here and the girl—he found himself doing all kinds of uncharacteristic things himself. Fact was he never went out to those fields before. Anyone going, he always let them go alone. But something about her pulled him right along. That much hope, that much determination, was contagious.

"What did you mean, Ooze," Rastus said, "a crazy robot?"

"That's Robert, that's who has her," Ooze said. "It's a crazy robot, that's the one whose filter's out of kilter. He's slower than the others, you know, and he forgets the rules of the game. They don't know what's wrong with him, but he sits out half the game. I don't even know why they didn't de-program him or re-program him long ago."

"Yes," Rastus said, "why didn't they?"

"Oh, I don't know," Ooze said. "You know every system has its quirks. Maybe they figure the trouble you know is better than the trouble you don't know."

Rastus looked at him. "Don't sound like no robot reasoning to me," he said.

53

"What's that?" the Genius said. They listened. *Clank, clank, clank.*
Some kind of metal, moving parts.

"Something's here," the Genius said. "It sounds like a tank." He
turned around. He had found his small blue flashlight and now in the
pitch blackness he saw it. Slowly he moved the flashlight, up up up,
then he saw the visored face. Eleven feet tall, and blue. Then he moved
it down slowly.

"Hotch——" His voice was a gasp. "Look there." Hotchkiss, alarmed
at his voice, turned. And he saw it.

"Don't be afraid," the robot said in a surprisingly human voice.
"I've come to help you. You're in robot territory," the Blue Robot said.
"My name is Robert. You have to get back to the spaceship quickly."

"Why?" the Genius said. "We just got here."

"Do you hear that?" Robert said. They did. It sounded like a herd
of tanks. "Come, I'll lead you," Robert said, reaching down for the
Genius's hand.

"Hotchkiss!" the Genius screamed, and Hotchkiss ran to him, but
the robot reached around, picked him up, and with one of them under
each arm, galloped, as only an eleven foot robot can, quickly across the
desert.

54

They heard, suddenly, a clank at the door. An unmistakable sound.

"The robots!" Ooze screamed. "They're not supposed to be able to
get to the door . . . they're not allowed in here."

"Shhh," Rastus said, listening. He heard a soft thud, and then the
sound of the clanking moving away. Slowly he went to the window, and

looked out. There was a large lump on the top of the steps, a beaten exhausted body. It was Amanda.

"Bring her in quickly," Ooze said, opening the door, and they carried her inside.

"She don't look too good," Rastus said.

"Well, she needs me," said Ooze. "She's a biological system, after all," and the Ooze hovered over Amanda.

Rastus was watching her. Slowly her eyes opened.

"You left me there," she said to him. "How could you . . . ? That big robot saved me—Robert what's-his-name—he saved me." Then she shivered. "Frankly I didn't think he was going to let me go. . . . He's awfully peculiar. But he helped me."

"Yes, I don't understand it myself," Ooze said, puzzling over this new wrinkle in the system.

"He knew you were losing energy," Rastus said. "No biological system can live too long in the region of the robots. He knew he had to get you away from him and back to Ooze. So he brought you here."

"Well thank heavens he did, and anyway it proves my theory," she said, getting up. She was feeling okay now. She thought she must have fainted.

"What theory?" said Ooze.

"Well, I mean it's not original with me, but you know, there are some very famous theories of altruism among insects, birds, and even social animals. I've always held it's an aspect of social intelligence, altruism. Built right into a species. But I must say I was surprised to see it was built into a robot."

"Maybe it wasn't built in," Rastus said.

"Why of course it was," Amanda said. "Why however could it get there?"

Rastus shrugged. "Some kinda mistake . . . you never know. Maybe he had other things designed for you . . . but you fainted and he had to bring you back here . . . half dead you weren't no good to him."

"What do you mean?" Amanda said, not liking the innuendo.

"Jus' what I said. I think he got somethin' in mind for you. . . . I wouldn't trust him a bit."

"Well, who can I trust?" she said. "You deserted me out there."

"I couldn't move you, no way. I had to get out or both of us be down, then, for sure."

55

The robot had deposited Donald and the Genius in the spaceship and promised to return with 342. They were of course amazed to learn he had been put into the robot's care.

"What do you make of that thing?" Hotchkiss asked. "Did you get a chance to inspect it?"

"I can't figure out where it's getting its energy from. I'm pretty sure it's electromagnetic. I just can't precisely locate its source. It's solid state—but I never saw anything like it before."

"He says he knows where Amanda is," Hotchkiss said, sighing. "At least he says she's okay."

"We got to figure a way past these things," the Genius said. "He says we're smack in the middle of millions of millions of them."

"It's not going to be easy. I think the only way is timing. He says they're going on a night raid. They're going to clear out of here, and then we have to run for it."

"Who are they raiding?"

"Beats me," Hotchkiss said. "The blue thing said he'll show us the way out of here as soon as they take off on the raid." He stared out at the spaceship. He didn't like what he saw—a cold barren place that offered few explanations for anything.

"You think he'll bring Three-forty-two?" the Genius said.

"He says he's bringing him here, he says the chimp is 'confounding explanations.' " Hotchkiss smiled.

"I bet he is. A robot who never saw a chimp before would be going absolutely crazy," the Genius said, grinning. "That chimp gets into everything."

"I can't figure out why he's helping us," Hotchkiss said. "It's clear the rest of these things are not at all friendly."

"I don't know," the Genius said. "It could be soft error. You know there could be some kind of light source that got in there and messed up its connections."

"I'd like to find out," Hotchkiss said. He saw the Genius had broken out the ice cream.

"You want some?"

"No, I'm not hungry," he said.

"Okay," the Genius said, "I'll save it for later." Suddenly he wasn't hungry either. He was feeling lonely. In such a state he automatically felt his shirt for the reassuring rectangle. But it wasn't there. He gasped. He'd lost her picture.

56

It is literally true that everything in our bodies except hydrogen has been processed through at least one star and at least a billion (thousand million) years ago. . . . some of the hydrogen on earth has been unchanged since the Big Bang itself.

—John Gribbin,
Genesis

Just then the Ooze screamed, apparently quite frantic, "MOVE, MOVE OVER, LET ME AT IT," he said, pushing Rastus from the console. "I have a crisis. I have to fix it before the GCB finds out; he'll have me hauled up there and chew me out. . . ." He pressed buttons frantically. "He'll coalesce me."

"Will you calm down," Amanda said. "What is the problem?"

"Indians . . . the Indians. I left them on a Pacific atoll which is being destroyed in a tropical rainstorm at oh eight hundred. I have got to get them off of it. They weren't s'posed to be there anyway . . . and now there's an electrical force at work. Rastus!" the Ooze shrieked. "Come and look—what is this? Come clear this damn thing. Clear it quickly. I'll be back." And the Ooze was off.

Rastus came and looked. "That's the influence of a night-dream," said Rastus.

"A what?"

He punched a key. "Comin' up red. Night-dream. Fixation. Somebody's fixated on these Indians. Thinkin' 'bout 'em day and night. You gonna have trouble movin' 'em, jes' like that. Oh, you could move in, no question, but there's a presence here gonna be disturbed."

"Oh," Amanda said, not sure what "oh" in this case meant. Then she said, "Well, who is it?"

"Who?" Rastus looked at her. "What difference it make if you know who?"

"I . . . I'm just curious," she said.

"Okay, give you a free ride," he said, and punched the console. Soon Eberly's face appeared, full of consternation.

"Lord, who is that?"

The console typed out:

NAME: EBERLY

OCCUPATION: SHERIFF

LOCALE: TEXAS, CONONGA COUNTY

TEMPERAMENT: ORNERY, GOODHEARTED, MEAN-SPIRITED, OVER-WHELMING SENSE OF DUTY TO PROTECT HIS TERRITORY

CHIEF CONCERN: "WHAT HAS HAPPENED TO MY STEPSON, ARNOLD DARTAN 4000."

CHIEF OBSESSION: "WHAT HAS HAPPENED TO THE INDIANS?"

HABITS: TALKS TO HEIFERS

ELECTRICAL FORCE: 4

"Four?" Amanda said aloud. "Why that's four more than the president of the United States, and he's only a sheriff. Why that must be Dartan's stepfather. . . . I always wondered about his family," she said. As she looked at the console she saw, on the edge of Eberly's mind, a faint, pinkish tinge.

"What's that?" she said, curious.

"Shared concern," said Rastus. "Fairly rare in that species. Some-body's worryin' with him, except"—he punched some more—"he ain't only worried about the Indians . . . he's worried about the boy."

"Oh," Amanda said, thinking it was rather nice that there was someone close enough to Eberly to be sharing such concern. "Who is that?"

Rastus punched again. "Just a cowhand. Name is Rufus," and they saw come up on the console a bright red-and-gold pattern of light.

"What beautiful colors," Amanda said, "but . . . but there. . . . Why is that black line—like a circle all around it?"

"Hmm," Rastus said, "ain't never seen nothin' quite like this before." He seemed to be interested in the pattern.

"Well, what is it?"

"Locked energy," Rastus said. "Usually by the time it got that much black around it, it dies out, you know, it don't hold on that way. It's glowing so much I got to say this be exceptional."

"Can I see more?"

"Sure you can. You can't see it all . . . but you can see aspects. What you wanna see? Prevailing dream?"

"Prevailing dream . . . what's that?"

"That's the organization of the person. They're organized around their prevailing dream. . . . 'Course ain't nobody aware what their own prevailing dream is . . . robots take care of that. Block it right out."

"What have the robots got to do with this?" she asked.

"They drew that black line," he said. "Can't get over it yet. That kinda line almost always puts the fire out." He kept clucking to himself.

Amanda for her part was relieved to see that there were surprises in the system. She figured that meant there were more ways out of here than they were saying. Or maybe even than they knew. She was not at all convinced that they—any of them—had the final scheme in view. She was uneasy now, about Hotchkiss and the Genius. Although she was thrilled by their effort to rescue her, she was nervous too. After all, she had had special protection coming through the robot fields. They would have none.

And the people she had seen in the robot fields.

And the colors of those faces. Ashen. The bending of the spine. None of them walked upright. It made Amanda shiver just to think of it.

"You wanna see this?" Rastus said. He had punched up the prevailing dream.

"Oh," she said softly, as she looked.

There, out in the center of Rufus's mind, was a lake. A beautiful lake, golden and shimmering with a reddish autumn glow. The sun had turned the leaves and fields around the lake to a rich shining orange gold. And there in the center of this lake, a surface still as glass, was a rock, and on the rock was a beautiful woman who was playing a lyre.

From the surface of the lake, a man periodically would rise up, a beautiful perfect man with flowers wound through his hair; and he would rise up as if by magic, as if catapulted from the depths of this magical lake, and sit on the rock by the woman's side. He would stroke her long fine hair, and she would play the lyre, and Amanda was struck by the resonance and the beauty of this pair, as if they were both very real indeed, as if this were in some way a scene you could pass going by a lake anytime, and at the same time you knew there were enchantments and magic and fairy tales here. She watched while the woman played, and she saw then suddenly some movement behind the woman, and on the shore she saw a small magnificent black horse. The horse unfettered and unsaddled was running up and back, whinnying and stomping and full of fire. She saw then another figure. It was a boy, and he was in the lake, too, just behind the rock, between the rock and the shore, and he was swimming and exhausted, and she saw then that both the lovers and the horse would come and they would go. As he swam toward the horse, getting closer, it would disappear. Simply disappear. And then he would turn, and stroking hard, swim toward the lovers, and as he approached the rock, just as his hand touched the rock, they too would disappear. Vanish, like fog, and then the horse would be there again, running down the shore, and the boy, disconcerted, hurt, confused, but most of all determined, would plunge into the water again and make for the shore.

There was something very beautiful, tragic, terrible, and hopeless about the scene. A scene of tortured promise, tempted return.

"How long can this go on?" Amanda asked finally, after having watched it for a while.

"Forever," said Rastus. "As long as his mind is the lake, that's it."

"Well," she said impatiently, "give him another mind. Another lake. Give him a field. . . . This is sort of awful, isn't it?"

"Can't do that," Rastus said.

"But is he stuck with that?" she said, feeling very annoyed with this entire place, wherever it was she had found herself.

"He could do it," Rastus said. "But he got to get out of the lake. Entirely. Got to stop swimmin'. Got to drown."

"Drown?" Amanda said. "He's got to drown?"

"About what it amounts to . . ."

"Will he die then . . . he'll die, you mean?"

"No," Rastus said. "If he give up swimmin', the lake will dry up. He be in the desert with no dreams."

"Well, that's no better than this, then." Amanda was feeling very uneasy now.

"For a time it ain't no better, no," he said quietly. "But it's the only way out."

"Well, what makes you think he'll ever get out of the desert?"

"He would get out if he ever wanted to . . . but a man like that swimmin' so long, so long in the water, he forgets how to walk, loses the will. The desert not be so long, but to him a mile is forever. He still wants the water." He turned the machine off then. "See, that's how it be sometimes," and he drifted off then to another room, another console, another time.

This was a terrible place, Amanda thought. If these were indeed the consoles reflecting the places in people's minds, the earth was in trouble for sure. The energy was low, there seemed to be few charges. There was only the one mind, that child's mind she had seen in the robot field, where every time the robots tried to get her, she threw herself down in a field of flowers and started laughing.

At that, the Ooze was back, yelling and screaming.

"Oh my God, let me at them—let me at them! Let me at my Indians!"

"Why'd you take them in the first place?" Amanda said.

"It's not my fault. He told me I could have them—I'm populating a planet—only I had to have a good reason. You know, everything up here has to have a cover story . . . I mean, you can't just go in there and do things for inexplicable reasons. . . . Well, I was trying to think of a reason, but I couldn't. So now he's taking them back. So I have to put them somewhere. I have to think," he said, pressing the buttons.

"Why don't you put them back where you found them?"

"I can't do that," Ooze said. "It was bad enough they disappeared— if I just put them back it will raise too many questions."

"Are you trying to tell me," Amanda said, "that all of those things that happen down there on earth, all that cause and effect, quite simply are a joke?"

"Well,"—Oozie looked genuinely embarrassed—"you don't have to put it that strongly. But more or less we do have a lot of influence."

"You mean that when we say the reason that people do this and that and the other thing, that even if a car crashes into another car, it isn't because the brakes failed, it's because you did it up here—you people or forces or whatever you are did it—but we'd never suspect, because you would pick only a car with rather worn brakes already so we'd think it was because of the brakes and all along it was because of you."

"Ohhh," the Ooze said, leaning forward with its hands, if that's what they were, over its face, if that's what it was, "you got it."

"So"—Amanda was getting excited—"everything that gets punched in on this machine . . . you punch it in here and it happens down there, is that it?"

"Well, more or less," Oozie said, "except of course for the GCB and Random Error."

"Random Error . . . you don't control Random Error?" Amanda asked.

"Oh goodness, no," Oozie said. "We don't even understand it. It just seems to be part of the system. The GCB, he has free access to any part of the system. Sometimes he changes things on a whim . . . but he has a fit over Random Error. He goes into an absolute tizzy."

"Why'd you take the Indians in the first place?" Amanda said.

"He said I could, but he's an Indian giver," the Ooze said. "Anything he gives he wants it back."

"I see . . . ," Amanda said, "including the Indians."

"Yeah . . . well, it wasn't clear, you know, exactly what he was giving. I was sort of reading between the lines." The Ooze looked around. "I have been known to take liberties."

"I should think so," Amanda said, "in addition to other things."

"Well, it's his atoms, you know. It's his atoms, after all."

"What is his atoms?" she said.

"The GCB—it's his atoms I'm mucking with. His atoms. Everything is his atoms. You're his atoms."

"I'm his atoms? What are you talking about?" she said.

"Well, you're his atoms, everything on earth is his atoms," Ooze said. "And now he's in a swivet, he wants them back."

"What do you mean, I'm his atoms? I'm me," Amanda said.

"You came from his stars . . . don't you know that?"

"Er, uh well, I suppose, indirectly, that . . ."

<hr />

348

"Indirectly, nothing!" said Ooze. "Directly. All his stardust is wound around your genes. He wants the stuff back now!"

"Well, really!" Amanda said, thinking about this. She had often thought of the notion that every atom in her body or anywhere had come out of the original hydrogen-helium Big Bang. But she had never expected a recall. The GCB wanted more than her atoms back; he wanted the magic molecules that she and Schrodinger had, some kind of evolutionary speed-up, she figured. She had to get a better fix on his scheme.

"Anyone else with influence?" Amanda asked suddenly.

"No no no," said the Ooze, Amanda thought somewhat defensively, and then lowering its voice, much softer, "except of course for the robots."

"The robots . . . they have access, too?" Amanda said. "Why then, you don't have any control at all—not with everyone mucking up your input like that."

"The robots screwed everything up. I had perfectly lovely biological destinies worked out, and now everything's a mess. Those NERPs require constant surveillance," said the Ooze. "And Random Error also causes problems. It sends the GCB into a swivet. He calls me on the carpet every time."

"You can't control Random Error?"

"No! We don't even know where it's coming from! I'm telling you it drives the GCB crazy. Nuts!"

"Really?" Amanda said.

"Oh," said Ooze, "he'll haul me into the palace for sure, unless I put those Indians back somewhere where they will raise absolutely no questions."

"The Indians . . ."—Amanda was thinking of something—"where are the Indians now?"

"I'll have to punch them up to see," Ooze said, hitting the keys. "There," it said.

"Hmmm," Amanda said. She was thinking. She had also watched the way Oozie punched the console. "Where are you thinking of putting them? And what about them . . . won't they protest?"

"No, I've worked out a deal with the Reds."

"The Reds?"

"The Red Robots—amnesia line. They'll forget everything. Wherever they wind up, they'll think it's the Happy Hunting Ground. They'll stay put . . ." —he was pacing the floor—"that's not the problem. The problem is quite simply where to put them. I was thinking of putting them back on the plains where I took them from."

"Why don't you, then?" Amanda asked. Not that she expected he would, but her curiosity was growing.

"Because if you put something back exactly from where you took it, you don't get an amnesia line. You can only get an amnesia line for ontological displacement."

"My goodness," Amanda said. "Sounds frighteningly Germanic and logical—that is, for an illogical system."

"Oh, everything has its rules, even the unruly," Ooze said.

Although Amanda was very upset—about herself, about Hotchkiss, and about Schrodinger—she was, after all, a human being as well as a scientist. And it is no small thing to see the alternate destinies of mankind paraded before your view, to have glimpsed, if not seen, into the future of mankind, without a deeply felt urgency to correct and alter its course, especially if one saw such fearful destruction as she saw here.

"The GCB," said the Ooze, "is in charge of species extinction. The only thing he's good at is endings." The Ooze had leaned over at this, and in a conspiratorial voice that had, Amanda thought, almost a hint of braggadocio in it, said, "Up here we call him the Finale Master, so he never, ever, never thought a species would decide to destroy itself—I mean, it's unheard of. I must say I never thought it could happen either—but when you started toxic dumping and then you built nuclear plants, he threw up his hands."

"He has hands?" Amanda said quickly.

"In a manner of speaking," said the Ooze, "only."

"Oh," Amanda said.

"So he just gave the Blue Robots and the Red Robots extra lines of entry, so it's just a question of whether you poison yourselves or blow yourselves up. He doesn't give a damn, although he is prejudiced, I happen to know, toward fireballs."

"Well"—Amanda was pacing the console room—"what about other forces? Doesn't anything else have power?"

"Oh," Ooze shrugged, "to be sure. There are powerful forces outside this spectrum. They are finding it harder and harder to get through. There is Radiant One and—"

"Who . . . what's Radiant One?" This was the force she had heard of in the heart fields.

"She's from the other system. She's a positive force."

"Well, why don't you let her in here? She'd help you populate another planet and everything."

"The GCB," Ooze said, looking frightened again, "would coalesce me. Radiant One can't get through crystals, see?" It pointed to the cobalt-blue sky high overhead. "Everything here is covered with crystals. The robots patrol them day and night. She can't get through." It shrugged.

"Look, there must be a way out of this," Amanda said. "I'm not going to sit here and accept the earth's demise. Can I get in touch with her—this Radiant One?"

"You are," said the Ooze in a whisper. "The molecules . . . the molecules are from Radiant One. That's why . . ."

All of a sudden there were alarms going off all over the console, and Ooze's antenna suddenly shot up over the side of its head.

"Oh-oh," it said, leaping off. "Galaxy collision. I've got to go. Galaxy collisions cannot wait. Back soon." And it turned its back, which it did because, of course, it was not at all used to having anyone in the vicinity of the console. It did not think about the fact that it was leaving the console running, and Amanda so close to it. Amanda looked at the machine. Well, if nothing else, she could decide the fate of the Indians. She did not really want to use them, as she thought the Indians had been used quite enough. On the other hand, if they knew her purpose she was sure they would agree to help her. She was going straight to this GCB.

She quickly looked about to be sure Ooze and Rastus were out of sight, and then she punched the console. Her fingers flew. Not for nothing did she have a photographic memory. She had carefully watched the Ooze's access code, and she knew from Rastus how to reach the place she wanted to put them. She hoped it worked.

"There," Amanda said, hitting the final button on the console. The console roared.

"EEEEEK!" the Ooze screamed, turning back. "Don't touch, don't touch, don't touch! Oh, my heavens, oh my heavens, oh my God, look what YOU'VE DONE—EEEEE!" it squealed again, more, Amanda thought, like a little stuck pig than anything as impressive as the Primal Ooze.

"Oh, I'm so sorry," Amanda said, quickly stepping back. "It's this terrible habit I've had ever since I've been a kid. I see a button, I push it." She bit her lip. "Did I do anything too terrible?"

Apparently she had. The Ooze was positively beside itself. Jumping up and down, and crying and pushing buttons, yelling the entire time "EEEEE!"

"Well, what is it? What's happening?" Amanda said, getting extremely nervous.

"You hit it, you hit it, the Indians, I told you I wasn't ready to move the Indians, oh my God my God my God!" It was still pushing buttons when Rastus came in.

"What in hell is going on? All my circuits are clouded. You ain't s'posed to do nothin' inexplicable. You ain't got an inexplicable sanction for another fifty years, Ooze." Rastus seemed highly irritated.

"Oh . . . I . . . I think it's my fault," Amanda said. "See, I have this thing, it's just terrible—they tried to get it out of me in the astronaut program, but they didn't really succeed," she said, breathless and embarrassed. "I guess. But it's this carry-over from my childhood," she said. "I see a button, I have to press it." She shrugged again.

"You see a button, you have to press it—what are you talking about?" Rastus said, roaring with anger.

Amanda, genuinely embarrassed, moved back from Rastus's furious glare. "Well," she said softly, "I don't know. It's something I do. I just do it," she stammered. " . . . I see it, and I push it."

"She sees it and she pushes it, oh my," Rastus said, holding his head. "Oh Lord, have mercy on us all." This last, which seemed to be a prayer, genuinely surprised Amanda, who had not, at least as of this moment, sensed any sort of religious tradition prevalent in this particular place.

Amanda saw that the Ooze had, for the time being, calmed down. It was lying on its back, if that's what it was, breathing heavily. "Oh my oh my oh my," it said, wiping its pink and hairless brow.

"You think he found out?" Rastus said.

There was an ominous silence. The terrible thing, Amanda thought, was that, upset though they were, she really didn't care about that, she was curious as to what had happened.

"What'd I do?" she said, simply.

"What did you do? I'll tell you, little miss snot-face, what you did," the Ooze said, angry now, so angry its antenna was flashing various colors.

"You're flashing," Amanda said, amused, and smiling.

"Flash, trash, now you shut up and listen to me," the Ooze said, jumping, surprisingly, quite up on her chest.

"Hey!" Amanda said, stepping back.

"You listen to me. You do not touch any more buttons on that console, do you understand?" the Ooze said. "Or you will be a gas. I will be a gas. We will all be gases. Instant. Presto. Vamoosed."

"Oh," she said. "How come?"

"Because this is how come: because he doesn't want anyone to find out, that's how come."

"Who doesn't want who to find out?"

"GCB," Ooze said, whispering. "GCB doesn't want anyone to get suspicious, so all this maneuvering goes on only in highly explicable circumstances, do you understand? When you push a button, things happen down there, but the right things have to happen. You need a cover. Something misleading. I don't care what you call it, but if you're going to do the inexplicables, you can only do them in religious communities. You do inexplicables in a scientific community, they get curious. They might find out."

"About you? Up here?" Amanda's eyes rolled. "Don't worry about it. Nobody would believe it."

"But they might, they might, they might!" the Ooze screamed. "So you need a cover—oh, EEEEE," it said again. "Look what you've done—the Indians. My God, you moved them—a store some-where . . ." and it turned back to the console again.

"A store?" Amanda said.

"Only for a minute, a minute . . . maybe no one saw them." The Ooze had hit the console, but Amanda, when it turned, had hit the console, too. The red buttons were all SEAT OF GOV'T buttons. There were two areas on the console. One for the United States and one for the Kremlin. Amanda had hit one of the U.S. buttons. Which one she couldn't be sure.

"Oh heavens, we'll have to divert them—we'll have to do weather. Weather's always a good diversion. Oh boy, this will have to be good." The Ooze worked away at the console for quite a while. "I'll have to do FLOOD—FLOOD, oh-oh—it's my last natural disaster. I am now out of natural disasters, with the exception of two lulus I would never use unless it was the Bitter End. I am out until 2004, earth time, anyway."

"What'd you do?"

"Not telling, not telling," said the Ooze. "You know too much already."

57

It was two nights after the Genius's disappearance that floods came. There were floods in Waco, the water had risen out of the Gulf in a storm and spread into the surrounding towns, turning the desert into a lake. But that, the flood, wasn't the worst of it. The worst of it was what the flood had uncovered. Driven from their homes, the families were living in tents and trailers up in the hills. Some of them weren't far from Reno. They had seen the trucks trailing the water jugs into there only yesterday. The government announced the people could not go back to Waco because there had been toxic dumps permitted into the soil for years, which had poisoned the well water, which of course they had all been drinking for years, but only now the news was out. The camera sped over the shocked stunned faces of those whose homes were flooded, only to be told the poison level spread by the rising water was so dangerous they could not return to retrieve anything.

Eberly sat in the café watching the television coverage—first speechless, then rising in his chair—as a "government spokesman" explained that the government had to find alternate energy resources, that they dumped the toxic waste there because they just hadn't figured out yet what to do with it, but that the resources were what counted.

"Resources? What kinda resources we talkin' 'bout here? I am asking you somethin', Rufus. I am askin' you, is George Washington gonna let things get this bad or not? Now answer me yes or no?"

Rufus did not know why the answer should fall on him. "I never said there was anybody decent in government, Eb."

The others wondered at this outburst in the sheriff. It was like him, of course. Yet it seemed to go further than Eberly had ever admitted he would go.

It was Silas who finally said, "What is it, Eb? These government people been ruinin' things for years. . . . Why all of a sudden you so out to stop 'em?"

"Ruin?" Eberly turned to him, his eyes ablaze. "They been ruinin' the East. To hell with the East. They want to poison it up, throwing cancer down people's well water, to hell with 'em. But this is Waco, Silas," Eberly said pounding the table, "and you forget, I'm the sheriff of Cononga County."

"Waco ain't in Cononga, Sheriff," Silas said. "It's in the next county."

"It was in Cononga," Eberly said, "until they redrew the lines in fifty-two."

"That was more than thirty years ago, Eb," Rufus said, wondering at this.

"Lemme tell you somethin'. They could redraw the lines, they could do what they could do, but I'm a here to tell you that once I'm sheriff of a place, I feel a responsibility. Effen it's Jesse James they need protectin' from, I gonna protect 'em, and effen it's that damn government talkin' man they need protection from, I'm gonna protect 'em against that. I'm gettin' my other holster," Eberly said, "and I'm goin' into Waco. And I am here to tell you, whoever put the poison in the water is just gonna get down there and get that poison out or he's gonna be dancin' to the tune of bullets under his feet." Eberly slid out of his chair. He was smokin', Rufus could see.

Rufus figured privately Eberly was all tuned up and upset over the Genius not coming back. To tell the truth, he was a mite upset himself. Not a clue, nothing. Only that laundry truck and that pathetic weird guy who called himself a magician. The magician told Eberly if he came out there and set on some old rug, the Genius would get back sooner. Of course, Eberly nearly shot at him saying something like that. But Rufus privately didn't think the old man was crazy. He didn't have the look that crazy people have in their eyes.

It was just that night, right after Eberly had taken the pickup truck to Waco, that the magician came through the door, talking and waving all excited like. Old Tom was there, and after they listened to the magician's story, Rufus turned to Old Tom and said, "You reckon he's crazy, Tom?" And Old Tom just looked at Rufus and said, "No."

The next day, Rufus figured, was what really did it. Set Eberly off like a shooting star. Bad enough the flood was in Waco, but the radioactivity had now drifted down through the entire water system. There was a warning out not to drink tap water, but Eberly had stepped out into his backyard to water his gladiolas, figuring that was all right, and as he did, he watched them curl like he was pouring lye on them. In three minutes it looked like the garden of hell.

Rufus figured Eberly'd gone plumb crazy over this poisoning question. Why the next morning he drove into Waco and crashed right into the meeting.

"Sheriff Eberly," he said, turning around, although Rufus figured there wasn't nobody in there didn't but know who Eb was except maybe the government people.

"Lemme tell you boys something," Eb said, "jus' so's you understand. You can flush the whole goddamn country down the sewer, if that's what you're aimin' to do, and iffen you asks me it is what you're aimin' to do; you can turn the whole place into a stinking sinkhole, and I'm gonna watch you go down, 'cause you ain't touchin' Cononga County. When you disappear down that poison drain, Cononga County gonna be here, clear and gleamin' like a pearl."

Of course later when questioned about this, Eberly would confess he didn't know how he was gonna keep the best bass fishing in Texas clean and clear when the water rushing down from above was bringing toxic chemicals and leakage from radioactive waste with it. He didn't know that at all. It was this that brought him down. That day he saw those dead bass washing up on the banks he was sick. He was sicker than he ever thought he could be. Those fish used to jump in the air, sometimes high as a man's head, and now they were dead. "No oxygen in the water," was what they said. Couldn't breathe. Things like that set up in a man when he started thinking, and it sent Eberly quivering if he didn't get hold of it somehow.

But in the meantime the government man was protesting Eberly's appearance. Protesting loud and clear, like he had it all worked out in advance, but Eberly interrupted him, surprising them all by firing his six-shooter straight into the air.

"Now you lissena me," Eb yelled. "I'm sick a' lissenin' to you. You

ain't nothin', nothin' but a lyin' cheatin' low-down good-for-nothin' no-
'ccount two-bit lily-livered chicken-hearted son of a bitch, who's tryin'
to git me and all a' Cononga County blown to smithereens. Well I ain't
gonna have it. You wanna send that there radiation out, you send it
out. You gonna blow bombs up killin' cattle and people and poisonin'
the water, you go ahead and do it. But don't bring none of that there
radiation in Cononga. Don't bring none of that poison water in Cononga.
We got one river here, and I mean to see there's still bass fishin' in it.
Ain't nobody gonna drink milk from no Cononga County cows and go
dyin' from it. No sir! Not so long's I am sheriff of Cononga County."
Eberly hitched his pants and drew his gun. "You betcher life on that.
Now git." He fired two shots at the government man's shoes.

"Now look," the government man said, his eyes wide with fear; he
was jumping up and down.

His assistant looked about, yelling, "He's crazy, he's crazy!" meaning, of course, the sheriff.

"Look," the government man said, backing toward the door with
his briefcase, "it . . . it might come in on the wind, it's not deliberate . . . it, the wind . . . we can't stop the wind."

Eberly had risen to the full heights of his indignation. He fired his
pistol again, again, again. The dust rose up in small whirlpools around
the government man's feet. "You got thirty billion dollars bustin' your
budget, you goddamn better figure out how to stop the wind, now git!"
and he fired again, this time over the government man's head, and when
the bullet sliced through his hat the two of them ran into the street,
hollerin' and yelling, flapping their arms as they raced toward their cars,
"screamin' and runnin' like a coupla plucked chickens," as Rufus would
describe it later.

"That was kinda close, Eb," Rufus said at the time, wonderingly.
"You coulda missed and shot the poor devil."

"Ah did miss," Eberly said. And Rufus couldn't tell whether he
meant it or not. It seemed to Rufus that Eberly was an altogether amazing
thing. When Eberly had that badge on, which he had most of the time,
why Eberly would go to his death protecting the citizens of Cononga
County. Even Hollis Weathers. Eberly hated Weathers with a passion,
but that night when some hooligan broke into Weathers' house, broke
it up and stole his stuff, Eberly was out three days and nights, running
high and low over the state of Texas. He wouldn't rest until he brought

him in. And he did. Everybody knew he would. Rufus supposed there wasn't a person in Cononga ever thought Eberly could get beat. He thought Eberly knew that, too, and somehow these things worked together so that Eberly never did get beat. Eberly, it seemed to Rufus, had been born for protection. He took to it so. That's why Rufus knew it was killing him about those Indians. Didn't seem like you could find them no how.

The president was taking a nap. He did this often. Naps, he had decided, were good for foreign policy. He had started many unpleasant things unnecessarily because he was grumpy. His wife had told him this. So now he took naps.

How many naps, exactly, no one was allowed to say. But we can assume there were, in the course of a day, many naps. Often these naps were interrupted by meetings. Occasionally meetings were interrupted by the naps, for the president was capable, in the midst of a heated discussion, of falling fast asleep.

However, today he was napping on his couch when he was interrupted by one of the presiding members of the Joint Chiefs of Staff, who rushed in unceremoniously, right past the two chargés d'affaires at the door and past the president's personal secretary, right past his wife, whom he nearly knocked over, rushed right into the presidential suite, and shaking the president hysterically until he awakened, cried, "There's ten thousand goddamn redskins in the basement!"

"What? Redskins?" the president said upon waking.

"Yes, Mr. President," the aide-de-camp said, terrified, "we got redskins, goddamn redskins in the basement."

"Redskins?" the president said. "Redskins in my basement?"

"Yessir—I mean no, sir," the aide-de-camp saluted. "Redskins in the basement of the Pentagon, sir." He whispered this very loudly.

"The Pentagon? In the basement of the Pentagon?" The president was aghast. "How the hell did they get in there?"

"We don't know, sir . . . but they're there, sir. . . . The thing is, sir . . . we don't know how to get them out, without the press finding it out, sir."

"The press?! Lord Jesus God almighty, you can't let the press know we got redskins in the Pentagon. Are you crazy, man?"

"No sir . . . I mean, yessir, I know that, sir. That's why I am here, sir. . . . What would you like us to do, sir?"

"How the hell do I know?" the president roared. "I need some advice, goddamn it. Go get my advisors."

"I spoke to them, sir," the aide-de-camp whispered. "They're working on it."

"Working on it. Get them the hell out! How the hell did they get in there anyhow?"

"I don't know, sir. No one saw them go in."

"NO ONE SAW THEM? Goddamn it, LIEUTENANT, ten thousand Indians are in the basement of the Pentagon and NO ONE SAW THEM?"

"No sir. They arrived last night, sir. They're very hungry. So we let them order in. We told the people making deliveries that they're Arabs. Well, we had to say something," the aide went on, "because the people making deliveries . . . they know someone's down there. They order in a lot. Quite a lot, sir."

"Order in . . . my God . . . can't you build a kitchen down there? You can't have them ordering in. Not ten thousand Indians."

"We're building the kitchen, sir . . . but in the meantime we had to say something . . . so we said it was Arabs, with lots of wives. It's okay, sir. It's going over. They believe it. Arabs like tacos, too."

"Hmmmm," the president said.

"It's also better for the budget."

"The budget? What budget?"

"Well, sir, the State Department thinks it's Arabs, so they're paying for it. It comes under the Oil Exploration Bureau. They'll never miss it, Mr. President. Otherwise," his voice dropped, "it would have to come out of the Bureau of Indian Affairs. Not a nickel in there. Not a dime." He stood up then and smiled. "It's working out actually very nicely."

"Hmmm," the president said.

"Which is why, sir," the aide-de-camp said, turning on his heel, "we have to ask you, sir . . . not to lower gasoline prices. We need to feed the Indians. If you lower the prices, it will eat up our budget. We've figured it out. If you lower it one cent a gallon, they'll be down to Cokes and fries. No burgers. If you keep it up, though," he smiled, "every Indian gets meat."

"Well now," the president said, smiling broadly. "Sonny boy," he said, "you can count on me." It made him feel damn good. The price might be dropping by the barrel, but he was gonna keep it up at the tanks. Anything to give an Indian a bellyful.

58

"I think this is great," Amanda said. The alarm system was still shrieking, "I'll just sneak out and pick Schrodinger up and go. I've been trying to get to him all along, but I thought it was so difficult."

The Ooze stared at her. "You won't like it when you get there."

"But I . . . I'll get Schrodinger," she said. "That's what I came for, after all." Although it was true that she had come for Schrodinger she was beginning to feel a strong obligation to clean up these robot wars. After all they seemed to be taking over large chunks of the earth and turning it to ruin. "Ruin the biology," the Ooze had said, "that's what they were up to—or else blowing it sky high."

"Well," the Ooze said, "you'll see when you get there." He looked strange all of a sudden, to Amanda. "You'll hate it. It's horrible. I hate to go."

"You're afraid of him," Amanda said, amazed that anything that had the powers Ooze had could be afraid.

"No, it's not fear," the Ooze said, beginning to shake.

"Why, you're shaking," Amanda said, surprised at the sympathy in her voice.

"Oh, I'm not afraid," said Ooze. "It's . . . it's . . ."

"It's what?" said Amanda

"He stinks," said the Ooze. "The stink. The stink from the GCB is just awful."

"The stink?"

"Oh," said the Ooze, "the GCB . . . oh no." It looked around, positively frantic, Amanda thought. "Anything but that. I won't go there . . . no no no, I won't do it, nothing doing."

"Well, isn't that disgusting," Amanda said. "You're positively intimidated by him! You, the Ooze!"

"I am not intimidated," the Ooze whispered loudly, looking around. "I just don't want to go."

"Because you're afraid," Amanda said, not concealing the disdain in her voice.

"I am not afraid!" the Ooze said, stamping its feet. It looked around again. "It's something else."

"What?"

"Oh, you can't imagine . . . you know it really gets the biologicals."

"The what?"

"The stink doesn't bother the chemicals or the electricals. It's only the biologicals."

"Oh," said Amanda, thinking this over. Here it was again, the constant refrain, the universe divided into chemical systems, electrical systems, and biologicals. With the Ooze the guardian of the biologicals. The guardian. And not. She clearly had to get to this GCB, whatever it was. Stink or no stink.

"So hold your nose, if that's what it is," Amanda said. "Besides the stink, you don't seem to like him."

"Oh, you know he needs me, because he starts these galaxies and he finishes them, but he leaves all the in-between work to me. He just starts them, you know, plays around with his fireball act, then he sends me in there. I never get to *start* anything." It appeared to be moping.

"Well, maybe you will," Amanda said, trying to cheer it up.

"Maybe maybe maybe. . . . You know how old I'm going to be next week, and I never had the chance yet?"

"No, how old?"

"Ten billion. I'm going to be ten billion years old, and I never once, once got to start my own universe, a galaxy, a solar system, or even a planet. He starts it and then I have to clean it up."

"How many does he have going at one time?" Amanda said.

"Oh heavens, I can't keep track. There's only one other biological, though I don't know if it's going to get to continue. It's on hold."

"On hold?" Amanda said quickly. "Well, where is it?"

"Over there," it said, pointing to Barnard's Star. "It's over there. It's more or less where earth was two hundred million years ago. He let me start that one, but he's never going to let me finish it."

"What do you want to do with it?" Amanda said.

"I want to make it conscious, you know. I want to start some mammals going in there. I had the earth, you know, up to the time of the dinosaurs. I was supposed to get them. I was just gettin' goin' and he knocked off the dinosaurs."

"What do you mean, knocked off?"

"Knocked them right off. Too many bilogical systems. Perish," he said, "in a snap. Get rid of it. Sent in a huge meteorite. The destruction was fantastic," Ooze said. "The ash was so thick the sun couldn't get through. Knocked photosynthesis right out of the park. You know, he goes for explosions. Then he got bored and went away. I didn't think I could get anything started again. Never mind the dinosaurs. I didn't think I could get a leaf to start again, in all that ash. But I did," it said simply, "and now you're all going to ruin it again."

"Well, maybe not," Amanda said. "There's still a chance."

"No chance," said the Ooze, clearly discouraged. "I was s'posed to get the Indians and I didn't. No chance as long as the robots are gaining. Every time they make a NERP the NERP makes another NERP. And they're planning another night raid."

"Well, we have to stop them," Amanda said determinedly.

The Ooze blinked. "You can't, they'll never let you. Oh, oh," it said, as Amanda saw an enormous Red Robot pounding down the hall toward them, a gigantic metal and brass-looking creature, with a pointed steel helmet and huge cyclical gold rolls about its thighs. It looked sort of like a futuristic version of a knight in armor, although its clear intention was menace. There was no saving grace here.

The robot had a voice like nothing Amanda had ever heard. It seemed to echo in a thousand chambers as he spoke. "The GCB has sent for you," he said. It was almost preposterous, except it was a trifle too frightening to be preposterous.

"Okay, okay," said the Ooze, turning to Amanda. "Get ready to disintegrate."

"Disintegrate!" she said. "Certainly not. I am certainly not ready to—"

"Shhh," it said, "it's electronic transport. You get into the Crystal Palace that way. There's no other way. You'd better cooperate," it said to her, " 'cause he'll do it anyway."

Amanda sighed. The robot turned to her and, raising some kind of gun, shot at her.

59

There was a terrible sound outside the door. The Genius looked out.

"Oh my God," he said, his face turning white. "Hotchkiss." Hotchkiss ran to the window to see hundreds of thousands of robots taking to the air on night wings, and hundreds more galloping across the desert toward their door. The night was full of stainless-steel gladiators, flashing eyes revolving, programmed for victory.

"What're we going to do?" The Genius thought his heart had stopped. In seconds, the robot army was at their door, pounding and breaking it down. The sounds of the clamoring robots were fierce outside. They were demanding Hotchkiss and the Genius. The Genius peered out. "We're cooked," he said.

Just as the door heaved in under their might, Hotchkiss heard a clarion call, a familiar scream. It was the chimp, and Hotchkiss looked out to see the big Blue Robot galloping toward them with 342 clinging to his neck.

"You are ordered to disperse. I'm guarding here," Robert said to the robots, "on orders from the GCB. He asks that you return to the game. They're in my custody."

No robot would lie. It was unheard of. The GCB had access to their programs. Each and every one. He'd have had them reprogrammed in a second. So the robots dispersed.

Except this one. Robert. This ineffectual, inefficient robot, the most unsuspected one of all, was the secret Maverick who could bring the system down. This was the one that would not, indeed, could not, obey. For he was a maverick, right down to his photovoltaic self. When he heard "right," he thought, Only if I want. If I want I can also go left. Left never entered the other robots' thinking at all. Right was right after all. As long as there was right, there was no left. Like that. Robert was robot enough to know he could not allow them to see his maverickness. Instead he had to pretend malfunction of operation, never malfunction of purpose. Purpose here was that dictated by the GCB.

60

The next thing Amanda knew, it seemed to her that no time at all had passed. She was simply standing in a palace of crystals that were shining and turning, and she and the Ooze were walking down a long mirrored hall. Amanda could see immediately what the Ooze was talking about. The stench was considerable, and it was getting worse.

"Is it much farther?" she said to it after a while, beginning to cough from the smell.

"Yes," said the Ooze. "We're still on the outskirts; we haven't even really gotten to it yet."

Suddenly the shining crystal walls changed. They went over a small bridge, and the smooth walls were shiny in a different way. They appeared soft and slimy; they appeared almost to be moving. The ground under their feet, too, was slimy and wet. The whole thing felt, Amanda thought privately, quite disgusting. Coupled with the stench, she thought she absolutely was going to retch.

They had not gone very far, slipping their way along the tunnels, along the stinking, slimy dark walls, when they came to a large cave. The stink was overwhelming. In the corner, Amanda thought she could discern a shape. She and the Ooze stood there as her eyes grew accustomed to the dimness, and then she saw there was something enormous and coiled there. It seemed to be miles of an enormous gray-green garden hose. It was mountains of gray-green garden hose, full of lumps and bumps—a mountainous heap of oozing pus and rheum.

"Good grief," Amanda said. "How revolting."

"Shhh," said the Ooze, as they stood there and confronted this large, lumpy, thumping, great gray-green snake piled up on itself.

"That's it," said the Ooze. Amanda stood there, her mouth open. This was too much to believe. This stinking thing, whatever it was, was running the universe!

This thing, master of the universe! That is, if any of this were to be believed. Amanda realized at once that her first reaction was anything but scientific.

"Yuck!" escaped from her before she knew it. The slimy, slithering, stench-filled mass before her was the essence of putrefaction. It was disgusting. The rank smell of its yellow gaseous fumes filled the air. It was a coiled, oily mass—warts and fissures steaming from every membrane. And the smell.

Amanda was holding her nose and trying not to retch. This, this essence of decay, could not be running the universe. From the mess a voice spoke.

"Revolted, are you?"

Amanda was vainly trying to see where the voice was coming from.

The coil moved, ever so slightly.

"Cat got your tongue?" the thing said, heaving so that each coil now slid one over the other, and the top one, the fastest, fell down the side, hanging loose. From the end of that one she could see there was an opening. So that's what Ooze meant. You couldn't tell the end from the beginning.

"No, the cat hasn't got my tongue," Amanda said. Then, firmly, "What do you want?"

"Want me to let the cat out of the bag?" the thing said.

"Yes," Amanda said. "Let the cat out of the bag."

"HO HO HO." It shook, all the coils shook at once, the stench increased, and then the coils fell, all into a huge pile. Amanda jumped back.

"The cat was never in the bag," the voice said. "The cat can't get into the bag, or out of the bag, as long as you're the cat's meow." It shivered then and gave out some squeaking noises, which Amanda supposed was some sort of laughter.

"Well," she said, uncertain as to how to proceed. "I don't know what you mean by that. I'm the cat's owner. I'm not the cat's meow. Unless, of course," she said, blushing slightly, "you're being personal."

"OF COURSE I'M BEING PERSONAL," the thing yelled. "Highly personal. I am nothing if not personal." When it said that, lights appeared all around, in the form of signs. Little signs then flashed on and off all around her. She thought that in fact there must have been hundreds of them, and all the signs said the same thing, I AM NOTHING IF NOT PERSONAL.

"Well," Amanda said, "thank you for the compliment, if that's what it is, but what I really want is my cat. Schrodinger. I understand you have him here, and I want him back."

There was silence for a moment, and then the voice burped. The wind and the stench from one burp almost knocked her down. "Puddy tat. Nice puddy tat." Then nothing.

"Yes," Amanda said. She noticed the lights had been dimming the entire time she was in this place, and now the darkness was proceeding quickly. "The puddy tat. He's my puddy tat and I want him back."

The thing began to shiver and shake, and as the dark came on it said to her, "No." Then it was dark. Amanda could see nothing. She felt a cold wind fall around her, and she felt the thing was moving away from her, or she from it; she felt this enormous rush of air you feel when something gigantic moves past you at great speed, as if she were on a platform and a train were rushing by, and she yelled to it.

"Look," Amanda said, ignoring the Ooze, who was punching her to keep quiet, "all I want is my cat, and I know how you feel about secrecy, so if you give me my cat, I won't tell anyone on earth, and you'll have your secret, okay?" Amanda was aware that she had taken on a tone as if she were addressing a small child, and this seemed right. There was something profoundly infantile about this shape before her, the essence of impulsive aggrandizement.

As far as she could tell, it was a twisted hose, with a lean look. It had no eyes.

"I want it," said the GCB, "so I'm gonna keep it."

"But," Amanda said, "I hear he isn't purring. You see, he doesn't want to stay. If you give me Schrodinger I . . . I'll give you another pussycat, a nicer one—one that purrs."

It was, Amanda thought, extremely difficult to be holding a meaningful conversation while you felt like throwing up. Every time the GCB opened his mouth, this fumous gas spewed forth. Even the Venus's-flytrap spat out its flies. It made everything retch. Amanda, however, remembered her biofeedback training, and carefully monitored her gag reflex, but the fact remained that this was a stench-filled palace. This, the source of this universe, was a stinking, blithering infantile mess, of great power and no follow-through, master of fissured hearts and lost memories. This was the beginning and the end. Of all things.

"I want Schrodinger, nice puddy tat," said the GCB, giving forth with a burp so powerful, the wind from it knocked Amanda down, the stench so bad she felt dizzy when she tried to stand. But now when she finally did, she was mad.

"Look, you big fat stinking mess, you can't have my cat. Now that's all there is to it. You can't go around taking whatever you want whenever you want, because he doesn't belong to you. Now I'll be glad to get you another one, but this one is mine and I'm taking him back. Do you understand?!" She was aware she was yelling, she was so angry.

"Yes," the GCB blurted, "I understand, but you, you're stupid." And it let out a huge burp.

"It burps?" Amanda whispered to Ooze. "My God, it keeps burping?" This struck her as so funny, she collapsed in laughter at once. It was hilarious, it was horrible, this huge cumbersome stink-filled, wart-covered mess, one of the greatest powers in the universe, with indigestion, yet!

"Oh my God," she said, recovering, trying to wipe the tears from her eyes.

"Shut up, girlie," the GCB said, "your attitude stinks."

"My attitude!" she yelled. "The whole palace stinks. It stinks beyond belief!" She was convulsed, and trying to stop laughing.

"It does?" She thought she saw an eye blink. "It stinks in here?" it said. "Ooze, does it stink?"

"Oh, why don't you shut up," Ooze whispered to Amanda. "He can't stand criticism. He doesn't know it stinks."

"Well it's about time he did. It's so revolting in here."

"There is a slight odor," said the Ooze, "which to most biologicals is offensive."

"Biologicals! To hell with them!" said the GCB. "Trouble, trouble, trouble."

"See, he doesn't like it because they start interfering with him. You know he doesn't like it. If he's going to remove the dinosaurs, it's one thing, but when the biologicals decide to remove themselves, that's trouble," said Ooze. "I know him like a book."

"He's an ass," Amanda hissed. "This is ridiculous. He can't possibly have all this power . . . he's an idiot, for God's sake. He—"

"Shhhhh," said Ooze.

"Hold your horses," said the GCB. "If you give me the cat," the GCB spewed forth, "I'll call the robots off."

"And Hotchkiss and the Genius—will they be safe, too?"

"Oh yes," he said. Quickly. Much too quickly.

"The GCB," she remembered Rastus had said, "he lies, he cheats, he steals."

"I'll give you back the earth," the GCB said. "Just leave me puddy tat."

What was this? Was the GCB giving Amanda a guarantee for the future security of the world in exchange for Schrodinger? Was this the Almighty Deal? Amanda was a scientist. If this were so, it was a mighty thing. Schrodinger was being asked to sacrifice himself for the world. It would be a great thing for the earth, Amanda reflected, but it was going to throw organized religion into a tizzy. She didn't think about it too long. Here was an opportunity to save the world. A simple thing. In exchange for her cat.

"No!" she said. "Certainly not!" Oozie blinked. The GCB snarled and turned.

"You're crazy," whispered the Ooze.

"He's *my* cat," Amanda said, "and I came to get him." She was sick of the GCB, of his cosmos and his deals.

61

The president had had a hell of a weekend. All the crazy things that had been going on in the goddamned country seemed to be getting worse. Ever since those Indians had disappeared and now of all things had wound up in the basement of the Pentagon, well, things had definitely been getting worse. First there was the weather. The weather had been peculiar, everybody knew that, for the last several years. But this weather was nuts. And there was the problem of California. California had always been a problem, but nothing quite like this: there was a lot less of California than there had been five years ago. A LOT less. Like a third. Yes, a third of California, an entire third of an entire state, and a Republican one at that, had slipped quietly into the sea without anyone making so much as a fuss. Well, hell, you know there's a silver lining in everything, and those people on the shore front felt they had been paying through the ole schnozzola as far as property taxes were concerned, so what the hell, but the *insurance* companies, my God— beachfront after beachfront slipping quietly into the old oil-slicked ocean no less. If the ocean over there had held up it wouldn't be so bad, but the gluck and the guck were rolling in fast and heavy, and the oil slick had washed over Highway 1 and sent things really into a tizzy. So there's always another highway. Soon they'd build a new one. But, there were problems here too. They said the soil erosion was so bad everytime you stuck a drill or a steam shovel into the ground houses were spilling down into it. Nothing was holding in the entire goddamn state.

"It's dust, the earth," said the environmentalists. "We've got to plant trees before it's too late." But, of course, it was too late, because it seemed they couldn't get the water down there out of the hills in any kind of condition to do the trees much good. Had too much something or other in it—he didn't know what—because the fish, who used to eat up some kind of algae or something, had gotten polished off by the oil rigs, and who knows, what with one thing and another, it just seemed they never could get that state straightened out.

So he let it slide. Some things, you have to let slide. Of course, it's only fair to say he didn't expect it to slide the whole way into the ocean, at least not so much of it.

But that was that. Let bygones be bygones, said the prez. The problem now was the weather. All those floods were one thing, but now there were even snowstorms occurring in Texas. Snowstorms with snowflakes the size of telephone books knocking people sideways if you got caught in them. Of course they hadn't killed anybody or anything like that, but nonetheless people were upset, having to wear hard hats in a snowstorm because of these strange inclement conditions. Nobody knew why these snowflakes were coming down so big and heavy chock-a-block out of the sky like that. And hell, they had earthquakes now in New York City. Earthquakes, and firestorms in Savannah, and heaven only knew what else. Typhoons were sweeping through Japan like never before; there had been fourteen feet, *feet* of snow in Germany in two weeks; people were drowning in their houses; why there were people who said the world was coming to an end.

All that was bad enough. Agreed. Then, on top of that, there were the sightings. Incredible! First, they had reports from a radar plane: the pilot saw ten thousand Indians flying through the sky heading for Washington, D.C. Nobody else saw them. Nobody at all. Next thing they knew, they got reports from three hundred witnesses—count them, all women it was sure—but nonetheless three hundred of them, attesting to the fact that ten thousand Indians, by God, had shown up in Bloomingdale's last Saturday afternoon. Now they weren't there long, less than two minutes, so nobody had a chance to ask them how they got there or anything, but they were there, at least if you could believe three hundred women shopping, and now those same Indians—well, they didn't know if they were exactly the same but they figured they probably were the same group of ten thousand—had shown up in the basement of the Pentagon. Thank God, the prez had said, thank God the media hadn't got wind of this one yet. They had thought of killing them. You know, just overdosing them with something down there, but then they had to get the bodies out. There were people in Washington highly experienced in getting bodies out, but even these people, with all their resources, felt that ten thousand was too much.

So that was that. Stuck with the Indians. Now the president was a man of action, and here he was with his hands tied. With ten thousand restless Indians running under the Pentagon, snowflakes knocking people sideways in Texas, and losing Republican states like California to things like oil slick and soil erosion every year. What *was* a man to do? The president was holding his head and crying when an aide entered the room and whispered in his ear.

"Oh no!" he said. The Indians had taken their tom-toms and were beating songs under the earth. Washingtonians thought it was an earthquake, because of the vibrations that they felt, but only the president and his aides knew the truth.

Somehow they had to get those Indians out. And they had to do it without telling anyone in the Pentagon what they were doing, because the Pentagon, as everyone knew, was not to be trusted in delicate decisions of this sort. Besides, the CIA reported that the Pentagon was riddled, positively riddled with KGB double agents, and since the president of the United States had had it on top-secret information that the Russians had stolen the Indians in the first place and he had delivered an ultimatum to Russia that if they did not return the Indians *intact* by June eighteenth he was going to ship ten thousand armored tanks to Afghanistan, which would put the ratio of armored tanks to people in Afghanistan in a ratio of four tanks to a family, it would be embarrassing, most embarrassing, indeed, if the KGB via the Pentagon ever got wind of this Indian thing.

Besides all that, how the hell did they get there in the first place? Unless . . . but that was unthinkable. He thought it anyway. The unthinkable was that the Russians had in fact stolen the Indians and to avoid the United States supplying every Afghanistan family with four armored personnel carriers, they had, with the aid of the Pentagon-KGB turncoats, smuggled the Indians back into the Pentagon. That was, based on the current level of *his* intelligence system, the only reason they could come up with.

But they were wrong. The Russians had figured they could blow the Afghans to hell and back again and the United States wouldn't make a move. They also didn't believe these Indians had disappeared. They had heard, on the most reliable basis for their intelligence, that the Indians were the last group of high-altitude labor available and the United States was building a nuclear missile station high up—at fifteen thousand feet to be exact—on top of a mountain in Alaska. Only the Indians could work there. Now *that* showed superior intelligence.

62

The Genius was happy to see 342, and the Chimp gratefully climbed inside the spaceship. It took him only minutes to sniff out the pistachio ice cream. They sat there now, the four of them, including the robot, eating the ice cream. The robot was strangely silent. He was staring at 342, who was practically taking a bath in it.

"It's very unusual," Hotchkiss said, making an effort at conversation, "to see a robot eating ice cream, or anything else."

"I can barely taste it," the robot said. "How come he can taste it?" He pointed to 342.

"Oh," the Genius said, "he can taste it because he's a mammal. See? You'll never really be able to taste it, because you might have a program for it, but you won't have any taste buds. . . . In fact," the Genius said, "I'm amazed you have any interest in it at all."

"A mammal," the robot said, as if it were a new word. He kept staring at them. It was some time later when it seemed he had been thinking about it that he said, "Mammals have more fun." The Genius nearly fell off his chair.

Ooze, at the console, was stymied for the first time in eight hundred billion years. It saw the Genius, Hotchkiss, and the chimp being held, it thought, as a kind of safe captives by a crazy robot in a rocket ship.

"Shhh," the Genius said suddenly, whispering, "what's that?" They listened.

"Night raid," said the Blue Robot. "Be quiet."

They huddled in the silence. All they could hear was the sound of whispering wings—the sound at first of metal and then rushing air, like a million aluminum moths beating their way through the sky. The robots were on a night raid. All of them with the exception of the Blue Robot held their breath as the sound began, and hearing it they started to shiver uncontrollably.

63

"I can guide you across the robot fields," the Blue Robot said. "I can offer you protection, but I cannot lead you to her." They were passing through the fields so far undetected.

No ships were landing now. The robots were playing a different game now. It looked like a huge screen for war games. They were bombing various sites, and then just as soon as they were destroyed, the scoreboard would tally up. They had little time to study this, however, as the Blue Robot was urging them on. "Hurry up, you only have so much time. When their games are over, they're going to be scanning again," and he rushed them to the edge.

"This is as far as I go," he said, "you'll have to take it alone from here."

"Well thanks a lot," Hotchkiss said, still trying to figure why he'd helped them.

"There's no path through the abyss. I don't know how you expect to find her," the robot said. "And there's no way into the Crystal Palace even if you do," he paused. "Not for you, anyway."

They were standing now on a black cliff, facing an abyss. There was a narrow path along the top of the cliff, which fell steeply down on either side.

"I suppose this is called walking the straight and narrow," Hotchkiss said glumly.

"Holy shit," the Genius said, "how we gonna walk along this? It's like walking along a knife edge."

"Once you get past that curve," the robot pointed, "it flattens out more."

"Great," Hotchkiss said, "then what?"

"Then you're in a huge cosmic circle," the robot said. "How you get out of there is your problem. I can't help. But I'll be here, on this edge if you need anything. I may . . ."—the robot seemed to be hesitating—"I may have to make a brief trip, but I won't be long."

"Oh, where are you going?" the Genius said, trying to figure where they got their energy from.

"I never know. Sometimes I get assignments. But it's unlikely."

"Okay," Hotchkiss said. "Well, thanks a lot. We'd better be going. I don't intend to walk the knife edge in the dark."

"You have excellent equilibrium," the robot said. "The dark shouldn't bother you."

"Yeah," Hotchkiss said, "well, thanks." It was the damnedest thing, but the robot made him uncomfortable.

"That robot is weird," the Genius said, as they walked along.

The knife edge was bad. But the cosmic circle, Hotchkiss noted, was no picnic either: another kind of desert, white and still, and end-less. . . .

"Shit," the Genius said, "which way do we go?"

"I don't know," Hotchkiss said. "Let's wait a minute and see what develops." But they were too impatient to wait. After a few minutes, they just strode off, hoping for luck.

They had gone quite a way when Hotchkiss and the Genius sat down to rest. Hotchkiss suddenly felt a big wet furry sticky mass.

"AAAAGH!" he said, knowing immediately what it was.

"What is it?" the Genius said, looking at the hairy mass.

"It's one of Schrodinger's hair balls," Hotchkiss said, with extremely mixed feelings. "He might have left it as a trail."

He looked about. Heavens, he had always wanted to be here. And yet. Yet he wondered. It was an impressive thing, or they were both impressive things, one might say—time and destiny. And still as he made his way he knew not a little disappointment. He had already run smack into a hair ball. And he knew, if he were to find Amanda, he needed to find another, and another. . . . So he searched.

But as he did so, he had reason to question the nature of his task. Despite the weight of questioning, his courage drove him on. There was always this hammering at the back of his mind—the incessant unan-swered cry: was this *destiny*, this, the goal of time? This slogging through the galactic firmament looking for *hair balls*?

"AGHHHHH!" Hotchkiss cried out, for right at that moment, an-other one hit him, smack in the kisser.

"I said, 'Catch,' " the Genius said. "Didn't you hear me? Boy, is that disgusting."

"Yes," Hotchkiss said, "that's another one of Schrodinger's hair balls."

"Are you sure?"

"Yeah," Hotchkiss said, "I'd recognize it anywhere."

"Great," the Genius said, "that means we're gainin' on 'im."

64

"He'll coalesce us, he'll coalesce us," Ooze said frantically. "Tell him you'll let him keep the cat . . . quickly!"

But Amanda was firm. The GCB would not and could not coalesce her. She knew that now. As long as she had the molecule. She did not know what terrible things they could do to her, but she had, she knew, in that molecule some powerful protection. And Schrodinger, with his two, had even more. Not till they escaped from this dreaded place would she give them up.

Except for Hotchkiss and the Genius. She was, in the back of her mind, and not very far back at all, worried about them. If they were in the robot fields, how would they ever get out?

She had asked Robert—the Maverick, she was convinced of that— to help them. He had certainly helped her. So. That was the only hope right now. That the Blue Robot might perform in an unrobot-like way. Amanda figured that his impulse toward rescue could not be an isolated phenomenon. He was programmed differently. Whatever was different in him would be their saving grace. She only wished she knew what it was.

"Look," said the GCB, "one last chance, girlie, or I'll keep you in the box."

"Box or no box," Amanda said spitefully, "the cat is mine and I'm not giving him up, I don't care what you do to me." Perhaps this was a provocative stance on her part, but it was extremely difficult to keep a clear head while you were monitoring your gag reflex. Everything near the Great Cosmic Brain that was biological was retching. She saw that even Ooze, who was biological after all, kept heaving. The stench was getting worse with every second. At her last remark, a horrible belching hit the air, clouds of yellow smoke spumed forth, and through the smoke a window appeared, and she heard the GCB yell.

"You want the cat?"

"Yes," she said.

"Is he very important to you?"

"Yes," she said.

"Very, very important?"

"Oh, yes," Amanda said.

"Good," said the GCB, "bring him in."

Two Red Robots came in with the clearly miserable Schrodinger in a small gold cage.

"Schrodinger!" Amanda cried, starting to move toward him, but the robots held her back.

"Hi, Ma!" she heard a voice say, startling her utterly. Ma? Who on earth would call her Ma??

"Hey, Ma," the voice said, "it's me, Schro."

"Oh, dear," Amanda said, despite herself. For she had never expected Schrodinger would call her Ma, or anything else for that matter. Apparently he had learned to talk, and the whole thing was most unsettling. She certainly was devoted to him, but this was most peculiar indeed. As Schrodinger rattled on, she wasn't at all sure she liked it. She had thought somehow that if Schrodinger ever could talk—although she hadn't realized that she had actually ever thought it, but now that he was talking, she realized that she had at one time thought it—that he would have a more refined manner, more like Richard Burton or Clarence Darrow, or someone like that. But this voice of Schrodinger's was something to behold. It was a fast-talking, street-wise kid from Brooklyn, it was a little bit hustler and con, and it also was dusted with the wisecracking rhythm of none other than Groucho Marx. It was a voice that meant business, start to last.

"Where did he get that voice?" she said, wonderingly, to Ooze.

Ooze shrugged. "Bits and pieces of whatever I could lay my hands on. That molecule gives you speech, but a cat's larynx needs work," it whispered. "I had to be very inventive to put that together."

Schrodinger was now talking to the GCB, whom he insisted on calling "Bud."

"Look, Bud," Schrodinger was saying, "we can make a deal."

"No deals!" said the GCB.

"But I can help you get your Indians back!" Schrodinger cried. "I got a plan, a great plan—wait'll you hear this."

They thought, each and all of them, that the GCB hesitated a moment to listen, but then he cried, "NO DEALS," and turning to Amanda, he said, "You want this cat, then go and get him," and he hurled poor Schrodinger, cage and all, through a window, a window that appeared out of nowhere, leading outside into some black and dense place. It was the memory fields.

"Stop!" Amanda had yelled, starting to run, but the Red and Blue Robots held her, holding her down. "STOP, BRING HIM BACK," she cried, but it was no use. They had pinned her so she couldn't move and brought her, dragging her really, once again to stand before the GCB. And then it started to happen. What the Ooze said would happen.

Even as she stood before the GCB, even as she looked at this mess before her, she was forgetting. She could see she was forgetting and worse than that, she saw she was disappearing. First her feet, then her legs, her arms—she was becoming invisible, and then she began to spin.

"Throw her in!" she heard him yell, and all she knew then was she was spinning in and out of something black and cold. It seemed like a well. And she would sink inevitably into a deeper and deeper despair.

"The death well," Rastus had told her. "The eternal black hole from which nothing, no light, no awareness, nothing could escape."

"I want my cat," she screamed into the increasing void. "He belongs to me. He's MINE," and then she heard the echo, "MINE . . . MINE . . . MINE . . . ," as if she were indeed at the bottom of a very long, dark well. She assumed this was an ordinary darkness and that her eyes eventually would get used to this level of light. It was not until sometime later that she noticed her watch was not glowing. At first she thought perhaps there was some material nearby that was interfering with the radium glow. And then she had another thought. From this dark nothing would or could escape. This was a black hole.

Technically and theoretically—two categories that frequently were sent awry here—she ought not to be alive. Perhaps, she thought, she no longer was. That is to say, if people who are said to be alive must be physically perceivable by other people, she was sure, since there was no light, she was not in fact physically perceivable. But she ought not to have any self-awareness or brain function whatsoever. She ought, in fact, in terms of what they knew about black holes, to be irreversibly dead. You do not use the term *irreversibly*, which in Universe One (which is our own) in connection with "dead" is a statement of the obvious. However, in this place, in this warp of time that Amanda was in, this corkscrew of the dark—up, down, in and out, and around—all took on different meanings. And time did not proceed forward or backward, often in any measurable way at all. Clocks were askew here, if there were clocks at all.

She had landed in what seemed to be a tar pit. She got up slowly, and as she looked around at this utterly strange and foreign place, she felt it was, in some way, familiar too. It was this that frightened her. She felt the fear beginning to envelop her. It was impossible not to be afraid here, and they knew it. That was how they got you. She looked about. No pathways, nothing. Schrodinger was out here. She must find him. She could not have taken two steps when she saw a figure emerge suddenly in the field.

"Where's my cat?" Amanda said to him on the edge of a dark and charred forest. There was a cold, dank wind blowing across from it. Rastus stood there, a sliver of hay in his lips, menacing. He frightened her now.

"It ain't me," he said to her. "It's you. I told you I am just the sum of your thinking: you think fear, I look fearful to you. I ain't nothing else but that."

"You're something else," Amanda said. "You're just trying to trick me." The truth was she wasn't sure now, anymore, of what was what.

"Where is Schrodinger?"

"You got to turn up and under every leaf. He camouflaged," and Rastus laughed then, a terrible piercing laugh. And Amanda began to shake. She knew now why she was shaking. It was perfectly clear to her. It was the pitch. The pitch and the tone in Rastus's laugh. It was the sound of victory. She stepped forward and sank. Her foot sank to her knee as Rastus uttered his terrible laugh again. She pulled her foot out laboriously and moved the other forward. This sank too. Up to her ankle. So it would be. Rise and sink. Sink and fall. Stumble and seek, always against the terrible mocking laughter. She was trembling now. It had gotten to her. Tears spilled down her cheeks. They intended her to die, surely, in this pursuit. She now doubted herself that she could do it. Her confidence was draining, like blood from a wound. She searched, through the blur of tears, for anything like a clue.

"Schro . . ." It came from her like a gasp, so constrained was her voice by her fear. The blackness now was deeper than night. There was nothing but the cold wind, the uncertain step, and the mire. "Schrodingerrr," her voice cracked. If she didn't make it she wanted him at least to know she was on her way to him. She would try. Every step now was uncertain; sometimes she would be in the quicksand, sometimes in the sludge, but the worst, she thought, the worst were the whirlpools. They would hit suddenly, striking her almost to the ground with their force. Head pounding, eyes burning, she dove to the ground, covering her head, but there was no blocking this pain. This was more than nerves. This was self. The sum total of unremembered memories, striking one again and again. Why did the molecule not protect her? What trick of fate was putting her through such agony now? She asked Rastus these questions when he would appear, but he would sometimes fade before he could answer her. She heard him now utter the word "transmuter," before he faded again. She didn't know what it was, she knew she simply had to go on, she told herself. She tried, even as she felt it, to forget the pain, but it only made it worse.

Rastus must be trying to tell her that the transmuter held the key, but the transmuter never worked alone. Always hand in hand with fate and time. It was that combination that held the trickery. Schrodinger had taken the two molecules. And Amanda was devoted, yes. But they were mean, these tricks of fate. Like all trickery, endless in its permutations. Endless in its deviations. Endless, like all trickery. And Schrodinger had taken more than the two molecules. The transmuter had been there, had worked through her house, uncovering in her pillows and her chairs the fine remnants of Amanda's feelings. Had transmuted these stray strands of feeling the way she turned the pillow, the consternation on her brow. Left now on the surface of the mirror, the transmuter had taken these effects of Amanda, those invisible unseen effects she had left, and woven them into threads of being, created these transmutations into a figure, into the very figure of her soul, had taken these transmutations of her soul and hammered them to the walls of the cat, spun them and condensed them into molecules, had taken them and hidden them in the smallest recesses of the ribcage of that cat. So it was again unknowing that Amanda went through the huge cavernous universe empty and calling out only to her own echoes, searching for Schrodinger and the lost remnants of her own soul. It was, she knew, the only way back. If she did not recover Schrodinger or the molecules, she was lost forever. To the reaches of time and destiny.

Everyone agreed the sheriff was looking terrible over this business with the Genius. It had been a bad time. It was as bad as the Indians disappearing. Maybe worse.

"I don't suppose you heard nothin' about my boy," Eberly said, walking into the café.

"No, didn't hear nothin'," Rufus said, "but that fella was here, the magician, he calls himself. He wants you to go out there, Eb. He says if you go out there the boy'll be home sooner."

"Now, Rufus," Eberly said, "you think I'm gonna do that?"

Rufus looked around. There was no one else but Silas in the café. Then he whispered. "Tom says he ain't crazy, Eb."

Eberly sat back. And looked. "That's what Tom said?"

Rufus shrugged. "That's what he said."

"What's he want me to do, this crazy feller?" Eberly said. He seemed weary. It made Rufus uneasy.

"Says you gotta go out there and do what he told you to do."

Eberly moved uneasily in the chair. "It don't make no sense, Rufus."

"No, it don't," Rufus said.

Eberly smoked and Rufus sat two, maybe three hours. Nobody said anything.

Finally Eberly said, pushing his chair back, "Well, I guess I'm gonna go."

Rufus stood up. "I'll go with you, Eb."

There was a pause. "You don't have to do that, Rufus. Ain't no reason for you to go."

"I got nothin' to do," Rufus said, following Eberly toward the door. Fact of it was, he didn't think you could let a man go off by himself on somethin' like this. It wouldn't be right.

"Look, Rufus," Eberly turned to him. They were both embarrassed.

"That's the way it is, Eb." And no one said anything more.

From the looks of things, Rufus had it figured. Eberly'd be willing now. Once, he wouldn't. But he'd be willing now to sit on a rug in the desert with a crazy man, and if he wound up wrapped around the stars, so be it.

Rufus and Eberly took up their vigil in the desert. The magician had come to them and explained, that is, as much as a magician could explain. They found the Genius's blue cap on the ground. Eberly held it tightly, looking at it. He thought sometimes it was the only real thing he could see.

Everyone knew about sun mirages, especially in the salt flats. The salt sparkled like a million stars, and people got so they thought they were looking at the sky: they saw gods there, chariots and men with melting wings. But at night, were there mirages at night? Could moonbeams cross you up as good as the sun? Or better? After all, sunlight came from its own source, moonbeams were all reflection, like mirrors. Perhaps it was the moonbeams then, playing tricks. This is one possible explanation for the things that they saw.

"This must be it," Hotchkiss said. They had stood outside the shining palace, full of shimmering cut surfaces, and looked in vain for an opening. It was sealed shut except at one place, where a huge glass window clearly led in. But they couldn't open it. Hotchkiss was heaving with all his might. The window would not budge.

"Leverage," Hotchkiss finally said. "It takes leverage . . . there," he pointed to a tall, slender pole not far away. It was the kind of pole he had seen lining the robot fields.

Together they dug down around the pole and carefully lifted it out. It was very heavy, so they dragged it across the sand and managed to wedge it under the window.

"We've got it," the Genius said, "I think," and using the sill for leverage, they stood side by side on the far end of the pole, weighing it down, hoping to budge it.

65

Rastus was an erratic guide. He appeared, suddenly now in another place. "Over here," he was saying to her, "over here. The lost door— it's down there," he said, pointing to a pool of water. It was the only clear water she had seen here. She leaned over to look in.

Before she knew it, she was in, slipping beneath the surface of the water. Amanda went down down down into dream's lost door, looking for the magic handle. Looking to see what steps, what way, would lead up from death. But there was no way. There were no steps. Here in this smooth glassed enclosure there was clearly no door either. She turned her head and struggled to go up. She couldn't. She felt her air tighten; exhausted, cut off, something held her down—she felt it. She was barely moving now. She tried to move, then couldn't—there was no room, her chest was crushed, no air, no breath, nothing. This was the way she slept. No dreams, she thought, I have no dreams. And she did not. Too deep for dreams was where she slept, where not the slightest memory could catch hold. The footholds were all icy and black and wet—one slip and it was over. So, no footholds, no knowledge, no awareness of the steep black climb in the darkness, the ever-present falling back into the well. Again again. Why did she not die, have it done with; why the endless torture, again, again, and again? She had had these dreams on earth too. Dreams so deep they were beyond all reckoning.

"I've never seen anything like it," Hotchkiss used to say; "one minute you're awake, the next wild elephants couldn't wake you. You wake up the same way, like you're shot from a cannon."

No transition zones, please, Amanda would think. No half-light places where I might remember. Please. And now she knew why. Here, in this museum of hell, were all the things people never wanted to remember: the deprivations, the robberies, the despair, the accusations, and finally the kill.

The Red Robot clanked in, the sound of his metal parts in a clamor, like a ghost in armor.

"Is she dead yet?" the robot said. He had eyes of green lights.

"Not yet," she heard someone say, and she heard the robot clank out. She could not speak, she could barely breathe. She felt them rolling her again in the dark cold window; they were going to hurtle her out again, into the black night, onto the tracks of a locomotive.

Again, again, again, night after night, they cut off her singed hair. Burning her, cutting her, demons devouring her whole.

The robot came again and felt her pulse. "She's still alive," he said. "It isn't possible."

"Perhaps . . . ," another said, "perhaps it's Radiant One."

"Radiant One . . ." The robot looked around. Amanda could see his head spinning like the turret on a tank. "Radiant One has been destroyed. We have the crystals up. Radiant One cannot get through here."

"What else?" There were whispers. "It must be something else."

"Please stop," she said much later, when she found her voice.

"Give us the cat," they said, and began the torture again.

"No," was all they heard. It was barely a whisper.

"Again! Again!" the GCB cried.

The next thing she knew she was hurtling along like a freight train into a long dark tunnel, breathless into the night she was spinning, faster than a bullet into the black well; it was sucking her black and down, blacker and blacker, her breath was lost; she couldn't get it, there was too much speed around her; it was whipping the air from her mouth. She could feel the huge thing speeding by her; it was hurtling at inconceivable speeds, its blackness and its weight threatening her the whole time, the weight, the speed, the blackness. . . . She was against a wall. She did not know how long she lay there or if she were dead or alive. That was what terror was. Not knowing if you were dead or alive.

Hotchkiss could sense now that the time was desperate. He and the boy were exhausted, but he could feel this terror gripping his heart. Amanda was suffering. He knew it. Knew it as he had never known anything before. He needed to find her, and soon. Frantic now, he paced up and down outside the huge glass window. The lever had not worked. The window was the size of a door that led, as far as he could tell, to nothing. Only a dark glassy sea on the other side.

"This is as far as you can come," said the Ooze, appearing suddenly. It had been worried about Amanda, but it could not protect her. It would warn Hotchkiss and the Genius because she'd asked. "You must wait now for them to open from the other side. There is no entry from this side."

"But it's late," Hotchkiss had said. "It's dangerous. Let me through."

"I can't," said Ooze. "I have no power." And it went then, leaving Hotchkiss and the Genius desperately trying to move the huge glass window.

Amanda knew they had untied her now. They had thrown her back into Memory Lane. If she would not give Schrodinger up by torture, they would destroy her here, by recollection.

She thought that as she crossed the memory fields, she must be a little closer to Schrodinger. Sometimes, the pain nearly killed her. Once she had sunk into a swoon thinking she had found him lying dead behind a cold, burned tree. But it was not Schrodinger. It was only an illusion.

She noticed that running along the other side of the swamp—the side that was not future time—was a fine gray curtain, a kind of permanent mist. She could see at times quite clearly through the curtain, although it did not occur to her, as it would not occur to anyone in Memory Lane—it being in the nature of Memory Lane not to have such things occur—to look more closely into it. It was the kind of odd border that one inevitably accepted. It was there but not to be looked into. The robots had designed it so that it was almost an inevitable part of the *Homo sapiens* system. One could go so far as to say that in the way that visible light made up only a small part of the spectrum, nonetheless, this was the only light that *Homo sapiens* could see, and therefore, unless one were a physicist or a scientist, or one who inquired into such matters, light would be taken as simply that part of the spectrum that could be *seen*, and not, in fact, as all the things that it *was*. In the same way that the visible spectrum was but a small part of the event called light, so too Memory Lane and the part that Amanda slogged so valiantly through were but part of the scene.

But Amanda was a scientist. Her curiosity, so fundamental to her temperament, was the true manifestation of those forces Rastus knew were outside the spectrum. So it was that even in the midst of her despair and her determination—two attributes that the robots knew only sank one deeper into the slime—she would glance up occasionally toward the mist-hung curtain and wonder, however briefly, what was going on there. It had appeared to her that this, like future time, was some kind of junkyard as well. At first it seemed like an automobile junkyard, with bits and pieces of things lying about. But there were very well-dressed people in there, too, people who looked, she thought, as if they were coming from church. She did not look for very long, partly because it took all of her strength to keep from sinking totally into the swamp.

She knew only this: that she was getting weaker. It was harder to walk, to manage, to move. She knew, too, that in this terrible place she was so consumed by the forces of the struggle that they were taking, quite literally, parts of her body in exchange for survival. She had slogged her way through the stinking swamp undaunted. At almost every turn, every new rock in the road, there would be a sign, one of the little signs that kept popping up all over the place, and the sign would say HAND IT OVER. She never knew what it was she was to hand over, but she knew it meant giving up. At first this had disturbed her, and then when she realized that her body, in any real sense of the word, could not survive this ordeal, but that *she* might, she gave up the parts of herself more readily. At first it had been small things. A finger here and there. But now, she was reduced to a crawling, clutching mess. She knew she was a walking nightmare, but she refused to look at herself. "I must go on," was the only message she could hear. Nonetheless there were times when she could not move at all. She lay there, the swamp sucking away, pulling down whatever it could, eating the flesh from her bones. With each part that disappeared she lost sight a little of her goal. Whereas at first she had had a clear picture of Schrodinger and could see him completely, now she only could watch fragments of him, darting here and there. A paw. An ear. Part of a tail. What she did see clearly, in the parallel universe, the one that ran alongside the swamp, were the people who had come from church picking their way through the junkyard.

In the mist a couple came toward her. The man was wearing a gray suit and a maroon-and-silver tie. The woman wore a pearl-gray dress that fluttered softly and longish below her knees and a small hat with a veil. The hat was gray, too, but had a dark winy rose in the side of it. The rose hung oddly and appeared to be of velvet, as if it had fallen off at one time and been attached with a pin. The woman carried a handbag, a small squarish black one, over her arm and she wore what appeared to be sensible shoes. They were walking toward Amanda, picking their way through the clutter that surrounded them. They were making their way through this junkyard as if they were at a flea market. As if they were looking for unexpected bargains. "Look at this," the woman would say, picking up a broken piece of something. "It's only five dollars; do you think we should take it?"

"Take it," her husband said, and the woman put the broken thing, whatever it was, into the shopping bag and made her way toward another.

Amanda did not know how long she had been watching these people through the gray, cloudless mist, but it seemed to her that quite some time had passed, that although they were coming toward her—occasionally the woman would raise a small gloved hand and prepare to greet her—although they would say, "We're coming," they never actually got there. They never seemed to get any closer.

Amanda realized at one point she had seen them doing this before, perhaps yesterday. She thought then the robots had done something to affect her memory, because it seemed to her that this was a feeling, rather than anything she could actually recall.

And then, one day, she saw. She saw that the junkyard was not a junkyard at all, that is to say, it did not contain the remains of automobiles. And those people had other people with them, picking over the things out there. What the things were, Amanda saw, were the very things she had lost: parts of herself, lost irrevocably to the swamp that had surfaced over there in that gray mist. She saw that it was full of parts, not only hers, of hearts and livers and twisted hope, and that the people picking their way through the rubble, taking what they could, were not terrible people at all, but good, upright, upstanding citizens. She saw more than this, that they did not know that every time they reached for something to put in their bags, that there was a part of her dying on the other side. She saw that they could not see it, and she wished she had not seen it either. Not as clearly. She saw as she looked around, that there were others in this swamp as well. Hundreds of others. They were staying alive by turning what little strength they had into some twisted shape of human intention. It was hideous and ineluctable. Amanda saw the twisted forms next to her rise up, surviving only by the mania in their eyes. Amanda knew she herself was dying.

She saw, behind the curtain, a field full of well-intentioned parents. They seemed like very well-meaning people. They were picking things up and putting them in their bags, with a great deal of worry. "We mustn't let anything accumulate," she heard one of them say; "it will look like a mess." So they were making things tidy, and they were experiencing relief. They seemed relieved, she saw, every time they put something into a sack. Of course, it was endless: every time they cleared things off, something else would arise, sticking out. They thought they were doing it for God and their country and some of them even for some tiny part of their lost selves. But they weren't. Behind them, invisible to them, were the stalking robots urging them on—move there, move there, pick that, pick this—and they did. So there they were thinking all along they had done the right thing, the proper thing, when all along there they were—the agents of thieves.

"Get that," she heard one of them say. Then another, "Oh, how awful, pick it up." They kept at it, with considerable determination and will. She saw, furthermore, how they were deluded. It was the essence of delusion, in fact, that drove them on. They thought they were doing the right thing, picking things clear like that. They thought they were clearing out the rubble. When what they were doing in fact was quite something else. Amanda could see from the other side of the swamp that they were picking flowers. Nipping them in the bud. Cutting them down before they bloomed. And worse than that. They didn't stop at the flowers. They dug into the earth with their shovels digging for more, pulling and yanking and stuffing as much as they could into their bags and their sacks. Sometimes they took the shovels out and hacked and hacked away, cutting what they thought were the roots of trees.

"We have to clear it of the underbrush," she heard a father say. "It looks such a mess," and at that she felt the shovel strike her knee, hacking and sawing her leg. She watched here now as parents assaulted their children.

"There," a mother said, appearing to be in the kitchen, having butchered a lamb and boned it and tying it neatly into a roast, "it's all cleaned up and ready to go." That mother bent now over the oven door, placing the small neat-rolled roast tied with thick kitchen twine, surrounded with potatoes and parsley, and saw only its simple surfaces, a piece of meat, containing in its preparation only mimicked acts, mimicked deeds that had gone before with such wretched and terrifying consequences.

As Amanda looked through the fine mesh of gray mist at the people who kept coming toward her but did not get any closer, she saw that she knew them. They were her parents. The shock was total. *Her* parents here, too? It could not be. And then she saw. She saw her mother was wounded. She kept falling to one side, and she saw then that a robot was there next to her bending down, like he was conducting some kind of operation. Amanda could see that blood was pouring from her side. She held her hand there and pinched her lips and tried not to cry, and the robot seeing this knew precisely what to do. The robots were expert at suffering. Her mother thought the robot was trying to help her. Bending down like he was a doctor or something, the robot cut and stitched. It took him quite a long time. He did it very artfully, so that the wound was closed now, there was hardly a scar, and from it he had fashioned something. He took the wounds from her mother's side and made cauls for her eyes.

She saw her mother searching now, looking for Amanda through the swamp, and she felt herself sink deeper. Her mother would never see her now. That much was clear. It was in the bag.

"Get the cat," said the Red Robot.

"Drug it," said the GCB.

As they did, Amanda saw the vision before her eyes begin to change.

"I can't . . ." Amanda gasped, "I can't watch anymore." She turned away.

"Cut the motor function," the robot said.

The Red Robot leaned through the glass. He saw Amanda, moving. She was crawling. Amanda below, knew only this: I must keep moving. Why she was moving, how she was moving, she didn't know. This was not simply spinal-cord damage; this was will. They're taking it, she thought, they're stealing it, even now, and she put everything in it then, in her crawling, hesitant, jerking movement toward escape. She saw a door.

It was emerald, glowing, the lost door. And not far. Think of nothing, she told herself; make it to the door. Think of nothing but move toward the door. With every thrust of her arms, her arms grew heavier, it became very difficult to breathe. Had they drugged her then, again, or was this simply death stealing across her bones, time's final wound, thrusting against her heart now. Oh God, she thought despite herself, Oh God, I'm not going to be able to. She reached finally with all her strength, lurching toward the door. Her fingers touched its edge, and the door swung open. Great bands of light came streaming through. So, she had made it then, her hand had touched the door. And this just now, just now this final trick: the door was there, and she had grasped its edge, but not in time. Her fingertips had grazed the door, but the light stopped just there, millimeters from their edge. She could not move at all now. So this, their final trick. Her eyes fought to keep the light as the heaviness grew in her, encasing her, and then nothing.

"Good," the robot said. "She must be dead now."

"She's nearly dead," the other robot said. "Although the cerebral activity is still significant. Sometimes it happens like that. Don't worry about it. It's like a chicken when you cut its head off. It will flip and squiggle for hours. But she can squiggle for hours," he said, getting up, "but she's finished."

But Amanda was not finished. She was struggling still. Oh God, why have you brought me here? This last was barely a whisper. Her strength drained, her voice almost gone, she implored the empty universe with a question as old as time. In this region, her trial of agonies had begun; in this region, nations and individuals had lived and died. In this region, cause escaped; the pattern moved on, nameless, aimless, pointless in its pain, uneasing suffering, it moved on here, in these dreaded hills as steady, as ineluctable as a wave. The thousands dead and those to come begged for mercy here. Have pity, they cried, the sound to circle, death-less, for as long as life prevailed, the sound to circle silent, unheard, ignored by those who could change it. Their comrades might share their suffering with them, but their oppressors would not lift it. Power and the knife it wielded ruled here, lancing love and trust; it gave only pain and suffering. And never only once. Again, again, again. The only mercy here was death, remembering nothing.

Was it the same force then that left Hiroshima in ashes, that left the homeless starving and the sick to die? Was it the same force? She felt it now, trembling through her. She wished not to feel it. It made it worse, feeling it; it rendered her powerless. She lost courage. Despair was no ally. Life was hope, and without it, life was gone. All this Amanda felt and knew. She was whipped and sobbing. It could not be contained. She couldn't take it. Too much input. Sensory overload. Feel too much and you wound up crackers. Everybody, everybody in the world knew that.

The moon, with the grade of its tides, its reflected light, would keep her steady. Reflected light. Everybody knew you couldn't stare directly at the sun. Except Schrodinger. She thought sometimes Schrodinger had stared at the sun, and this explained the glazed look in his eyes. It wasn't that you got blinded. It was that you saw, and then forgot it. So much for the heat. So much for the light. She knew, too, that Schro-dinger had divined her secret. Once she had seen the sun. Right to its

389 _____

center. And then she forgot. Sometimes you had to forget. It had hurt her, looking at the sun. It burned through your eyes, down through your throat, around your heart, and rocketed through the center of you to your toes. Like being hit by lightning. There was illumination and there was death. And sometimes they were close. There was death at the center of a certain kind of light. In the center of the light she saw her heart, a battered wreck of tears and fissures, swollen and deformed from cease-less striving; valiant, trying always to mend itself, but tattered, torn, and shredded. Stitched and patched, corroded and swollen, like a fine Ferrari rusting in a junkyard, its once-smooth engine holding promise only to an angel or a magician or one whose memory was so fierce in its passion it confidently began repair. Only to those. Magic stalkers. Those who defied all natural laws. Natural, unnatural and supernatural, enemies and allies all at once.

66

"WILL YOU GIVE IT UP?" screamed the GCB through the dark and fumous wall.

"No," Amanda said, her voice barely a whisper.

"GIVE HER FEAR," screamed the GCB.

"We did," said the robots.

"Give her doubt," said the GCB.

"We did," said the robots.

"Give her loss," said the GCB.

"We did," said the robots.

"Give her death, then!" said the GCB, slithering toward the door, the gaseous fumes forming a dark wall behind him.

Things had gone too far. The Ooze was going into the Memory Fields. It had made a deal with the cat. It thought it might be too late.

"There are forces," it said to Amanda, trying to pull her to her feet. "Hurry hurry hurry."

"No strength," Amanda said, slipping into the mire. "You have to help me."

"I'm not strong enough here," Ooze said. "You have to walk." It looked about nervously. "I've sent for help, but I don't think she can get in, all the shields are closed."

"Hotchkiss," Amanda said, slowly. Her mouth could barely move.

"Don't know, don't know," said Ooze, trying to lift her. "Lost them . . . lost news." He saw the robots coming.

"Save them, please," she said hoarsely, sinking. "You must."

"Trying," the Ooze said. "I'm trying, but the odds are terrible. No time. The time is very bad, a dangerous hour. Come on, you must."

"Can't," Amanda said, slipping back into the sludge, "can't," and she passed out. That was the doorway to death, and the robots knew it.

"The man be strong," Rastus said, letting out a long whistle. He was looking at Hotchkiss's lion heart on the screen in the console room. It might be strong enough to do it.

"Do you think so?" said Ooze. "Really think he's that strong he could bring *her* in?"

"Radiant One be *looking* to come in," Rastus said.

"It takes such a strong masculine element," Ooze said, "to bring her in, right now. . . ." Ooze was frantic and worrying. The system was so complicated. At other times in other hours, Radiant One could come in alone.

But not now. Not at the hour near death. Equal forces were needed. The balance was everything now.

"I see it," Rastus said pointing to the screen, "she's coming."

"But the crystals," Ooze said, "she can't get through . . . crystals. . . ." Its voice faded off as it saw all hopes of populating its new planet collapse.

Rastus saw it, too. The crystal dome was closed.

"Amanda's gonna die," Rastus said, and he turned the console off. He didn't want to watch this.

The robots saw her coming.

"I never thought she'd give up," said the first one.

"But she did," said the second.

As Amanda approached the black door—eyes vacant, feet barely moving, face white, hair white—the robots opened the doorway to death, and just as the robots reached to pull her inside, at that precise instant: She heard Schrodinger's cry.

It was more than a cry. It was a scream. She had never heard Schrodinger scream like that before. It was the sound of a vibration that sent the heavens reeling. Amanda stopped and turned. Schrodinger, in his heavily weighted doubled-hemispheric self, didn't know what made him cry out. Deep in his animal self was some primitive twisting pain, some forewarning of a sense of loss that his simple self could not sustain. Schrodinger, sniffing the surface of the air, had smelled the approach of death, and lifting his head high into the blackness, smelling the fear raining down, had let out this terrible wail, a desperate lament from the depths of his stricken soul. Schrodinger's screaming squall split the air with its ringing; a great caterwauling screaming shook the heavens and the palace of the GCB, a screaming so tortured, so profound, a vibration of such consequence, it threatened the crystals, hanging in the air.

"Stop him, stop him, stop him!" cried the GCB, throwing his huge, stinking hulk about the floor. "Great heavens above, stop that screaming cat! Look out—the crystals!"

It was too late. Above him the crystals were swinging now; all out of line and turning and spinning, the crystals clashed; with each bashing crystal, lightning struck the floor of the glass palace, sizzling up the spines of the GCB and all the palace guardians, frosting and searing all at once the doors, the ceiling, the floor and setting forth energies the GCB could not defeat. It shook the universe in all its quadrants and rearranged the sounds.

Where Hotchkiss and the Genius stood, on the cold barren hills outside the window, the energy changed there too. The window began to glow, and the Genius said "Look" in almost a whisper as they watched the window glide open in a silken move, and they shot through to rescue.

Amanda, on her way to death, knew only Schrodinger's screaming cry—and then a great blast shook the doors and the robots leaped back as Hotchkiss stood there, in on a beam of loyalty and love, a frequency cleared of all confusion by the desperateness of the hour. Pure energy faster than light had sped him here. His manhood held him true. The boy lay in his arms, only a boy yet and buffeted to near ruin by the rigors of the journey. Hotchkiss was exhausted, but he was standing. Exhaustion dripped from every pore. Shining in the light of sweat, he held the exhausted boy in his arms, his legs trembling from the effort, but he had made it. He slung the boy around his neck, and with his last remaining strength gathered Amanda into his arms.

The GCB, the palace, and the robots were in an uproar. Radiant One had swept Hotchkiss in and was holding the shields open until Hotchkiss and Amanda came through.

"We can't," Amanda said, seeing the opening in the cobalt sky. "We can't leave Schrodinger." They could hear his screaming still.

"Hurry, only seconds left," said Radiant One. The GCB had recovered now and the ceiling was closing quickly.

We have art, in order not to die of the truth.

— Friedrich Nietzsche

Beauty is a simple passion
But oh my friends
In the end you will dance
The fire dance
In iron shoes

—Anne Sexton

67

The GCB was not a GCB for nothing. He knew how to hang on to an empire. Seeing Amanda's imminent escape he had slithered and slathered, burpled and brawled his way into the console room and called up Amanda's mind. He hit the button that ensured if he could not get her one way he would do it another. He struck TEMPERAMENT, the button guaranteed to raise an incipient drive into a consuming passion. And soon the Dancer appeared.

The Dancer flashed quickly across the screen, and the GCB, screaming triumph, slathered out. But there were a pair of eyes watching from the corner, a pair of burned-out eyes, the eyes of a man with forgotten dreams. And Rastus had seen it all. He was surprised. He should have had it figured. The Dancer. It was a natural.

When Amanda woke up she saw she was in the hut of Robert, the Blue Robot. Hotchkiss, the Genius, and Ooze were there looking very worried. Rastus was there, too, lounging against the wall. Amanda was very weak. She attempted to lift her head from the pillow but it only fell back again.

"Hotch," she said, holding out her hand, and then it too fell limply by her side.

"Amanda, I'm here," he said, rushing to her. Hotchkiss was shaken: he had never seen her this way—this was more and worse than physical fatigue. The Genius saw it too, and it frightened him. He almost didn't know her, such a look in her eyes.

Amanda's eyes were open again now and trained on Rastus.

"I trusted you," she said quietly, feebly. "You led me in there," and then she collapsed back again on the bed.

Hotchkiss turned questioningly to Rastus.

"I didn't do nothing. I thought I knew where the cat was. Tried to find it. I was wrong," he said, and leaned back against the wall.

Hotchkiss was beside himself. "What did they do to her?" he demanded of Ooze.

But Ooze only said, "It's what the robots do. At least she's alive."

"You have to do something," Hotchkiss implored. And the Ooze did what it could do best. It attempted to restore the body. It attempted to give her life. But the body here was firmly wedded to the mind, and it knew it could only bring her so far.

"There is nothing more I can do," it said upon leaving the hut. Amanda was still sleeping. She seemed to sleep a lot now. Hotchkiss almost preferred it when she slept. At least then he could touch her, stroke her hair. When she was awake, the slightest human contact made her cry.

"How long, Ooze," Hotchkiss asked, "until she's . . . she's better?"

"It's beyond me now . . . I don't know," the funny thing said. Hotchkiss thought it seemed very sad.

In the meantime Hotchkiss did what he must. He assigned the Genius certain tasks. Together they attempted to understand the system. They observed. They *analyzed*. The Genius interrogated the Blue Robot. Hotchkiss attempted to map their positions. It was clear to him that they had to get to Schrodinger—for Amanda—and to get out.

68

Schrodinger, in the meantime, was taking matters into his own paws. He had a plan the next time that robot came by. There was a changing of the robot guard every twelve hours. The Reds and the Blues. He sighed and curled up in his tail. He didn't like to give it up, no. But he would have to. He knew Amanda was in pain. And he thought, unless those Indians were put back where they came from, they'd never get out. The GCB was wild over it. Maybe if he could placate him with that, he could make some deal.

He climbed into the dungeon window and waited now until the robot change of guard came by.

Ooze was back at the console. What was the damn cat up to? It could see that the cat had already given up a half molecule to that stupid robot, Robert. Of all things. It could see by the glow that the cat was down to one and a half, and Oozie aimed to get them. Well that explained why the stupid robot was sitting in the spaceship eating all their ice cream. With that half molecule, the Ooze figured the robot was in an unheard-of place. He was an electrochemical unit, in metal housing, that was to some degree, by one half molecule (although a half molecule of admittedly inordinate powers), on his way to becoming a biological system.

Well, one half was all that robot would ever get. Ooze would see to that. It had to get that cat to cough up the rest for it. Amanda's molecule it was sure of, once it got her safely back. The problem of course was, would she ever get back? The GCB could care less. He didn't care what she was—gas, dust, cosmic rays, or *Homo sapiens*— he'd just as soon have her atoms one way as another. GCB was fed up with *Homo sapiens* anyway. The only species ever to dare to take extinction into its own hands. Such a thought! Even the Ooze rolled its eyes at this. And then the questions! The questions were what got the GCB so crazy. It would have been all right, her asking all those questions, if she didn't have the molecule. He had to get it out of her. And if he just coalesced her or killed her, he'd never get it out of her. It would be gone forever.

This depressed the Ooze no end. It had taken zillions of years for those molecules to evolve. And it only had three. It was using them for its other planet, the one in which it planned the Leap. Well, it wanted to get that planet going before the universe started contracting again, which, with the GCB in the mood he was in, could happen any minute.

Schrodinger sat in the window of the dungeon watching the robot changing of the guard. The Blue would be coming in, and he knew he'd be there waiting for the right one, so he watched them clank by. Understanding so much, having seen so much, he knew what he must do. Soon he saw it, the rather stumbling gait, now, which distinguished it from the others. He was lagging behind, and soon the huge metal thing was inches from his window.

"PSSST . . . hey fella," he said. The robot stopped and turned, its eyes swinging in its head like turrets, searching. They beamed like searchlights down on Schrodinger.

"Hey, fella, I gotta talk to you—over here," Schrodinger said. The one thing he had learned was you could always make a deal. He could see that now. Frankly, the whole planet down there was going to hell in a basket, and he really could care less. He knew his life-span. But he felt differently about Amanda. They had to get out soon, and the only way to calm the big brain down, he figured, was to move the damn Indians back to where they came from. With no questions asked.

This was a problem that had worried the Ooze. But not Schrodinger. With the help of the stupid robot, he saw how it could be done. The Indians, the Ooze had said, were of high priority to two unlikely people: a sheriff and the prez. All he had to do was get them together. And Schrodinger was about to do precisely that.

"Hey, fella," he said to the robot, "you really dig the ice cream, huh?"

Schrodinger, for himself, wouldn't be caught dead eating pistachio. Or chocolate. He liked vanilla, and that was it. He wasn't crazy about the stuff, period.

The robot jerked toward him. His memory searched for something comparable to the talking thing addressing him. Nothing was there. Furry, four-footed, and talking. Nothing. Not a thing.

"It's me . . . Schrodinger," the cat said. "I gave you half of the ice-cream molecule."

"Oh yes," said the robot. "I don't have a classification for you, though."

"Take it easy," Schrodinger said. "If you think the ice cream's good . . . how would you like a hot dog?"

"A hot dog?" the robot said. It searched its memory. Nothing.

"It's better than ice cream," Schrodinger said. Then something went off in Schrodinger's brain.

"And how about girls? You wanna go for girls?" Schrodinger said. The robot searched again. Girl—nothing much, and then there, back over there, the scanner lit. A light buzzing.

"Girls," the robot said, seeming to smile.

"Step over here, fella," Schrodinger said. "Tell ya what we're gonna do."

Maybe, the robot thought, trying to categorize Schrodinger, it's a fossil gap. Fossil gaps were the places when scientists figured there had to be intermittent species, only there were no recorded fossils. There was just this gap. Sometimes the gap was as long as one hundred million years. So, the robot thought, this must be a fossil gap.

"I'm no gap, fella," Schrodinger said, who of course could see and hear almost everything. "Now look. I wanna make you a deal. A deal you're going to like. It's a sweetheart of a deal," Schrodinger said, "but you gotta do what I say."

The robot listened. That is to say he listened with even more attention than usual, because his system had gone into a stage known as "Please Repeat Instructions." Robert always went into "Please Repeat Instructions" when stymied, which he was by talking to a four-footed furry thing.

The Ooze couldn't believe it, watching the console. Why, that cat had done it! The cat had called it on the console only a few hours ago, and made a deal with it: if he got the Indians back in place, the Ooze had agreed to do Schrodinger a favor. A BIG favor. The Ooze finally agreed, because after all, it didn't think the cat would be able to do it. Commandeering a stupid robot like that. Well, it was amazing. It thought only the GCB could commandeer those robots. That cat had made some kind of a deal with the Blue Robot, the retarded one, as it was fond of calling him. Perhaps it'd judged the robot too harshly.

Well, maybe when the GCB heard this he would ease up. A tiny bit. In any event, Ooze wouldn't be turned into a gas. And of course it'd be able to keep its part of the deal.

The crazy old magician was setting out there on the Texas desert the night it happened, was the way Eberly told it, the night it happened with Rufus, Eberly, and the Indian, Old Tom.

The way Eberly told it this big ole ship opened up all of a sudden and this here eleven-, twelve-foot tall kinda knight-in-armor-looking thing comes outta there pointin' some kinda gun thing straight at Eberly.

The robot had been programmed that all *Homo sapiens* respond to intimidation. He had no time to refine his program, so he used what in his judgment was reliable. Brandishing his obliterator, he advanced on Eberly.

"You see this?" the Blue Robot said. "This is an obliterator. If you don't do what I say, I'll obliterate you."

"Now, son," Eberly said, hitching up his pants and hauling up his huge steer-horn belt buckle, "lemme tell you somethin'. You gotta be able to understan' this. An' I want you to lissen real hard. Now my name is Sheriff Eberly, and I'm sheriff of Cononga County. And you just put that damn obliterator away, fella, 'cause we don't tolerate carryin' no obliterators in Cononga without a license. And I kin tell," Eberly said, full in the power of his stature, "you ain't got a license for thet thing."

The Blue Robot appeared to stare at Eberly. Rufus gulped.

"How very amusing," the Blue Robot said, putting down the obliterator. "This creature doesn't recognize my superior power. This won't be much satisfaction, after all. Because I do have superior power, but no one here is advanced enough to recognize it."

Eberly was watching and listening.

When the robot was done with his talking, Eberly said, "I'll take Tom with me. If those Indians are under there like you say, Ole Tom can hear 'em, but how you gonna get me into the White House?"

"Let me worry about that," the Blue Robot said. "I have a lot of experience with the White House."

Sure enough, Eb and Old Tom flew to Washington, and when they got out of the taxi in front of the Pentagon, Old Tom put his ear to the ground. He came up nodding, and Eberly went straight to the White House.

"How I gonna git into the White House?" Eberly had said.

"I'll take care of that," the robot said, and he did.

Eberly walked right through the front door. The guard on the left was looking at the sky. The guard on the right was looking to his left. He pushed open the doors and strode down the hall. The secretary on the left was looking at her desk. Preoccupied, she heard nothing. The guard on the other side was tying his shoe, the second secretary was looking in her drawers for aspirin, so Eberly strolled right down to the next pair of doors.

Never did see so many goddamn doors in all my goddamn life, he said to himself, hitching his holster up and looking around just in case.

When he got to the Oval Office, he thought he should knock, and so he did, and then he walked right in.

"Evenin', Mr. President," he said. "Name's Sheriff Eberly, Cononga County. I came to see you 'bout some Indians."

The president, when he reflected upon this later, remembered only that he thought his head was going to blow off.

"How . . . how'd you get in here?" he said, pressing his emergency buzzer. Or so he thought. In his fluster he was actually pressing only the desk.

"I just walked in, Mr. President. . . . Now the thing is, I know you got my Indians stashed under the Pentagon there, and I want 'em back, and I'm willin' to take 'em back too, without causin' no kinda trouble with the press or nothin' like that. Keepin' it nice and quiet, jes' between you and me. But"—he had taken off his hat and was twirling it in his hand—"you got to clean up the water first."

The president was dumbfounded. Where were the guards? Where were the aides? Where was everybody?

"Well sir, Sheriff, nice to see you," he said, "but we don't have any Indians. I'm afraid you're mistaken." He tried to smile.

"Don't go lyin' in your teeth like that," Eberly said. "Ain't right in a president. I know you got 'em, and you know you got 'em, you got 'em under the Pentagon." He took a sheaf of copies of telegrams out of his shirt. "And iffen you don't git 'em out and back to me, mah frien' Rufus is gonna send all these here telegrams to every goddamn newspaper and TV station in the country, tellin' 'em that's where they is." Eberly checked his watch. "And he gonna do it iffen he don't hear from me in a half an hour."

The president was pale. "What . . . what . . . what will we say," he said, "when they see the Indians . . . ? The reporters—they'll know."

"Well, you jes' give 'em some kinda government talk. You tell 'em it's national Indian Memorial Day or somethin' like that, and you have yerself a parade down main street, parade 'em right to the airport. Jes' so they gets back."

"Parade . . ." The president appeared to be mumbling. Frankly, Eberly would say later, he thought the fella was a mite tetched. They did a lot in a half an hour. It was amazing, Eberly thought, just how efficient a government could be. They got the Indians out with a band and flags and all in exactly twenty minutes, and they also had these bills of some kind or other sitting in all their drawers, and they filled in the blanks on these bills, called them executive orders or something, and they promised to clean the radioactive water out of Cononga County as soon as was "humanly possible," which was the only part Rufus, who was on the phone to Eberly through this whole thing, didn't like.

"What is it, Rufe?" Eberly said.

"Some humans is more possible 'n others," Rufus said. And Eberly acknowledged how this was true. But they took it anyway. Eberly didn't like the place, the White House, and he didn't care none for this president either, so he wanted to get on down to the airport and get home.

When he got back, he found Rufus sitting with the Blue Robot in the kitchen. The robot had eaten an entire quart of ice cream and was about to start another.

"He gonna get sick," Rufus said. "But he says he got to git back there wherever he come from. Only got one more day. I tole him I never saw anythin' metal eatin' ice cream before. Specially a whole quart, and he tole me the reason he's eatin' so much is he only gets a very faint, he says, idea of what it's like. Tell you the truth, Eb, I felt sorry for it. It ain't as smart as all that. It figured if it ate more ice cream it would taste it more. It went out feeling frustrated, if you ask me. And that ain't all."

"What're you talkin' about, Rufus?"

"He was lookin' at that there magazine. I'm tellin' you he was really lookin' at it. I mean like the ice cream, he sort of got it but he didn't quite."

Eberly stared. "*That* magazine?"

Rufus nodded. Eberly shook his head. That was a girlie magazine. Now what in hell was a robot doin' lookin' at that?

"He tole you where he come from yet?" Eberly asked.

"He tole me a lotta things, Eb."

"You believe it, Rufus?"

"Don't know, Eb, don't know if I do."

69

Rastus wasn't placing any bets. The odds here were fixed. Still he had to hand it to them. Didn't think they'd get this far. They'd had some kind of assist. What kind he didn't exactly know. There were forces he'd heard of.

As Rastus peered into the console he saw something new arising now, something altogether unexpected. Female Principle Rising. He let out a low whistle. Now *that* was a powerful thing. That put a different fix on things entirely. In his mind he looked at the odds: already he saw the numbers were beginning to move.

He went back to the console and punched again. Where was it coming from?

> *Does this explain the action of the mind? Can reflex action in the end, account for it? After years of studying the emerging mechanisms within the human brain, my own answer is "no." Mind comes into action and goes out of action with the highest brain-mechanism, it is true. But the mind has energy. The form of that energy is different from that of neuronal potentials that travel along the axone pathways. There I must leave it.*
>
> —Wilder Penfield,
> *The Mystery of the Mind*

Rastus watched with wonder. He had heard tell. Heard tell of things outside the spectrum.

He stared now out into the black sea. The black sea was on fire. Galaxies, stars, supernova looped and spiraled through time. Explosions resounded through the night. Fusions. Radiations. Energies released.

Matter out of nothing. Things he had never seen before. The forces out there were bending the light with their power. The forces out there were calling to their own. The atmosphere crackled with its sound.

Hotchkiss could bear it no longer. Lying there nights while she slept fitfully, starting, sitting up, staring straight ahead. Some nights she woke up screaming, telling him they had stolen her bones.

But tonight as he lay there, he felt something happen, and he took a chance. He stroked her, at first barely touching her arm, then her shoulder, then her neck, and he felt his heart quicken as she turned to him for a kiss. He kissed her as she slept and then turned away on his side. Sometime during the night, he did not know when, he felt her stir and reach for him. He thought she had been so long from him she must be dreaming, as she rolled toward him and nestled her chest into the curve of his spine.

To Hotchkiss, it was wondrous. Such energies poured forth. Amanda could not contain herself. When Hotchkiss touched her, she was a tidal riot. The moon was moaning through her, the mons olympus rising and falling, aching for his touch, pulling from her and then releasing, like the rise and fall of a wave, carried high then hurried, Hotchkiss all around her.

Sometimes she didn't know where he was, above her, below her, in her, or out of her, the wavelengths of her pleasure surrounding her like an aurora, mind-blow, electric light, then out. One time, she actually thought she had passed out. She was neon curtain.

She was surprised to see the room was not on fire from them, as she lay there caressing the back of his shoulders, kissing his neck. She saw that Hotchkiss had changed. He was softer now.

He seemed to her almost feminine then; if it hadn't been Hotchkiss she would have thought it *was* feminine, it was such a soft curved line, the line of his back, his shoulders—it was soft and strong, like the neck of a swan, and she thought it amazing that combined in the bristled toughness of his fore should be the amazing curvature of his aft. It struck her as wondrous to lie against it, as though it were indeed not feminine, but a feminine aspect that hovered just outside the outlines of Hotchkiss's very male presence, like a glow or a shadow, or something thrown off that came from Hotchkiss and yet was the very opposite of him. It was the kind of opposite that didn't clash or break down her concept of Hotchkiss, but balanced it in some perfect way. This loving had gone through to the center of her, like the sun through ice, swiftly lifting the hardened edges, making them flow. Her need, unleashed and naked, no longer menaced her. She loved Hotchkiss completely now. With all her heart and soul.

She loved his fore, she loved his aft, lying there as his aft sunk sleepily, dreamily into the pocket of her thighs, locked and floating, encased and swollen, they became a floating dirigible of time.

It seemed to her that she and Hotchkiss simply floated there, just above the surface, defying all laws of motion, celestial and otherwise, by the power of their connection. She could never forget the rapture of that night. She did not know what Hotchkiss dreamed. She could not sleep but lay there, simply quivering with love, as Hotchkiss, dreaming of who knew what, gently curled his fingers around hers and heaved a deep, nocturnal sigh.

The robot, having gained the second half of Schrodinger's molecule, was more fully, although not entirely, into ice cream. He had now eaten through the chimp's entire supply.

"There's no doubt about it," the robot said to the chimp, who certainly wouldn't understand it, "mammals have more fun." The robot acutely felt that this was only the beginning. He wanted more.

Hotchkiss was overjoyed. Amanda was restored.

For her part, Amanda knew only this: that morning when she awakened, she saw the sun shining on her wrist. The blue veins streamed with life. She touched it. "I'm alive. . . ." she said. It was the most present sense of herself she had ever had.

"We've got to make a plan," the Genius was saying. "We've got to get out of here. I've been studying the robots. They're a bitch to get past."

"Last night it got worse," said Ooze.

"How could it get worse?" Amanda said.

"Night Raid. Robots went on a night raid. They NERPed another thousand last night."

"NERPed a thousand? What's he talking about?" Hotchkiss asked.

"For every NERP they convert, there's another ten robots up here. The NERPs give the robots energy."

"I thought they got it from the GCB," Amanda said.

"They do," said Ooze, "but the NERPS give them energy, too. Last night they made one thousand NERPs, and now there's ten thousand more robots here."

"This is murder," said the Genius.

"What in hell is a NERP?" Hotchkiss demanded to know.

"A NERP is . . ."—the Ooze paused, taking a deep breath—"a Nerve Ending Reversal Program. Instead of jumping the synapse the energy falls back on itself. Low energy. Comes to the wrong conclusions that way every time."

"Wow!" the Genius said. "How do they do that?"

"I told you they're very clever. Mankind is very easy to convert," the Ooze said with disgust. "Even the most primitive animal knows not to drink soiled water. HAH! HAH!" The Ooze started to laugh then. It occasionally expressed contempt for mankind, which it regarded as some basic perversion of biological development. There were moments, and this was one of them, when Amanda was tempted to agree with it. By a terrific twist of circumstance, mankind was changing the laws of nature. Everyone knew that a mutation, such as a black moth, could and would only survive when environmental conditions encouraged it, such as the soot covering the trees in Manchester. Otherwise the mutation would die. It would flourish, of course, when the trees were black. And now there was a new mutation, a NERP. A quasi-biological system, a robot that, by manipulating the environment—by painting the trees black, so to speak—would ensure its own survival. They were clever, these robots, manufacturing their own mutations and the environments to spawn them. But they were destroying life. There was no doubt about that either. Could, would biology win? Or would the planet be destroyed? Would there be nothing but dust and ashes and toxic oceans, a planet fit for the Red Robots? Like hasty and gifted ministers, they knew how to make their conversions. They picked their subects carefully, and by dangling greed, dangling fear, dangling hopelessness, and dangling "there is nothing I can do" before them, they made their conversions. The pumping station was piling up. Hearts burned out fast on hopelessness; societies burned out too.

The smell of sulfurous wastes wafted across Amanda's nostrils. The wind of future time was sweeping down on her now. She could smell it burning. It was coating her throat. The others—she must tell the others. There was still time.

"If we got rid of the NERPS . . ." Amanda said, thinking out loud.

"Oh, you'd cut down their energy a lot," Ooze said.

"By how much?" she asked. "I mean . . . What if we got that list and de-NERPed the world?"

"You couldn't do it," said Ooze, "he'd never give that list up."

"Suppose we *could* do it," Amanda said.

"If you could do it?" Ooze asked. It calculated. "Well, you could probably guarantee at least another million years to the planet's life, if you got all the NERPs."

"Gosh," said the Genius, "we've got to get that list . . . we've got to go in there for Schrodinger anyway." And then he looked discouraged. "But I don't know how we'll get past the robots."

"There's something missing in all this," Hotchkiss finally said quietly.

"What do you mean?" the Genius asked.

"I've been watching them," Hotchkiss said. "Their energies aren't always the same. There's something else that can influence them. Something besides these NERPs and the GCB. Something that seems to slow them down. We just have to find out what it is."

"I've been trying to; I've been interrogating Robert," said the Genius. "He even let me take his head apart. He's wild. Absolutely wild. He ate all of Three-forty-two's ice cream."

Amanda was thinking about what Hotchkiss had said. She knew there was something going on, too. The GCB, when he had her in his power, had convinced her he was All. Now she saw how foolish it was. The GCB was powerful, yes. The robots had nearly killed her, yes. But there was *more*. The GCB could not turn darkness into light. But something could. Some force had given her this power. She had felt it last night.

The GCB was throwing a fit. Temporarily mollified by the replacement of the Indians, he was incensed to see the cat had given up a molecule to one of his robots, because it meant first of all he would never get it back, and to the degree the robot had that particular molecule, which was very high indeed on the sensor scale, the GCB would have little control, if any, over him.

Not that it really mattered, thought the GCB. One robot more or less was not going to make any difference.

But about this matter the GCB was wrong. Very wrong indeed.

"Amanda," Hotchkiss said to her that night, "maybe we just have to run for it."

She shook her head. "Impossible . . . you can't get past them." He felt her shudder beside him. "You've never been up against them . . . you have no idea . . . they're totally negative. Completely negative energy." And even as she said it they both had the same idea.

"Reverse the fields." They said it simultaneously.

"You think we could do it?" Amanda asked.

"Sure we can do it . . . I think," Hotchkiss said. "There must be a way."

"It's not like ordinary energy," Amanda said. "It's some weird thing, not strictly electromagnetic or anything like that." They were both excited now at the prospect. "If it can be done, I guarantee you one of these acts up here—Ooze or somebody—must know how to do it." She was, for the first time, beginning to feel optimistic. "I miss Schrodinger so much," she said.

"We'll get him soon," Hotchkiss said. He spoke with real confidence now. He thought some of this must come from his feelings about Amanda. He had never felt confident about her before. Things had changed.

Amanda felt it too. Something had quite literally come together. She didn't know yet what it was. But the feelings she had thought she could only feel for McCloud and the feelings she reserved for Hotchkiss alone, blended now, and they astonished her.

70

The robot solution was not to be simple. The Ooze said it never heard of such a thing, and it didn't think it could be done. Rastus pretended to know nothing. The Genius took apart the Blue Robot, put him together, took him apart, and said it just didn't add up. It didn't make any sense whatsoever. "I never saw a robot like this," he said. He was feeling discouraged.

"Be patient," Hotchkiss said, "there's got to be a break in the system. Somewhere."

Amanda, too, thought this must be so.

It was shortly after Hotchkiss had left one morning that Amanda turned toward the door with a start. It was Robert, who was usually so polite. But this morning he simply clanked his way in rather brashly, while Amanda was still in bed.

"What do you want?" she said suddenly, uneasy at the expression she saw in his eyes. For Robert now, maybe it was the early light, but no, more likely his renewed ambition. Robert in the early light no longer had glassy envelopes on his retinas. Robert now had expression.

"I want it," Robert said.

"What?" she said, feeling extremely uncomfortable, "what do you mean?" Her heart began to race.

"You know . . . I want to do what you do," Robert said, the jealousy, the envy burning through his eyes. Amanda pulled the sheet up under her chin.

"Uh . . . what exactly is that?" Amanda said, unwilling to believe what she had already guessed.

"*Melt*," the robot said.

For the first time in her life Amanda forgot any scientific response when confronting a previously unobserved phenomenon. She grabbed the sheet around her and bolted for the door.

"Wait," the robot said, "listen to what I have to say."

Amanda listened dumbfounded as the robot talked on.

"I can see the flowers," the robot was saying, "and I can register their scent, and I can write a poem about flowers," he said.

Did she see something then in those cathode-ray-tube eyes? Some indication of something more than cybernetics?

"But I know that I cannot experience the smell of flowers"—he looked at them—"not the way you do."

"Why'd you want to do that?" Amanda said suspiciously.

"I do not know," the robot said.

Amanda turned, amazed. She didn't think this robot had an "I do not know" in its program.

"Were you programmed to want to smell flowers? Were you programmed to desire to imitate *Homo sapiens*?" Amanda interrogated him.

"No," the robot said. "I was programmed to record the smell of flowers and to register it and report this . . . but somewhere, I do not know why, this program mixed with another program. Although all the circuits are working properly, dissatisfaction occurs."

"Dissatisfaction?" Amanda snapped. "A robot can't be dissatisfied. A robot can be in error or not in error. What are you talking about?"

"The systems don't add up," the robot said. "The visual system sees, the smell system registers the smell as a category, but the flower itself is just a series of inputs. I know there are other systems," he said, "and I want to see how they work."

Was it, Amanda wondered, that everything intelligent eventually required experience? Or was it simply some "unconscious" leftover of its human programmer, some prejudice that had inadvertently worked its way into the system, some ineffable gap in the robot's own brain workings. So. Well Amanda was all for it.

"I know enough," the Blue Robot said, "to hear the birds. I remember the smell of flowers. I have all that stuff up here, I just don't have the sensory outlets. I want to go back to the originals. Somewhere somehow the formulas got lost. All the flowers are in black and white. I can't remember the smell, the aroma. I have to go deeper into the biological system to recover the memory, to make it operable. But I want it. There's enough memory there to remember that I want it."

It wants pleasure, Amanda thought. The robot wants to touch, smell, and taste. Intelligence isn't enough. He wants to be animal.

He wants a biological system, she thought, while all around her on earth, biology was in contempt. While machines polluted the air and water, while men killed off plants and animals and running streams to profit in real estate and oil, while the earth was ruining what it had, this robot was out to plunder the one treasure the earth had chosen to ruin for itself: life.

A robot who wants to feel. What strange evolutionary quirk was this? A robot yearning to feel, jealous of biology, while on earth they ruined it.

Amanda suddenly remembered the remarkable experiment she had seen in a biology laboratory when she was eighteen years old. Biology had been her first love. There in a tube, inorganic molecules of oxygen and hydrogen had been placed. Then a bolt of lightning had been shot through the tube—or a bolt of electricity equalling lightning—and *presto*, the molecules were then organic. That afternoon in the laboratory, life had been created in a way that they surmised it had first started on earth. And now, now there was something different afoot. Quite different. A bolt of lightning. The Ooze once told her the robot had been struck by lightning. Was it, then, strictly an accident of nature, of a plan afoot by an unknown source to render life into the robot, to give life to an otherwise inorganic system? What powers of electricity were truly at work here Amanda could not be sure. The point was this: the robot before her was a clever mutation of a sort. In that same leap—that lightning bolt that had first stirred those droppings of the stars, those strange molecular inorganic structures of hydrogen and oxygen—that same force had moved into the robot, converting the electricity in him to something other. For the Blue Robot was not robot alone: he was a mutation in the link of nonliving intelligence; for the intelligence itself to endure it had to become biological. Without wish, without pleasure, without all the perverse permutations of those things, without the drive for experience the robot had no need to continue. He was programmed to reproduce, but he needed a goal.

It is so intelligent, Amanda thought, it knows it is really not experiencing ice cream. Everyone else was ready to abandon experience, and this robot wanted it. He wanted it as a condition of intelligence, of curiosity, of operability. A pleasure system. If the environment were not pleasurable there was no need for this robot to go on. Even he, this strained weird cyborg, knew that clever programming was not enough. If he was to have a future, he must have the wish to endure.

The robot told Amanda that Schrodinger had given him one molecule, which Amanda realized had inspired the robot this way.

The robot wanted Amanda's. He thought one more might make him more of a mammal.

"I really don't think another one is going to do that much for you," Amanda said cautiously. "Where would you go?" she asked. "Even if I gave it to you? To Earth?"

"Oh no," the robot said. Holding only one sweet molecule of life, even with that he didn't want to go anywhere polluted. "I'm going to Ooze's new planet."

At that the Ooze itself came barging in.

"That damn cat," said Ooze, "that damn cat made me promise I'd give the robot a place if he moved the Indians. I never thought he'd do it! I don't want cyborgs on the planet. I wanted to make the Leap. Advanced mammals. With the molecules I was going to make the Leap. A beautiful planet. Green and wonderful. With advanced mammals. Now that thing will be there." The Ooze was so upset it started to cry.

Amanda was thinking fast. The robot might be of use to them.

"Ooze," she said, "come over here." She attempted logic. With Schrodinger's molecule and hers, the robot really wasn't a robot anymore. He was on his way to being an advanced biological unit. What kind, they couldn't be sure. The Ooze would have to settle for him on its new planet.

"Nothing doing," said the Ooze. "I want to make my leap. I don't want a robot leap. I might get more molecules. . . ." It eyed Hotchkiss and Amanda.

"Don't look at me," Amanda said. "Besides I thought you were fed up with *sapiens*. I thought that was the whole idea."

"The Leap was the idea, ninny," the Ooze said, "but since I can't leap, I may just have to start over again." It looked gloomy. "But with all these robots up here and all the NERPs making more robots, it won't be long until it starts all over again—war, murder, the works."

"Look," Amanda said, "I have a plan. A de-NERP plan. But you've got to help. You've got to be willing to let me give my molecule over to Robert. He might not be so bad," she said to Ooze. "Besides, there won't be so many robots, because if we got rid of the NERPs we'd gain a million years—isn't that what you said?"

"Well, yes," said the Ooze reluctantly. "Hell's bells," it was thinking. Nothing ever worked out like it planned. It was going to wind up compromising. As usual.

"And you can still have Schrodinger's molecule. He has one left." The Ooze decided to say nothing about that.

"Look," Amanda said when she thought the timing was right, "I'd be willing to give you my molecule"—for she had figured now that Ooze would have to play along—"if you tell me how to reverse the other robots' fields."

The robot was shocked. He was still part robot after all. He felt some commitment to the secrets of the system.

"I can't tell you that," he said.

"Why not?" Amanda said. "There's no honor among thieves."

At that the robot got mad. "Look, I have standards, rules, guidelines. I have laws to observe."

"I thought you were a maverick," she said simply, and at that the robot's head began to turn; it turned and turned and twirled around. When it stopped he looked at her and seemed to be almost smiling. "How'd you guess?" he said.

They talked all night. The Ooze listened. Hotchkiss implored. The Genius was perfectly brilliant. By morning the deal was struck. They waited for the robot to speak.

"Okay, okay," said the Genius, "now tell us how to reverse their fields."

"First give me the molecule," the robot said.

"No, you have to go first," Amanda said.

The robot paused. "Okay," he said. "It's Radiant One. She can reverse their fields; she only has to be within fifty yards."

"Well that's great," said the Genius. "Where do we find her?"

Amanda looked very concerned. "Look, that's not fair. We have to know where she is, and Ooze said she's been captured."

"I don't know where she is," said the robot. "That wasn't part of the deal. You owe me the molecule."

Rastus watched all this on the screen. The odds had already moved on the big board, where the odds only moved slightly if they moved at all. A Female Principle in the aura of Radiant One would be a very powerful force indeed. Rastus felt something in him come alive. He would confess this to no one, but he was, deep inside, beside, and aside from being a burned-out man, a man who could not resist a long shot.

"It's the Dancer," he said, astonishing them all when he walked into the hut. "The Dancer has her." And then he pointed out across the robot fields, past the huge mouth of the croupier robot, out there into oblivion.

He turned to Amanda. "And she's out there waiting for you now."

71

Hotchkiss listened in amazement. "An eleven million mile high dancer?" he said. "I'll have to go with her; she can't go alone out there."

"You can't," Rastus said; "she has to go it alone. If she does it, if she releases Radiant One, with a Female Principle Rising, she'll be strong. Very strong. You can reverse the robots, get to the GCB, get out. Only thing is . . ." He paused.

"What?"

"I don't know how long Radiant One can remain in this system, even if you get her."

"What do you mean?"

"She loses energy here . . . but this is the right time. Only time you stand a chance of breaking her out of the Dancer."

"Do you know what in hell he's talking about?" Hotchkiss asked Amanda. He was surprised to see her so quiet. Yes, she knew. The Dancer, Hooper had told her about the Dancer. She drove men mad.

"Why do I stand a better chance?" she asked. "What does it mean, Female Principle Rising?"

"It means," Rastus said, "a certain kind of strength. A tolerance for ambiguities. That's what it means."

"Look, I still think it's better if both of us go," Hotchkiss said.

"You can't," Rastus said. "Enlightment comes through the Female Principle," Rastus said, "at least in this hour. This hour here, you need maximum tolerance of ambiguities, you need a force that can be torn apart and still hold. It's not just strength, it's the *kind* of strength, the way of holding. Female Principle Rising, if anything rise." He stood back there, in challenge, she saw that; in sadness, she saw that; and in awe, that surprised her, but she saw that too.

"You stand a chance, if you go now," Rastus said, "but the Dancer is a . . . very high roller," he said, whistling low. "There's only one way," he said, "you're gonna make it."

"How's that?" Amanda said.

"You got to go in at high speed. Very fast. She moves like lightning."

"How can I do that? Ooze can't take us in. It can only take us back. How can I go in at high speed? You told me I had to go alone."

"You got to go alone, it's true," he said, "but you got to go in with momentum. Got to."

"Where would I get momentum *here*?" Amanda said. "That's impossible. I'll just go. I mean to hell with it. How tough can she be? I'm pretty tough myself."

"You don't understand," Rastus said, "this is not like the robots. Tough don't matter here."

"What matters?" she asked.

"The right move. Balance. It's all balance."

"Why that's good!" Amanda said excitedly. "I have perfect balance!"

Rastus saw the odds move ahead with that. But there was still the other question, the question of momentum.

Hotchkiss and the Genius and Amanda thought all night. Where in this place of burned-out hopes and dying energies would they find anything that could do it? They thought of mechanical solutions—of levers—of taking the odds and ends they found in the rubble and fashioning some kind of catapult. But the Ooze said this wouldn't work.

"You don't understand. You can only use yourself. You have to make your own momentum. That's the only way to meet the Dancer."

"Beat the Dancer," Rastus said, slowly, then, "maybe."

It was just then that 342 came into the hut. He was wearing Amanda's skates.

72

"I can do it, I'm sure," Amanda said now, lacing up her skates.

"Keep your eyes on the Dancer's belt," Rastus whispered to her, leaning down.

"Why?" she said. Dare she trust him, still?

"I saw him hit your mind up on the screen. . . . Watch the belt," he said to her.

"Is he going to coalesce you for telling me this?" she asked him.

He shook his head. "He can't coalesce me, exactly. I'm not alive."

"You're not alive?" she said shocked. "What do you mean?"

"Not in your sense," he said. "I'm a hologram . . . a cerebral system. I'm not real, you know . . ." he paused, "no eating, drinking, fucking, or shitting."

"That," Amanda said catching her breath, "is a bit reductive, wouldn't you say?" But she had caught the terrible jealousy in his eyes.

She took off at a dead run, gaining speed in the fields. The robots did not stand a chance of stopping her.

"You got to go as fast as you can," Rastus said. "You got to give it *all* you got. Do not look into the Dancer's eyes. Remember."

She whizzed past the dread croupier. It was there at the edge of oblivion, that the jump had to be made. She found herself hurtling toward it faster than she had ever known and then, almost before she knew it, she took off. She was flying high, high through the spectacular night, tilting, falling, flying, turning, spinning, what seemed here to be impossible maneuvers, zillions of maneuvers in fractions of seconds. She was blazing through the skies with the most amazing machine of all: she was piloting herself.

And then she was in a spin, a spin that went fast and faster and fast—this tight skater's spin—until she absolutely disappeared. She was in the well. Always the well. Black and deep. But she was calm; she knew the trip by now. The preceding motions. Ascent and descent. She was familiar with the ride. But this was the place. The place Hooper had talked about, the place where men went mad.

It wasn't long before all the movement stopped. It was very quiet. And it was night. All she could see and hear and feel was the cold blackness. Not even a stir of wind. Soon through the dark, she saw the stars come up. She didn't recognize them, these patterns of stars in the dark. There were no constellations that she knew. Another system. She waited.

It was not too long before she heard it. A faint sweet song, barely discernible, coming from an instrument that seemed to her familiar, high and light and lilting, and yet utterly strange. The sound put her on her guard. There was a kind of seductive sweetness to it, a high register of appeal, calling. She heard it more clearly now, the sound; the musical sound was calling her. Amanda. She heard her name.

And then she saw it. Suddenly, like a thunderbolt, the blaze of sound erupted from the soft sweet calls into a thunderous blare, but the blare was as nothing to what she saw before her in staggering show, the almost unbearable beauty of the Dancer. There she was, her arms, her legs in starry array, spinning and pirouetting and balancing on one toe, wearing a tiara of ten million stars. The eleven million mile high Dancer was in the sky, and she was there dancing for Amanda, for only she could see her, and she felt this flood of warmth run through her, a sense of perfect happiness. A joyous light swept through her, causing her to raise spontaneously on her toes, to spin as the Dancer spun, to imitate, to do the same. The Dancer held out her arms, Amanda held out *her* arms, and she heard the sweet calling music again. She was overwhelmed by the Dancer's beauty, by the incredible pleasure in her smile, by the arms outstretched to her, and she barely remembered Rastus's warning.

She could not resist the Dancer. Because the Dancer was beautiful, the Dancer was powerful, and the Dancer was, of course, perfect.

Amanda felt light-headed, transcendent, beautiful herself, caught in the perfect glow that the Dancer was known to bestow. This was joyous, wonderful. Why had they all warned her? For what? She felt invigorated, happy, well, almost giddy. She remembered once, when scuba diving, being on the edge of what was called "narcosis of the deep," when you giggle and laugh from excess nitrogen in your blood, you prepare quite happily to drown. They have to haul you up. Of course, here there would be no one to help haul her up. She was not doing what Rastus said, but, after all, what did he know? She felt herself slowing down within the circle of the Dancer. She began to doubt. She didn't even know what she was skating on. What was holding her *up?*

The Dancer's eyes were gleaming. Amanda so much wanted to look there. . . .

Forcefully, her memory, her instruction, was working for her. She caused her eyes to drop away from the Dancer's calling glow and down to the belt. The belt was beautiful too, but not as hypnotic as the eyes. The belt was moving, and she saw when she looked closely a very familiar pattern, a weaving pattern, lilting and falling in an even rhythm through the sky—the belt was Radiant One. She had been, she realized, about to faint, about to pass out, but her eyes focused on the belt, which stopped the hypnosis and made her realize that the joyous, overwhelming feeling was changing. The more she looked at the belt, the more she felt, well, different. She wasn't as happy, for sure. Perhaps one last look. She heard the Dancer calling her. "Amanda." It was the most beautiful voice she'd ever heard, and the most wondrous spectacle, this grand dance in the sky.

But she had been trained, and Rastus had said to her, "It is life and death now. Remember one thing: do not take your eyes off the belt," and so sighing, reluctantly, she kept her eyes on the belt, and then . . . she saw it.

"My God," escaped from her before she knew it. She saw something and it was glittering, yes. The Dancer's hand rested lightly on it. There on the side of the wondrous weaving belt was a sheath of red and blue and golden stars, a sheath of insufferable beauty; and in it, she could see too, for this beauty was transparent, was what they undeniably had prepared for her—a knife. And the Dancer, Amanda realized, this Dancer was prepared to kill.

Amanda started skating faster now. She had to pick up speed. It was difficult to keep the Dancer in front. The Dancer was moving incredibly fast, trying to get behind Amanda. A rush of icy air passed on her right. Then it slashed past her on the left. The belt, Amanda thought. She saw the wonderful weaving movement in the starry girdle. It seemed to be moving away. It *was* moving away.

And as she watched it move, she saw how hard it was to see it. It appeared always to be closer than it was. That was the Dancer's trick. The Dancer was untying it now and wrapping it around her brow. It floated now just above her eyes. Amanda would have to go up there to get it.

The Dancer was moving toward her now. Moving like lightning streaks across the sky. A bright green flash assaulted her shoulders, striking a glancing blow. Amanda ducked. A blue blaze of fire erupted on her left, and she skated harder, skating fast, rapid circles around the Dancer, and as she skated faster and faster, Amanda began to spiral upward.

"I've got the rhythm now," she thought excitedly. Something was helping her move as she glided past the Dancer, Amanda *behind* her now, the Dancer moving in a fury, and Amanda spiraled up and around her. Amanda skated through the sky, her speed, her determination, her love supplying surface to her flight as she climbed higher and higher around the Dancer until she was opposite the eyes. She looked into them. Beauty, truth, illusion—they danced so closely there, you could not tell them one from the other. Amanda was transfixed, caught in the weave of their spell. Blue, orange, and purple flames engulfed her. The blaze was startling in its brightness. Luminous purple transparencies, blue ghosts, and red ethers floated there surrounding her like a corona; fire of gold, fire of green, Amanda a borealis of swirling light. It was a gyre and it was spinning; she was sinking faster into the bottom of it. As the gyre rose higher, she melded to the Dancer. She saw the trap too late, she tried to break loose, to move, she could not; to breathe, she could not. Her arms had stretched as far as the Dancer's own. Her legs had jetted down through the sky until Amanda too was eleven million miles high, the Dancer's dance her very own. All looking gone, Amanda was on fire. There was nothing there but the fire of light and her fading presence. She was disappearing into it.

And then two strands of light fell, only two frail strands, across the Dancer's eyes. Fate, history, will or revolution; something had brought them down. It was enough. They broke apart. Amanda was free. She could move again and she was gaining speed. Speed and distance were amok here in the Dancer's glow. The Dancer was out to win, but the beautiful dangerous Dancer, so capable of savage deceits, was not counting on the coalition of Radiant One and this girl.

"When you decide to reach for it, you got to give it everything," Rastus had said, "it's farther, much farther than it looks."

Amanda knew for certain she had held this light before, and she knew now how to claim it. Amanda sprang and reached, flying through the space of infinite time, hoping her aim was true.

Instinctively her hand reached out, and Radiant One was released. She enveloped Amanda just as the knife came down.

73

Amanda came streaming in, swinging down through the sky on a curtain full of stars. Hotchkiss and the Genius raced to meet her, and together the three of them sped down the field, Amanda skating, Hotchkiss and the Genius running, the reversed robots thundering behind them, as Amanda led triumphant, Radiant One held high above her head, winding out behind her like the tail of a golden dragon. The armies of robots poured down behind them, their negative charges converted to positive, as they raced toward the Crystal Palace to claim Schrodinger and the NERP list from the GCB inside.

The robots held open the doors of the Crystal Palace. It took thousands of them to pry open its shining walls, and Hotchkiss, Amanda, and the Genius bounded forth into the steaming mess. The Ooze was at their side.

"Get the NERP list!" Amanda said, pointing Hotchkiss and the Genius one way. "I'll get Schrodinger."

Now that they were inside, Radiant One was gone. "I'll stay as long as I can," she had said, and she had left Amanda's hand just as she'd gone through the door.

"This is the absolute limit," said the GCB, running for cover.

Amanda's eyes were rolling from the stench; the fetid air made the tears fall down her face, but she had strength, and soon she saw the dungeon door. And therein lay the turning point. There was a huge Red Robot there, and Radiant One was gone; the robot was guarding the door. Schrodinger had given up his last molecule. But Amanda didn't know that. She assumed that Schrodinger still had the special magic she had ascribed to him, even before he had ever swallowed a single molecule. The robot raised his obliterator, and, furious, Amanda kicked it from his hand, picked it up, and shot him with it. Then she blew the door off. These obliterators, she thought in passing—for at the speed and the panic in which she was passing it was difficult to think anything at all, but she thought—these obliterators were terrific things.

Schrodinger was in the corner. Without food or drink, the GCB's revenge, he was too weak to even cry out.

"Oh, Schro," she said scooping him into her arms and kissing his face. Schrodinger's eyes were shining. And then she ran. The stench was powerful and deep; she was dizzy and crawling from the smoke, when she reached the last gate. Once again, who knows how, who knows why, who knows where, Rastus himself, in a twist of unexpected complexity, had thrown her a rope. She could barely gather the strength to hang on, Schrodinger buttoned inside her jacket, as he pulled her along the steaming floor, out into the sun.

Rastus had seen on the console that the cat had given up the molecule. And more than that. Amanda had given hers to the Blue Robot. Rastus wanted them out of there. Things had been in a mess ever since they landed. Of course he liked the mess, in a way, too. Had to say it had been lively. But he was the only one at this point who knew what she was really up against.

With Radiant One gone, the robots were reversing to negative again. Hotchkiss and the Genius saw the signs flashing green ALERT ALERT ALERT just as they reached the GCB's Crystal Tower. Racing inside to the field of blinking buttons they saw the one they wanted. DUMP, the button read. "GET IT!" yelled Hotchkiss, and the Genius jumped toward it just as a corps of Red Robots approached the tower door and pounded inside. As the robots raised their rifles, the Genius reached the button and held it. It was the most incredible racket anyone had ever heard. Some of the robots had been programmed for print, something Hotchkiss and the Genius had not anticipated, and reams and miles of paper poured out of the backs of their heads, falling in streams, piling up thicker and thicker in spirals on the floor. The NERP list was there. It was *very* long.

"We'd better get out," Hotchkiss said, seeing them drowning in a sea of paper, and they bolted for the door.

"Radiant One is out," Rastus whispered to her, guiding her through the fields. "The robots are going into reverse. You got to get that cat purring," he said to her; "he can destroy their frequency."

"He can't—he's weak. He must have given up his last molecule," she said. Amanda was feeling sick. Radiant One was gone. And they had given away their magic powers. The robots were running all over the fields, in every direction. They were confused, but their heads were turning. They were reversing.

"The cat can," Rastus said, holding her arm. "You can get him to do it."

"But he's so weak," she said looking down at the limp Schrodinger.

"You *got* to do it!" Rastus was fierce now.

"If I sing . . . if I sing this song . . ." she said, "but I don't know if I can . . ." Fear was closing her throat as she looked at the robots. Rastus, seeing this, would not let her look back until he had steered her almost into the middle of the field. Then she turned and saw them coming. Hundreds, thousands of them were bearing down on her, their intention very clear. She felt the old fear again, sweeping over her. She could hardly speak or move. And then she saw Hotchkiss and the Genius, struggling on the other side. They had reached the field, but the robots were gunning for them too.

Rastus shouted at her. "SING," he yelled. "SING, or you'll wind up just a cerebral system like me," and she saw then the terrible recognition in his eyes.

Amanda held Schrodinger in her arms. And then Amanda sang.

As the fields of Red Robots bore down on her, marching like Nazi soldiers in file from the right, and she felt the snap and pound of the steel heels of the Blue Robots approaching from the left, and the ground began to heave under her, Amanda stood firm and held Schrodinger tightly to her, softly singing to him. At first, he did not respond, but as the robots closed in, relentless and drawing nearer, she thought she heard the flicker of a purr. She continued to sing, and as the stars went out one by one behind her and the night got blacker and blacker, she saw then at the far end of the fields the lights come up, like a landing field. She saw the fields double and triple and quadruple and knew they were playing with hundreds of minds that night. Her singing grew stronger and she felt brave, despite their advance, and she sang and sang the most beautifully, she thought, she had ever sung, and Schrodinger began to purr. His purr grew, and the vibrations shook the sky, struck the stars out of their blackness into light, and the robots, still marching, marched in place now, for with Amanda singing and Schrodinger purring they could not advance. They had never been stopped in their tracks, and old, antique buttons in their heads began to go off. Antiquated, unused buttons, red and ringing, lit the air. "Alarm! Alarm!" the buttons announced as Amanda sang, and soon the robots stopped moving altogether. They stood there, their heads moving about in 360-degree revolutions, attempting to find a wavelength that might recharge them.

Amanda held Schrodinger firmly. The robots stopped now and

began to crackle and smoke. Millions of electrical conjunctions flew through the air as the robots spewed forth everything they had ever known. The minefields at the end cracked and sputtered like lightning striking a powerhouse. It had to be one hell of a night on earth, Amanda thought. But at least they were safe. Seeing the robots emptied now, standing like shells in a row, the lights getting feebler as all their systems went down, she felt better than she'd ever felt before.

It's nearly over, she thought, tears in her eyes, holding Schrodinger tightly to her chest and running across the fields to meet Hotchkiss and the Genius. Behind them she could see Memory Lane. It looked different now.

It had been Schrodinger's most impressive purr—and then Amanda suddenly felt him stop.

"Schro . . . ?" she said, it was almost a gasp. She felt something in the sudden stillness. "Schro?" There was no sound. The little body was still and cold.

"SCHRODINGER!" Amanda screamed, putting her head to his chest. "Schro . . . Schro . . ." The screams collapsed as she fell to the ground. It couldn't be . . . no, not Schrodinger . . . not now . . . no. "Schro," she cried again. But it was no use. Schrodinger was dead. Amanda's grief spilled down in tears as she fell across him onto the robot floor.

74

The Ooze rushed to her. "He's all right . . . it's all right, you'll get him back. Necessary transaction for molecular conversion. He's not dead . . . I mean not to you in *your* world anyway. I had to coalesce him, his mind, his spirit anyway. There was no other way. He was a very complicated construction."

Amanda looked up through the tears, her face stained with dirt and ice. Was this Ooze lying to her?

"Are you . . . are you . . . ?"

"Have I lied? I never lie. I misconstrue, sometimes don't tell the whole truth, but never lie. I'm incapable," it said, blinking.

"Why didn't you tell me that before?" Amanda asked. She was still shaking. "I want his body at least," she said, clutching the little cold form, although in fact it didn't seem like Schrodinger's body even. It seemed like a shell, a plaster cast. In minutes she saw that it was.

"It's nothing," the Ooze said, touching it. "See?" And the cast shattered then, turning to dust in her arms.

Hotchkiss came running up. "Where's Schrodinger?" he said.

"I'm sending him back another way," Ooze said. "I had to coalesce him through a dematerialization zone. Once he didn't have the molecules there was no way to get him back. It takes ninety-six hours for that kind of conversion to be complete."

"Well what about us then?" Hotchkiss asked. "How will we get back?"

"This way," said the Ooze. "You've got to use two different lines of exit. Amanda, you go that way, Hotchkiss and the Genius, you go down on the Horses of Heaven, the stables over there."

"Wow," said the Genius.

"I don't know how to ride," said Hotchkiss.

"Yes, you do," said the Ooze. "You'll see. Everybody knows how to ride these horses, it's the chance of a lifetime." This was odd, Amanda noted; the Ooze was talking as if it were selling insurance. Must be Piranski creeping in again.

"Why do I have to go alone?" Amanda said.

"The Red Robots are still after you; I have to send you out on a special exit line; and you have to pick up Three-forty-two." The Ooze looked nervous.

"Hey look, is she safe?" Hotchkiss said.

"Now she is—except she might forget. I mean there's a certain region where you pass by a Red Robot with a lance. He'll try to lance you. It's strictly luck."

"That's not good enough," Hotchkiss said.

"It's all right," Amanda said. "I must be lucky or I wouldn't be here now."

"The worse that can happen is that you'll forget," Ooze said. "You'll arrive. I promise you that."

"Well," Hotchkiss said, "that's good enough for me."

"Hurry," said the Ooze.

"All I can do," Oozie said, "is set you down where you'll find somebody receptive. You'll have to do the rest yourself. Good luck," the little thing said. "Keep on truckin'."

"Can I do it?" she asked, afraid of the answer.

"What?" the Ooze said.

"Can I save it, the earth? Can I keep the oceans blue and the grass green? Can I?"

The Ooze shrugged. "You should have asked the console when you had the molecule," it said.

"I couldn't," Amanda said, "in case it said no."

"An interesting group of connections," Oozie said, looking at her, "destined never to be repeated . . . at least in a millennium."

"Thanks a lot," Amanda said, "for the compliment. Now where's the tunnel? Show me."

Ooze said, "It's a tunnel, but it's also a corkscrew. But first," he said, "you have to get Three-forty-two, where the Blue Robot left him, and cross the chasm. All that takes is confidence."

"You'll send Schrodinger?" she said.

"I promise, very soon," said the Ooze, "and I never make promises. But that cat trapped me into it."

"How's that?" Amanda said, smiling.

"I told him I'd *promise* to get you all back if he moved the Indians back and gave me a molecule," said Ooze, "and he did it!"

"Where's the GCB?" said Amanda.

"Preparing to materialize, no doubt," said the Ooze. "You know," it said, "he wasn't so bad before."

"Before what?" Amanda said.

"Before *sapiens*, I mean, he did get peeved at the dinosaurs and took them out," it said. "He was always something of a stinker, but he was never *rotten*."

"Well, what happened?" Amanda said, thinking that although she was in a hurry, she shouldn't miss this story.

"I don't know," said Ooze, "but something coincided. Either the robots made the first NERP or the first NERP made the first robot. I never got the answer to that question."

Part of the way was familiar to her. But most of it wasn't. Still, she had found 342, following Ooze's instructions. It was dark, as it told her it would be. Soon, she would come to the chasm. The chasm, the leap, and then the tunnel out. Not far now. But it was hard to see. She kept bumping into things, so her pace was slow.

She was in the darkness, though she was not cold. She had learned to listen now, and she thought she heard the sound. The sound of Radiant One. And then she saw the white light, the bleep coming near her.

"I am Radiant One," she heard the bleep say, "follow me." And Amanda, glad to see anything offering confidence and purpose, immediately did. Sometimes she thought it was a star, sometimes she thought it was a quasar. She did not have difficulty following it; it seemed to pull her along in some kind of magnetic jet stream. They kept hitting walls. Amanda could see even in the dark. The entire place was a labyrinth.

"It looks like a labyrinth," said Amanda.

"All the territories between universes are labyrinths."

"How do you know the way?" Amanda said.

"That's what I am," the white bleep said, "knowing the way. We are coming to the chasm. This you must cross alone," and the white bleep disappeared. Amanda was alone. This was the place Ooze said where there would be a tunnel on the other side that would lead her out. But first the leap, it had said.

"You've got to go across that by yourself," said Ooze. "Nothing I can do can help you there, until you get to the tunnel entrance. It's all a matter of confidence."

"Confidence," she said under her breath. Confidence. That was too much. Or was it. She looked out into the huge black chasm. It seemed to her she was looking out at the very edge of the universe. She had come, she had told Rastus, because of Schrodinger, yes. And because she wanted to see.

"You just might," he had said to her, "and then you might be sorry you did."

But she didn't think she would be sorry. She did still want to see. And as she stared out into the chasm she saw it there.

It was a fireball. A fireball of swirling quarks. She saw that. And she saw broken symmetries. She saw life and she saw death. She saw the flow. One into the other. She reached out into the black space as she saw the river running by, and she pulled it back and saw the river shining in her hand. The diamonds of eternity glittered in her hand, and then slipped through back into the sky, like stars of sand. Stolen.

From where? From whom? "The sands of eternity had been stolen," Rastus had said. From whom then? She saw the cosmic circle now, the eternal band, weaving and twisted and ineluctable, snaking its way through the galaxy in a hypnotic dawn. It threw her down, the power of this view. Like a horse kick in the midsection, it knocked the air from her. It gave her fear; it gave her glory. Watching that glittering serpent snaking its way through the sky, sinuous and weaving through the stars, the endless space of time, space finally without time, the never never ever ever land—it made you want to die, right where you were, to pass out and over and beyond, where you like the serpent would simply twirl and swirl, twist and plummet, rise and fall. Each breath would be your being; feeling only the rhythm of your rise and fall you would *be*, knowing nothing.

It slammed into her gut like a fist.

75

"Wait till the light is right, be *sure*," Rastus had whispered to her, "before you go for it." But how could she be sure? So, she took a running jump, leapt into space. False light, half light, dead light, any light would be seized on; this was a tale as old as the night. And as tricky. But there are times when the move *must* hold. Amanda took a running leap, 342 in her arms, focusing, leaping with everything in her, and hoping, hope gathering in her with a force as free as the wind and as mighty, and she leapt and sped across the gap. Radiant One was leading ahead into the long dark tunnel, and Amanda, behind her, was holding fast, wedded to the promise of delivery, knit as tightly into this as a knot into its string, she sped behind Radiant One, braided into its filaments, twisting and turning yes, but each twist and turn now braided more strength into the line.

Each twist now bound her to safety, her face buried in the neck of 342, bound to protect his animal hide. Arms wrapped tightly to hold him, she did not know she was free, and clear.

76

Amanda was in orbit, and unclassified, twinkling and spinning at a mystifying rate. Perhaps it was an unexplained ephemeron, which was something the astronomers observed in the skies and which did not last long enough to allow explanation. She would normally have been safe once in that orbit. Rastus had done his best. But there had been an electromagnetic gap in movements in the world. The secretary of the interior had just given up all the wilderness to the polluters. Cries were raised in protest, and just as quickly, the robots shut them down. This caused, however, a delay in her point of entry. She would have to circle now, one more time, before the final leap. This gave the Red Robot his single last chance. Powerfully he raised his lance. He knew it would strike true. Amanda would forget. Events conspired to gain him ground. The list would flutter from her hands. No warning would take hold.

Desert

"Rufe, hey Rufe." Eberly had an expression on his face Rufus had never seen before. It was the expression of someone scared.

"Yeh, Eb?" Rufus said, turning slowly around. The mountains had turned orange, and the floor of the desert was beginning to move slowly, in a strange undulation; the desert floor had turned into a serpent. Rufus felt it rise and fall beneath his feet.

"Rufe," Eberly's voice was catching now, barely able to come out, "you ever seen, ever heard anything like this?" Rufus said nothing. Where was the head of the serpent, he wanted to know. Rufus was not afraid. He was beyond fear, somewhere near acceptance, but not quite. He was willing to fight. He was prepared to find it fightable. Eberly had already concluded there wasn't a chance.

*A strange wail began, like the scream of an anguished animal, but
it was more metallic than that. Rufus thought suddenly it was a cross
between the terrible tremblings of the jets that crossed their houses and
the agonizing cry of a dying bull. He had heard a bull once in horrible
pain trumpet its own death. It wasn't anything he'd ever want to hear
again.*

*"Oh God, Rufus," Eberly said, sitting now on the ground in a pool
of sweat. Rufus had never heard him say that either. There was a smell,
too, a God-awful smell, something so rank, so putrefacted, it smelled like
evil itself.*

*"You reckon, you reckon"—Eberly was whispering—"it's one a them
bombs, hydrogen or nucleers or whatever?"*

*Rufus shook his head slowly. No, this was too supernatural to be
the workings of science. A spell had fallen on the landscape. Some dreadful
threat was working its way into their bones even as they stood there; some
renewing memory was being taken from them even then as they stood
there in their terror. They were each becoming less than what they were,
and they knew it, and they couldn't stop it. All sacraments had been
destroyed, all sacraments and superstition. They had slipped beyond the
crevass of evil, into the void, a world of putrefactions and serpents of
death, whose heads lay in unknown directions, as did the manner of their
strike.*

But there was something that neither the robot nor history had anticipated.

There was a point. A gap. So infinitesimal a fraction of a moment
that one might say it was the pause before the synapse, the spark of time
when the impulse jumped across the space to trigger the response, or
understanding. In just such a fraction of time, at the precise moment
when the Red Robot raised his lance, sending the piercing signal through
the sky, destined for Amanda's mind to carry to earth, this arrow of
forgetfulness was stayed by one small thing: an inhalation of the breath.
For it was the way that it was in this world that robots had no power
where there was no breath. They came in and out on exhalations and
inhalations, and since these were things routinely done by living things,
there was always a time when they could gain entry. So the robot was
of course alarmed, surprised to see his lance had been held off, and with
it, his future. For Amanda was holding her breath, and why? No one

told her to do this. Oozie offered no protection against the Red Robot's aim; he had his region and Amanda had passed through. Was it yet some primal "instinct" that had protected her before? No. It was this: Amanda was holding her breath in awe; she was gasping at the beauty of the whirling ball of blue below her, struck dumb and quiet by the magnificence of the view. This gasp, this soaring sense of beauty, had been built, too, into the human genes. Inspired, spirited, and stilled all at once by this teeming ball of life, so blue, so brilliant, so spectacular; this gasp of wonder was what at last held off the robot's line. She saw the teeming ball, replete with life. Three hundred fifty thousand varieties of plants, four thousand three hundred twenty varieties of mammals, eight hundred sixty thousand varieties of insects, two hundred fifty thousand varieties of flowers, twenty-eight thousand fifty varieties of fishes, eight thousand six hundred thirty varieties of birds, six thousand one hundred twenty-seven kinds of reptiles, proliferations of species of every kind of living thing, and there, most impressive of all, at the center of the blue ball, the gleaming console. There was the mind of man lighting up the center of the earth as she came through the clouds. The earth was bursting with light.

"She made it," Rastus said with a smile. "Is that somethin'? The odds were three trillion, nine million, seven hundred thousand and six to one."

She was smiling as she broke through the clouds. And then as she came closer she saw the dark patches, here, there, everywhere. The power being turned off, the light being cut down. The robots had been effective in their work. There were dark patches everywhere.

The Horses of Heaven had fire in their eyes, and they glinted like red lights in the dark, like lights streaking across the tails of planes, or cars receding around a curve, night actions of unknown destinations and speeds.

The big wall rolled back, and the horses were loose. In a thundering herd they leapt across the great cavern, Hotchkiss and the Genius hanging on as they sped them to earth.

Rufus woke up that night, took out his car, and drove, alone, into the mountains. He had with him a silver lasso and a gun. He hoped he wouldn't use the gun, but there were grizzly now as well as bobcat, and he would be sitting alone.

It was not long before he heard them, the team of wild hooves, striking the canyon floor, feet sparking, like fire and brimstone they ran, and he knew soon they would pass him. The wind did not change, and he waited, and soon the horses came, and he stepped forward then, the lasso singing in a circle in the air, his voice crying out "Maria! Maria!" and the loop sang up and floated, floated only a fraction of a second as if waiting, waiting for the right head to appear beneath its circle, and then it sank, and he felt it grow taut.

But it wasn't Maria. It was Donald Hotchkiss.

How many venturers after a lost dream have felt the lasso sail and rise convinced, certain, hovering seconds over its proper target only to fall and capture a totally unexpected quarry? In this case the dream of the black horse died with the discovery that all that Rufus had captured was an astronaut in a time-warp, at first sight simply technology gone awry.

"Sorry, fella," Rufus said, releasing the coil in a daze. Moon mavericks, that was what was out. Seeing things that weren't there. But he had smelled them. The horses. They *were* here. "What are you doing here?" he said.

"I'm coming back from the stars," Hotchkiss said. "Don't try to understand it."

"Nope," he said, pulling the silken lariat through his fingers. What was lost was lost, never to be recovered. Looking for answers bleeds the heart away, the rope sang through his hands.

Amanda and 342 had landed with a *thwack* and a *thump*, smack dab in the middle of the desert, at the feet of a pair of scrolled purple boots.

"Where in hell choo coming from?" Amanda heard a voice and looked up.

Damn that Oozie. It said someone receptive. This was a weather-beaten cowboy. Had it screwed up again? She smiled, and looked at her boots. They were charred and burning.

"Hi," Amanda said.

"You an American?" the fat one said, leaning down. She saw the badge star gleaming on his pocket.

"Yeah," she said, getting up. "I'm an astronaut, and this," she said, patting the chimp's head, "is my copilot."

"Oh," Eberly said. "Ain't you s'posed to have a ship or a rocket or something?"

"I lost it," she said, getting up and dusting herself off. "Can't you see the condition of my boots? They're burned." She pointed to them.

"Came in on the boots, that it?" Eberly said, squinting. "Well now," Eberly said, "this piece of property's turning into a regular landin' field for them there outer-spacers."

"What do you mean?" she asked suddenly.

"Fella came down only minutes ago, brought my boy back with him, came straight down from heaven swinging on some long kinda rope it looked like, swung on down here lookin' like Tarzan and smellin' like smoke. Never could see what he was hangin' from, and Rufus swears he heard horses."

"Hotchkiss!" Amanda said. "Where is he?"

"You know that fella?" Eberly said.

"Where is he!" Amanda was almost screaming.

"Take it easy now. Fella's all right. Over to my house. Says he don't wanna talk to nobody yit. Waitin' to git some kinda message or something like that. Looks to me like he mighta been waitin' for you."

"Is there . . . does he have a cat with him?" Amanda said brightly.

The sheriff shook his head. "Not that I seen."

"Oh." Oozie wouldn't break a deal. She was sure of it. Still, she was a little uneasy.

The magician was running back and forth in leaps of joy across the desert, wrapping his cape in a swirl as he spun himself into ecstasies, shouting, "Round trip, round trip, round trip!"

They were all sitting there, wondering how to do it.

"It's hopeless," Amanda said. "We can't de-NERP the world. There are too many."

"We're sunk," Hotchkiss said.

"We ought to try," the Genius said, not very convincingly. Three-forty-two was yelling and screaming and pulling at their hands.

"What does he want?" Rufus said, looking at him.

"He wants us to try, I guess," Amanda said.

"Wal now," Eberly said, "I been thinking." They all turned and looked at him. His voice sounded different from usual.

He stood up then, did Sheriff Eberly, sheriff and chief investigating officer of Cononga County, and he said, "I know what we have to do, and we just have to go out and do it. How many you figure there be?"

Amanda pushed the list across the table. "Look at this," she said dejectedly.

Eberly studied the list. "Hmmm, it's a lot," he said, "but you know a good cowboy can always round up three thousand cattle and brand 'em in a night"—he winked—"if he has to."

"What?" Amanda said.

"Yessir," Eberly said, standing up and hitching his pants. "Looks to me like what we need is a good ole Texas roundup. Yessir. 'At's what I'd call it all right. We got to go out, git 'em, turn 'em upside down, and burn those blue dots right outa the little heifers."

They all stood there speechless. Could it be this simple? Even Einstein said the solution was simple. What wasn't simple was getting to it.

"It's not possible," Amanda said, discouraged. "Do you realize how hard it is to change people's minds? It'll take centuries."

"We ain't got centuries," Eberly said. "We don't have to git everybody. The Indians is all right. We ain't got to do them. Mebbe all we got to git is the policy people. Now in my day," Eberly said, continuing, still hitching his pants, "I could hog-tie and brand fifteen hundred heifers in a day. Now I figure it ain't so different from that. A roundup, that's what we got to do."

They stared at Eberly.

"Eb, they's all over the world," Rufus said. Three-forty-two by now was absolutely beside himself, screaming and yelling and hammering on the door.

"What in tarnation's wrong with thet thang anyways?" Eberly said. "Mebbe he needs to run around." He opened the door, and they saw to their surprise, the Blue Robot standing there.

"I'm going to help you," he said. "May I come in?"

"Wal now," Eberly said, "whaddya know?"

"Woww-ee," said the Genius under his breath.

"Why?" said Amanda wonderingly.

"Holy shit," said Hotchkiss, yet again another way of viewing phenomena.

Three-forty-two kept leaping up and down for joy. The robot clanked in and explained the deal.

The Ooze, it seems, had gotten the molecules back from the robot in exchange for the following deal. It had promised the Blue Robot a biological planet and it was about to start one. But Oozie wanted some mammals too. That was a problem. The Ooze was plucking a *Homo sapiens* right off the planet Earth. "Two pairs: one chimp pair, and a *Homo sapiens* pair." He'd sent the robot to get them, "to populate the planet. That way it'll skip the intervening million years or so and go right to NOW."

"Oh," Amanda said, feeling her heart beat faster, "who is it going to take?"

She looked at Hotchkiss.

"It's made the arrangements. It got a pair. It found a female in the San Diego zoo that's willing to mate with Three-forty-two."

"Oh," Amanda said. That's why the chimp had been so happy. "Well," she went on, "the, uh, people . . . did it say who?" This couldn't be the last final trick, could it?

"It didn't say," the robot said, seeing her thoughts. "I'm going to meet them later." Then the robot went on to explain what he would do for them.

"I told Schrodinger I'd get you two horses and a night line," he said. "You can travel anywhere on them at any speed you choose. You can materialize, dematerialize, do absolutely anything you want on this particular frequency." His blue eyes glowed. "But you only have it for twenty-four hours. That's it."

"Twenty-four hours?" Hotchkiss said. "We can't do all of this in twenty-four hours . . . ."

"I tole you afore and I'll tell you again," Eberly said, "iffen I kin do fifteen hundred heifers in a day I damn well can go three thousand folks in twenty-four. We gonna have ourselves a real ole-fashioned Texas roundup."

"It might work," Hotchkiss said.

"Do you think?" Amanda said, beginning to smile.

"YIPPPEE IIIII OOOOOOO, YIPPEE IIIII AY AY AY AY," said the magician, which startled Rufus and the sheriff no end.

"Where'd you learn that cowboy song, boy?" Eberly said. But the magician only smiled.

It was a night to remember, as the storybooks say, and the little troupe of Eberly, Rufus, and the Genius, and Amanda, the chimp and Hotch-kiss, rode high in the night on the Horses of Heaven, and working with the magic of Blue Robot entry, they entered the bedrooms and the salons, turning the blue dotters upside down.

The first target of course was Delko and Delko's wife. Delko's wife, her hair in curlers, heard a noise. She got up and went out into the living room.

"Uhhh," she said, gasping and taking a step back.

"I won't hurt you," Amanda said, "but I need to see Delko."

"It's three A.M.," Delko's wife said, "and I thought you were dead."

"I'm not dead," Amanda said. "Where is he?" She started to move toward the door.

"I'll get him," Delko's wife said, hugging her bathrobe about her neck, and bolting back into the bedroom. She shook her sleeping husband awake. "That crazy girl is here," she said, whispering to Delko and shaking him awake.

"Huh? Who?" Delko in a daze sat up.

"You know, the one who went to the stars." Delko's wife looked around. "She's here."

"Amanda!" He screamed and yelled it all at once as he leaped out of bed. "It can't be. She's dead."

"That's what I told her, but she wouldn't listen—she wants to talk to you . . . she wants to talk to you," Delko's wife was still whispering. "She's here with some funny people."

"People?" Delko's eyes were round. "If she isn't dead, she must be under arrest—probably M.P.s. Hah!" he said, climbing into his bathrobe and making for the door.

"I don't think so," his wife said, following him with mincing steps and still whispering. "They look like cowboys."

"Cowboys?" Delko roared. "Hell, they can't be cowboys." He was saying this as he stepped into his living room and saw Amanda there and the chimp in a kind of glow, and just outside the window, a wild rearing thing. It was a cowboy on a horse, all right.

Too late, he saw the lasso. With a flick of her wrist she turned him upside down and burned the blue dot away. They did Delko's wife too, who finally said, "I'm tickled to death," which was more or less the case. With all of them.

By morning the little band returned. They had done their job, but they were all exhausted. And unsure, despite their valor, that the cure had worked.

"Look, Doris," Beedle Hobbs said, "there ain't that much doin' here anyway."

"Well," Doris said, rolling her eyes, "I don't know . . . outer space is awfully far from my mother . . . and that *thing* is weird."

"Not any weirder than your mother," Beedle said.

"Welllll, that's true of course, but Beedle . . ." Doris said, lighting a cigarette and wondering. Robots, spaceships, and that funny-talking thing. What was the world coming to anyway? "I'm not packed, Beedle—he said we had to go in twenty-four hours, *immediately*. I mean, I can't pack for the rest of my life in only a day."

"You won't need much, Doris," Beedle said.

"Maybe I can pick up a few things once we get there," Doris said.

"Doris," Beedle said, "there's *nothing* there."

"No stores at all?" Doris said.

"No stores," Beedle said. "I dunno. He said once we get there we ain' gonna wanna buy anything anyway. Anything we don't know, he says, Three-forty-two's gonna teach us."

"That sounds backward, doesn't it?" Doris said.

"What the hell's the difference, Doris? We'll teach 'im a little, he'll teach us a little . . . I mean, the important thing is we're gonna have a *real* good time. Isn't that what counts?"

"I guess so," Doris said. That meant, Beedle knew, she was ready.

They were sitting there in front of the fireplace.

"You figure we got 'em all?" Eberly said to Amanda and Hotchkiss.

"I don't know," Hotchkiss said. "We got all the decision-makers."

"This has been exhausting," said the magician, who fell fast asleep on the sofa.

Amanda was looking very sad.

"I just don't understand," she said softly. "It said it would send Schrodinger."

"It'll do it. Something probably got fouled up. You know how fouled up things are up there."

"Yes," she said, unconvinced. She got up dejectedly and went into the kitchen.

The astronomers looked at the sky. Thousands flocked to their telescopes. It wasn't Halley's and it wasn't predicted, but there was no doubt there was a *comet* in the sky.

Comets, of course, are known by their tails, which is usually the only part one can see. Never had they seen a tail like this one.

"Good grief," said Tim Purse, which he thought was a curse word.

"Holy mackerel," said another.

"Oh my stars and garters," said a third.

"It's a cat . . . it's not a comet, it's a cat that seems to be on fire," Tim Purse said, stepping back from the telescope. He had come to *see*. Sound was not up to this.

"By jove, a fiery cat," said the third, looking intently into the glass.

"Is it alive, or is it dead?" said the second.

"It can't be alive, not at that speed," said another. No one knew, of course, precisely what the speed of a cat could be or would be, but it was safe to presume, from a scientific point of view, that a readily discernible cat whose tail was streaming out behind it like a comet could not be said to be "living," in the ordinary course of things.

Tim Purse ran to the phone.

Hotchkiss picked up the ringing phone.

"Amanda," he cried, "Tim Purse says that Schrodinger is streaking like a comet across the sky."

She raced with Hotchkiss at her heels into the backyard. And there they saw him, lit up like the aurora borealis itself, but unmistakably the puss of Schrodinger beaming across the stars.

"Oh," Amanda said, gasping, "isn't he beautiful." That was, it so happened, just the first thing that came to mind. Then she said, "My God, is he okay?"

"I don't know," Hotchkiss was whispering.

"Oh!" Amanda said. This was somewhere between a wail, a cry of joy, and a lament. He must be alive, she thought, but she couldn't tell, just at this juncture, simply by observation alone.

"Look out," Hotchkiss said pointing, as the tail of the Schrodinger comet turned. It appeared to be heading directly for the field across the road.

Quickly they raced across the street, just in time to hear a loud WHUMP as Schrodinger landed covered with dust, but all smiles and a loud greeting.

"Schrodinger lives!" Amanda cried, tears streaming down her face as she raced to him and picked him up. She squeezed him so tightly he squealed. "Thank heavens . . . thank Oozie . . . oh my God, I'm so glad to see you." Then she held him off. "Can you still talk? Can you draw?" But Schrodinger only uttered a very catlike meow and spun his hind legs in the air.

"He's cured!" Hotchkiss said joyously.

Eberly was looking up at the sky. "Never saw a cat fall outa the sky like that, did you, Rufe?"

"Nope, never did, Eb," Rufus said.

It wasn't the first and it wasn't the last of things Rufus had never seen before. He knew that now. And he knew he wasn't loco for seeing it. Seeing things that nobody else saw wasn't the stuff that made a man loco. Rufus knew that now. Not seeing things was what made men loco. He thought about that. Thought they'd gotten all of it, the blue dots, the NERPs. But you never knew. Had to keep your ear out. And your eye. Catch 'em quick as you could, turn 'em upside down, and clear 'em. The only way. He was feeling better about things now. He knew he'd never see Maria again. But here was something. Hope. A little vigilance, and there was hope. He figured they might just make it now. Mebbe.

Around the Nation

Fireball Streaks Across Southern California Sky

LOS ANGELES, April 3 (AP) — The authorities said today that they could not determine the origin of a large flaming white object that streaked across Southern California skies, prompting dozens of calls to law enforcement agencies in at least five counties.

The object, which was sighted Saturday evening, may have been a meteorite or space debris, said Dick Hallen, a Federal Aviation Administration duty officer. "This sounds very much like something from outer space."

Lieut. Col. Frank Luciani of the Air Force said, "We looked into the possibility of a satellite entering in the quadrant at that time and found nothing."

The object crossed the sky from southeast to north and disappeared over the Pacific Ocean, witnesses said.

"Something this big is very rare," said Dianne Sayre, a supervisor at the Griffith Park Observatory in Los Angeles. "It was very spectacular."

Author's Afterword

Max Planck's discovery of "quanta" in 1900, Einstein's theory of relativity, and the findings of Werner Heisenberg, Niehls Bohr, Louis deBroglie and Erwin Schrödinger, to mention just a few, form the basis of quantum theory. The discovery and development of this theory revolutionized the world of both scientists and philosophers and left an impact that ranked with the discoveries of Isaac Newton.

In the subatomic realm, absolute notions of space and time disappear. The idea of matter as "something" disappears. Matter ultimately is intense units of energy; in the subatomic world there is pattern, energy, and probability. Events are not predictable. The role of the observer was dramatically altered by the discoveries of quantum mechanics. The world could no longer be said to be "there," and the observer "here." Rather, the observer, in this realm was found to influence what he observed.

He became a participant in the outcome. His observation actually brought into being either one "reality," or another. This finding, in addition to the others, turned classical physics, as well as common sense, completely upside down. Erwin Schrödinger, a physicist and philosopher, described the cat-in-the-box experiment as a way of demonstrating the utter "weirdness" of the quantum world. This is a description of Schrödinger's experiment:

SCHRÖDINGER'S CAT

A cat is placed in a sealed box with a device that can release a gas which will kill the cat. A random event (the decay of a radioactive atom) determines whether or not the device will go off. There is no way to know whether or not the cat is dead or alive, unless you look in the box. The box is sealed and the experiment is activated. Moments later, either the gas has been released and the cat is dead, or it hasn't and the cat is alive. There is no way of knowing without looking into the box. According to the classical theory of physics, the cat is already in one state or the other. When you open the box you will see which one it is. According to quantum theory, the situation is very different. The Copenhagen Interpretation of Quantum Mechanics has it that the cat is in a kind of "potential" state of being both alive and dead, and only at the moment when the box is opened and the cat is actually observed will it "occur" as either one reality or the other. From the point of view of "common sense," this is of course absurd. Nonetheless in the subatomic realm this is what happens.

Schrödinger's original idea was to demonstrate that these "absurdities," which correctly describe the subatomic world, do not apply to the larger macro (cat) world. The cat is used as an example of a statistical probability. It has been used often however to describe quite the opposite. Today there is an intense debate among physicists about the nature of "reality" and to what extent the discoveries of subatomic physics do apply to the larger world. It is a theory that has brought us the horror of the atom bomb and a potential for technological revolution that can only be imagined. A leading scientist has written, "No single set of ideas has ever had a greater impact on technology and its practical implications will continue to shape the social and political destiny of our civilization. . . . When the history of this century is written, we shall see that political events—in spite of their immense costs in human lives and money—will not be the most influential events. Instead the main event will be the first human contact with the invisible quantum world and the subsequent biological and computer revolutions." (Heinz Pagels, *The Cosmic Code*)

Although the laws of quantum theory apply only to the subatomic world, the striking parallel findings between Eastern mysticism and quantum physics suggest hopeful possibilities, as elegantly expressed by the physicist Fritzjof Capra in *The Tao of Physics*.

Science does not need mysticism and mysticism does not need science; but man needs both. Mystical experience is necessary to understand the deepest nature of things and science is essential for modern life. What we need therefore is not a synthesis but a dynamic interplay between mystical intuition and scientific analysis. . . . Most of today's physicists do not seem to realize the philosophical, cultural, and spiritual implications of their theories. Many of them actively support a society which is still based on the mechanistic fragmented world view, without seeing that science points beyond such a view, towards a oneness of the universe which includes not only our natural environment but also our fellow human beings. I believe that the world view implied by modern physics is inconsistent with our present society, which does not reflect the harmonious interrelations we observe in nature. To achieve such a state of dynamic balance, a radically different social and economic structure will be needed: a cultural revolution in the true sense of the word. The survival of our whole civilization may depend on whether or not we can bring about such a change. It will depend, ultimately, on our ability to adopt some of the *yin* attitudes of Eastern mysticism; to experience the wholeness of nature and the art of living with it in harmony.